A DANGEROUS MAN

"You're so used to dealing with men you can control that you don't know what it's like to be with a real man," Ben said.

"Then show me," she said.

For a moment he stared at her. "I don't think it would be a very good idea," he murmured even as he moved a step closer, even as his hands slid around to her hips. "Your mother was right about me. I'm not what you need."

She raised her hands to his shoulders, then slid her arms around his neck. "You're wrong. You're exactly what I need . . . exactly what I wan—"

He kissed her, a greedy, blood-stirring kiss that made her knees weak and sent a rush of heat sizzling through her body.

He broke off the kiss, rested his forehead against hers. "This is your second chance, sugar, and I don't give third chances. If you're going to change your mind, now's the time to do it. If you don't, I'm going to take you upstairs to your bedroom and get rid of those clothes and make love to you." He brought his mouth close to her ear, making her shudder. "And then I'm going to do it all over again. It's your decision. What do you want?"

"You," she murmured, eyes closed, her mouth seeking his.

"Open your eyes and say that again," he commanded. "Look at me and say it."

He wanted to be sure she was choosing him—not merely giving in to need and desire. "I want you, Ben E-doesn't-stand-for-anything-or-maybe-it-stands-for-everything Foster. I want you to kiss me again and again. I want you to go upstairs to my bedroom with me—or, hell, right here on the porch is fine."

He kissed her once, hard, then reached past her and opened the door. They stumbled up the stairs, then finally reached the cool, quiet darkness of her bedroom.

He turned on the lamp, holding her, hands on her waist, at arm's length.

"Last chance, darlin'."

Bantam Books by Marilyn Pappano

SOME ENCHANTED SEASON

FATHER TO BE

FIRST KISS

GETTING LUCKY

GETTING LUCKY

Marilyn Pappano

BANTAM BOOKS

New York Toronto London Sydney Auckland

GETTING LUCKY
A Bantam Book / September 2001

Cover art by Ann Bauer.

ISBN 0-553-58232-1

Published simultaneously in the United States and Canada

Bantam Books are published by Bantam Books, a division of Random House, Inc. Its trademark, consisting of the words "Bantam Books" and the portrayal of a rooster, is Registered in U.S. Patent and Trademark Office and in other countries. Marca Registrada. Bantam Books, 1540 Broadway, New York, New York 10036.

PRINTED IN THE UNITED STATES OF AMERICA

OPM 10 9 8 7 6 5 4 3 2 1

GETTING LUCKY

Chapter One

As the school bus turned the corner onto Fourth Street, Ben Foster pulled to the curb fifteen feet before the stop sign and shut off the engine. There was something inherently wrong with what he was doing—spying on a bunch of schoolkids in hopes of catching a glimpse of a twelve-year-old girl. It was creepy. Perverse.

And the fact that the girl was his never-before-seen daughter didn't make it feel any less strange. But what was the alternative? Walk up to the house, knock on the door, and say, "Hey, darlin', say hello to your long-lost father"?

Maybe sometime, but not today. All he wanted today was to see her.

The bus came to a stop with a squeal of brakes, the doors opened, and a half-dozen kids tumbled out. The two he was interested in looked both ways, then ran across the street in front of the bus. They were both blonde-haired and fair-skinned, both pretty, but it was the older one who held Ben's attention.

Her hair fell past her shoulders and was pulled back in a fancy braid. She carried her backpack as if it were too heavy, and she moved with the unconscious ease of a girl who wasn't yet fully aware of her body. She was beautiful. Delicate. Perfect.

He'd learned quite a bit about her in the past few weeks—that she lived here in Bethlehem, New York, in the blue house down the street, with her sister and brother, their aunt, uncle, and cousin. She was in the sixth grade, made A's and B's, and had a best friend named Susan. Her aunt Emilie worked at the local inn and had risked prison to keep the kids together when their mother, Berry, got locked up, and her uncle Nathan was a cop. Her name was Alanna Marie Dalton.

And she was *his daughter.*

Ben had had about thirteen years to get used to the idea of having a daughter, but truthfully he'd rarely spared her a thought. The day Berry had told him she was pregnant, he'd told her good-bye and he'd never seen her again. He'd never seen Alanna, either, and at odd times he suspected that might have been his loss.

It had definitely been his grandmother's loss. She'd gone to her grave regretting that she'd never been able to meet her only great-grandchild.

His throat tightened at the thought of her. Emmaline Bodine had been the most important woman in his life. She'd taken him in every time his mother had taken off, and she'd done her best to teach him things his parents hadn't. The fact that she'd failed was his fault, not hers. He'd been too wild, had had too many bad examples to counteract her good one. But she'd never stopped loving him, until the day she died two months ago. If he knew her, she was probably watching over him somewhere up in heaven, waiting, hoping for him to finally, just once in his life, do the right thing.

Whatever that was.

Refocusing his attention, he looked across the street just as the Victorian's front door closed behind the two girls. He thought about staying there a while longer, in case they came back out, then decided against it. The last thing he needed was some housewife calling the cops on him. Hell, with his luck, it would be Alanna's uncle who showed up to haul him off to jail.

He started the engine and pulled away from the curb, driving slowly past the Victorian and the house where Alanna lived. He headed back to Main Street, then downtown, making an illegal turn to park in front of the diner he'd noticed earlier. It was late for lunch, early for dinner, which meant he had the place mostly to himself, and that suited him just fine. In small towns like Bethlehem, people tended to pay a lot of attention to strangers. At the moment, he'd just as soon do without that.

He slid into a booth, turned the coffee cup right side up, then gazed out the window. May in New York was more pleasant than back home in Georgia. Summer days in Georgia weren't fit for anything but stretching out in the shade or under a ceiling fan with an endless supply of ice-cold beer and doing a lot of nothing.

And that summed up his life—a lot of nothing. He'd lived in a lot of places, worked at going-nowhere jobs that required brawn rather than brains, drunk a lot of beer, amused himself with a lot of women. He'd had no ambitions, no thoughts for the future, no strings but Emmaline. He hadn't amounted to anything, and his grandmother had died knowing that.

The steamy aroma of coffee drew his gaze from the town outside and his thoughts back to the north. "Welcome to Henry's," the waitress said, her voice too cheerful by half. "Do you need a few minutes to look over the menu?"

Ben glanced down at the plastic-encased menu with the name—Harry's Diner—printed across the front. Flipping it open, he scanned the offerings. "I'll have the pot roast."

"Good choice. You can't go wrong with Hank's pot roast."

"Hank?"

"He owns Henry's." She glanced at the menu and frowned. "Harry's. I said Harry's, didn't I? Of course I did. Henry owns Harry's. The other waitress is . . . Mary? Maude? Marva? And I'm Gloria."

"Are you sure about that?"

With a flush and a smile, she checked her name tag. "I'm sure. Who are you?"

"Ben Foster." He couldn't ignore the hand she offered without being rude, and his grandmother hadn't raised him to be rude, especially to women of a certain age.

"Welcome to Bethlehem, Ben Foster. You're not from around here, are you? Not with an accent like that."

"No, ma'am. I'm from Georgia."

"And what brings you to this part of New York?"

It was a simple question, and he was going to give a simple lie. There was no reason to feel guilty about it, except that Emmaline had hated his lies. "It looks like a good place to stop a while."

"Oh, it is. Bethlehem's the best place on earth to live. Of course, you'll see that for yourself soon enough. I'd best get your order in to Harold. I'd hate to see a man faint dead away from hunger when the best food in town is just a few steps away."

Ben watched her go, then turned back to the window with a grin. He wouldn't go so far as to proclaim Bethlehem the best place on earth—he was rather partial to hot days, the scent of magnolias, kudzu run wild, and lazy Southern drawls—but it wasn't bad. Solid old buildings surrounded the town square, where kids played in the grass. Shoppers strolled along the sidewalks, and mothers rocked babies on park benches. It was almost too wholesome, clean, and prosperous a scene to believe.

If it was as good as it looked, Alanna was lucky to have ended up there.

As he watched, a car pulled into the space next to his and emphasized his thought about prosperity. The silver Mercedes gleamed so brightly in the afternoon sunlight that it almost hurt to look at it. The woman who drove it damn near gleamed, too, unfolding from the sports car more gracefully than he would have thought possible for an Amazon. She stood at least six feet tall, most of her height taken up by long, long legs of the sort men built erotic fantasies around. Her hair was black, parted in the middle, and fell in a sleek, undisturbed line past her shoulders. Her pale skin looked so fine that his fingers itched to touch it, just to feel for himself if it could possibly be as soft as it looked. But he was no fool. He'd wager that no man with calloused hands had ever touched the woman. In fact, he wouldn't risk money on the odds that any man had ever touched her—at least, not without an engraved invitation.

She moved so gracefully that she seemed to glide across the sidewalk and in the door, sparing no attention for anyone or anything as she took a seat in the booth next to his. Immediately she took a folder from the black bag she carried and bent her head over its contents, looking up only when the waitress approached.

"What can I get you, hon?"

"Just coffee, please." Her voice was low, smooth, lacking the Southern accent he was fond of, but not unpleasant. If wealth and power had a sound, her voice was it.

"Can I interest you in a slice of fresh-baked apple pie?" Gloria asked. "It's Howard's specialty."

"No, thank you."

Gloria filled her coffee cup, topped off Ben's, then went behind the counter to trade the carafe for his food. After setting it in front of him, she folded her arms across her middle and watched him take the first bite. "Good, no?"

He nodded.

"So, Ben, you said you'll be stopping a while. How long is that?"

He'd thought he would come to Bethlehem, maybe see Alanna, maybe not. He'd intended to give Emmaline's locket, the only heirloom the Bodine family had ever had, to Emilie Bishop to give Alanna someday, then head back down south, his obligation fulfilled. Now he wasn't so sure. He thought he might like to meet Alanna, to see just once how it felt to be a father. He didn't have any idea. If he cared enough to think about it, he could probably count the number of times in his life he'd laid eyes on his old man—fewer than fifteen for sure.

He was pretty sure he wasn't looking to take on the role of father. He was years too late for that, and Alanna didn't need him. She may have been cursed with worthless parents, but her aunt and uncle were good people, and they loved her like their own. What use could she possibly have for *him*?

He might as well stick around until he figured it out. "I don't rightly know," he said in response to Gloria's question. "A few days, a few weeks. Maybe long enough to see if it really is the best place on earth."

"Then you'll be needing a place to stay. Let's see . . . Mrs. Laramie has that garage apartment, or . . . No, it's been rented. There are the new apartments over by the hospital—nice enough, but no personality. And the old apartments on the other side of town . . . I believe 'genteelly shabby' would be a polite way to describe them."

Ben grinned. Genteelly shabby, he was familiar with. Much of his home state could be so described. "Hold off on apartments, Gloria. I'm not moving here. Just staying a while. Is there a motel in town?"

Her smile was broad enough to add extra wrinkles to an already generous number. "Talk about good fortune. Bethlehem now has a motel. Just opened its doors last week. For years the only place to stay was

Hallie McFlynn's inn. Lovely place—old farmhouse, pastoral setting, beautiful rooms, best food in town."

"I thought the best food in town was right here," he teased.

"Oh, it is, it is. Molly's place is lovely, but a little on the pricey side. But the motel is perfect for travelers just passing through or for folks on a budget. It's right along Main, just a few blocks in that direction." She pointed back in the direction he'd come, frowned, then pointed the opposite way. "I'm not much on directions, but I can find my way anywhere, given enough chances. The motel's that way. You can't miss it. Now . . . What about a job? You'll be needing one of those, too. What can you do?"

He could raise hell with the best of them, drink most people under the table and still get home under his own power, and give a beating as well as he took one. But those talents weren't likely to be of any interest to a prospective employer. "I'm good with my hands. There's not an engine made I can't fix. I can frame a house, wire it, plumb it, drywall and finish it. I can put on a roof, take out a wall, build cabinets and stairs and porches and chairs."

"Why, you're just a jack-of-all-trades, aren't you?"

"Yes, ma'am."

"There's a lot of construction going on in Bethlehem. Let me think and see what I can come up with." She looked toward the door an instant before the bell rang, then called, "Have a seat, and someone will be right with you. Ben, you be sure to save room for some apple pie."

He watched her disappear into the kitchen, then shifted his attention to the new customer, on his way to the Amazon's table. He was tall, dark-haired, and carried a briefcase in one hand and a baby carrier, complete with baby, in the other. It was an incongruous sight—obviously successful businessman with bald-headed munchkin, Armani or something similar versus white bunnies and pastel flowers on a green background. Where was the nanny responsible for raising the child?

An older waitress whose pale red hair color was straight from a bottle came from the kitchen and greeted the man warmly. Maeve, according to the name tag she wore. Both waitress and businessman seemed genuinely friendly, but the Amazon merely waited for their conversation to end.

At last, the man ordered coffee and pie, laid the briefcase on the bench opposite the woman, and put the baby seat on the table. "Lynda," he said, a cool greeting if the two of them had created the munchkin together. "Watch Rachel for a moment, will you? I've got recycled apple juice on my jacket."

"But, Ross—"

He was headed for the door marked Restrooms before she could go any further with her objection, and she was left looking appalled. Maybe she wasn't the kid's mother, Ben decided—hoped. Surely even the worst mother ever wouldn't look at her own baby as if it were the nasty little creature from *Alien,* especially when the kid was being quiet and trouble-free.

But he didn't know much more about mothers and babies than he did about fathers. The only way he knew to get in touch with his own mother was to visit the bars she frequented, and he hadn't even been in the same state when Alanna was that tiny. By then Berry had gone off to Nashville, and he had damn near forgotten about her. They had both moved on—to other people, other promises for better futures, other problems. From what he understood, Alanna had paid the price.

Maybe it wasn't too late to make it up to her. Or maybe it had been too late the day he'd told Berry good-bye.

Either way, he supposed he would soon find out.

RACHEL ELIZABETH MCKINNEY WAS ONLY eight weeks old and not much more than ten pounds, but she had a remarkable ability to intimidate a grown woman. Who did that say more about? Lynda Barone wondered. Rachel? Or her?

The baby sat in her seat in the middle of the table where Ross—her father, Lynda's boss—had left her, gazing at Lynda with sleepy blue eyes. She wasn't fussing or crying, responses Lynda had been known to cause in coldhearted businessmen decades older. In fact, Rachel didn't even seem to notice that her father had left her with a stranger. She was pretty laid-back about it.

Lynda hoped the baby kept that attitude, because if there was one thing she knew nothing about, it was babies. She could strike fear in the coldest, most profit-hungry hearts in the business world, could reduce powerful men to quivering masses . . . but she couldn't remember the last time she'd held an infant, and she'd never changed a diaper, given a bottle, or voluntarily gotten within ten feet of one. They spoke a language she didn't speak, had customs she wasn't interested in learning, and required care she didn't know how to give.

"Isn't she a little angel?" the waitress, Maeve, cooed as she brought Ross's order. She flashed a smile at Lynda. "And trust me, I know my angels." After fussing over the baby a moment longer, Maeve returned to the kitchen. Lynda resisted the urge to grab hold of the woman, to insist that she stay until Ross returned. But she'd learned early in her career to never plead, show fear, or admit to weakness. The lessons had stood her in good stead.

She looked at Rachel, grateful to see her yawn as if she might drift right off to sleep, and also resisted the urge to smile. The child was prettier than a person might reasonably expect for a small, chubby, bald girl. She had her father's eyes in her mother's face, and was living proof of the miracles that could be worked in Bethlehem. A few years earlier, no one had given Ross and Maggie's marriage the slightest chance of lasting out the year, especially Ross and Maggie themselves. But there they were, not only still together but happier than ever, more in love, doting on each other and now Rachel as if nothing else in the world mattered.

At one time, back when she was young and naive, she'd thought she could have it all—husband, family, satisfying career. But eighteen-hour workdays, a schedule heavy on travel and light on free time, and the take-no-prisoners drive necessary to not only survive but excel in a man's world weren't exactly conducive to sustaining personal relationships. She couldn't remember the last time she'd had a date, or even just a fling.

Her gaze shifted to the man in the next booth. If she were going to fantasize about a fling, he would be a good candidate. Handsome, a stranger and destined to stay one, in town for a few days, a few weeks, and then gone again. His voice—all soft, rounded sounds, warm honey, and lazy hot nights—was amazingly easy on the ears, and his face—blond hair, stubborn jaw, angular lines, incredible green eyes that crinkled at the corners as if he smiled too much . . .

Abruptly she realized he was watching her watch him, and she jerked her gaze away, though not before catching his grin. No doubt, he was accustomed to being ogled everyplace he went, but she wasn't accustomed to ogling. Almost immediately, though, she sneaked another look as he slid out of the booth, checked his ticket, then tossed a bill on top of it. His body was long and lean, gloved by a white T-shirt and faded denim that clung to well-developed muscles and stretched taut in the right places, and his moves were languid and lazy, as if he knew exactly how to pace himself.

As he moved slowly past her table, he nodded toward Rachel. "Pretty baby."

Though she knew it was utterly ridiculous—pure feminine vanity—Lynda couldn't shake the odd feeling that he wasn't necessarily talking about Rachel.

The bell over the door rang, then he appeared on the sidewalk outside. He didn't so much walk as . . . amble. *Lazily.* His T-shirt stretched across broad shoulders and tapered over a narrow, flat middle, and his faded jeans looked as good from behind as from the front. What little skin that showed was golden brown, and looked silky and hot to the touch . . . and that was more than she'd noticed at one time about any one man in more years than she could recall.

He climbed into the car beside hers and started the engine with a powerful rumble. Without so much as a glance inside the café, he backed out across both lanes of traffic, then headed, presumably, for the motel on the edge of town. With a soft sigh—of admiration? longing? wistfulness?—she turned her attention back and barely controlled her surprise at seeing Ross seated across from her, holding Rachel against one shoulder. "I—I didn't hear you come back."

"You were distracted." He glanced out the window in the direction the stranger had gone, then smiled. "I don't believe I've ever seen you distracted before."

The heat of embarrassment warmed her cheeks and stiffened her spine, but she offered no excuses, no explanation.

"Sorry for bringing Rachel. Maggie had a meeting, too, and they never get anything accomplished if the kids are there. Oh, and Tom isn't going to make it. He got tied up on a call from Hong Kong."

Tom Flynn was chief counsel for McKinney Industries and Ross's top advisor. He was forty, brilliant, and had once had a reputation that spanned the globe as the toughest, most ruthless bastard in business. Lynda had detested him, competed with him, envied him, and wanted to be just like him. But his recent marriage to Holly McBride had mellowed him significantly. She couldn't even remember the last time he'd insulted her, tested her patience, or made her mad enough to spit. Sometimes she missed the old Tom. Mostly she envied the new one.

"Did you get a chance to look over the reports?" she asked. It was a rhetorical question. Ross had taught her by example to be painstakingly thorough. It was how he'd built his fortune, which had enabled her to build her own.

"Some of them," he replied. "Just give me the short version."

For one long moment, she wasn't sure what to say. She knew the answer, of course. She'd put the reports together herself and could quote numbers, percentages, profits, losses, expenses, and countless other details, mundane and not so.

What she couldn't grasp was Ross's willingness to settle for the "short" version. This was a complicated project that involved the acquisition of a manufacturing plant in Osaka, which would be paid for in part with the transfer of ownership of various small enterprises on three continents, along with shares in other M.I. interests. There were dozens of factors to consider, hundreds of minor details to work out along the way.

But all he wanted was the "short" version.

"Well . . . Before the parties involved will agree to the deal as laid out, the mediators will have to resolve the problems with the workers in Malaysia, which will, of course, entail a substantial increase in salary and benefits packages, which will decrease profits but should have the reciprocal effect of increasing productivity. Then we'll need to begin negotiations with—"

Ross looked up from Rachel with a grin. "Bottom line, Lynda."

"Bottom line?"

"Your recommendation is somewhere in all those pages. What is it?"

She was mystified. "That we move ahead. But that's simply my opinion. You really should weigh all the options for yourself."

"Have you weighed them?"

"Yes, but—"

"So why should I do it again? Repeating the whole process doesn't strike me as a very efficient use of time."

"But that's the way we've always worked." At least, until Rachel was born. And Tom got married. To go back even further, until Ross and Maggie put their marriage back together.

"Change is good," Ross said simply. "So do we give this project the green light?"

She wanted to hesitate and hedge her bets, and opened her mouth to do so. Instead, she answered simply. "Yes."

"Good. Is there anything else we need to discuss?"

She did have a few minor issues to bring up, but decided against it. If he wasn't interested in the Osaka deal, he certainly wasn't going to care about her petty concerns. "No, not at the moment. Are you going back to the office now?"

"I think Rachel and I are going to go home and take a nap." He gazed tenderly at his daughter in a way that had once been reserved for Maggie. "If you could tell my secretary, I'd appreciate it."

He naturally assumed that she had no place better to go and nothing better to do than work. She was tempted to prove him wrong, but unless the world came to an end between then and five P.M., he wouldn't even know. And all she would do at home was work. Of course she would go back to the office, deliver his message, and be the last one to go home that evening. As usual.

"I'll do that," she said as he stood up and shifted Rachel to his other arm. She kept her sigh inside until they were gone, then it slipped out.

"Something wrong, hon?" the chubbier waitress, Gloria, asked.

Lynda glanced at the swinging door that led into the kitchen, standing utterly still, and wondered where the woman had come from. Had she been so distracted again that she hadn't noticed she wasn't alone? That wasn't like her.

"No, everything's fine. I . . . I just got the go-ahead on the biggest deal I've ever put together." And had no one to share the news with but a stranger.

"Congratulations! That's cause for celebration! You should grab your husband and—"

Lynda interrupted, though she didn't have a clue why. "I'm not married."

"Oh . . . well, then your sweetheart—"

With a rueful smile, she shook her head.

"A pretty girl like you . . . Well, surely you've got friends or family you can celebrate with."

"My family lives in Binghamton, and my best friend is in Buffalo."

Gloria looked flustered. "Well . . . well . . . congratulations anyway. You should be very proud of yourself. And I'll tell you what—" She took a small Styrofoam box from the counter. "Have the last piece of Harold's best pie as a reward. It's on the house. Take it home, heat it in the microwave, spoon vanilla ice cream over it . . . ah, it's heavenly."

"I don't—"

Gloria pressed the box into her hands. "Go on, indulge yourself. You deserve it."

Lynda smiled reluctantly. "Thanks." She did deserve it. And she would enjoy it.

All by herself.

ANGELS LODGE, BEN DISCOVERED, WAS MORE than Gloria's "few blocks" away—closer to two miles, in a clearing after the road began its climb out of the valley. The place had just opened its doors last week, she'd said, and she hadn't been kidding. Though the office and what looked like about ten rooms were completed and open for business, the rest of the two-story building was still under construction. If he decided to stick around, he might hunt up the foreman and apply for a job. He couldn't ask for a better commute than a few hundred feet down the sidewalk.

From the outside, the lodge looked like ten thousand other motels. Inside, though, was a surprise. The lobby was a scaled-down version of a much more expensive place, with a marble-topped registration desk, wood paneling, and furniture that were antiques or good reproductions, and the photographs on the walls were of local sights, all elaborately framed and signed by the same artist.

A young woman was working the desk—early twenties, brown hair, pretty, with a name tag that said Bree. In a summer dress that reminded him of some famous watercolor painting he'd once seen, she looked right at home in the elegant surroundings. "Can I help you?"

"I need a room for a few nights, maybe longer."

She asked the usual questions, then studied the information displayed on her computer screen. "Some of our rooms have small kitchens, Mr. Foster. Since you may be here a while, would you be interested in one of them?"

He wasn't much of a cook, but he could handle soup and sandwiches. And since he wasn't fond of eating alone in restaurants and had noticed an absence of fast-food places in town, it seemed a reasonable solution. He said as much to the woman as she took his credit card.

"Are you in town on business?"

"Yes, ma'am." That little Emmaline-guilt twinge tickled down his spine again, and he hadn't even really lied. It *was* business. Just not the kind she meant.

The printer spit out a page, and she X-ed the two places he should sign. "I hope you have time to enjoy the town while you're here. Bethlehem's a great place."

"So I've been told. I plan to take some time."

"Great. If you can start tonight, the high school jazz band is giving a concert in the town square at seven. Practically everyone in town will be there. A lot of them make an evening of it and have dinner at one of the restaurants downtown, and some bring blankets and dinners for a picnic in the grass. It's really nice."

"Sounds like fun." Now, that truly was a lie. He didn't like high school bands, or jazz, or anything that involved big crowds. He was fond of picnics, but on hot days with pretty women, a lot of privacy, and an entire afternoon to pass.

"You can't miss the square. It's—"

"Right across the street from Harry's."

"You've found Harry's. It's the heart of Bethlehem." Her smile was broad and charming. "Here's your key and your credit card. Your room is around the corner here to the left. If you need anything, don't hesitate to ask. And welcome to town. I hope you enjoy your stay."

Ben returned to his car and moved it to the east side of the building. She'd given him an easy number to remember—111—with a window that looked down on the town. It was a pretty scene, with lots of rich green from the trees, roofs, and a fair number of church steeples.

He carried his duffel into the room, then took a look around. Like most motels, it was close quarters, but the quality was a step or two above the usual. The carpet was better-than-average quality, the pad a bit thicker. The dresser, night tables, and cabinets were good-quality, paint-grade plywood, simple in design, and painted a smooth, hard white. There were more framed photographs on the walls, and the kitchenette and bathroom were both designed for efficiency.

He closed the sheers but left the heavy drapes open, then began unpacking. His kit bag went on the counter in the bathroom, his clothes in the dresser and closet. The last item in the duffel, a wooden box, would go back in the car trunk—safer there than in the room. It held the only things he owned that he couldn't afford to lose.

The box wasn't anything fancy, just a small cedar chest with a lock. Finding the key on his key chain, he unlocked then opened the box. The aroma of cedar drifted up, making him sneeze. There wasn't much inside—a handful of photographs, a card bearing a twelve-year-old postmark and a Nashville return address, and the locket. The photos, copies of originals back home, were of Emmaline, old and wrinkled in the earliest; older, more wrinkled, but still vital in the last one. The card was to her from Berry, an impersonal announcement that she'd given birth to a girl. It had included a poorly lit photo of one-month-old Alanna.

The locket was gold, engraved on the front with hearts and flowers and on the back with some long-dead Bodine's message to his beloved wife, Sally, dated 1860. When Ben was a kid, Emmaline had entertained them both for hours with stories about Sally, her husband, and the Civil War. The Recent Unpleasantness, she'd sometimes called it, or simply the War, as if there had been no other in the last two centuries.

She had worn the locket every single day he could remember except the last one. When he'd visited her the night before she died, she'd taken it off and pressed it into his hands. "For Alanna," she'd whispered weakly before dozing off.

It might have been the first time in his adult life he'd ever cried.

But it hadn't been the last.

His fingers felt big and clumsy as he pressed the latch that opened the locket. In the tiny oval frames inside were pictures—My babies, Emmaline had often said with pride. Ben and Alanna, each only weeks old. Face-to-face in the locket, but never in real life.

Despite the age of the photos, the resemblance was strong enough to be certain that Berry hadn't lied. He'd wondered when she'd announced her pregnancy. Fidelity was only one of the qualities she'd lacked in great measure. But once he'd seen these photos, he'd known it was true. Alanna had his hair, jaw, nose, and the shape of his eyes, but the features that fitted into an okay face on him went together beautifully on her. She was clearly his daughter, only sweetly, delicately better.

Feeling more alone than he had even when he'd watched Emmaline's casket lowered into the ground, Ben returned everything to the box and locked it, then slid the box into the duffel. He stretched out on the bed, pillowing his arms under his head, and closed his eyes. If he dozed off, fine. If he didn't, he could drive himself nuts for a few more hours, thinking about what he should do, wondering what he wanted to do, wishing the "right" thing Emmaline had always urged on him could, just this once, also be the easy thing.

The next time he opened his eyes, the clock on the night table showed that the concert in the square had just started. He combed his fingers through his hair, changed into a clean T-shirt, picked up the duffel, and headed to his car.

The streets surrounding the square were closed to traffic and cars were parked everywhere. He found a space at the edge of downtown, in front of a dusty bookstore, then walked the half-dozen blocks to the square. Bree had predicted that practically everyone would be there, and it appeared she was right. The park benches were full, and every blade of grass was home to a blanket or a lawn chair. People stood on the sidewalks and sat on the courthouse steps, leaned against buildings and hunkered down on curbs. Some listened to the music, while others talked with friends or watched the kids play. It was the sort of thing Emmaline would have loved.

Ben found a relatively isolated spot across the street from the bandstand. He was scanning the crowd, checking out every blonde when four of them together—a woman and three kids—caught his attention. He didn't know Emilie Bishop from the man in the moon, but the tightening in his gut told him that was her. That meant the oldest of those kids was Alanna.

His guess was confirmed when she turned his way. For an instant he felt a jolt, as if she were looking right at him, then she laughed, let a dark-haired girl pull her to her feet, and disappeared into the crowd with her.

"You can't ask for anything better than this, can you?"

Swallowing hard, Ben turned to see an older man sitting on the steps nearby. He looked like somebody's doting grandfather, another of those family positions Ben knew nothing about.

"It's nice," he said noncommittally before trying to locate Alanna in the crowd again.

"You're new in town."

"Just visiting."

The man laughed. "I came for a visit last summer to help my son with his kids, and here I still am, nearly a year later. Something about this town gets to you. . . ." His gaze shifted past Ben, and a smile lit his entire face. "Or maybe it's something about the ladies here that gets to you."

Ben glanced over his shoulder to see a pink-cheeked, white-haired woman approaching, arms around two girls—Alanna and her friend. His heart rate increased a few beats, and the tightness in his stomach spread to his chest.

"I'm Bud Grayson."

"Ben." He tore his gaze from Alanna, dried his palm on his jeans, and shook hands with the man. "Ben Foster."

"And these lovely ladies are among the lights of my life. Miss Alanna Dalton, Miss Susan Walker, and Miss Agatha Winchester, may I present Ben Foster, a visitor to our fair town."

"Welcome to Bethlehem, Ben," Agatha said, releasing the girls to take his hand in both of hers. "Foster . . . Are you related to Horace Foster over at the city engineer's office?"

"No, ma'am, I'm afraid not."

"Say hello to Mr. Foster, girls," she directed as she let go of his hand.

"Hello," they said dutifully.

Acutely aware of Alanna in his peripheral vision, Ben focused on Susan first—shorter than Alanna, sturdier, darker, with brown hair and eyes, and the air of a tomboy. She looked strong and resilient. He could easily see her climbing trees, sliding into home plate, and holding her own with any boy around.

He spoke her name with a nod, then slowly let his gaze slide across to Alanna. The resemblance that was so noticeable in their baby pictures had been diluted by the years. She still had his hair, his jaw, his nose, but he could see hints of Berry in her, too, as well as features that were purely her own. He wanted to touch her, to offer his hand and wrap his fingers around hers and wait for it to sink in that this was his *daughter.* This child shared his blood, his genes. He had helped create her.

But he didn't reach out. He didn't even speak her name. He simply nodded.

"Hi," she said politely, then turned her attention to the older man. "Grandpa Bud, where's Dr. J.D. and the kids?"

Her voice was sweet, feminine, and flat-out stunned him. There wasn't so much as a hint of the South in it—not surprising when her mother had dragged her all over the eastern half of the country—but it was pleasing anyway. Soft. Rich with promise.

Then his thoughts turned regretful. The first words most fathers heard their daughters speak were usually *Mama* or *Daddy. He* got *Hi,* spoken one stranger to another. And there was no one to blame but himself.

"I believe you'll find them over by Harry's."

Ben watched the girls exchange looks and giggles, then take off. Once they'd been swallowed up by the crowd, he asked, "Your granddaughter?"

"Oh, no. Though maybe someday." With a grin, Bud explained. "Alanna's got a bit of a crush on my grandson Caleb, and the feelings are reciprocated. Maybe they'll outgrow it—after all, they're still young. Or maybe they won't. Either way, any grandfather in the world would be proud to claim Alanna for his own."

Any except her own. His father would care no more about a granddaughter than he had about his son, and Berry's father had abandoned her and Emilie after their mother's death. He wasn't likely to feel any more paternal toward their kids than he had toward them.

"Do you have any children, Ben?" Agatha asked.

Through sheer will, he kept himself from taking a telltale look toward Harry's. "I've never been married."

She didn't point out that one had nothing to do with the other. Instead, she smiled a sly woman-with-an-idea sort of smile. "Stick around Bethlehem long enough, dear, and we just might change that."

Her words brought a great laugh from Bud. "Watch

out, Ben. Agatha and her sister, Corinna, fancy themselves matchmakers. If they set their sights on you, you'll never have a moment's peace until there's a ring on your finger."

"Oh, you," Agatha scolded. "I didn't notice you complaining when I set my sights on you."

Taking her in his arms, Bud twirled her around in time to the music, then kissed her flushed cheek. "That's because I was a goner the first time I laid eyes on you. Agatha's the reason, Ben, that my visit to Bethlehem became permanent. She's going to become my bride next month."

"Congratulations. Bud, Miss Agatha, it's nice to meet you. I'm going to wander back that way and see if I can find someone." Ben gestured in the general direction of Harry's, then took a few backward steps before turning.

He wanted to see this grandson Caleb—wanted to see how he looked at Alanna. He knew how young boys thought, and what they wanted. Hell, he'd been one himself. From the time he'd turned thirteen, any father who had let him near his daughter had been asking for trouble. No matter how nice Caleb's grandfather appeared to be, that said nothing for the boy's character. One lifelong troublemaker could easily recognize a younger version in the making.

And, if necessary, he could deal with him, too.

Chapter Two

As the sun moved lower in the western sky, the temperatures cooled. Many of the younger children started settling down, curling up on blankets and in laps. The streetlights buzzed softly, audible only when the music paused, and the sweet scent of pipe smoke drifted on the air. It was a relaxing scene, but Lynda knew another relaxing scene she preferred—in her house high on the hill. The house was old, isolated, and in need of substantial repairs—once she was able to lure a competent workman away from Bethlehem's booming construction business—but it was her sanctuary. Her safe place.

A few feet away, Ross stood with his wife, Maggie, and Tom and Holly Flynn. The five of them—six, counting the baby—had come to the concert from dinner at Holly's inn. The food had been wonderful, as usual, and the setting—the terrace outside the dining room—had been lovely, but Lynda had found the experience awkward. Maybe it was because there was bad history between her and Maggie, or because she didn't really know Holly at all. Or maybe it had something to do with the fact that the evening had been unbearably romantic, and she'd been the odd one out.

With the old Ross and Tom, the wives would have entertained themselves while Lynda and the men talked business. That sort of meal she could handle without batting an eye. But one where business was designated off-limits as a topic of discussion . . . *Not* her forte.

She was about to interrupt the conversation to tell them she was going home, when a figure across the street caught her attention. Ben, the waitress had called him in the café that afternoon. Who was good with his hands and had amazing green eyes, a body to die for, and a lazy, graceful way of using it. Who could look at an infant and say, "Pretty baby," and make a full-grown woman think he might be referring to her—or wish he was.

He stood near the corner, leaning against the stone facade of an antiques store below, an insurance office above. She was surprised to see him. He didn't seem the type to go in for family-oriented community entertainment. His preferred music, she would guess, was blues—soulful, hot, smoky—and his preferred environment a dimly lit room, with unmade bed, tangled sheets, windows open, and ceiling fan stirring heavy, lazy air, redolent with the scent of jasmine.

He was alone in the crowd, gazing intently at a scene on her side of the street. She glanced in that direction, but without his vantage point, there was no way she could see what, or who, had caught his attention.

Just as she wasn't sure why he had caught hers. Maybe because he was incredibly handsome in a bad-boy sort of way, or because he gave her an achy little tickle deep in the pit of her stomach, something she hadn't felt for far too long.

Slowly his gaze shifted in her direction. At six feet without shoes, she was impossible to miss but easy to overlook. She expected him to do just that, but he didn't. Across the width of the street, under the glow of the street lamps, she felt his steady, warm gaze. It sent a tiny shiver of heat through her and brought color to her face. It made her want to sink into the wall, dissolving into brick and mortar, at the same time she considered walking across the street to him.

And say what? *How about that stock market? D'ya think the interest rates will go up or slide down? What's your take on the trade agreement before Congress?* It had been so long since she'd talked about anything but business with a man that she wasn't sure she remembered how.

Besides, she knew better than to approach someone like him. Her type was steady, career-oriented, an MBA; wore suits and ties, carried a briefcase everywhere, and considered his cell phone an extension of his hand. Ben looked as if he didn't even own any of the above.

She knew without looking when the man turned his gaze elsewhere—felt the heat cool, the tingle fade. He was once more looking at whatever had caught his attention before, and that was as good a cue as any for her to leave.

When an opportunity to break into Ross's conversation presented itself, she took it. "Holly, I enjoyed the dinner. Maggie, it was nice seeing you and Rachel. Ross, Tom, I'll see you tomorrow."

Everyone murmured the appropriate responses, including a cooing sound from Rachel, whose infant's oblivion was more likely the source of her toothless grin than any pleasure at seeing Lynda.

As she left the crowd behind, she drew in a deep breath, then blew out all the tension. The music faded into the distance, and she slowly became aware of other sounds. A bobwhite's sweet call. The sputter of a streetlight about to burn out. The flap of a flag in the gentle breeze. And footsteps, heavier, more solid than her own.

As she reached her car, she glanced over her shoulder and spotted him immediately on the opposite side of the street. Ben. Had he followed her?

Her fingers tightened around the keyless remote attached to her key ring. One of the buttons was a personal safety alarm. In a town like Bethlehem, it would bring plenty of people running. Of course, if there was no reason for them to come running, wouldn't she feel like a fool?

Her thumb hovered above the panic button as he stepped off the curb and started, without looking, across the street. He appeared to be deep in thought . . . but appearances were often deceiving.

When she disarmed the car alarm, it chirped twice, and brought his head up. He looked surprised to see her and altered his course so he would pass at an angle away from her—to reach his car, which, she noticed for the first time, was parked one space down from hers. His smile was distant, distracted, his comment polite and nothing more. "Nice night for a concert."

There were a dozen intelligent responses to such a comment, but like some easily flustered schoolgirl, she couldn't think of one, and so, as she unlocked the car door, she simply agreed. "Yes, it is." Settling in the seat, she watched discreetly as he got into his own car, backed out with that powerful engine rumbling, then headed out of town toward Angels Lodge.

Within fifteen minutes, she was home, changed into a skinny tank top and pajama bottoms, and curled up in her favorite chair, with the telephone, and vanilla ice cream melting over warm apple pie.

" 'Yes, it is'?" Melina Dimitris echoed. "Jeez, Lyn, such snappy repartee. It's a wonder some guy hasn't grabbed you up—and Ross McKinney doesn't count. He's only interested in your brain, which seems a bit feeble tonight. You need someone who's interested in your body."

"Have *you* gotten lucky since we last talked?"

"Are you kidding? I would have bought commercial time on the networks to tell the world."

"Then don't preach at me."

Melina didn't take offense. She never did. She was the only person in the world Lynda could be totally natural and open with. "So just how good-looking is this guy?"

Lynda licked the spoon clean before letting it fall into the bowl. "Not ice-cream cute."

Melina snorted. "Like any guy is?"

"Let me think. . . ." It was their version of a rating system, one developed soon after they'd met their freshman year in college. A man was only as good as whatever they would give up to have him, and Melina was right. No man was ice-cream worthy. "Maybe sushi for six weeks."

Another snort. "Down South where he comes from, they call that bait. Besides, since you moved out into the wilds, you don't get to have it for weeks at a time anyway."

"Maybe three-inch heels—but not my Jimmy Choos."

"The last guy you were willing to give up three-inch heels for was . . . Oh, my, I'm impressed. If you can't get the nerve to approach him, would you please send him my way?"

" 'Get the nerve'?" Lynda repeated, feigning insult. "Do you remember to whom you speak? The woman who has been cursed to the devil in twelve languages? And you think I lack the nerve to talk to a carpenter from Atlanta?"

"To a gorgeous, three-inch-heel-worthy bad-boy hunk from Hotlanta? Yeah, I think you're afraid."

Lynda waited a moment, two, then just as heatedly said, "You're absolutely right."

They both laughed. "And if you're chicken to pick him up for yourself, you're sure not gonna send him to me. It's just as well," Melina said philosophically. "If he said yes, I'd have to shave my legs, and you know how I try to avoid that."

Lynda rolled her eyes. Since her sixteenth birthday, Melina's motto had been *Be prepared*. She could get intimate with some guy two minutes after meeting him and have everything she could possibly need at her fingertips. Whereas Lynda found it damn near impossible to get intimate, no matter how many times she slept with a man. She didn't have a personal motto, but if she did, it would probably be something like *Look, don't touch. Keep back. Hands off.*

"I've enjoyed this," Melina said, "but my ice-cream bowl is empty, my cordless phone is nearly dead, and I have to pee. Take my advice—find some courage and go after this Southern James Dean. Have I ever steered you wrong?"

"Have you ever steered me wrong? Let me count the ways."

"Yeah, yeah, yeah. Sheesh, I set you up with *one* blind date from hell—"

"How many?"

"Okay, two. Well, maybe four."

"Try seven. Every date you ever sent me on."

"—and I get treated like a junkyard dog at a poodle convention. At least I tried to do something about your abysmal social life, which is more than you can say."

"But when I handle my social life, it's merely abysmal. When you get involved, it becomes ghastly."

"You say that like ghastly is *so* much worse. At least for a while it was *different*."

"I don't like *different*. Not changing is good. Now . . . you'd better head to the bathroom—and recharge your phone. I'll talk to you later." Lynda hung up, then sighed heavily. Moving to Bethlehem and leaving behind all Buffalo had to offer had meant some serious adjustments, which she'd made. But she hadn't yet adjusted to not having Melina nearby. They visited each other often and talked more often, but it wasn't the same. It was as if she'd left the better part of herself behind in Buffalo.

And that was as sentimental as she allowed herself to get. With an encouraging breath, she took her dishes in the kitchen, then settled at her desk in the room that served as her home office. So her best friend—her only friend, a devious voice inside her head amended—lived five hours away, she couldn't remember the last time she'd been kissed, and every time she spoke to her parents they found five thousand ways to let her know that this was *not* the life they'd envisioned for her. She had her work, and that was all she needed to be successful, fulfilled, and happy.

She was. She really was.

BEN HAD LAIN AWAKE LATE INTO THE NIGHT, but every time he'd made a decision, he'd found some compelling argument against it. He wanted to meet Alanna, but after neglecting her all her life, did he even have the right? He wanted to go back to Georgia and forget her again . . . but what kind of man was capable of that? One like his own father, and he damn sure didn't want to be like him. Besides, what were the odds that he could forget her now that he'd seen her, heard her voice, gotten close enough to touch her?

And what were the odds that he had anything of value to offer her? That appearing in her life after all these years would do more harm than good? That she reasonably, realistically, had no use for a father who couldn't begin to compete on any level with the uncle who was raising her?

He got up Tuesday morning, showered, shaved, and dressed, then nuked a cup of coffee in the microwave to drink while staring out the window. Distant sounds of construction came from the other end of the building, along with the occasional rumble of a truck passing by on the highway. The sky was bright and sunny over Bethlehem, but on the mountainside above the motel, gray clouds were moving in, drifting lazily, as if in no hurry to get where they were going.

He would pack his bags, Ben decided, and head back home to Atlanta. Alanna had gotten along just fine without him. No doubt, she was a hell of a lot better off than she would have been if he'd always been around. He knew nothing about raising a kid, had taken too many whippings as a kid himself to care about disciplining anyone, and had no wisdom to impart and no character to pass on. Nathan Bishop was a good man, where the word most consistently applied to Ben was *bad*.

Alanna couldn't do better than Nathan . . . or much worse than Ben.

As he looked over his shoulder at the unmade bed and last night's clothes dumped on a chair, his stomach growled. He would get some breakfast first, then deliver the cedar chest to Emilie Bishop. Then he would come back and pack, and be well on his way home by noon.

Breakfast was doughnuts from a little place downtown, where he also got directions to McBride Inn. He started to walk away, then, on impulse, turned back. "What about the schools? The junior high or middle school?"

"They're all together," the woman behind the counter replied. "Turn right at the corner out here and go straight until you run into them."

"Thanks." As he left the shop and walked to his car,

he warned himself to forget about the school, to stick to his original plan. He concentrated on the directions to the inn and tried to shove the others out of his mind, and five minutes later he found himself parked in front of the school complex.

Yellow buses lined the drive, waiting their turns to unload. Cars were bumper to bumper, too, and the sidewalks carried plenty of foot traffic from the surrounding neighborhood. Ben watched for a moment, then decided to move to the parking lot next to the elementary school. The sign said Staff Only, but he'd never had any problem with disregarding minor rules that stood between him and what he wanted. Besides, he wouldn't need the space for any longer than it took the buses to unload.

Alanna was on the third bus. Laughing at something Susan was saying, she stepped to the ground, switched her backpack to her other shoulder, then tucked her hair behind one ear. She waited for her sister to get off—Josie, three years younger, also born of a worthless father—then the three of them started toward the grade school building. Halfway there, they were met by a small gang of kids—Caleb from the night before, a taller, older boy, and three younger kids. Ben had seen them all at the concert, with the man Alanna called Dr. J.D.

Caleb was a thin, gangly kid with brown hair and a shy smile. He looked about as innocent as a boy his age could be, but Ben knew well that looks were often deceiving. He could pass for God's own favorite angel himself, given the incentive, when he'd always had a friendlier acquaintance with the horns-and-tail guy down below.

The younger kids wandered off while the older four settled on the steps to talk. Ben had never been the sentimental type—had never looked at a little girl and wondered, Does my daughter look like that? Does she giggle and act silly? Is she a tomboy or a prissy little girl? He'd never given a thought to whether she played soccer or studied dance or liked boys yet, had never considered her first words, first steps, first date, first broken heart.

Now it all seemed more important than he could have imagined. Seeing her made the difference. It made her *real*.

A woman who reminded him of every sour-faced school secretary he'd ever known—and being a frequent visitor to the principal's office, he'd known plenty—passed his car and gave him a narrowed look. Deciding it was a good time to leave, he drove out of the parking lot, but he didn't head for McBride Inn or the Bishop house on Fourth or even the lodge. He went to the hardware store across the street from the doughnut shop and felt a comfortable sense of familiarity the instant he walked through the door. He might not belong in a lot of places, but after fifteen years in construction, he knew hardware stores well. He could hold his own in any of them.

This one was nothing like the huge building centers that could be found all over, which gave it that much more personality. The checkout counter was located in the center of the building and also served as office space. Just past it was a circle of lawn chairs, price tags taped to the backs and ignored by the men who sat in them, drinking coffee and talking. Most of them were elderly and dressed in work clothes, and all turned to watch as he approached.

"Morning."

A couple repeated his greeting. The others simply nodded.

"Think it's going to rain this morning?"

Everyone turned to look at the oldest man in the group, who removed his John Deere cap, scratched his head, then replaced it. "Might. My bones have been hurtin' this mornin'. Then again, that could just be my arthritis flarin' up."

"Or bein' ninety-four years old," mumbled the man beside him, a youngster probably in his seventies.

"Ain't nothin' wrong with my hearing." The old man scowled before turning his attention back to Ben. "You new in town?"

"Yes, sir. Name's Ben Foster. I'm up here for a while from Atlanta."

"Isn't young Nathan's wife from Atlanta or somewheres down that way?" The question came from the man nearest Ben, with thinning white hair, the name Melvin embroidered above his shirt pocket, and missing parts of three fingers on his right hand. "You know Emilie Bishop? Used to be Dalton?"

"No, sir."

"Huh. I don't believe I'd live someplace where I didn't know my neighbors."

Ben liked the anonymity of the city. He'd known plenty of people and hadn't needed to know more. Plus, it had been easy to avoid his mother when one of her rare maternal urges struck, or his father when he needed to be bailed out of jail at three in the morning.

"You lookin' for a job while you're here?" the old man asked.

"Yes, sir, I am. Thought maybe someone in here could point me in the right direction."

"What can you do?"

"Just about everything on a building site." He wasn't boasting—there was no need to. Besides, he knew better. Any one of these men would spot a fraud a mile away.

"Pull up a chair and we'll see what we can come up with," the old man said, waving a bony hand in the direction of a display of lawn chairs.

Ben chose a five-gallon bucket of drywall mud instead. No sooner had he settled in than Melvin was passing him a Styrofoam cup of steaming black coffee brewed strong enough to strip paint.

The conversation meandered from debating the merits of the new construction in town to forecasting the weather to occasional questions about Ben's previous jobs, what he was best at, what he disliked most. He admitted to a fondness for framing and building cabinetry, along with a strong dislike for painting and outright loathing for taping and mudding, choked down the coffee in small sips, and listened. Somewhere in the conversation, he decided there was something to be said about small-town familiarity. These men had known each other virtually their entire lives. They knew all the important events and embarrassing moments in each other's lives. They had a history with each other.

Emmaline was the only person Ben had shared that kind of history with. Between his practically nonexistent relationship with his father, his on-again, mostly off-again relationship with his mother, and his absentee-father act with Alanna, he was alone. No one who was a part of his life today had been a part of it ten years ago or ten years before that. No one who knew him now knew that his parents had more or less abandoned him before he could talk, that his grandmother had done most of his raising, or that he'd abandoned his own child before she was even born.

Maybe someone knowing all his secrets wasn't such a good thing, after all.

He'd swallowed the last gulp of coffee and felt as if the hole it was eating through his stomach was just about complete when the bell over the door rang. Every man around him looked to the front, so he did, too. Unfortunately, from his vantage point all he could see was a freestanding display of saws.

"Well, would you look at that," the old man murmured.

"What do ya think she's doin' here?"

"Probably come to ask for advice. I heard she's been turned down by every contractor and sub in town," Melvin remarked. For Ben's benefit, he explained, "She bought the old Hope place outside of town. It needs a lot of work, but no sub wants to take on a small job like that when they can sign on with one of the contractors and have work guaranteed into next year."

"I heard she was bringing in somebody from Howland."

"She was gonna try," the old man said. "Would *you* drive ninety miles round-trip through the mountains for a short-term job, or spend most of your profits to move here until the work was done?"

There was a chorus of no's, then slowly the old man

turned to look at Ben. So did Melvin and, one by one, all the others. The old man removed the John Deere cap once more, scratched his head, then grinned. "Son, this just might be your lucky day. Provided you're as good as you say and you meet with her approval"—someone snorted—"you just might get yourself a job. You'd even get to be your own boss."

Someone snorted again.

Finally the click of heels on concrete circled the display and came to a stop at the counter. Ben leaned forward to see past Melvin and found he had to look six inches higher than he normally would to see the mystery woman's face.

The Amazon.

Her manner was so cool and detached that she might as well wear a sign that said Keep Your Distance. Her posture was rigid, her clothes—a navy-blue jacket and skirt, pin-striped vest, and heels—unimaginative. Her black hair was pulled back and secured at her nape, but her skin was too pale, her features too delicate, for the style to look harsh, as intended.

As she waited, showing no visible signs of impatience, Melvin pushed himself to his feet. "Pardon me, boys, I've got a customer. If I can, I'll steer her your way, sonny."

Ben looked at her again. She was confident, intimidating, and judging from those earlier snorts, presumably difficult. But there was more to her than that. In the café the afternoon before, she'd been the one intimidated, and by nothing more than a tiny baby, and at her car last evening, when she'd thought he was following her, she'd looked vulnerable. Neither response was quite what he would have expected.

"You do that," he replied. Hey, a job was a job, and considering his real purpose for staying in Bethlehem, being his own boss just might come in real handy. As for working for the Amazon . . . She was a beautiful woman, and like most Southern men, he had a weakness for beautiful women. She was a bit of a puzzle, too, and as a kid, he'd always been good at solving puzzles. Besides, it wouldn't be for long. Only until he found the courage to approach Alanna.

What would happen then was anyone's guess.

LYNDA WAITED AT THE COUNTER, DELIBERATELY ignoring the men off to her right. She hadn't been pleased when she'd checked her schedule immediately after arriving at the office and discovered that the deadline she'd set for finding someone to work on her house had arrived. She wasn't at all pleased that she'd had three weeks to look, had made countless calls to every contractor, carpenter, plumber, electrician, and self-proclaimed handyman in a hundred-mile radius, and had gotten the same answer from every one of them. *No.*

Oh, most of them had couched it differently. *Call back in October or December or after New Year's. I can give you an estimate in August. I'm all booked up until next spring. I just don't have the time.* No one wanted to tie himself up on a one-time remodel, not even for premium wages, exceptional benefits, and bonuses.

But she refused to accept defeat. There must be *someone* willing to handle at least the most pressing repairs. Her big plans, such as the laundry room, the new floors, and the bathroom remodels, could wait, but the leaky roof, the faulty wiring, and the rotted porch boards were priorities. She would see them fixed immediately, even if it meant buying a shelfful of how-to books and doing the work herself.

The idea made her smile. If there was one thing she knew nothing about—besides babies—it was construction. Any roofing, wiring, or carpentry she might do would surely result in conditions more dangerous than she currently faced.

"What can I do for you, miss?"

She turned up the competence, the capable confidence in the smile, a few megawatts. "I'm looking for someone to handle a few small jobs for me, Mr. Fitzgerald, and I was told you might be able to help."

"What kind of jobs?"

As she detailed the priorities, he started to grin and sent several sneaky glances toward his cronies in back. Lynda felt the heat rising up her neck, as if she were giving them great cause for amusement without knowing why. The bigger he grinned, the stiffer she got. By the time she finished, she was barely moving her mouth.

"Well, now . . . " The old man tilted his head to one side and scratched his jaw. "You know, Bethlehem's got something of a boom goin' on right now in construction. Anybody can hammer a nail straight won't have no problem finding steady, long-term work with any of the builders round here. And you wouldn't want somebody can't hammer a nail straight. Somebody who doesn't like taping and mudding—that's okay, 'cause nobody likes it. That's why the fellas that do it get paid so well. What kinda money are you planning to offer?"

"I . . . don't know." She couldn't remember saying those words at any time in the last twelve years. She'd learned instead to reply, I'll find out, and do so. But she hadn't found out this time. She'd assumed she would pay a fair price for good work.

"I'll warn you, it's a seller's market." The old man pitched his voice unnecessarily loud. "Anyone you find who's both qualified and willing will set his own price, and it likely won't be cheap."

She smiled faintly. She hadn't dickered over the price of the house. She certainly wasn't going to fuss over the cost of making it the perfect home she wanted it to be.

Lowering his voice to normal once again, the old man went on. "There's a young 'un over there, new in town, talks all the right talk. 'Course, that don't mean he's as good as he says, but a few calls to Georgia can prove that."

Lynda felt as if her smile were frozen in place. What were the odds that it wasn't Ben of the green eyes, the sensual Southern drawl, and the lazy, heat-inducing way of moving? Ben, the good candidate for fantasies, if she were the fantasy-indulging type.

"Why don't I call him over and introduce you, then the two of you can reach an agreement amongst yourselves."

She wanted to say no, forget it, she'd changed her mind. But the notation on her calendar—to say nothing of the fact that rain was forecast for the day and into the night, with one of those roof leaks directly above her bed—kept the words inside. Instead she simply nodded in agreement.

"Come on over here, son," he called, beckoning with his mangled hand. "Lady's got a proposition to discuss with you."

She tried not to watch, but did anyway, as Ben stood up and . . . oh, yes, ambled lazily around the old men in their lawn chairs. He stopped at the end of the counter, a respectable distance between them, and waited for someone to speak.

"Ben Foster, this is . . . " Mr. Fitzgerald scratched his jaw again. "Sorry, miss. I don't believe I know your name."

She was opening her mouth to speak when Ben did. "Lynda." He extended his hand, leaving her no choice but to take it. The palm was calloused, the fingers long and slender, the nails blunt cut. The knuckle of his middle finger was swollen and the finger made a distinct bend from there to the tip, leaving a gap between it and the ring finger. This was a hand that had done a lot of hard work . . . and had probably delivered some incredible pleasure.

She slid her palm against his, curved her fingers ever so slightly around his. She realized with a mental shiver that she was cool and clammy, but his heat was seeping slowly through her veins, stirring her blood, bringing with it a sense of . . . potential.

"I'll leave you two young 'uns to work out the details yourself," Mr. Fitzgerald said as he headed back to his chair.

A moment passed before she realized the old man was gone, another moment before she understood that every eye in the place was on them. She tugged her hand free and gestured toward the door, and they started walking in that direction. "How do you know my name?"

"I heard it at the café yesterday. But I didn't catch your last name."

"Barone."

"I bet that's the first time anyone called you young 'un," he remarked as they approached the door.

"But not you." From the corner of her eye, she saw him shrug—saw the snug-fitting T-shirt stretch over muscles that rippled—and warned herself to forget her self-imposed deadline, buy a few large buckets, and get out before it was too late. But the only thing she forgot as he laughed was her own warning.

"I've been called every name you can think of"—his gaze slid over her all-business suit and no-nonsense hair style—"and a few you've probably never heard." He laid his hand on the door, then raised his brows in silent question. When she nodded, he pushed the door open, then followed her outside.

The air was muggy and wrapped itself around her. The sun was still shining in patches, but dark clouds had moved over the valley, bringing with them a slight breeze and a suffocating closeness. She didn't mind, though. It was better than the hardware store and the grinning old men.

"Melvin said you have a proposition to make. Sounds interesting."

"Actually, I have a job to offer, provided you're interested and your references check out." She kept her gaze on the brick buildings across the street. "I recently bought an older house. It's in fairly good shape, but the previous owners did no maintenance or repairs for fifty years or so. I have plans to completely redo the place—"

"When you're able to hire a real crew."

She wasted a moment analyzing the comment, certain it was just a little mocking but unable to find proof in his calm, steady voice. "In the meantime," she finally went on, "there are some repairs that really can't wait. The job will involve some roofing, some rewiring, replacing rotted floorboards, and maybe a few other small repairs. As for salary—" Abruptly, she realized why the old man had all but shouted his piece about a seller's market, and a flush warmed the back of her neck again as her jaw tightened. "As Mr. Fitzgerald made a point of letting you know, you can set your own price . . . within reason."

He was grinning again. She could hear it in his voice. "Relax, Ms. Barone. I'm just looking for a temporary job. I'm not planning on getting rich. So . . . Why don't we go to Harry's, have a cup of coffee, and talk? I can tell you whether I'm qualified and willing, and you can get the information you need to check out my references. Deal?"

She finally looked at him again, and felt the strangest sensation in her stomach. Butterflies. As if she hadn't made a thousand deals a million times more significant with men immeasurably more important. As if there were some sort of potential between them. As if he could not only fix her house but might even fix her life.

Then she came back to her senses. She was behaving foolishly. Her life didn't need fixing. It was perfectly fine as it was. This was merely a simple job interview, prospective employer to prospective employee—business, plain and simple. And so, as she turned toward Harry's, she gave him her standard aloof business smile and called on her standard business voice. "It's a deal, Mr. Foster."

Chapter Three

One hot summer night when he was fifteen, Ben had gone for a ride with some friends. They'd stopped at a convenience store for beer and cigarettes, and they'd cruised a few back roads. He hadn't had a clue, he'd told Emmaline later that night at the jail, that the car, the beer, and the cigarettes were all stolen, along with the contents of the store's cash register. For once, he'd been telling the truth, and she'd believed him. But she'd warned him on the way out of the police station that he was a lousy judge of character, and it was going to get him in serious trouble someday.

Truth was, he was a damn good judge of character. He'd known those kids he went joyriding with were thieves and troublemakers. He just hadn't cared.

He didn't know exactly what Lynda Barone was. As they waited for the red-haired waitress to bring their drinks, he studied her, seeking answers. The fact that she had money was obvious in ways that had nothing to do with the hundred-fifty-grand car parked back at the hardware store. She looked, acted, even smelled rich.

He didn't have any automatic prejudices in favor of or against wealth. Some of the most down-to-earth good ol' boys in Georgia had money to burn, and some of the sorriest excuses for wasting oxygen didn't have two dimes to call their own. How important the wealth was to her would determine how important it was to him, and he didn't know that yet.

Money aside, he couldn't quite get a feel for her. She apparently had a reputation for being difficult, and yet she could be intimidated by a baby. She was evidently successful in her career, but on the short walk to Harry's, he'd asked her the usual getting-to-know-you questions, and she'd answered in words of one syllable without ever looking at him. Was she shy? Private? Too busy to waste time on idle chatter? Or disdainful of fraternizing with the help?

He was still trying to figure it out.

Maeve greeted them both, filled Lynda's coffee cup, and set a glass of iced tea in front of him. He gave the pale liquid a long, sorry look before reaching for the sugar. "You Yankees may have won the war, but you still haven't learned the secret to making good iced tea." He doubted the sugar would improve it much. Sweetness could hide only so many flaws—a fact that applied to life as well as tea.

She smiled an all-purpose smile, thin and quick. "If you don't object, Mr. Foster, I'd like to get right to business. I have a busy schedule today."

And she didn't want to disrupt it any longer than

necessary with him. He could understand that . . . though he wondered what was the point of having all that money if she couldn't take a few hours off when she needed to.

"My first priority on the house is the roof. It leaks."

He glanced at the clouds settling over the valley, as if the weight of the rain they carried was slowly forcing them to the ground.

She looked out, too, and a scowl wrinkled the fine skin across her forehead. "Additionally, I have electrical problems. Lightbulbs burn out fairly quickly, and the circuits overload on a regular basis. There are also some rotted boards on the porch." She grimaced as if she'd gone through a couple of them.

"That's it?"

"Those are the priorities. There's also a leak under the kitchen sink and a drip in the bathroom sink, and one of the toilets runs constantly. There are no shelves and not enough electrical outlets in my office, the kitchen needs additional outlets and cabinets as well, the floors are in need of work, some of the molding is missing, the banister is wobbly, the front door sticks, some windows need replacing, and—"

"I get the picture."

She drew a breath. "Can you handle the priorities and, time allowing, some of the lesser jobs?"

"Yes." Fact was, any reasonably skilled handyman could do most of them.

"Would you like to see the house so you can prepare an estimate, and then we can—"

The first raindrops were fat and landed with audible plops on the flat surfaces outside the window. The wrinkles returned to her forehead as she watched them, and he took advantage of her preoccupation to speak. "We can do it two ways, Ms. Barone. I can give you one price that covers everything. You pay me, I buy the supplies and hire whatever help I need. Or you can buy the supplies and hire my help, and pay me an hourly wage. Since I don't know how long I'll be in Bethlehem, that's what I would prefer." He didn't want to be stuck there until a specific job was finished, and he didn't want to be accountable for her money.

In the moment that she looked at him, he would bet she'd realized it was harder to get ripped off if she controlled the money. "All right," she agreed. From her bag, she withdrew a notebook and pen, made a few notes inside, then slid both across the table to him. "If you'll fill out that information, I'll make the necessary calls today, and provided that everything checks out, perhaps you can start tomorrow."

The leather binding on the notebook was so soft he wanted to stroke it for a moment. The pen inside was silver, heavily engraved, a fountain pen filled with peacock blue ink. She looked as if she might have been born clutching it in one hand. He was tempted to lay it aside and borrow the waitress's #2 pencil instead.

The information was standard—name, social security number, current and previous addresses, job history, references, emergency contact. He filled in most of the blanks, then handed the notebook back to her.

"You list your name as Ben E. Foster. What does the *E* stand for?"

He gave the answer his drunken mother had once given him, deliberately slurring the words in an overdone backwoods-Georgia-mountains accent. "Enythang you want."

She didn't smile.

He didn't, either. "It doesn't stand for anything. My old man liked Ben E. King."

She looked as if she didn't know who that was, and didn't care. "There's a period of five months before your last job that are unaccounted for. Were you unemployed at the time?"

Ben resisted the urge to squirm on the bench. "No, ma'am. But I can guarantee you won't get a good recommendation from the man I worked for then."

"Why not?"

"He fired me." It hadn't been the first time he was fired and probably wouldn't be the last. It had, however, been the first time the boss had tried to kill him before firing him.

"Why?"

He wished he'd said he'd been out of work. He didn't want to get into the details of what definitely wasn't one of his finer moments. "Let's just say . . . she never told me she was engaged."

A look of distaste crossed her dark eyes. With a slow blink, she returned her gaze to the notebook. "You left the emergency contact blank."

He had parents who'd never wanted him, other relatives who hardly knew him, and a daughter to whom he'd never existed. "There's no one."

She looked up again. The distaste was gone and replaced by something even worse—pity. But it disappeared as quickly as it came, and she closed the notebook with a snap. "You didn't tell me the salary you require."

He wasn't looking to get rich, he'd told her, but he saw no reason to sell himself cheap just to prove it. He named a reasonable range, using his best wage back in Georgia for the low figure and adding a few bucks to it for the high. Her expression was so cool that it was impossible to tell whether she'd been considering the same range, higher or lower, but it didn't matter. The amount was more than fair, and he could live on it. That was all that counted.

"Agreed," she said. "Once I speak to your former employers, I'll have our legal department draw up a contract, and you can have your own attorney review it. Bethlehem has only a few lawyers. Any one of them will do it for a reasonable fee."

"I'll take your word, and your legal department's word, for it." He wasn't a contracts sort of person. Back home, his handshake was more binding than a piece of paper could ever be.

"Very well." She returned the pad and pen to her bag, tossed a five on the table, then pulled out a compact umbrella. Ben would have given a lot if it were orange with yellow daisies or even a nice solid hot pink or lime green. But, like her suit and heels, it was a dull, drab navy-blue. "I'll be in touch with you, Mr. Foster."

He doubted it. Oh, she would call and tell him the job was his—after all, he was good and she was desperate—but he would wager his first week's salary that she hadn't connected with anyone in a long time. All work and no play had made Lynda one cool, distant lady.

He watched her leave, expertly opening the umbrella as she went through the door so not even one raindrop touched her. She headed toward the hardware store without a look back. Her back was straight, her head high, her strides long and purposeful. She moved like someone who knew exactly where she was going.

But what would she have when she got there? Any friends? Family? Lovers?

"So you're going to be working for Ms. Baron."

Ben gazed at Gloria, sliding into the seat across from him. "You eavesdropping back there?"

"I prefer to call it using the ears the good Lord gave me. When do you start?"

"She hasn't hired me yet."

"She will. Have you seen the house yet? Lovely place. Sits on a hill looking down on the town. The place might be a little run-down now, but when it was new, it was a gem. Teak, mahogany, ebony. Imported marble, stained-glass windows, silk wall coverings all the way from Paris . . . It was beautiful," she said with a sigh, as if remembering it firsthand. "When did you say you'll start?"

He didn't bother pointing out again that he wasn't officially hired yet. "Tomorrow."

"You should go out there today—have a look around, get to know the place. Get a feel for it. Let me draw you a map." She pulled a pencil from behind her ear and a napkin from the dispenser, then her face fell. "I forgot . . . Ms. Brown put a fancy security gate across the road. All you can see is trees, trees, and more trees. I swear, that woman's got more Keep Away signs than anyone I've ever met—and I don't mean just the kind that hang on the gate out there. Do you suppose she's deliberately trying to keep people at a distance, or just doesn't know how to let them near?"

"You're asking the wrong person. I just met her."

"And actually had a conversation with her. That's

more than most people in town can say, and she's been living here for months. She needs to loosen up. You should tell her."

Oh, yeah, that would go over well—the new handyman telling the rich lady boss to loosen up. She would fire him before she ever hired him.

"So . . . things appear to be going your way, Ben Foster. You got into town yesterday, and you have a job today, and you'll be your own boss . . . well, as much as anyone working for Lydia Barone can be his own boss, I imagine. Anything else you need while God's smiling down on you?"

How about an answer to the question of what he was supposed to do about Alanna? Given a gentle shove in the right direction, eventually he'd be able to figure out the rest on his own.

"Keeping your questions to yourself?" she asked with a knowing smile. "That's all right. Well . . . Welcome to Bethlehem, Ben. I just know it'll prove to be everything you need."

Wishing he were half as optimistic, he stood up. "Guess I'll be seeing you around."

"Oh, you will."

As the door closed behind him, Ben imagined he heard the sentiment repeated in a soft whisper. "You certainly will."

AT THE MCKINNEY INDUSTRIES BUILDING THAT housed her office on the third floor, Lynda skipped the elevator and took the stairs to her floor. Along the broad corridor, she passed secretaries, minor and not-so-minor corporate officers, and a board member or two, who all greeted her impersonally. When her own secretary said, "Ms. Barone," in a snooty sort of voice, Lynda asked her to get Melina on the phone, then waited until she closed the office door behind her to roll her eyes. Were Ross and Tom the only people in the entire company who dared call her by her first name?

She'd never thought about it before, but it seemed so. Even Ben Foster had called her by her first name only until he'd learned her last name. Of course, she hadn't called him by his first name at all. It seemed so . . . intimate. *Mr. Foster* was someone you could easily keep at arm's length, but *Ben* was the sort you climbed into the backseat and did wicked things with under the cool moonlight. *Mr. Foster* could be a teacher, a lawyer, a boss. *Ben* was fun, lust, sex.

"Ms. Dimitris is on the line," her secretary called over the intercom.

Lynda slipped out of her jacket, then braced the phone between her shoulder and ear while she dug in her purse for the notebook. "Hi, Melina. I have a job for you. I want whatever information you can get on Ben E-doesn't-stand-for-anything Foster. His social security number—"

"Whoa, hold up. Ben E. Foster? The Southern lad? The devil in blue jeans? What are you up to, Lynda?"

"Nothing," she replied defensively. "I'm making a purely business arrangement—"

Melina gave a whoop that vibrated over the phone line. "You're buying yourself a man! Wow, I hadn't thought of that. It's one way to solve the shortage of dates, isn't it?"

"Calm yourself, Melina. I'm considering hiring Mr. Foster to do some work for me around the house. The roof leaks, and it's raining today. He's a carpenter—sort of a jack-of-all-trades, really—and I can't find anyone here who'll do the work for me, so I'm hiring him as a handyman."

"Uh-huh. I agree, any man who can take care of the 'work' around the house is definitely handy. How are you paying him?"

"I think the more important question is, am I paying you for doing a background check for me, or do I pass my business on to your competition?"

"Rico would charge you double what I do, only get you the easy stuff, and come on to you in the process."

"And that's supposed to warn me off? Do you know how long it's been since any man's come on to me?"

"Yeah, but he's not worth it. And I speak from experience."

Lynda's smile was faint with sympathy. Once upon a time Melina and Rico had been partners in the private investigations business as well as in their personal lives. Melina had thought they would marry and live happily ever after . . . until one of her own employees had caught him on film, checking out the local motels with about half of their female client list. She'd kicked him out of the agency and her life, and claimed it was no big deal, but Lynda knew she'd cried more than a few tears over the rat.

"Okay, give me Ben Foster's info," Melina said, sounding all business. As soon as Lynda finished reading, Melina asked, "What about those unaccounted-for months? Want me to find out what he was doing?"

Lynda thought of his explanation. Did he know he'd blushed when he'd given it? Not the sort of full-face, beet-red blush she was cursed with, but just a bit of crimson darkening his high cheekbones. It was charming. "No. Don't bother with it."

"Okay," Melina agreed before returning to the teasing. "Let's pretend you really are hiring him only to work on your house. This means you'll get to see him whenever you want, right?"

"Wrong. You forget, I work during the day. Most mornings I leave the house by seven and I usually don't get home until about seven in the evening."

"But you're pretty much free to come and go as you please."

"What do you want me to do, Melina? Pull a chair out into the grass, get a Diet Coke and a pair of binoculars, and spend my days watching him work?"

"Sounds like a plan to me. Just be sure to grab a second Diet Coke for me."

"You're all talk, you know that? Listen, I know you're busy, but can you get on this as quickly as possible? I'd like him to start on the roof tomorrow."

"Not a problem. I'll get back to you in a few hours."

After thanking her, Lynda hung up and turned to work. She hated her day feeling so fractured. Sometime in the past five years, she'd become a creature of habit. At one time, it hadn't been unusual for her to walk into the office at seven only to find out that she had an hour to catch a flight to Singapore, London, or Manila. She'd loved jumping on a plane and going someplace new, arriving in some exotic country without even a toothbrush, never knowing for sure that her day would end in the same city, or even on the same continent, where it had begun.

Lately, though, she'd noticed that she liked a little

advance planning. Three or four weeks was ideal, forty-eight hours mandatory. Maybe she was getting old. Settling in.

After a while, she succeeded in immersing herself in work. She stayed at her desk through lunch, as she usually did unless meeting with Ross or Tom, munching on a salad from the dining room downstairs. She'd made up for the morning's lost hours by three o'clock and was actually ahead of schedule when Melina called.

"Sorry for the interruption," Melina said cheerfully. "I'm sure, in your head, you were off in some other time zone, finalizing some incredibly complex deal, but I've got the scoop on the handyman. You want all the juicy details or just the bottom line?"

Every time Melina conducted a background check for M.I., she asked that question. Every time, Lynda opted for the juicy details—which, more often than not, weren't—in a written report and the bottom line on the phone. This time she surprised herself. "Spill the juice."

"Well, from a strictly business viewpoint, he's everything he claims to be. He does good work, is reliable and trustworthy, and knows his stuff. He doesn't waste the customer's time or money, he gets it right the first time, can do damn near anything that needs doing, and he plays well with others."

As long as they keep their fiancées a safe distance away. Like in the next state.

"He's never been married and is an only child. He pays his bills on time, doesn't vote, and has only one credit card. He's never owned a house, but he's got a midnight-blue '65 GTO that I'd give a week's salary to take out on the highway with no cops around." She sighed wistfully, then grew serious. "Now, don't be a prig, Lyn—you know how you are—but he, uh, *does* have an arrest record."

Lynda's disappointment was stronger than the situation called for. "For what?"

"Nothing major. Public drunk a few times. A couple of barroom brawls. There was an incident about fourteen years ago involving a fast car, too much booze, a Georgia state trooper, and a few DeKalb County good-ol'-boy deputies—oh, and the trooper's eighteen-year-old daughter. He doesn't have any recent arrests—just a couple of speeding tickets. Apparently, he got over his fascination with fast girls, but not with fast cars. Lyn, I think you've hired yourself a bona fide, certified bad boy, Southern drawl, tight jeans, and all."

"I haven't hired him yet."

"Oh, come on. So he was a high-spirited lad. You can't hold that against him. They raise 'em that way on purpose down South. Besides, he's all grown up now." When Lynda remained silent, Melina's voice turned sly and coaxing. "Think about those green eyes and that body to die for. Imagine that husky voice calling you pretty baby in the middle of a sultry hot night." Then, in a normal voice, "Think about that tub on your bed overflowing and flooding the entire house."

"Gee, thanks for putting things into perspective for me," Lynda said dryly. "Send me a report and a bill. And thanks for the quick service."

"We aim to please, ma'am. Talk to you later."

Lynda depressed the disconnect switch, then dialed Angels Lodge. Ben was out, and she was relieved to get voice mail instead. She wasn't at all disappointed at missing the chance to hear his lazy, honey-smooth voice. Really, she wasn't.

Besides, she thought after leaving a message along with directions to her house for a Wednesday morning meeting, there was always tomorrow.

EVERY DAY AFTER SCHOOL, ALANNA AND JOSIE Dalton rode the bus to the Winchester house, where they had cookies and lemonade, did their homework, then played outside or helped Miss Agatha and Miss Corinna until Aunt Emilie came home. It was a big change from the way things were when they lived with their mom, Alanna thought, and she liked it, even if liking it made her feel bad.

It wasn't that she didn't love her mom, Berry. She did. But it was so much easier living with Aunt Emilie and Uncle Nathan. No matter what happened, no matter how bad things got, Emilie and Nathan would never leave them the way Berry used to. Even when they were poor and homeless, before Nathan, Emilie had never let them go hungry and she'd always been there to take care of them.

But their mom had done the best she could, Alanna reminded herself with a sigh as she curled her feet under her on the glider. She was sitting under the big maple tree in the sisters' front yard with a pad of paper and an ink pen. Brendan was driving his dump truck, with his bear Earnest inside, and a few feet away Josie was playing in the grass with their cousin Michael. Because it was warm and he'd just woke up from his nap, Michael wasn't wearing anything but his diaper, and he giggled every time Josie tickled his tummy.

"Are you writing to Mama?" Josie asked.

"Yes." At least once every week since they'd moved

into Uncle Nathan's house across the street, she'd written a letter to their mother. Sometimes the letters went to apartments in Boston, Providence, or Hartford. Sometimes they went to hospitals or jails. Their mom had a problem with drugs and alcohol and men and life. Most the time she couldn't take care of herself, so she sure couldn't take care of Alanna and the kids. Most of the time she was real sorry about that.

Usually Alanna was, too. But lately she'd mostly been mad.

"If you have room, tell her I love her," Josie said, then started Michael's favorite game, peekaboo.

Alanna had room. So far, all she'd written was the date and *Dear Mama.* Usually she told her all about school and the silly things Josie and Brendan said and did. She'd already told her that in July she was going to camp with her best friend, Susan, and some other girls from school. The camp was in Massachusetts and was named Woolaroc—for *woo*ds, *la*ke, and *roc*ks—but Susan kept calling it Camp Woe-Is-Me and Woe-Be-Gone. She'd told Berry about all her friends and how good her grades had gotten, and about Miss Maggie's baby, Rachel, who lived across the street, and being in Miss Holly's wedding and all the plans for Miss Agatha's wedding.

She always told her everything, because she knew Berry didn't like missing out on their lives, even if it was her own fault. But at that moment, she couldn't think of anything to say besides *Dear Mama.* Except *Why aren't you here?*

And *Why are we living with Aunt Emilie and Uncle Nathan instead of with you?*

And *Why do they love us better than you do?*

Alanna's face grew hot, and she felt funny deep inside, like she'd done something wrong. The questions were mean, and she didn't want to be mean to her mother. It was just that it wasn't fair. Practically every kid she knew lived with both his mother and father. Even the kids whose parents were divorced lived with one of them and usually saw the other. But they didn't even get to live with the one parent they had because she loved her drugs more than them.

It just wasn't fair.

With a sigh, she laid the pad and pen aside and got down on the grass with Josie and Michael. The ground was still damp from the morning's rain, but she didn't mind.

"Are you already done writing to Mama?"

"I'll do it later."

"Ask her when she's gonna come see us. She said she would this summer."

Berry was always making promises, but the only times they'd seen her in three years were when Emilie took them to wherever she was living—or locked up. Alanna didn't believe her anymore, but Josie did, and Emilie said it was good for her to have faith.

"Tell her she can have my bed when she comes," Josie announced. "I'll sleep on the floor. And I'll clean my room and show her the picture I got an A on in Art. And we'll have a picnic out at Dr. J.D.'s creek, and I'm gonna ask Miss Maggie to help me bake a cake for her, for all the birthdays we've been gone. We'll go to church, and maybe if we save our allowances, you and me can take her to a special dinner at the inn and have candles and real napkins and ever'thing, but don't tell her that so's it can be a s'prise. And then we can . . ."

Alanna quit paying attention. There was no use getting her hopes up, 'cause their mom wasn't gonna come. It was easier to admit she'd lied from the start than to believe her and then be disappointed. Josie didn't mind the disappointments so much. She'd be sad for a bit, and would make excuses for Berry, and then she'd forget about it. But Alanna was tired of being sad, and of making excuses. Her mother was a bad mother. No mother at all was better than a bad one, and an aunt who really loved them was a hundred times better than a mother who didn't.

She didn't need her mother anymore.

And she didn't *want* her anymore.

Chapter Four

Ben lay on the bed, hands folded behind his head, and listened to Lynda's message play out. So her background check was completed, and she'd found no excuse to not offer him the job. In spite of her need to get the work completed, he suspected she would have preferred to hire someone else—anyone else—over him. But, as Emmaline used to say, beggars couldn't be choosers. Although Lynda Barone had surely never begged in her life, this time she certainly wasn't swamped with options.

Rising from the bed, he grabbed his keys from the table, then left the room for his car. Once he reached the edge of town, he took a meandering route that approached Alanna's baby-sitter's house from behind. Seeing kids in the yard, he slowed, then impulsively stopped when he drew even with them. "Hey there," he called through the open window.

Alanna and her sister were sitting on the grass with a

chubby, dark-haired baby between them. A few yards behind them, an older child—their brother, he guessed—was playing by himself, providing appropriate sound effects.

"We're not supposed to talk to strangers," the younger girl announced. "Uncle Nathan says so."

"That's good advice. Do you think—" Feeling like the lowest of liars, he looked at Alanna as if he'd just recognized her. "Hey, you're Miss Agatha's friend, aren't you? We met at the band concert."

She brushed a strand of hair from her face, then nodded with a vague smile. He'd bet the Amazon's stock portfolio that Alanna remembered next to nothing about him. She'd been too intent on finding young Caleb.

Josie looked from Alanna to him, her expression miffed. "How come you met her without meeting me?"

"You weren't there," Alanna said, giving her a poke. "We're really not supposed to talk to strangers."

"Uncle Nathan says so," Ben said agreeably. "I understand. Do you think he'd mind if you gave directions to one? I hear there's a grocery store around here, but I guess I missed it."

"You talk like Aunt Emilie," Josie announced. "She says she's a Southerner by birth, but she lives in Bethlehem by the grace of God."

"I'm from Atlanta."

"Hey, so's Aunt Emi—"

Alanna clamped her hand over her sister's mouth. "You haven't missed the grocery store. You just didn't go far enough. It's straight ahead on the right."

"Thanks," he said. "I appreciate it."

The chatty sister waved as he pulled away, then exclaimed, "Sheesh, Lannie, you didn't have to . . . "

His daughter was beautiful, responsible enough to be entrusted with a baby's care, had clear blue eyes, wore a crystal around her neck in the shape of a star, and answered to the nickname of Lannie. She was a real person, with her own personality, wants, and needs, and not just some abstract unwanted nuisance, and she had the ability to make him feel guilty for thinking of her that way the last thirteen years.

He would never think of her that way again.

The grocery store was downtown, across the street from the large stone building that housed the courthouse, the police and sheriff's departments, and the jail. To Emmaline's great distress, Ben had become as familiar with Southern jails as his old man had. He intended to stay hell and gone from Bethlehem's jail, for Alanna's sake if not his own.

Fortunately he wasn't a picky eater, he thought as he made his way through the store aisles, because he wasn't much of a cook. Other than a good Southern breakfast of fried ham, biscuits and gravy, his only talents in the kitchen lay in the washing of dishes and the mopping of floors. But he could live just fine on sandwiches and canned soup, scrambled eggs, and frozen pizza.

"Is that your favorite brand?"

Ben looked at the pizza boxes in his hand, then at the girl who'd spoken—no, woman, he corrected. She was in her early twenties, slender, wearing shorts and a T-shirt that had seen better days and a ball cap that covered most of her curly blonde hair. Pretty, innocent, and very young in spite of her age, she reminded him of Alanna, and particularly Josie.

He tossed the pizza into the cart. "Frozen pizza's frozen pizza."

"Actually, it's not." She returned the boxes to the freezer shelf, then took out the same variety in a different brand. "These are the best, and they're cheaper. Trust me."

"You're a frozen pizza connoisseur?"

"An expert judge of all convenience foods. I love to eat and hate to cook." She extended her hand across the shopping cart. "I'm Sophy."

"Ben."

"You're new in town."

"Let me guess. The accent gave me away."

"Bethlehem's a small town. I know everyone here. I would have remembered seeing you."

He gave her a sidelong glance as he pushed his cart toward the ice-cream display. He'd been picked up by his share of women in grocery stores, but he was hard put to say that Sophy was coming on to him. If so, she was too subtle by half—and way too young for his tastes.

"You have family here?" she asked as he added a half gallon of ice cream to the cart.

He thought of Alanna and, with a twinge of guilt, shook his head. It wasn't as if he were truly denying her existence. He had no obligation to share the personal details of his life with anyone, especially a stranger. Hell, he hadn't even decided yet if he was going to share them with Alanna herself, but if so, she certainly deserved to know before everyone else.

"So if it's not family, what brings you to our fair town?"

"Luck. Fate."

"Around here we call those things miracles. O little town of Bethlehem, and all that. Do you believe in miracles?"

"You bet." He might not have set foot in church in the last twenty years for any reason but Emmaline's funeral, but he'd been raised there. He believed in God, miracles, salvation, and damnation.

"Are you looking for work?"

"Already found a job."

"Really? Doing— Working for Ms. Barone, I bet. I heard the old men at the hardware store talking." At the end of the frozen foods aisle, she picked up a couple of insulated bags and slid his pizzas inside, then neatly folded the tops over. "Have you seen her house yet? It's a lovely old place, in spite of all its problems."

"So I've heard. I'll see for myself tomorrow. I'm meeting Lynda there in the morning."

"Lynda," she repeated. "It's a fairly common name for a very uncommon woman. When you first meet her, you expect her to be named something exotic. Alia, maybe, or Kailani."

He chose the checkout with the shortest line and began unloading his cart. "I don't know. I think Lynda suits her. It's Spanish for pretty, isn't it?" And she was definitely that. Not that it mattered. He wouldn't be seeing much of her, and when he did, he would be keeping his distance.

"She's an interesting woman. You wouldn't believe how much moving to Bethlehem has softened her. The Ms. Barone today is so much warmer and friendlier than the one five years ago."

If that was the warmer, friendlier version he'd talked to this morning, she must have been encased in the polar ice cap five years ago.

"She wasn't really living then. She was just going through the motions. But that's changing." She gave him a grin that lit up her entire face. "You'll help it change."

The disinterested checker read out the total of his purchases, and he paid her before fixing a frown on Sophy. "The only thing I'm interested in changing while I'm here is that old house." And *maybe* the relationship he'd never had with his daughter.

He pocketed his change, then picked up two of his bags. Sophy swept up the other two before he could reach them, and fell into step beside him as he headed for his car. "Do you work here?"

"Nope."

"Then why are you masquerading as a dispenser of advice and a bag girl?"

"At least you didn't say 'bag lady,' " she teased. "But dispenser of advice . . . I like that. Sophia Jones, dispenser of advice. She sees all, knows all—"

"But has a knack for avoiding telling all."

"Is this your car?" She touched the GTO's paint job lightly. "Pretty. I bet it purrs like a big, dangerous cat."

He put his bags in the backseat, then leaned against the car and crossed his arms over his chest. She smiled prettily, but when he didn't respond, she put the bags she carried inside, too, then slid her hands into her pockets. "All right. Truth is, I'm looking for work, and I know some of the jobs you'll be doing up there require more than one person."

He looked her over again. She didn't look particularly strong—too slender, too delicate, too blonde—but with most of the work he would be doing, physical strength wasn't as important as know-how and the willingness to follow directions. He'd never worked with a female helper before, but then he'd never done this sort of one-on-one job before, either. He'd always been part of a crew with little, if any, contact with the homeowner.

And there was the clincher—she looked as if she needed the job.

"I assume you've done this kind of work before?"

She nodded enthusiastically enough to make her curls bounce. "I've done lots of building and making repairs. It's really all I've ever done."

"So you know the business end of a hammer."

"They're both business ends, depending on what your business is."

He grinned. "Okay. Tomorrow, at the house, around ten. You have a car?"

"No, but I can get a ride. Thanks, Ben. You won't regret it."

He watched her cross the street, headed for the town square, and wondered if her promise might be right. There wasn't much in his life that he didn't regret, and *that* had been one of Emmaline's great regrets. It was too late to change for her sake . . . but was it too late to do it for himself?

THE SKY WAS STILL DARK WHEN LYNDA'S alarm went off Wednesday morning. She shut it off, then got up and dressed in running clothes. She did an easy five miles on the treadmill before jumping in the shower, where she focused her attention on the day ahead. As usual, there were meetings to attend, reports to study, and proposals to evaluate, as well as a hundred and one problems to solve. She had a conference call scheduled for one P.M. with their offices in Tokyo and London, as well as lunch with Ross, Tom, and the U.S. senator sponsoring a bill they seriously wanted to get through Congress.

Oh, yes, and the meeting with Ben Foster. Funny that it was the one she was most uneasy about. Of course, that couldn't have anything to do with the fact that he was, as Melina had so aptly put it, a bona fide, certified bad boy, now could it? Or how about the fact that she hadn't been on a date in . . . jeez, this century? Or that her hormones had decided to come out of dormancy at the first sight of a vastly inappropriate male?

It was just a business meeting, like all the others—less than all the others. No fortune rode on the outcome. No futures hung in the balance. It was hardly even worthy of her time.

She reminded herself of that as she dressed in a conservative steel-gray skirt and jacket, and reminded herself more emphatically as she traded the suit for a softer, collarless jacket in lavender and matching slacks. The change had nothing to do with him. It was just that she'd worn traditional suits in dark colors both days that week, and she was ready for something lighter, more summery.

As she twisted her hair into a chignon, the creak of the back door opening drifted up the stairs, followed by a brusque call. "It's me, Ms. Barone," Mathilda Martin, Lynda's housekeeper, said loudly.

Inserting pins in her hair as she went, Lynda walked as far as the landing at the top of the back stairs. "I have a man coming out to start work on the house this morning. Could you put on a pot of coffee, Mrs. Martin?"

"Yes'm."

Back in the bathroom, she did her makeup, spritzed herself with perfume, and stepped into her heels before studying her reflection in the mirror. She looked the way she always did, she assured herself—professional, no-nonsense, definitely not someone to underestimate merely because of her gender.

Fastening a watch around her wrist, she headed for the kitchen via the back stairs. "Mrs. Martin, this man that I've hired to work on the house—" She took the last step into the kitchen and came to an abrupt halt.

"Is sitting at your kitchen table," Ben finished for her.

She hadn't heard the intercom buzz, or Mrs. Martin ask for his name, or the back door's creak. His unexpected presence put her off balance. She'd thought she would have time for a cup of coffee and to review her notes on the repairs, but he was early, nearly ten minutes so, leaving her unprepared and irrationally annoyed.

As she slowly moved farther into the room, he stood. For a born-and-bred hell-raiser, he had better manners than most men she came into contact with. Her parents, who had insisted on all the social niceties from her and her brother, would be impressed.

Not that it mattered, of course. Not that they would ever even meet him to know.

"We'll take our coffee in the offi—" She broke off as Mrs. Martin thunked a cup of steaming brew and a plate of sticky buns onto the table across from Ben, and smiled uneasily. "Or right here will be fine. Mrs. Martin, did you bake these rolls?"

"No'm." Picking up a plastic tote filled with cleaning supplies, the woman left the kitchen.

"She's a woman of few words," Ben remarked with a grin. "I got a 'G'morning' and 'Sit there' from her, but that was all."

Lynda slid into a worn, smooth chair, took a moment to sweeten her coffee, then drew a breath and looked up. "I don't have the contract from Legal yet. It was mid-afternoon by the time I asked, and no one could fit it into his schedule. They like to go home by six."

"Slackers."

The corners of her mouth twitched with a smile she barely managed to restrain. "I apologize for the delay. They'll have it ready for me today. As I told you yesterday, the first priority is the roof. I assume that's one of the jobs you'll need an assistant for. Frankly, I don't know where you'll be able to find anyone with experience, but—"

"I already hired someone, but we didn't discuss salary. I figured I'd see how good she is first."

Lynda blinked. "She? You hired a woman?"

"A kid by the name of Sophy Jones. She's about twenty, twenty-two. She says she has experience."

"Did you check with her last employer?"

He broke one of the buns into pieces, then popped a chunk into his mouth. "Not as good as my grandmother's," he said when he swallowed, "but good enough. No, I didn't check with her last boss, ask for references or a social security number or fingerprints or a vial of blood for DNA testing. I just hired her. And if she doesn't work out, I'll fire her."

Lynda opened her mouth to protest, saw the muscles in his jaw tighten, and closed it again. She might be the client paying the bills, but he was the boss. He had to get the work done, and if he wanted to do it with a twenty-year-old woman he knew nothing about—except, no doubt, that she was pretty—that was his prerogative.

Which didn't stop her from politely asking, "Did

you make certain she doesn't have a fiancé to watch out for?"

A hint of bronze crept across his cheeks. "She's ten or twelve years too young for me to care. But"—his expression turned wicked, his voice silky—"I forgot to ask whether *you* have one. You know, someone who might come home, not expecting me to be here."

"No, I don't." She had to swallow to get the words out, which made her sound stiff, even when she got the conversation back on track. "There's a garage out back you can turn into a workshop or storage area or whatever. I presume you'll need to buy and/or rent tools and equipment. There's a place called A-1 Rentals on the west side of town. Anything you can't get at Mr. Fitzgerald's you can probably pick up there. How do you want to handle expenses?"

"More than likely you can set up an account at the hardware store, and I can just charge whatever I need."

She nodded once in agreement, then awkwardly gestured. "Do you want to take a look around?"

"Sure."

She led the way out the back door onto the wrap-around porch. The rotted boards were to the left of the door. She'd gotten into the habit of laying her briefcase and shoulder bag on a bench there while she unlocked the door, and one day last week they'd given way beneath her. Need to lose a few pounds? Melina had teased. Glad my bruised and scraped leg amuses you, Lynda had retorted. *I'd hate to get hurt for no reason.*

Ben glanced at the hole, stepped over it, and walked the length of the porch. She followed, watching as he tested the railing and made it wobble precariously, circled the corner and did it again, then reached the front section of the porch, where brick steps stretched from one end to the other. Chunks of mortar were missing, and in places entire bricks were gone. When he went down the half-dozen steps and across the grass, Lynda waited. She might give up her heels for a fling with this man, but she wasn't wearing them in wet grass.

Standing in the middle of the front lawn, he studied the house, turned once to take in the view of the town in the valley below, then faced her again. "Nice house."

That wasn't most people's first response. The real estate agent hadn't even wanted to show the place to her. The man who'd inspected it told her it had once been a great old house and she really should buy one of the new houses going up in town. Ross had suggested the same.

It wasn't that there was anything terribly wrong with the house. It was old and needed a great deal of work. It was, according to Ross, much too big for a woman living alone—according to the real estate agent, much too isolated and lonely for a woman alone. It would require regular maintenance and upkeep. It would be a burden.

But she had more than enough money to make most burdens go away. And she'd wanted the house from the moment she'd seen it. It was going to be her home—not a place to live, as every other residence she'd ever maintained had been, but *home.*

"Along with the repairs to the roof, you have some rafters up in the attic that need replacing," Ben said. "See the way the roof dips?"

She glanced at the grass, then her lovely, soft, buttery leather shoes, and stayed on the top step. "I'll take your word for it."

"The fascia boards are rotted, too. If I'm going to climb up there, I may as well replace them at the same time." He returned to the porch, leaving wet footprints on each step. "You need to get some landscaping guys out here and see what they can do about the drainage. Your yard's holding way too much water for no more rain than we had, and that can cause problems with your foundation. You said you wanted some windows replaced. What's wrong with them?"

"They don't open."

"You mean they're stuck."

"If I'd meant they were stuck—" Lynda caught herself. He didn't know her well enough to know that she said exactly what she meant. "No, I mean they're not made to open. I want windows I can open in nice weather."

"Not a problem." He said it in such a bland, emotionless way that she wondered if he thought she was a silly woman, wanting to replace perfectly good windows just so she could open them. Not that it mattered what he thought. It was *her* perfect home, or would be when he was finished with it.

He took another long look around, then asked, "Are there any restrictions on what we do? Is the place on the National Register, or is the local historical society going to kick up a fuss?"

"No, but I don't want to make sweeping changes. I like the house the way it is. I just want it fixed."

"What kind of budget are you looking at?"

The question amused Lynda. People rarely thought of her and the word *budget* in the same sentence. Her personal resources were virtually limitless, especially when something was important to her, as this project was. "Money's not a problem."

"For me it is, if you expect top-quality work on a nickel-and-dime budget."

She rephrased. "Money's not a consideration. I'll pay whatever it takes."

He gave her a look that started at the top of her head and slowly eased toward her toes. She wasn't accustomed to such scrutiny and resisted the urge to squirm under the weight of his green gaze. But when he was finished looking, all he did was murmur, "Must be nice," then continue around the porch.

At the back of the house, he leaned against the railing, then rested his hands on the flaking paint. He looked supremely comfortable and at ease. She didn't know what to do with her hands.

"I'll do the roof, the rafters, and the fascia boards first. I'll need to get into the attic."

"Mrs. Martin will be here until five. I'll instruct her to prepare lunch for you and your . . . assistant."

"Sophy," he said absently. "You can call her by her name."

She would rather not, Lynda thought, unwilling to consider why every thought she had of the woman was snide. She didn't have a jealous bone in her body. Even if she were going to be jealous, it would be over someone she had at least a hint of a relationship with. "I'll stop by Mr. Fitzgerald's and A-1 Rentals and set up accounts at both on my way to the office. And you'll . . . ?"

"Get started." He offered his hand, belatedly solving the problem of what to do with hers. She took his.

And held it too long.

And enjoyed it too much.

Chapter Five

"It's quite a view, isn't it?"

Ben knew better than to startle when sitting fifty feet in the air with nothing to break a fall but the unforgiving ground. Still, Sophy's question had caught him off guard. He'd thought she was leaving with Mrs. Martin.

"It reminds me of the town in north Georgia where my grandmother was born," he said. "In the summer, everything was green and overgrown, all hills and valleys like this with a roof here, a steeple there."

Sophy sat cross-legged beside him at the roof peak. "It's been a good week, hasn't it?"

He shrugged, though truth was, it had. They had accumulated a small fortune in tools and supplies and were well on their way to getting the old roof repaired. They'd put in three solid days of work, and it had felt good. He'd seen Alanna again, coming out of the police station Thursday afternoon with her uncle, and that had felt good, too, in an odd way.

But he hadn't seen Lynda at all. No matter how early he got to work, she left earlier. The night before he'd stayed until seven o'clock, doing piddling little jobs like organizing the garage workshop, but she'd stayed away longer.

He wasn't egotistical enough to believe she was avoiding him. He figured she worked long hours routinely and wondered why, if money wasn't a consideration. He'd never known anyone so fortunate, although he considered himself lucky enough. He was never going to get rich, but he'd always had enough for his needs.

Of course, he'd lived alone and accepted no responsibility for anyone but himself. Now he had a daughter, and even if he never tried to be a part of her life, he owed her something.

"Do you miss Georgia?"

He glanced at Sophy. "Why do you ask?"

"You'd gotten so quiet that I thought maybe you were still in that little town where your grandmother was born. Do you miss it?"

They had talked a lot in the past few days, but hadn't said much. She wasn't any more eager to share personal information than he was. He considered her too young to have any secrets . . . though he'd been about her age when Alanna was born. Old enough to create a child, but way too young to father one.

Rather than answer her question seriously, he grinned as he stood up, then offered her a hand. "Crank up the heat and humidity a few notches and learn how to talk right, and I'd feel right at home."

"We do talk right. You're the one with the funny accent."

"Back home, people like this accent."

"Especially the women, I bet," called out a voice from below.

Ben approached the back edge of the roof with care and looked down to see a woman standing in the driveway next to a vintage Volkswagen Beetle convertible.

"You must be Ben. You're awfully cute. I'd hire you to work on my house . . . if I had a house."

Wondering how she knew his name, he made his way down the scaffolding, with Sophy right behind him. By the time they reached the ground, the woman was waiting, offering a handshake. "Hi. I'm Melina Dimitris, Lyn's best friend."

"Lyn?" Sophy echoed.

"Lynda Barone. The owner of this monstrosity? Your boss? A bit on the tall side, pretty, dresses as if the word *casual* were stricken from her vocabulary?"

"Ms. Barone," Sophy said to Ben as if he'd been too slow to catch on.

Melina was a bit on the tall side herself—five eight, maybe five nine—with wildly curling black hair that reached halfway down her back. She was pretty, too, and dressed as if the word *modest* had been stricken from *her* vocabulary. She was slender, muscular, her skin a warm gold a few shades lighter than his own, and she had a healthy appreciation for men. He recognized it in her dark eyes.

"I take it Lynda's not home yet. I knew I should have gone by her office and dragged her out. I swear, she'd work twenty-four hours a day if her body would just give up sleep for a while."

"Hey, Ben, I'm gonna go," Sophy said.

"Can I give you a ride?"

"Nah. I'll catch one down the hill."

He didn't point out that it was nearly a mile down the hill to the electronic gate that kept the world out, or ask who was picking her up or where they were taking her. He'd learned already that she would merely smile and remind him that he was her boss—not her father, her brother, or her guardian angel. "I'll see you Monday."

She waved in acknowledgment, gave Melina Dimitris a nod, then started down the blacktop drive.

"Pretty girl," Melina remarked as Sophy disappeared around the first curve. Then she turned her appreciative smile on him. "So, handsome, what time does Lynda get in?"

"I don't know. I've been here as late as seven. She hasn't."

"It's rude of her to leave her weekend guest unwelcomed like this. Of course, some might say it was rude of me to not tell her I was coming for the weekend."

"Some might," he agreed as he picked up an armload of tools and started for the garage. He was surprised when Melina grabbed the paint bucket filled with trays of fasteners and the circular saw and followed.

"Tell me something," she said as they walked into the garage's cool, shadowy interior. "Was buying this house the biggest mistake Lynda ever made?"

He looked back at the house, at the roof that no

longer sagged, the rows of new shingles, and the unpainted fascia boards. "What was her biggest mistake before the house?"

Melina rolled her eyes. "Agreeing to marry this idiot lawyer back in Buffalo. They both worked twenty-hour days, they never saw each other, and—I'm not kidding—they actually had to pencil in their lovemak—um, their personal time—on their schedules or they never got together."

An ambitious lawyer. Yes, that was the sort of man he could see Lynda with. Someone who thought contracts, negotiations, and profits were more important than her, who would rather broker a corporate merger than spend a lazy afternoon working out his own merger with her.

Ben had never been ambitious, but he'd always known there were more important things in life. All the money in the world couldn't make a person happy, or any less lonely, or any more loved.

He thought Lynda needed to be less lonely, and more loved.

"No," he replied in response to her question. "Buying this house can't begin to compete with that." Then, after a moment, "Did she marry him?"

"No. He—" Abruptly she looked at him. "I probably shouldn't be discussing this with you. Lynda doesn't like being talked about."

He could have guessed that. He could also guess that Melina wouldn't mind it one bit. She liked being the center of attention.

Pulling his keys from his pocket, he started toward the GTO. "I'd let you in to wait, but I don't have a key."

"I have one. You want me to make a copy for you?"

"No, thanks."

She leaned against the driver's door, blocking his way. "Why don't you stick around and have dinner with us? I promise, we'll be much better company than going back to the motel alone."

"How'd you know I'm staying at the motel? As far as that goes, how'd you know my name?"

After studying him for a minute, she opened the small bag slung bandolier-style across her chest, pulled out a business card, and offered it to him. Dimitris Investigations, it read in raised black letters. Underneath was her name, along with a Buffalo address and phone numbers.

"You're a private detective."

"We prefer *investigator.*"

Lynda high-power-super-conservative-business-woman Barone's best friend was a P.I. That was difficult to wrap his mind around. Lynda was so—stuffy? elegant?—and there was something inherently sleazy about the private detective business.

"And you investigate prospective employees for her. So you know pretty much all there is to know about me."

"Pretty much."

Which meant Lynda did, too.

"Hey, don't hold it against her. She was hiring you to work on her precious house. She had to be certain you were what you claimed to be."

He didn't blame her at all for checking him out. It was just common sense. In her place, he would have done the same thing. But he wasn't in her place. He was the one whose life had been snooped through. Just how much, he wondered, was "pretty much"? Did she know about his arrest record? Did she know that his parents had abandoned him or that he'd turned his back on his own kid? None of it was a secret, but he preferred to think that at least some details wouldn't follow him out of state.

"Don't take it so seriously—and please don't get mad and quit," Melina said, exaggerating the seductive tone that seemed to come naturally to her. "Lynda would kill me, and I couldn't even blame her. She says I have a big mouth, but I don't, really. Normally I'm the soul of discretion. It's just that you're so much handsomer than I expected, and there's just something about a Southern drawl, and I'm a sucker for men with blond hair and green eyes, and—" She gave him a sidelong look. "Are you buying any of this?"

"Nope."

"I didn't think so." She pouted more prettily than any Georgia girl he'd ever known. "And here I thought you Southern gentlemen were highly susceptible to the dim-witted female routine."

"I'm a Southerner, but I'm not a gentleman. That was your first mistake." He glanced down the hill as the sound of a finely tuned engine broke the silence. Looking back, he tapped his finger below Melina's full lower lip. "Poke that lip out any farther and you're gonna trip on it. Suck it in, darlin'. I'm not quitting, and I don't see any reason to tell Ms. Barone you blabbed."

She rewarded him with a brilliant smile. "I knew you were a sweetheart. So how about dinner? Just you and two beautiful women. You'll be the envy of every single man in this whole county."

Ben chuckled at her confidence. If he had a weakness for black curls, big doe eyes, long lashes just perfect for batting, and a megawatt smile, he would accept her invitation without hesitation. Since he was beginning to think his biggest weaknesses were straight black hair, intense dark eyes, long legs, a husky voice, and neither talent for nor interest in batting lashes, he had no doubt the wisest action would be to refuse.

Before he could do either, the Mercedes crested the hill, then pulled into the space on the far side of the Beetle. When Lynda got out, she was wearing a blinding smile of her own that made her look younger, softer, prettier. Of course, her clothes helped with the softer part. Her snug-fitting dress was sleeveless, the same color as the flesh of a freshly picked peach off the tree in Emmaline's yard back home, and exposed an awful lot of shapely leg.

"Why didn't you tell me you were coming?" she asked, juggling jacket, briefcase, and purse to hug the shorter woman.

"Because I didn't decide until about five hours ago." Grinning, Melina said for his benefit, "It's a five-hour drive from Buffalo to Bethlehem."

"For anyone who doesn't drive like a bat out of hell," Lynda said dryly.

"Don't insult me to a man who obviously has a well-developed appreciation for fast cars and fine engines." Melina drew her fingertips lightly over the GTO's front fender. "What do you have under here?"

"A 389 with tri-power."

"Three deuces," she murmured appreciatively.

He nodded toward the Beetle. "What do you have? A couple of rubber bands attached to bicycle pedals?"

She feigned a wounded expression. "That is the best automobile I've ever owned. She's a classic."

"Back home we'd park it in the front yard, fill it with dirt, and call it a planter."

After smacking his upper arm, Melina said dramatically, "It's only due to the fact that my mother did a better job raising me than the wild animals did with you that I don't rescind my dinner invitation. But I'll be gracious in spite of your insults and let you escort us anyway. Lyn, the three of us are going to dinner. Change your clothes, let your hair down, and put on your dancing shoes. Let's find some nightlife."

If Ben hadn't been watching, he would have missed the emotions that flashed across Lynda's face—surprise, discomfort, aloofness, disapproval. It made a part of him want to say no, thanks, then get out before he got frostbite. The rebel in him, though, wanted to second Melina's instructions and make her squirm.

"I don't own any dancing shoes," Lynda said, "and the nearest nightlife is forty-five miles away in Howland. Feel free to go and enjoy, but I'm staying here."

"Aw, come on, Lyn. Dinner, a drink or two, maybe a twirl around the dance floor." Melina smiled slyly. "You could wear your heels. Ben's tall enough to handle them."

He was that, Ben thought, though just barely. He stood two inches over six feet. In her heels, she was about an inch taller. Fortunately, his ego had never been tied to meaningless things like height.

The discomfort returned to Lynda's expression—at the idea of dancing with him? Or was it the prospect of socializing with the hired help in general that made her look as if she'd rather parade down Main Street in a housecoat, pink foam rollers, and flip-flops?

Feeling the flush of heat starting at the back of his neck, Ben politely moved Melina away from the car. "You came to visit"—he wondered which name would annoy his boss most—"Lyn, remember? And I've put in a long day. I don't really feel much like dancing tonight. Enjoy your weekend, darlin'. See you Monday, Ms. Barone."

Chapter Six

THOUGH HE'D HAD EVERY INTENTION OF going back to the motel and staying there until Saturday morning, a few hours later Ben found himself at the Starlite Lounge, the most reputable of the few bars in town, sharing a beer with a pretty woman named Leanne while she waited for a friend who was a half hour late and counting. She hadn't said whether the friend was male or female, but he suspected male—and *she* suspected he wasn't coming.

He didn't care that her mind was on someone else, because his was, too—on the two women who'd just walked into the tavern. He could imagine Melina going damn near anywhere she pleased, but not Lynda. If asked to describe her preferred hangout, he would have said quiet, elegant, with fancy hors d'oeuvres, expensive wines, and not a square of denim anywhere in the place. The only time places like the Starlite were quiet was when they closed up for the night, they didn't have even a wave-from-a-distance acquaintance with elegance, and the hors d'oeuvres were pretzels and peanuts. As for any wine they might serve, it was cheaper by the gallon than a single glass of her kind.

The two women sat at a table away from the dance floor, giving him a side view of them both. Melina hadn't changed clothes—she wore khaki shorts that were a scant inch from indecent and a snug-fitting top—but Lynda had traded her dress for navy pants and an ivory blouse, probably linen and silk. The outfit was dressier than most of the women in the place would choose for work or a date, but somehow she didn't look out of place. In fact, she made the others look underdressed for the occasion. You could do that when you were rich and accustomed to setting standards rather than meeting them.

"See someone you'd like an introduction to?"

"No," he replied, feeling foolish at having been caught watching Lynda. "I just noticed my boss over there."

"Who?"

"Lynda Barone."

"Really?" Leanne looked and sounded surprised. "I didn't know she ever put in public appearances, except when mandated by *her* boss. I'd heard she spent her days at the office working and her nights at home working. I don't think I've ever even seen her at the grocery store, though I have heard of a sighting or two at Harry's—unconfirmed, of course."

"You don't know her?"

"Never met her. Of course, she's only lived in Bethlehem a year and a half or so. And I'm hardly of her standing. But who is, besides the McKinneys and the Flynns?" Leanne gave him a curious look. "What do you do for Ms. Barone?"

"I'm working on her house."

"Is it befitting a multimillionaire?"

He wanted to ask how many millions *multi* covered. He'd known she was wealthy, but he hadn't considered that she might be gaspingly, eye-poppingly, downright filthy rich. "It's a great house."

"So what have you found out about her?" Leanne asked, resting her arms on the tabletop. "Is she as difficult as people say? Does she live up to her reputation as an ice maiden? Is it true she's kissin' cousins with the Big Bad Wolf and considers the Wicked Witch of the West her role model?"

Ben glanced at Lynda, sitting quietly while Melina flirted with a lumberjack. Did she know she was the subject of gossip around town? Probably. Did she care? Most people would guess no. Why should she? But Ben thought she probably did.

Leanne laughed, lightening up for the first time since she'd joined him. "What's that saying? 'If you can't say anything nice, come sit by me.' "

Ben shrugged. "I hardly ever see her. She works long hours."

"With nothing secret, wicked, or decadent going on at home, huh? So she's as boring as she seems."

Not boring. Never that. But before he could say so, her gaze shifted to the door and a smile stole across her face. "I appreciate the company, Ben," she said as she gathered her purse and drink. "You're a great distraction. Maybe I'll see you around."

He responded with a nod, then watched her weave

her way between tables to meet the man who'd just come in. He also caught the guy slipping a gold band from his left hand and sliding it into his pocket. Who was he fooling? Leanne? Or everyone else in the place? Not that it was any of his business. He just thought if a person was going to make promises to someone else, he should do his best to honor them.

He drained his beer, ordered another from a passing waitress, then glanced around the bar again. Of course, his attention ended up on Lynda again. Naturally.

She sat alone while Melina danced with Paul Bunyan, and she looked as if she'd rather be anyplace else in the world than alone in a bar. It wasn't her expression that gave her away, at least not overtly. No, she looked poised, cool. But there was a muscle in her jaw clenched too tightly for cool, a rigidity to her posture, and the hint of desperation that underlaid her steady gaze.

He watched her until one song ended and another began. When Melina didn't return, he picked up his beer and made his way to her table. "Mind if I join you?"

Faint relief joined the nearly invisible desperation as she gestured toward the empty chairs. He chose the one to her right and dangled the bottle above the table.

She was watching Melina, but her gaze kept shifting to him, obviously waiting for him to initiate a conversation. Deliberately he remained silent and drank his beer.

After the fourth or fifth glance in thirty seconds, she smiled awkwardly. "I imagine, somewhere in this room, there are wagers being made even as we speak."

He glanced around and saw that they did, indeed, seem to be the topic of more than one discussion. "On how long it takes you to run me off?"

"Or how long it takes you to decide I'm not worth the effort."

Maybe it was the long day he'd worked, or being alone in a strange town on a Friday night, or hell, maybe it was the beer. But at that moment, Ben honestly couldn't imagine ever making that decision. Maybe she was difficult, but Emmaline always said the harder you worked to get something, the sweeter the having was.

"We could outwait all of them," he remarked. "Or we could walk out the door together. That would blow their minds."

She gave an acknowledging nod, then silence settled between them. After a time, she glanced his way again. "I thought you didn't feel like dancing tonight."

"I'm not dancing. I came in for a beer. This is my second."

"And is that your limit?"

He'd never set limits for himself before, which explained the times he'd been arrested, as well as the barroom brawls and most other troubles in his life. But in Bethlehem, limits seemed like a good thing. No getting drunk, in fights, or arrested . . . or involved in unwise affairs. No doing anything that might embarrass his daughter, if she ever found out she was his daughter.

"Yeah," he said, giving the bottle a long look. "That's my limit."

But avoiding unwise affairs didn't mean he couldn't enjoy a slow dance or two in a crowded bar with her best friend nearby, did it?

He looked at Lynda and imagined sliding her chair back, taking her into his arms. Feeling the cool soft silk of her blouse covering the warm soft silk of her skin. Breathing deeply of the rich fragrance that perfumed the long line of her throat. Hearing the slow, steady rhythm of her breathing. Discovering how snugly her body fitted against his. Seeing the slow, lazy awareness seep into her dark eyes. Touching his mouth to the lush curve of hers and tasting . . .

Swallowing hard, he finished the beer in one drink, but it didn't provide the cooling he needed. Okay, so asking her to dance was out of the question. Apparently, even thinking about it was off-limits. What did that leave? Polite, friendly conversation. Surely he could handle that for a few minutes.

"I wouldn't have pegged this for your kind of place," he said, half-surprised that his voice sounded normal and didn't echo the raw, achy way he suddenly felt inside.

"You think I'd prefer someplace elegant and quiet where the dress code is only slightly south of formal?" She folded her hands on the tabletop. "What would you say if I told you our first stop tonight was going to be Five Pines Lounge, but we came here instead because Melina wanted to?"

"And Five Pines Lounge is . . . ?"

"A bar outside town. The kind of bar where, instead of a hat-check girl, they have a pistol-check guy named Vito."

"I'd say you're full of crap. Or you think I am."

For a long, still moment she looked at him, then quietly said, "No, I don't think you are. Truthfully, I don't like bars of any kind. The music's too loud, the air's too smoky, and I'd rather have ice cream than liquor anytime."

"Then why are you here?"

"Melina thinks I need more of a social life. She thinks she can take me to places like this, and some of her gregariousness will automatically rub off." Her smile was rueful. "So far it hasn't worked."

"Do *you* think you need more of a social life?"

She looked at the couples on the dance floor for a moment before smiling that little smile again. "I like my life the way it is. I have everything I want—a great job, a great house, a great friend, financial security, a good relationship with my family. What else is there?"

Someone to share it with. Someone to go home to. More than one friend. But who was he to give advice? He was currently living in a motel, and when he returned to Atlanta, he would rent an apartment as he always had. He had plenty of buddies, but not one really good friend, and at the moment he wasn't on speaking terms with his family. He should fix his own life, and then maybe he'd have the right to tell her how to fix hers.

"Yeah, what else?" he murmured.

After another silence, she asked, "How is the work on the house going?"

He figured she was asking because she found the silence awkward. He answered for the same reason. "It's fine. Considering how long the place has been neglected, it's not in bad shape."

"And how is your assis—Sophy working out?"

"She's fine, too." And she was, at handing him tools, steadying boards, helping to carry supplies. Unfortunately, her construction experience had been just a little bit exaggerated. She didn't know how to use half the tools on the site and couldn't level a board to save her life. He was afraid to let her use the power tools, figuring she'd reduce their entire supply of lumber to kindling or slice off a few body parts. She'd already narrowly missed tacking his hand to the sheathing the day before, instead of the roofing felt.

"She's not from around here, is she? I can't recall ever seeing her before, or hearing of her."

"And do you know everyone in town?"

"I'm . . . familiar with a lot of people."

"Then why doesn't anyone know you?" he asked mildly.

Discomfort wrinkled her forehead and tightened her jaw. "Believe it or not, some people do."

Ben shook his head. "People know of you. They know who you are. No one I've met actually knows you besides Melina."

"And how many people have you met in your few days in town?"

"More than you, I think." Inwardly, Ben grimaced. He hadn't meant for the conversation to veer off like that. He was trying to think of a way to redirect it when soft warm hands grasped his shoulders from behind. When he glanced over his left shoulder, the woman bent around the right and gave him a sexy smile.

"Hi. Remember me?"

She was blonde, tanned, flashy, and he would certainly remember her if he'd met her. Blankly, he shook his head, and her smile turned seductive. "Give me tonight, and you will. I'm Kelli. Want to dance?"

Ben glanced at Lynda, who was looking aloof again,

then he smiled at Kelli. She was pretty, but didn't interest him; sexy, but didn't turn him on. In other words, she was safe.

"Sure," he agreed, letting her pull him to his feet. "See you later," he said to Lynda, whose face could have been carved from stone for all the emotion she showed.

The music was slow, the dancing intimate, and Kelli, he'd bet, was willing to get more so. But when the dance was over, he'd have no trouble telling her no and going home alone.

He wasn't sure he could say the same about Lynda.

YOU'VE FORGOTTEN HOW TO FLIRT."

Lynda gave Melina a long, dry look. "I never knew how to flirt."

"Sure, you did. Remember back in high school?"

"*You* may have been an accomplished flirt in high school, but I was six feet tall by my fifteenth birthday. There were only three boys in my senior class who were taller than me. Believe me, in high school, size matters."

"Size *always* matters," Melina said with a giggle.

It was after ten o'clock, and they were driving out of the valley surrounding Bethlehem with the Mercedes' top down. Melina's seat was reclined a few inches, and her hair was blowing in the breeze. Lynda sat up straight behind the wheel, her hair pulled back and neatly contained. Warm air blasted out of the heating vents, taking the chill off the night, and music from the stereo lost its battle against the night wind, blowing away unheard into the darkness.

They were going nowhere, doing nothing. Melina's idea.

"Hey, there's Angels Lodge," she said, flinging an arm out the open window. "Pull in. Let's see if Ben's home."

Scowling, Lynda continued up the hillside.

"Come on, Lyn. What if he is? And what if he invited you in?"

"And what if Hi-I'm-Kelli-let-me-jump-your-bones is there?"

"He left alone."

"And she left five minutes later." Not that she'd been keeping track. It had been impossible to miss the collective sigh of feminine disappointment when he left, and the echoing sigh of feminine relief when Kelli left—neither of them Lynda's. She didn't care what her employee did on his free time, as long as it didn't affect his job performance. Ben could have a half-dozen Kellis all at once, and as long as he still had the energy to finish her roof, that was fine with her.

"Why didn't you dance with him?" Melina asked, futilely brushing corkscrew strands of hair from her face.

"Well, gee, let's see . . . he didn't ask me?" Maybe she was hopelessly out of date, but she liked men making the first move, calling for dates, risking the rejection. Like any levelheaded person, she preferred to minimize the risk of rejection.

"He didn't ask Blondie, either," Melina said, gazing up at the sky. "But she damn sure got to cuddle up close to him anyway, because she had the nerve to make the first move and you didn't. . . . Man, there are a lot of stars in the sky. No wonder Buffalo doesn't have any stars. You guys are hogging them all. Look at that one. Make a wish on it, quick."

Lynda took her gaze from the road long enough to follow Melina's pointing finger. "That bright one? The one that's *moving*? I seriously doubt Delta's late-night flight to Buffalo will make our wishes come true."

"You never know," Melina said with a contented sigh. "Some passenger on that plane could be on his way to Bethlehem. His final destination could be your heart."

After giving her a disbelieving look, Lynda slowed the car, swung onto the shoulder, and made a tight U-turn. "That's it. You've definitely had too much to drink this evening. I'm taking you home, and we're both getting some sleep."

Melina didn't protest. In fact, she didn't say anything at all until the electronic gate was closing behind them and they were on their way up the drive. She returned the seat to its upright position, combed her curls back, then twisted to face Lynda. "Don't you get lonely, Lyn? Not just for sex, but for companionship. For someone to listen to how your day went, to miss you when you're gone, to give you a solid, safe *someone* to reach out and touch in the middle of a long, dark night. Don't you wish you had someone to share this place with?"

Lynda parked beside the Beetle, put up the convertible's top, then shut off the engine. For a moment, the silence seemed deafening. "I don't need a man to make my life meaningful."

"I do."

Melina couldn't have surprised her more if she'd tried. For a moment, Lynda stared at her, then she choked back a laugh. "*You?* Come on. You're the most self-sufficient woman I know besides me. You own your own business. You carry a gun. Men fall at your feet. You use them, then lose them. Melina, you're a walking advertisement for the we-don't-need-no-stinking-men feminist movement."

"It's not about feminism or self-sufficiency or even sex. Humans are meant to love. It's basic to our very nature. Without it, we're not fulfilling our potential. Part of me is empty because I don't have that kind of love. Part of you is, too."

Lynda got out of the car, waited for Melina to get out, too, then they started across the flagstone path together. "Is this your biological clock ticking?" The idea provided her with some measure of relief. The need for a child . . . that she could understand. But the need for a man, a husband . . . even for someone who considered herself old-fashioned, the notion seemed terribly dated.

"No, it's not the bio clock. I've got plenty of time," Melina said as they went into the kitchen where a dim light burned. "Truth is, it's loneliness. Emptiness. I'm not looking for just great sex anymore—though I certainly wouldn't turn it down. But I want more, Lyn. I want love, marriage, commitment. I want to have it all."

With a shrug and raised brows, she headed up the back stairs, wiggling her fingers in a wave just before disappearing from sight.

Lynda locked up, then wandered into her office. The message light on the machine was blinking, so she pressed Play, then curled up in her desk chair.

"Hi, honey, it's Mom. I sent you the latest issue of *Prospects* this afternoon and realized later that a couple of the notes fell out. When you get it, remember to check out Darnell on page twenty-nine and Raphael on page eighty-three. I realize he's a bit younger than you, and, well, there is the small problem of his lack of a job, but you've got plenty of money and he's awfully cute and ten years isn't really such a lot. Just keep an open mind, and think of the *adorable* grandbabies he can give me. That's all I wanted, sweetie. Take care. Love you."

Shaking her head, Lynda swiveled around to look out the dark window.

The subscription to *Prospects* was one of the more harmless of Janice's efforts to get grandchildren. The magazine, subtitled *Catalog Shopping for the Perfect Mate,* was delivered to the Barone house in Binghamton—thank God. Janice went through it with avid interest and flagged all who showed potential, then sent it on to Lynda, complete with her comments.

Maybe, instead of tossing them into a corner, she should pass them on to Melina. When and how had Melina gotten the idea that only a man could make her life complete? That was such a chauvinistic, traditional belief. She and Melina earned great salaries and respect. They had influence, power, could go anywhere and do anything. They already had it all.

Didn't they?

It was late on a Friday evening, and there was no one to answer the question. Not that time mattered. It could be high noon on a busy weekday, and she would still have no one to answer. For someone who had it *all,* she was sadly short of friends.

Maybe that fact provided part of the answer.

With a shake of her head, she forced her attention to her mother's message. Consider Darnell, and look closely at Raphael. Darnell wasn't in the running, based on nothing more than his name. She liked simple, short names—Joe, John, Dave, Sam, Ben . . . *Ben?*

Shaking her head, she refocused again. As for Raphael . . . Oh, yes, she could see herself with a twenty-four-year-old boy toy who was unemployed and no doubt pretty, in order to produce the absolutely adorable grand-babies. She wouldn't even know what to say to someone like that, though in her head she could hear Melina's seductive advice: *Worry about that after the first anniversary.*

She wasn't planning on any anniversary, at least of that sort. What would she do with a husband besides have hopefully great and regular sex? She would see him for an hour or two each evening, spend a short night beside him, and maybe get to kiss him good-bye in the morning. She might get a bit more time with him on weekends, unless she went out of town or he did. He would get angry at being ignored, and she would feel guilty, but at the same time she would resent him for loading on the guilt, and before they knew it, they would be divorced.

No thanks. Melina could risk it if she wanted, but not Lynda. Self-protection was important to her. So was maintaining her dignity. Since marriage didn't come with lifetime guarantees, and since she didn't buy into the garbage that a woman wasn't complete without a man, she would remain single, thank you. And successful. Happy. Not lonely.

She had it all, and she wouldn't forget it.

BEN AWOKE SATURDAY MORNING TO FIND SUNLIGHT filtering into the room around the edge of the rubber-backed drapes. He sat up in bed and caught his reflection in the mirror that topped the dresser—his jaw dark with beard stubble, his hair standing every which way. He'd come home from the bar last night smelling of cigarette smoke, beer, and Kelli's perfume, a combination that left him queasy, so he'd taken a shower before stretching out in bed to watch TV. If the way his hair had dried was any indication, his sleep had been restless or his dreams had been hot . . . and they hadn't involved Kelli.

He hadn't made it to his feet yet when a knock sounded. "Ben? You up yet?"

Easing out of bed, he went to open the door to Sophy. "Come on in," he said by way of invitation, as he headed toward the kitchenette. "Want some coffee?"

"No thanks. Should I wait out here until you get dressed?"

He glanced down at himself. "I'm wearing boxers. Even Emmaline didn't mind boxers."

"Maybe not, but I'm not your grandmother."

While a cup of water heated in the microwave, Ben put on a pair of jeans, then pulled a shirt over his head. "Okay, Soph, I'm decent."

She peeked, then came into the room. "Well, you're dressed," she corrected him with a smile.

"Aren't you going to close the door?"

"I wasn't planning on it. It might appear improper."

"You're practically young enough to be my daughter," he said dryly. "Unless you've got something planned, I don't think we have to worry about propriety."

Ignoring the door, she opened the drapes, then sat at

the table, where sunlight made her curls gleam golden. "I wouldn't think you could have a daughter much older than . . . oh, twelve or so. Unless you started very young."

For a moment Ben's hand froze in midair, delicately balancing a heaping spoonful of coffee crystals. Once the tightness in his chest eased and he could breathe again, he dumped the coffee into the mug and stirred. "As a matter of fact, I did."

He'd just turned fifteen the week before, and she'd been nineteen, the girlfriend of some distant cousin he hardly knew. They'd had a fight, and she'd seduced Ben to get back at him. Ben had known it at the time and hadn't cared. When you were fifteen and a virgin, and a beautiful woman was stripping off your clothes, you didn't care why. You just thanked your lucky stars.

"No details, please," Sophy said. "I want to know you better, but everyone should be allowed a few secrets. What are your plans for today?"

He sat down at the foot of the bed and sipped his coffee. "Don't have any."

"You like soccer?"

He shrugged. When he was a kid, soccer wasn't played in his neighborhood. Any kid who'd tried to introduce it likely would have gotten the crap beat out of him.

"There's a soccer game at one of the parks right now—the season opener for last year's champs. They're eleven- to fourteen-year-old girls, and they're good. Want to go?"

Off the top of his head, he could think of seventeen things he would rather do than watch a bunch of little girls kick a ball around . . . unless one of those girls was

Alanna. "Sure. Why not? Beats watching television here in the room." Even if watching Saturday-morning TV was one of his favorite ways to pass a lazy weekend. "Let me brush my teeth—"

"And comb your hair. But don't bother to shave. It's cute."

It took him less than five minutes to get ready and out the door. Sophy gave him directions to a park in a middle-class neighborhood on the north side of town. There was a gravel parking lot in the center of the six-block park, with baseball and soccer fields, tennis and basketball courts, several small playgrounds, and plenty of wide open space all around.

There were games going on at three soccer fields, but before he'd moved five feet from the car, he zeroed in on one game, and one player in particular. Alanna was the goalie and wore her team's blue and yellow colors underneath the protective gear. Her blonde hair was in a ponytail, and her skin was a soft, healthy-looking gold. She looked so young . . . and so grown up.

Collapsible bleachers were set up on one side of the field, one set at each end. As he followed Sophy to a seat, he gave the crowd a quick scan and identified Emilie Bishop, holding her little boy while Alanna's brother, Brendan, played beside her. Miss Agatha was there, too, with another elderly woman—her sister, the other matchmaker, he presumed—and so were Bud Grayson and young Caleb.

"Nice turnout," Ben remarked.

"Bethlehem's like that. It's a great community." Sophy twisted to look all around. "Usually, someone from McKinney Industries is here—they sponsor the

Seraphim. That's the blue-and-gold team, last year's champs."

"The Seraphim?"

"It's a fancier way of saying angel, though I suppose most Seraphim feel they deserve a fancier name. After all, they do stand in the presence of God. Me, I'm happy with plain, old angel. Oh, there's the M.I. people. It's Mr. Flynn and Mr. McKinney. I thought maybe Ms. Barone might be here."

Ben fixed a stern look on her. "Is that why you invited me?"

"No." But she sounded a bit too innocent. "I just thought you'd like to do something besides watch PBS."

He'd mentioned the television back in his room, but he hadn't told her what he watched was the cooking and home-improvement shows on public television. How had she guessed?

"Besides, it's a beautiful day, and you shouldn't spend it in a motel room. The sun's shining, it's not too warm, there are no clouds in the sky, and"—jumping to her feet, she yelled—"Woo-hoo! Good save, Alanna!"

Everyone around them was applauding, whistling, and stomping their feet—for *his* daughter. Had Emmaline ever heard applause for her daughter, or for him? Probably the only applause his mother had ever received was on those occasions when she'd finished bringing . . . uh, pleasure and diversion to a group of lusty young men, and *he'd* never done anything applause-worthy in his life. The closest he'd ever come was fishing off the banks of the Chattahoochee River or driving like a rocket fueled by moonshine through the streets of Atlanta.

Of course, he thought with a grin, down South, fishing and driving fast both qualified as sporting events any red-blooded Southerner would be proud to excel in. Ben hadn't been the greatest fisherman, but he'd been pretty damn good at driving fast.

"Watch Alanna," Sophy said. "The blonde goalie for the Seraphim. She's very good."

Ben couldn't say about good, but Alanna was quick, agile, and focused. Her concentration was intense, her reflexes sharp, and she didn't shy away from aggressively defending the goal. He was impressed.

"You got a buck?" Sophy asked, extending her hand palm-up.

He dug in his pocket and pulled out a crumpled bill.

"Thanks. I'll get us something to drink."

"You'll need more—"

She walked to the end of the row, jumped to the ground, and disappeared.

The instant she was gone, Ben started feeling way out of place. He was the only person in this section of bleachers who was alone, and it was kind of a creepy feeling. Though no one in the surrounding rows appeared to notice, he couldn't help but feel he stood out in the wholesome family crowd.

The discomfort faded immediately when the bench shifted and Miss Agatha sat down beside him. "Well, hello, Mr. Foster."

"Miss Agatha. Please call me Ben."

She laid her hand briefly over his. "I understand you like our town so well that you've taken a job and plan to stay."

"Only until the work on the Hope place is done."

She laughed. "Take it from one who knows—work on an old house is *never* done. As soon as you get one thing fixed, another starts showing its age."

"True. But I'm only taking care of the major repairs. Lynda will have to hire someone else for the routine maintenance."

"Lynda Barone. She's an interesting girl. Full of contradictions. A real puzzle." The old lady's smile turned sly. "You look like a young man who enjoys puzzles."

The last thing Ben needed was to have Agatha and her sister turn their matchmaking attention to him. He leaned close and lowered his voice to soft, silky. "I've been warned about you, Miss Agatha," he murmured. "Unless you'll consider giving up Bud and giving me a chance at winning you for myself, you'd better look elsewhere."

Her cheeks turned pink as she laughed. "You flatter an old woman, Ben."

"And you flatter a young man." He claimed her hand and pressed a kiss to the back of it.

"Ah, if I had a granddaughter . . ."

"And if I had a grandfather . . ." He changed the subject. "What brings you out to a soccer game, Miss Agatha? Love of the sport?"

"Oh, heavens, no. I barely understand it. I come for Alanna. You met her the other night. She and her sister, brother, and cousin are as close to grandchildren as I'll ever have. So I go to dance recitals, school plays, soccer and Little League games, karate classes, and concerts."

"Sounds demanding."

She patted his arm. "Spoken like a man who hasn't yet held his firstborn in his arms."

And never would, Ben thought—at least, not the way she meant. He'd missed so much of Alanna's life, so many experiences that could never be replaced.

"Speaking of fathers, where is Alanna's?"

"Her sister, Josie, fell from the bleachers before the game started, and their uncle Nathan took her to the hospital for X rays."

"Her uncle." Ben swallowed hard, but didn't let it drop. "What about her father?"

The set of Miss Agatha's mouth became grim and disapproving. "He's chosen to play no role in his daughter's life. Someday, I hope, he'll realize his mistake, but who's to say if she can ever forgive him?"

"If he realizes his mistake, then he probably won't be foolish enough to expect forgiveness," he said quietly.

"Oh, dear, I didn't mean to sound so—"

"Miss Agatha, look!" Josie Dalton scrambled up the steps, her left arm encased in a bulky splint. "It's not broke or nothin', but look what I get to wear." She fixed her gaze on Ben. "Hey, I 'member you. Did you find the grocery store?"

"Yes, I did."

"He got losted, Miss Agatha, and had to get directions to the store from me and Lannie. Well, mostly Lannie, on account of she had her hand over my mouth so's I couldn't talk." She wrapped her good arm around Agatha's neck. "I gotta go tell Aunt Emilie I'm okay so she won't worry. Uncle Nathan said it was okay to cry if I wanted, but I didn't—well, not very much—'cause cryin's for babies, and there wasn't any reason to cry with him there, 'cause he'd never let anything bad happen to me. See ya, mister. See ya, Miss Agatha."

After she was gone, Agatha sighed softly, stood to leave, then turned back. "Can you imagine how it must feel, Ben, for a child to have such unwavering faith in you?"

He could—barely. The only thing he'd ever trusted his parents to do was let him down. Alanna didn't expect even that much from him.

"It would be pretty scary," he said, watching Josie with Emilie and a dark-haired man whom he assumed was perfect-father, perfect-uncle Nathan Bishop.

"Oh, no," she disagreed. "It would give you something to live up to. Expectations to meet. A precious little heart to not break. A good father works hard to become the person his child believes him to already be."

What did Alanna believe him to be? he wondered as Agatha returned to her seat and Sophy came back carrying two cups of lemonade.

Irresponsible. Selfish. Uncaring. Absent.

He could live up—or was it down?—to those expectations. He'd been doing it all his life.

But could he become better than he'd already proven himself to be?

More important, would anyone care if he did?

Chapter Seven

"I wish you didn't have to go back."

It was Sunday afternoon and Lynda was sitting on the bed in the guest room, watching as Melina packed her bag.

"Me, too. But the job that pays the bills and supports Melina in the way she likes is in Buffalo."

"If you'd met Mr. Right while you were here, you wouldn't think twice about staying."

"If I met Mr. Right, I wouldn't think twice about moving to Timbuktu." Melina glanced around the room, then closed the bag. "Let's get some food before I leave."

"It's already four o'clock. You won't get home until—" Remembering how fast she drove, Lynda broke off. "Where do you want to go?"

"Harry's. I'll get some pie to take home with me."

Melina picked up her bag, and Lynda followed her downstairs. They took separate cars into town, parking side by side. Lynda tried not to notice the midnight-blue GTO parked a few spaces down, but Melina wouldn't let it go unmentioned.

"Well, well, our Southern bad-boy is here and probably anxious for some company. Let's take pity on him, Lyn—and no transforming into the ice maiden."

"Let's don't," Lynda countered. "Let's enjoy your last evening here without strangers."

"But Ben—"

Lynda gave her friend a stern look. "All right," Melina grumbled. "Whatever you say."

Her compliance lasted only for the length of time it took them to walk inside and locate Ben's booth. The instant she saw him, she plastered on a delighted smile and stopped beside his table. "Fancy meeting you here. Mind if we join you?"

He gestured to the opposite bench and Melina slid in. Barely. Leaving Lynda to, presumably, sit next to Ben. She wasn't doing it.

"Your hips are expanding, but you don't need that much room . . . yet," she said dryly. "Slide on over."

"My hips— What— Aaahhh!" Melina slid across, scowling at her, then turned on the smile again for Ben. "How was your weekend?"

"Good. How was yours?"

"Oh, great. Lynda's always such fun."

"I'm sure she is," he replied in that lazy, honey-smooth drawl. "When are you heading back to the city, darlin'?"

"Darlin'," Melina echoed with a sigh. "Tell me, do you call me that because I'm so adorable? Or because it's easier than remembering my name?"

"I remember your name. It's Melina." He barely

touched on the *M* and slid right into the *L* M'lina. All liquid and soft and slurry.

While he said *her* name matter-of-factly. No sliding, no gliding, no soft, sensuous sounds. Just *Lynda*.

"I'm heading home after dinner," Melina said in answer to his question.

"Hope the rubber band doesn't break."

She gave him a saccharine smile. "Jealousy isn't pretty. But I realize I have this great, classic Beetle and all you have is an old GTO."

"Jealousy? Over your turtle-on-wheels?"

Lynda listened to them with a faint stirring of her own jealousy. Why was it so easy for Melina to talk to him? Why was he so willing to flirt with her? And why did he call Melina *darlin'* and her just plain *Lynda*?

The waitress came, took their orders, and told Ben his meal was about ready. He asked her to hold it until theirs was ready also. "Isn't he a sweetheart?" the woman said, directing the comment to Lynda.

"Oh . . . sure. A sweetheart."

"Don't sound too enthusiastic," Ben drawled. "You give the hired help such extravagant compliments, and they might start thinking they're actually worth something."

The comment was uncalled for, and it stung. She didn't respond, though, other than to meet his gaze for one cool moment before looking away.

"Well . . . Maeve, I'm Melina." Sounding unnaturally cheery, Melina offered the waitress her hand. "I'm Lyn's best friend, occasional employee, and the little voice in her head that keeps her from getting too stuffy."

Maeve took her hand. "I'm pleased to meet you, Melina. Let me get these orders in, or you all might fade away from hunger."

After she left, silence settled over the table. Melina looked from Lynda to Ben. "We're a quiet bunch, aren't we? Let's see . . . Ben, why don't you tell us something about yourself we don't already know?"

"You mean there's something in my past you might have missed? Some private something that escaped your snooping?"

Heat flooded Lynda's face. She hadn't known he was aware of Melina's occupation. He'd understood that she was going to check his references . . . but checking references and doing a full-scale background investigation were two totally different things. One was accepted business practice. The other wasn't.

"So much for not telling that I blabbed," Melina said tartly, then continued, not the least bit apologetic.

"Nothing escaped my snooping. If I wanted to know it, I found out. But I imagine you do have a few secrets left. Everyone's entitled to that. Don't be cranky, Ben. You have to admit, it's not unreasonable. She's a woman living alone, and you have access to her house. She couldn't hire just anyone—"

Lynda stopped the flow of her words with a hand on her arm. "It's all right, Melina. If Mr. Foster is offended, he can ask for his paycheck and quit."

His green gaze was impossible to read. So was his expression. Even when he slowly smiled, she still didn't have a clue what he was thinking. She knew she wouldn't trust that smile, though. It was about as friendly an expression as an alligator might wear just before he bit off your fingers. "Why would I quit a steady job with good pay where I get to work without supervision, just because the boss lady is nosy?"

"I'm not—"

This time it was Melina who cut her off. "She's not nosy. She's like a computer, though, that collects data constantly, files and stores it for later use. She can give you chapter and verse on anyone in here right off the top of her head. Test her."

"Melina—"

"Go ahead."

Ben glanced around, then gestured to a man sitting alone at a table against the wall. "What's his story?"

"Drop it," Lynda said.

"Don't you know? Or is the database down? The hard drive giving an error message?"

His mocking tone set her teeth on edge. In a quiet, controlled voice, she said, "His name is Sebastian Knight. He lives on the family farm a few miles outside of town, but he's a carpenter by trade. He was married, but his wife left a few years ago, leaving their little girl, Chrissy, with him. He has family in town and a few friends, but mostly he keeps to himself."

Ben nodded once, as if something she'd said had meant something. She didn't waste any time trying to figure it out.

"Obviously, Mr. Foster, you aren't in the mood for company—at least *my* company. For whatever it's worth, it wasn't my idea to join you. If you'll excuse me. . . ." Rising from the seat, she moved to the booth farthest from where he sat. Huffily, she slid onto the bench so her back was to the room, dropped her purse, and covered her face with both hands. When she heard Melina sit down across from her, she gritted out, "Damned insufferable Southern pig."

There was a moment's silence, then, "One thing I like about you Yankees—when you insult somebody, there's no doubt."

Silently, Lynda groaned.

Ben sat across from her, looking not at all insulted and just the slightest bit ashamed. "If you're wondering what that was about"—he gestured toward the other booth—"it was me, being an ass. It's just . . ." For a moment he seemed to contemplate his excuse, then made a dismissive gesture. "Never mind. I'm sorry."

She wished he hadn't apologized—wished she could continue thinking of him as rude, because that justified her own rudeness. But now that he'd apologized, she had no recourse but to do the same, when the truth was, she didn't feel the least bit sorry.

"I—I shouldn't have said what I did." It was such a shabby apology that her face turned hot again. Her parents never would have let her get by with such a poor substitute for a simple, sincere apology. She could hear Janice in her head, admonishing, We taught you better than that.

But Ben seemed satisfied. "Want to move back over there or call Melina over here?"

"I think it would be best if I cancel my order and go on home, and you and Melina can have dinner together. I've got a lot of work to catch up on, and I don't have much of an appetite anyway, and—"

He was studying her so intently that her words dried up. The silence dragged out—one beat, two, four—then he silkily broke it. "I can't figure you out. Are you afraid of me, or do you believe the hired help's place is as far away from you as possible?"

"I'm not a snob." She hated sounding so prim and snooty—hated more that he thought she sounded that way, too.

"You're rich. You can't help but be a snob to some extent."

"I have money, but I've *earned* every dime of it. I wasn't raised rich. I'm sure my upbringing was hardly different from yours."

"You think so?" he asked cynically. "Put a dollar on the table."

Warily she did so. He added one from his pocket.

"Describe a typical day in grade school," he challenged.

Lynda thought about it a moment, then shrugged. "Mom would get us up for breakfast—my brother, Lucas, and me—and make our lunches. We lived only two blocks from the school, so we walked. After school, Mom always had cookies and milk waiting, and dinner cooking. She sat down with us at the kitchen table, and we told her everything we'd done, then we did our homework, and then we played. When Dad got home, we had dinner, watched a little television, played a bit more, then it was bedtime." She smiled self-consciously. "Sounds like something off *The Donna Reed Show,* doesn't it?"

He didn't smile back. "I missed a lot of school because my mother was usually too hungover to get herself up, much less me. Breakfast was usually a candy bar swiped from the convenience store down the street. I mostly remember getting into trouble because I hadn't done my homework or I'd fallen asleep in class. Most days I went home to an empty apartment, and I entertained myself until she came home or I fell asleep. If I got too hungry, or too scared, like the time in second grade when someone broke in while I was there, I called my grandmother, who came and got me and kept me until my mother realized I was gone.

"Hardly different from yours? I don't think so." He picked up the two dollar bills, slid them into his pocket, then stood up. "Come on. Our food's on the other side of the room, and I *do* have an appetite tonight."

She wanted to refuse, to walk out the door and go home. She wanted him to admit that the tale he'd just told wasn't true. She wanted him to smirk, say "Gotcha," and laugh at her gullibility.

But he wasn't smirking, and when she moved, she didn't leave but got up and walked across the room with him. She slid in beside Melina, and Ben sat across from them. They both ignored Melina's curious looks and began eating.

A few minutes was all Melina could stand. "Well?"

Ben glanced up. "What? You want company *and* conversation?"

"Are you two going to make nice?"

"Is this nice enough for you? How long have you had that turtle-on-wheels?"

"The Beetle's the only car I've ever had. She was a gift from my parents for my sixteenth birthday." Melina pouted. "I've had nothing but good to say about your GTO. It seems only fair that you return the courtesy."

"Darlin', we're talking about a *GTO* versus a *Beetle.* Of course you've said good things about it. She'll turn one-eighteen in the quarter mile in the low twelves. It takes more than twelve seconds for your Bug to get rolling."

For a moment, Lynda thought Melina was going to drool at the prospect of such speed. Then she grinned wickedly. "Okay. So the Bug doesn't fly. But you can't park the GTO at the top of the world on a balmy summer night, put the top down, strip down naked, and make hot, lazy, crazy love under the stars." She fanned herself languidly with one hand. "Take my word for it—it's a completely different way of flying . . . and the only punishment for going too fast is doing it all over again. Sloooowly."

When had the diner become so warm? Lynda wondered dazedly. Harry must be baking back in the kitchen, or Maeve hadn't adjusted the thermostat for the body heat generated by the crowd of . . . seven diners. Okay, so maybe the heat was hers, and hers alone.

One thing was for sure. She would never put the top down on the Mercedes again without thinking of Melina's words . . . and Ben.

He took a long drink of iced tea, but his voice was still husky when he spoke. "Fair enough. Each car has its advantages and its limitations. I guess when a vehicle's as ugly as that Bug, it's got to have some redeeming grace."

Oh, yeah, Lynda thought grimly—jealously—as she caught a glimpse of the look in his eyes. She would think of Melina's words, and Ben making them a reality. *With* Melina.

It was no big deal. It wasn't as if she'd been interested in anything more than a short-term fling. Just a brief reminder that she was a woman, with womanly needs and desires that couldn't be satisfied by a good hostile takeover. But, hey, what did she need sex for? She'd gone without it for so long that soon, feelings like lust and arousal would be leached from her system, like files deleted from the computer she apparently reminded both Ben and Melina of. Then she would officially be a spinster.

"Hey." Melina's elbow applied to her ribs brought her attention back to the present. "I've got to head home. Slide out, give me a hug, then have some dessert for me."

"No, I'd better go, too." Lynda stood up, and all three of them reached for the ticket.

Ben got it first. Before Lynda could protest, Melina grinned. "Why, thank you, sugar," she said in a bad imitation of a Georgia peach. "You Southern gentlemen are so kind." Offering her hand, she reverted to her own voice. "It was a pleasure meeting you, Ben Foster. I like you, and impressions to the contrary, I can't often say that about men I meet. Have Lynda bring you to Buffalo soon. We'll introduce you to the big city, Yankee-style."

"Be careful on your way home," he said, accepting her hand, not even blinking when she kissed his cheek.

Feeling very much like an interloper, Lynda didn't know where to look or what to say when it was her turn. "Thank you for dinner." Oh, God, she sounded stilted and formal.

While Ben took care of the check, thankfully Melina pulled her outside. "Aw, Lyn, you're a hoot, you know? *Relax*. Treat him like a person."

An attractive male person who made her hot, whose own temperature was affected by her best friend. Sure, that would help her relax. "I wish you'd spend the night and go home in the morning."

"I'll be fine. I'm wide awake, and I've got my cell phone, my gun, and my pepper spray. I'm ready for anything." She wrapped her arms around Lynda, hugging her tightly. "Be good—but if pretty boy in there gives you a chance to be bad, be *real* bad. I love you."

"I love you, too." Lynda stepped back and watched Melina settle in behind the wheel. As she backed out, Lynda raised her hand in a wave that looked a lot more lonesome than intended. "Be careful," she called, and Melina responded with an exuberant wave out the window.

Once the car was out of sight, Lynda glanced inside. Ben was talking to Sebastian Knight. Their conversation apparently pleased him. They shook hands, then with a grin, Ben ambled out. He slowed his pace when he saw her standing on the sidewalk between him and his car.

"I thought you were anxious to get home."

"I am. I wanted to give you this." She pulled a card from a pocket inside her bag and handed it to him.

He studied it a moment before looking at her. "Melina's business card? I don't need a private detective."

He offered it back, but Lynda didn't take it. "It's got her cell phone number as well as her home number. In case . . . in case you want to get in touch with her."

Slowly, he began moving again, stopping only when he drew even with her. "I imagine I'll see her again next time she comes for a visit. Other than that, I can't imagine wanting to get in touch with her." He looked for a place to put the card, then reached for her hand and folded it into her palm.

His fingers were strong, warm, most assuredly talented. Standing there on the sidewalk in downtown Bethlehem on a warm May evening, she wouldn't protest if he wanted to touch any other part of her with those long, calloused fingers.

But he released her hand and slid his hands into his hip pockets. "You never answered my question in there. Are you afraid of me, do you dislike me, or do you think I'm too fresh for a mere employee?"

"N-no." That was all she could say, all she could think.

"Then why don't you give me *your* number, Lynda? In case I want to"—his emerald gaze drifted down from her face, then back up again —"get in touch with you?"

She tried to swallow, but her throat had gone dry, tried to treat it as a joke, but her sense of humor had disappeared. "You—you have my number."

His laughter was sudden, unexpected, charming, "I certainly do, darlin'," he said, brushing his fingers lightly over her arm as he walked past her to his car. There he looked back. "Why don't you go to work at a decent hour some morning and have breakfast on the porch before you go? I'll be on my best behavior. Promise."

He didn't wait for an answer, but got in his car and started the engine. He didn't leave right away, though, not until she'd locked herself inside her own car and backed into the street.

As invitations went, she'd had more interesting ones,

certainly more flattering ones, but none more tempting. *I'll be on my best behavior. Promise.*

But she didn't want him on his best behavior. She wanted him at his smuggest, wickedest, Southern bad-boy best. She wanted to be bad.

And she wanted him to make it so good.

IT WAS THE FIRST MONDAY OF SUMMER VACAtion, and the weather was suitably warm. Corinna Winchester Humphries sat in a creaky wicker chair on the front porch and watched her sister and the Dalton children playing in the yard. Sometimes it was difficult to tell who looked forward to summer more—Agatha or the children.

Beside her, Emilie Bishop looked up from her snuggling-with-Michael-before-leaving-for-work. "Are you sure the kids aren't too much trouble?"

It wasn't the first time she had asked the question, or Corinna had insistently responded, "Absolutely. They're no trouble at all, Emilie. You know that."

"But aren't there times you'd like to do things with your friends? Play bridge at Mrs. Larrabee's or attend the Ladies Society meetings over at the lodge?"

Corinna chuckled. "Heavens, why would we want to spend our time with stuffy old women when we could be having fun with the children instead? They're like grandbabies to Agatha and me both. They're fond of us, and we're crazy about them." That was a masterpiece of understatement. She and Agatha loved the Dalton/Bishop brood dearly, and the children loved them, too. They were woefully short of family, and

Corinna hoped the children thought of them as the grandmothers they'd never had.

"They're crazy about you, too," Emilie said with a smile. "We all are." The smile slowly faded as she watched them play. "Has Josie said anything about seeing her mother?"

"She says Berry told them she would come to Bethlehem this summer."

"I've asked Berry not to say things like that. If she can come, she should do it and surprise us all. But when she tells them she'll come, then doesn't . . . The disappointment is so hard for them to bear."

Corinna understood that Berry had problems. Being abandoned by her father after the death of her mother, then growing up in foster homes, had led to a less-than-exemplary lifestyle. But the woman was a *mother,* for heaven's sake. She couldn't put herself ahead of her children and expect to gain more than a twinge of sympathy from Corinna.

"It's easiest on Brendan," Emilie went on. "I'm not sure he knows exactly who Berry is."

"He's lived more of his life in your care than his mother's. As far as he's concerned, 'Aunt Emilie' is just another way of saying 'Mama.' "

Emilie smiled bittersweetly. "Josie gets hurt, she cries, she pouts, she gets over it. But Lannie . . ."

"Alanna is getting tired of excuses." Corinna had noticed the subtle changes in the girl. She no longer indulged Josie when she wanted to talk about Mama. She refused to discuss the promised visit. She treated all mentions of her mother as if they were of no consequence and often used the occasion to cast Emilie in a mother's light instead. And who could blame her? Emilie had been willing to sacrifice everything for them—her job, her home in Atlanta, her money, even her freedom. She'd been willing to face life in prison for them. They *should* love her more.

Emilie nodded in response to Corinna's observation. "Until I moved in with them, all the obligations Berry couldn't or wouldn't handle fell to Alanna. At six years old she was more a mother to Josie and Brendan than Berry ever was. She had so much responsibility for a child. . . . If Berry doesn't get herself under control soon, I think Alanna will write her off. Berry will lose her for good, and I don't know how to stop that from happening."

"You can't stop it, dear," Corinna said, watching as Alanna swung a laughing Brendan in circles. "You've done all you can. You've been honest with the children about their mother. You've acknowledged her problems, and you've helped them deal with the effects. I suspect you're right, that Berry *is* losing Alanna. She has no one to blame but herself. And let's be frank, Emilie. The loss is Berry's, not Alanna's."

"True. I just can't help but wonder what these kids did to deserve a mother like Berry and fathers who are just as bad or worse."

Corinna smiled serenely. "And the children can't help but marvel at how blessed they are to have surrogate parents like you and Nathan."

Emilie gazed at Michael, who looked more like his father every day. "We're *all* blessed to have Nathan. And on that note, I'd better get to work." She kissed Michael and handed him over, then kissed the other children on the way to her car.

As she drove away, Alanna slid into the empty chair. "Were you and Aunt Emilie talking about my mother?"

"What makes you ask?"

"It's the look Aunt Emilie gets. All worried and upset and angry. The look she used to get when Mama didn't come home for days at a time, or when she'd get sick from the drugs and booze she bought with our grocery money."

"Yes, we were talking about your mother."

"She still says she's coming to visit, but I don't care whether she does." Alanna's look was filled with defiance. "I really mean that. She can stay away forever for all I care. We don't need her here. I wish Aunt Emilie was my mom and Uncle Nathan was my dad. They are in every way that counts, and I wish more than anything they were for real, and then we could be a real family."

Corinna laid her hand on Alanna's arm and squeezed gently. Families, and the feelings about them, were a complicated thing. She had always been surrounded by family and treasured them. Emilie, who'd been five when she was placed in the foster-care system, had grown up on the outside looking in. She'd always been alone until she'd taken over the care of her nieces and nephew, and now she wouldn't know how to live without them. Berry, a product of the same upbringing, cared only for herself, and the children's fathers apparently felt the same, since none of the three had ever been a part of their lives.

"You *are* a real family, dear," Corinna gently stressed. "It doesn't matter that Emilie and Nathan aren't your birth parents. You know too well that it's possible to give birth to a child and feel no love or responsibility for him, just as it's possible to never give birth and love someone else's child as if you had."

It was a difficult lesson, one that no child should ever have to learn, regardless of age. But if great quantities of love could lessen its effect, then Alanna would be all right, because she was certainly well loved.

Breathless from a game of ring-around-the-rosy, Agatha dropped down on the porch steps. "Alanna, how would you like to go on a picnic today? Bud tells me there's a lovely place along the stream that runs through Dr. J.D.'s property and is perfect for snacking on sandwiches and brownies and wading in the cool water."

The cloud that had descended over Alanna's features lifted in an instant, and she smiled her prettiest smile. "Sounds like fun, Miss Agatha. Can I help you with the food?"

"You certainly can. In fact, if you're willing, I believe I'll let you fix it all, and I'll supervise. Everyone will be impressed by your talents."

"Okay. I'll wait for you in the kitchen."

As the screen door banged behind Alanna, Corinna gave her sister a dry look. "I suppose a picnic at J.D.'s will include the Brown/Grayson bunch—and, of course, Bud." Hence Agatha's silly grin. "Let me tell you a little secret, Agatha. Caleb's not the least bit interested in Alanna's picnic-making abilities, and Bud's not the least bit interested in yours. You could take a loaf of store-bought bread and a package of bologna, and they both would be perfectly satisfied as long as they shared it with you."

"I know. Isn't that a wonder?"

It was no wonder at all. Agatha had much to offer a

man, even though she'd chosen to remain single until now. Corinna had always known it, and Bud Grayson had needed only a few seconds to realize it. He'd fallen head over heels in love with her, and she with him. Corinna wished them all the happiness in the world and, honesty forced her to acknowledge, envied them a little, too. It had been so long since her Henry had died. So many years that she'd loved him, so many years that she'd missed him. Sometimes she felt as if her life were behind her and Agatha's was just beginning, and in a sense, she was right. So was her sister.

Agatha had fallen in love. Was there anything in the world more worthy of wonder than that?

THE MERCEDES WAS GONE WHEN BEN ARRIVED at work Monday morning. He wasn't really surprised . . . just a little disappointed. Even that was uncalled for. Lynda was his boss. Period. His presence in town was temporary. He wasn't looking for any kind of emotional entanglement—needed to avoid them, in fact, in case he decided he wanted to meet Alanna. Even if he were looking, she wasn't his type, and he for damn sure wasn't hers.

All that acknowledged and understood, he was still a little disappointed.

The morning was half passed and he was setting the table saw near the foot of the steps when the kitchen door opened and Mrs. Martin, came out, apron tied around her middle, handbag over one arm. "Isn't it a beautiful morning, Mr. Foster?" she called in a voice that boomed with friendliness.

He gave her a curious look. In the past week, he was fairly certain she hadn't said more than ten, maybe fifteen, words to him, consisting mostly of Coffee's ready and Lunch is ready, and even those had been grunted rather than spoken. He hadn't imagined that she could actually sound human, or that she could smile, or that she ever had a pleasant thought. "Yes, ma'am, it is," he replied as she came down the steps. "Are you going somewhere?"

"To Trenton. I just got a call from my son-in-law. My daughter's gone into labor. Her first child. My first grandchild. I'll be gone for a week or two, maybe four. Heavens, if I like being a nana well enough, I just might stay!"

No matter how he tried, he couldn't picture the staid, sour woman as a doting grandmother willingly answering to "Nana." It just wasn't possible. "Does Lynda—Ms. Barone—know you're leaving?"

"Everything's all taken care of. My replacement is inside. She's quite suitable. She knows the schedule and has the key, and she knows to fix lunch for you and Sophy. By the time I get to Trenton, my grandbaby will have been welcomed into the world!"

Ben watched her leave, then gazed at the back door. What exactly constituted "suitable" in Mrs. Martin's mind? Another unsmiling, prison-matron type?

Oh, no. There was nothing harsh or stern about the woman who appeared in the doorway. Motherly, yes. Matronly, no way. As for smiling, her face was split by a broad grin. "Good morning, Ben Forester."

He couldn't help but grin back. "Good morning, Gloria."

"What would you like for lunch today? I've got the makings for my special chicken salad with walnuts."

"Sounds great."

"And how about a pecan pie?" She pronounced it *pee-can,* the way Emmaline always had. "I can stir one up in no time."

"You're a woman after my own heart," he teased, but she took him literally.

"Oh, no. I think someone else has her sights set on it. I'll give you a holler when lunch is ready."

Great. Another matchmaker type. Just what he needed.

As she closed the door, Sophy climbed down the scaffolding to join him. She wore overalls and a sleeveless T-shirt, with a baseball cap over her curls and paint splatters everywhere. She painted enthusiastically, if not neatly. "Did I hear Gloria's voice, or was I imagining things?"

"No, you heard her. She's filling in for Mrs. Martin, who's gone to be with her daughter in Trenton."

"Oh, yes, the grandson. Today's his birth date. So Gloria's filling in. That'll be fun. I like working with her." Before Ben could ask any of several questions—how did she know the baby would be a boy, what had she meant by that birth date remark, and when had she worked with Gloria before?—she went on. "I'm finished with the fascia boards. What's next?"

"Let's do the porch—replace the rotted boards, tighten the railings." When they were done, the porch would need a coat of paint, as would the entire house, and then there were the front steps to repair, but that wasn't a priority. Far as he could tell, no one used the front door, anyway.

He'd already moved his equipment to the grass near the back steps. With Sophy's help, he carried a stack of wood over. When she saw the saw and the nail gun, her eyes lit up. "Can I cut the wood?"

"Uh . . . we'll see."

Her features were fluid, shifting from anticipation to pout in an instant. "I bet if I were a man, you wouldn't say that."

"Darlin', man or woman, if you were half as experienced as you told me you were, I wouldn't say it."

"Aw, you didn't hire me because of my experience," she teased. "You felt sorry for me because I needed a job."

Ben's cheeks warmed. "I hired you because I needed help. Experienced or not, you *do* help."

"Thank you. So teach me to use the saw."

"Sorry. I'm not that brave."

In addition to the spot where someone had broken through the floor, his inspection had turned up another five places where the wood was in sorry shape. Fortunately, the repairs were a simple matter of prying off old boards, cutting new ones to fit, and nailing them in place. By the time they were halfway through, he'd given in to Sophy's wheedling and agreed to let her operate the saw. He had everything lined up, the cut clearly marked. All she had to do was lower the saw blade, cut through the plank, then raise it again. What could go wrong?

He didn't know, but if anyone could figure it out, it was Sophy.

He gave her a pair of safety glasses, showed her how to start and stop the saw, then stood behind her, watching over her shoulder. When she shut off the saw, she flashed him a grin. "I think that one's a tiny bit off. I probably need to do it again."

"It's fine," Ben murmured, his gaze on the car that had driven up while the blade was running. Wearing a blindingly white jacket and skirt with matching heels that made her several inches taller than him, Lynda unfolded from the vehicle and crossed the flagstone path that led to where they were working.

"I'll take this board around front." Sophy traded safety glasses for board, nearly knocked Ben in the head, then bumped the rail on her way up the steps.

Lynda stood silent until Sophy's footsteps faded, then she came a step closer. "How is she working out?"

"She's fine."

"A little . . . clumsy?"

"Most of us mere mortals are." He glanced pointedly at his watch. "Has the world come to an end?"

She acknowledged his meaning with a smirk. "Ross decided he wanted my proposal that was due next week today instead."

"And, of course, you just happen to have it ready."

"I just need to pick it up."

"When you were in school and the teacher announced at the beginning of the semester that you had a paper due at the end, I bet you started it right away, didn't you?"

She nodded again. "And I bet you waited until the night before it was due."

His response was a shrug. "If a carton of milk says Use by June 15, you do."

"And if a sign says Do Not Enter, you do, too."

"What can I say? I'm a rebel by birth."

"And I'm . . . what? A conformist?" She smiled faintly. "I've been called worse."

What? By whom and why? he wondered, but he didn't ask. "What if you hadn't had this proposal ready a week early?"

"I did, though."

"But what if you didn't?"

"I've never failed to have something ready."

Failed. Interesting choice of words. How could anyone consider it a failure to not have work ready a week before it was due? At the very least, she'd deserved a day's notice. "You should have told Ross you'd give it to him tomorrow or the next day or, hey, how about next week when it's *supposed* to be ready."

"I'm not an obstructive person."

"Maybe you should be." He glanced at his watch again. "As long as you're here, why don't you have lunch with us? Gloria is making—"

"Gloria?"

"Your substitute housekeeper." When the blankness didn't leave her expression, he went on. "Mrs. Martin's daughter in Trenton is having her first baby, and she's gone to help out. She said everything was taken care of, that Gloria was quite suitable. I assumed that meant she'd cleared it with you."

Lynda's forehead wrinkled in a frown. "I don't recall . . . I'm sure she mentioned it and I simply forgot. She's very reliable."

And, according to Melina, Lynda was a walking, talking computer. He doubted she ever forgot anything, but if she wanted to give Mrs. Martin the benefit of the doubt, that was fine with him. "Anyway, Gloria's fixing chicken salad sandwiches, pecan pie, and—"

A crash from the side of the house interrupted his words. He cleared the steps in two leaps and raced around the corner of the porch to find Sophy lying on her back in the grass, staring at the sky, her legs resting on an eight-foot section of railing that lay crookedly across the bushes growing next to the porch.

"Remember I said that *later* we'd tighten the railings?" he asked as Lynda came to a stop beside him. "We don't have to remove them to do it."

"Are you all right?" Lynda demanded.

"Oh, sure. You know, I've spent so much time up there looking down"— Sophy airily waved at the sky —"I'm just enjoying being down here looking up." Her face crimson, she sat up, then easily got to her feet. She brushed her clothes, removed her cap, and combed her fingers through her hair, then replaced it. "Sorry about that," she said as she moved between two bushes. "I wasn't thinking."

Ben gave her a hand up to the porch. She took the big step easily, with no sign of injury, unless bruised pride counted.

"Maybe you should see a doctor," Lynda said.

"Really, I'm fine. Just embarrassed, that's all." She gestured toward the back door. "I—I think I'll see how lunch is coming along."

"I hope she's more proficient in the kitchen than she is out here," Lynda murmured after Sophy had disappeared from sight.

"The homeowner and employer who would be sued if Sophy were so inclined shouldn't be snide about her abilities," Ben said, crouching to examine where the section of railing had broken loose. "Some people, including whoever fell through the porch by the back door, might say these premises are a tad unsafe." As long as he was down on the floor, he let his gaze slide the length of her legs, from the heels he estimated at four inches, over slender ankles, shapely calves, nice knees. That was as far as he could go, since the hem of her skirt grazed just above her knees. Too bad she didn't dress more like the lady lawyers on *Ally McBeal,* Emmaline's favorite show, with skirts so short that a deep breath could lead to a little unplanned exposure.

But as soon as the image formed, he pushed it away. That was Melina's style, not Lynda's. No doubt she could make a man weak in the right clothes, but right for *her.* Elegant. Classy. Tasteful.

Lynda cleared her throat, drawing his gaze higher. She raised one delicately arched brow, a silent comment on his interest in her legs, and said in that low, husky voice of hers, "The bruises have finally healed, and, yes, I'll agree the porch isn't the safest place, which is why I've hired the two of you to make it so. One might argue that Sophy was aware of the risk and should have been more careful."

"One might." He stood up again. "On the other hand, one might argue that she's young and poor, and you're richer than sin. Not that it matters. Sophy's not the lawsuit type."

"You know that for a fact?"

"I'll bet you a buck."

"And how do you prove it? Ask her if she wants the afternoon off to see a lawyer about possible legal action? No, thanks. If the idea hasn't already entered her head, your question would put it there."

"You don't have much faith in people, do you?"

"Of course I—" As they started toward the back of the house, she broke off. "I have a world of faith in certain people."

"Your parents, your brother, Melina, Ross. Who else?"

Because she didn't like the answer, he suspected, she turned the question back on him. "And who do you have faith in? Your parents? Brothers or sisters? Friends?"

"My mother, my father, and I are happiest never acknowledging the others' existence. Fortunately, in a city the size of Atlanta, that's fairly easy to do. I don't have any brothers or sisters, and no friends like Melina." He held the back door for her, then followed her inside. "I have faith in myself."

And that was one sad fact.

In the week he'd been working there, he hadn't seen much of the house's interior, but he didn't imagine he'd like any of the other rooms as much as the kitchen. The room was large, with a fourteen-foot ceiling, glass-fronted cabinets of fine old oak, marble countertops, and a black-and-white checkerboard floor. A long, broad oak table stood in the center of the room, home to a row of cookbooks without so much as a splatter on them, and hanging from a rack above was an expensive-looking set of cookware that looked as if it hadn't seen any more use than the cookbooks.

This was a room that could easily be the heart of the house. It needed children coming home from school, sitting at the table for a snack, and sharing the details of their day while dinner simmered on the stove. But in this house, they would have to share with the housekeeper, since Mom—man, picturing Lynda as a mother wasn't an easy jump to make—would be busy conquering the business world.

Sophy was leaning against the island, her hands and face scrubbed clean of the paint that dotted her arms and clothing, while Gloria cut thick slices of homemade bread and explained the secret of French onion soup. "It's the onions," she said, lifting the knife to emphasize her point. "You have to—"

"Caramelize the onions." Ben reached past her to snitch the discarded end of the loaf.

Gloria fixed a surprised gaze on him. "You hammer, you saw, you make incredible noise, and French onion soup, too?"

"Nope. But it was one of Emmaline's favorites. We had to have something to keep us going when we ran out of possum. You know, roadkill's not always that easy to find."

She studied him a long time before waving the knife again. "You're teasing me, aren't you?"

"Yes, ma'am, I'm teasing. I've never had possum in my life. I was raised on biscuits and gravy, fried chicken, pork barbecue, grits, sweet cornbread, and Krispy Kreme doughnuts."

"Well, that explains a lot," Lynda murmured from the table, where she was sorting through the mail. When they all turned her way, she looked up as if just realizing that she'd spoken aloud. A blush colored her cheeks an appealing shade of rose. Instead of explaining or apologizing, though, she changed the subject as she approached the housekeeper. "I'm Lynda Barone, Mrs. . . . ?"

"Just Gloria. Muriel did clear this with you, didn't she? She's so excited about the new grandbaby that she's just tickled pink. Wouldn't surprise me none at all if the whole thing slipped her mind. 'Course, it's good for grandmas to be excited—shows the little ones how much they're wanted. I can provide references if you like. My most recent job was at the café in town. I'm sure Hank will be glad to speak for me."

"Hank?" Lynda echoed.

"Harry," Ben replied.

Gloria beamed at him. "Isn't that what I just said? Henry will be more than happy to give me a recommendation. And Sophy and I work well together, and I get along just fine with Mr. Forester, don't I?"

"Yes, ma'am, you do . . . but it's Foster."

"What's Foster?"

"My name."

"I thought it was Ben," she said, her brow wrinkled in puzzlement. "I'm not too good at names until I've known someone a decade or two, but I don't know how even I could confuse Foster with Ben."

Lynda stepped into the conversation again. "Mrs.—Gloria, if you could give me a list of references—"

"Already on your desk. At least, I think that's where Millicent said she was putting it."

"I'll check those out, then we'll talk in the morning. Now I'd better get my papers and go back to work."

"To do what?" Gloria asked. "Have a salad and a piece of fruit delivered to your desk so you won't have to take a real break or carry on a conversation with people actually in the same room and not on the other side of the world?"

"I don't—"

Don't what? Ben wanted to prompt. Eat at her desk? Work through her lunch hour? Avoid even the most casual conversation with some of her coworkers?

"Come on, Ms. Brown," Gloria coaxed. "Forget work for thirty minutes. Relax and have some comfort food with some nice people. We *are* nice, if we say so ourselves."

"And we do say so," Sophy chimed in.

"Well . . . I suppose it wouldn't hurt."

"Good! Just let me clear this table, and—" Gloria reached for the mail on the breakfast table, but Lynda picked it up first.

"I'll put this in my office."

Intending to wash up in the downstairs bathroom, Ben followed her from the room. When a piece of lavender paper drifted to the floor from the mail she carried, he swept it up, then scanned the handwritten note as he straightened. *Anton, page 43. Do you think those green eyes are real? If they aren't, who cares? The muscles are, and they're quite impressive. Mercy, I'd love a job oiling these bodies for the pictures. My heart might give out, but I'm willing to take that risk.*

"I, uh, think this is yours," he said, suppressing a grin as he held out the paper.

Instead of rose, this time she turned crimson. She snatched the note from him, crumpling it in her fist. "It's not— My mother—" She drew a deep breath. "My mother sends me this magazine, with notes about the guys pictured inside."

"Muscular, oily guys."

To his surprise, she laughed. "For the most part, yes. It's not pornography. They're not naked. They're just . . . trying to sell a product."

If it was just good-looking model types in ads, Ben thought, there was no reason for her to be embarrassed. Whatever their product, her mother thought she should be buying, or at least looking. But instead of trying to eke out more information from her, he changed the subject a bit. "The late Lewis Grizzard, a fellow Georgian and a damn funny man, once explained the difference between being naked and nekkid. Naked means you don't have any clothes on. Nekkid"—he laid his drawl on thick—"means you don't have any clothes on and you up to somethin'."

She laughed again. "Well, these men aren't even naked." With that she turned into her office and he continued toward the bathroom. He would have sworn he heard one more comment from her, though, in a murmur surely not intended for his ears.

"Maybe I would enjoy it more if they were."

Chapter Eight

WEDNESDAY WAS THE SORT OF DAY Lynda remembered from her summers growing up—bright and sunny, warm but not so much that a person couldn't be comfortable sitting in the shade, not doing much of anything. Back then, life had seemed so far away. Her entire world had revolved, for three short months, around the local swimming pool, the sun, her friends and family, backyard barbecues, vacations to the beach. She'd never thought any further ahead than the inevitable end of summer, never had any concerns more pressing than who her new teachers would be, or whether she was going to grow any taller.

"That's an interesting reaction to the news," Tom Flynn remarked, jerking her twenty-five years forward into the M.I. conference room. It was the midweek staff meeting for all department heads and their assistants, and she'd just been caught staring out the window daydreaming about lazy days and utter contentment.

Of course, the possibility that she'd been woolgathering wouldn't cross Tom's mind. He didn't believe she was capable of it, no more than she'd believed six months ago *he* was capable of falling in love.

What news was he talking about, and what reaction was she supposed to have? Considering that she'd rather tap dance the length of the conference table than admit she hadn't been paying attention, she decided to give bluffing a try. "What reaction did you expect from me?"

"Oh, I don't know. Considering how much time you put into this deal, a display of temper. A few choice words for those idiots in Malaysia. Better yet, an order for the pilots to get the Gulfstream ready for a trans-Pacific flight."

The Osaka-Malaysia deal! She couldn't believe it had fallen through—and after Ross had relied on her to decide whether to go ahead or drop it. Now she would have to admit that her mind had been wandering, because she wanted details. She needed to know who was to blame and whether anything could be salvaged.

Ross, who'd been gazing out the same window, swiveled his chair around to face them. His dark gaze was amused as it brushed across her face. "If we can find a new buyer who will agree to the same deal as the Malaysians, or get the Osaka people to bend a bit more, we'll be all right. Tom, why don't you give her the letters and contracts, and Lynda, you can see what can be done." He nodded once to signal that the meeting was over.

Lynda accepted the file Tom slid across the table, then started to rise, but Ross gestured for her to stay. He waited until everyone else had gone before he spoke. "You got a little distracted again, didn't you?" His tone was mild, not the least bit intimidating or threatening. The Ross who had never tolerated weakness or distraction in an employee had disappeared after Maggie's accident and wasn't likely to ever return. Still, Lynda felt as embarrassed as if she'd been soundly chastised.

"I'm sorry, Ross. I was paying attention, honestly. It's just that . . ."

"At some point, something more interesting sneaked into your mind. Like what a beautiful day it is, and doesn't a tall glass of lemonade and a hammock tied between two hundred-year-old shade trees sound a lot more appealing than yet another staff meeting."

She knew from her last visit to the McKinney house that he had just such a hammock in the backyard. With Maggie's flower beds in profuse bloom, and her and Rachel close at hand, he probably found it a most relaxing place.

"I heard you hired the distraction from Harry's to work on your house," Ross went on. "How is that going?"

She pretended she wasn't blushing. "He's very qualified for the job."

"I have no doubt."

"Seriously. I had Melina check his references, and she got nothing but glowing reports."

"Lynda, I wasn't teasing. I have no doubt he's qualified. I can't imagine you hiring someone who wasn't."

She thought of Sophy, whose enthusiasm for the job

far exceeded her experience, but remained silent. After all, it wasn't as if *she'd* hired the girl.

"I—I wasn't thinking about him," she solemnly assured Ross.

He nodded. "Does he have a name—this eminently qualified person?"

"Ben. Ben Foster. . . . He's from Atlanta. . . . He's worked in construction for years. . . . Mr. Fitzgerald at the hardware store recommended him." Realizing that she was blurting out information in spurts, she caught her breath and clamped her jaw shut.

"What was on your mind, if you don't mind my asking?"

She didn't mind. She was simply surprised. In all the years she'd worked for him, he'd never asked personal questions and she'd never volunteered such details. Rather than admit to daydreaming about the summers of her youth, she gave a vaguely honest answer. "I was just thinking that Bethlehem doesn't have a community swimming pool." She would have arrived at that acknowledgment eventually if she hadn't been interrupted. At least, she probably would have.

"No, they don't," Ross agreed. "You know, City Park has plenty of empty space. A couple of acres would be enough for a really great setup. Why don't you look into it? Talk to the mayor and the council, get some figures."

"But the Malaysia deal—"

"Just got a major setback. It's on the back burner for the moment, until you find some new buyers or decide to forget it. Take an easy job for once, Lynda. See about getting Bethlehem a pool."

It wasn't a bad idea, she admitted. The company was

always involved in some sort of community project, usually one that benefitted children, and when she was a child, she couldn't have imagined anything better than the pool on a hot summer day. "All right," she agreed. "I'll have a report on your desk—" She was about to say tomorrow when she remembered Monday's conversation with Ben. He was a rebel—the very word implying intriguing, wild, reckless, dangerous. And she was a conformist, a fancy way of saying *boring.* "How about Monday?"

"Sounds fine. Maybe Ben Foster can help. Feel free to put him on the payroll if you can use him."

"I don't think that will be necessary, but I'll keep it in mind."

"I bet you will. Now that you've found someone to work on your house, you just don't want to share him, do you?" Ross chuckled. "Does he have family here in town?"

"No. As far as I know, he doesn't have ties anywhere."

"Hmm. I saw him at the soccer match Saturday with a blonde woman, and I just wondered if he's related to one of the girls on the team."

He didn't strike her as the soccer type, but the blonde-woman type . . . Oh, yeah, she could imagine that. No, wait, she didn't have to imagine it. She'd *seen* him with the sultry blonde Kelli at the bar Friday night. Had she gone home with him? Spent the night? Taken him to the game the next morning?

It was none of her business. He could have a half-dozen Kellis and she wouldn't care, remember?

Gathering her papers, she stood. "I'll have the preliminary work on the pool for you by Monday, and I'll see what I can do about the Malaysia deal." She was halfway to the door when, against her will, she turned back. "This woman . . ."

Ross didn't try very hard to restrain his grin. "Cute, curly hair, probably twenty or so but looks fifteen."

Sophy, Lynda thought with a rush of relief. Of course, it was possible he could have something going with his assistant, but she didn't think so. His behavior with Sophy was more big brother to little sister than man to woman. He was patient, teasing, affectionate—exactly the way Lucas treated *her.*

"That's Sophy Jones. She works for me, too. And I just got a new housekeeper, named Gloria. I'm becoming a one-woman enterprise."

"You've always been that." He glanced out the window, then rose from his chair. "I believe I'm going home to stretch out in that hammock and have some lemonade with my two best girls. You should head out, too."

"I've got work to do."

"You have a comfortable lawn chair?" When she nodded, he went on. "And I know you've got a laptop and a cell phone. What more do you need? Or—don't be too shocked; this is only a suggestion—how about simply taking off the rest of the afternoon? There aren't any major crises or disasters anywhere. The office probably wouldn't miss you at all."

"I'll think about it," she said dubiously. "Enjoy your hammock."

She returned to her office down the hall, getting a stuffy "Ms. Barone" greeting from her secretary as she passed. Inside she took off her jacket, sat down, then eased off her shoes and stretched out her legs. If she swiveled her chair ninety degrees, looked out the window, and squinted really hard, she could barely make out her house, a dark spot surrounded by a green clearing and a mountainside of trees. The temperature was usually a few degrees cooler up there, and most of the time a breeze rustled through the leaves, making it seem even cooler.

When was the last time she'd taken off early? Not scheduled time off, comped time to make up for a trip, time for a doctor's appointment or a funeral, but honest-to-God, spur-of-the-moment I'm-outta-here time. It was an easy answer—never. Not once in thirteen years.

Maybe it was time to break a perfect record.

With her jacket and briefcase in one hand, her purse in the other, she stopped by the secretary's desk. "I'm going home now, Tasha."

"What do you mean, you're going home?"

"That house out there on the hill—it's home, and that's where I'm going." She gestured, though Tasha's window faced the wrong direction. "I'll have my cell phone, so if anything important comes up, you can refer calls to it. Would you make an appointment for me with the mayor for tomorrow morning? Also, find out who the best swimming pool people are and get me an appointment with them, too—no later than Friday afternoon."

"But—but—" Tasha jumped to her feet and followed Lynda to the elevator. "Ms. Barone, I don't know what's important! You always said everything was! This is very irregular! You can't— You've never— *Ms. Barone!*"

The closing elevator doors cut off her protest.

Lynda watched the numbers light up, then flash off. She figured she had worked virtually every day of the last thirteen years, putting in eighty-hour weeks and more. She'd taken fewer than five vacations, and all of them had been combined, to some extent, with business. Leaving like this *was* very irregular. Unheard of. Some might even say peculiar.

Others might say it was no big deal. Just a complete and utter conformist . . . caught up in the smallest act of rebellion.

WHEN HE WAS SIXTEEN YEARS OLD, BEN HAD developed a crush on a pretty little redhead by the name of Peggy Louise Boudreaux. She'd been nearly a foot shorter than him, her waist so tiny he could circle it with both hands, and she'd kissed . . . Oh, man, just the memory of her luscious mouth made him hot all these years later. They'd had a couple of serious encounters of the most intimate kind before she'd remembered to mention that she was going steady with the captain of the football team.

Unfortunately, she'd remembered *after* the guy had beaten the living daylights out of Ben for messing with his girl. Studying him, with his black eye, broken nose, and bruised ribs, Emmaline had shaken her head and unsympathetically announced, "I hope you learned a lesson."

He'd learned several of them. Never fool around with someone whose boyfriend outweighed you by fifty pounds of solid muscle. Never let him sucker punch you. And never risk life and limb for any girl unless you were sure from the get-go she was worth it.

Peggy Louise Boudreaux had definitely been worth it.

Not that she had any bearing whatsoever on the situation he found himself in at the moment. Actually, it was the pain Earl the football star had inflicted on him that had brought the memory to mind. Pain much worse than what he was feeling right now, but at least then he'd had the pleasure of Peggy Louise to make it worthwhile.

He was sitting on a chaise longue in Lynda's backyard, his T-shirt wrapped around his right arm and the arm cradled protectively to his chest, his head tilted back, eyes closed. He thought the bleeding might have stopped, and the pain in his wrist had eased to a dull agony, though it would be quick to leap back into the swearing zone with the slightest movement. He'd already done plenty of swearing, widening both Sophy's and Gloria's eyes before they hustled inside to put together an ice pack.

"So this is how you spend your days—resting in the sun, working on your tan."

He opened first one eye, then the other, and squinted at Lynda. When he was reclined like this and she was standing in her heels beside him, she looked about ten feet tall and intimidating as hell—though not in the she-could-unman-him-without-breaking-a-sweat way she was probably shooting for. This was more of a jeez-she-was-one-hell-of-a-beautiful-woman thing. "So our secret's out," he said, hearing the strain in his voice. "We work an hour a day, then eat your food, use up all your ice, and bask in your sun until it's time to go home. Guess you'll have to either fire us . . . or join us."

"Watch it. I may decide to join you, and then you'd have to give me that chair. I don't bask in anything less than ultimate comfort."

"Yes, ma'am." He started to salute, winced, and let his hand sink back down.

"What did you do to your arm?"

"I, uh, fell." It wasn't an easy admission to make to a woman who moved as gracefully as any world-class dancer. "I took a dive off the roof, scraped my arm on something on the way down, then tried to catch myself, with limited success."

She looked toward the house, at the tools on the first-floor roof and the ragged-looking bushes immediately below them, then gazed back at him. "You guys are hard on my landscaping. It's a good thing I was planning to replace all that shrubbery when everything's done."

"Oh, Ms. Barone, you're here!" Sophy's voice was heavy with relief as she came out of the house carrying towels, a plastic bag filled with ice, and an elastic bandage. "Gloria and I told him he needs to go to the emergency room, but he's being stubborn. He probably needs stitches . . . and a cast . . . and something for the pain."

Lynda laid her things aside and crouched next to the chair. His wrist was swollen and starting to discolor. She wrapped one clean dish-towel around it, molded the ice bag to fit, and used the second towel to hold it in place, then secured the elastic bandage over his shirt and the laceration that started at his elbow. "They're right. You need to go to the hospital."

"I'll stop by on my way home." Provided he could get himself home. The GTO was a stick, which would make for some interesting one-handed, left-handed driving.

"I can take you," Sophy volunteered.

In spite of himself, Ben laughed. "No offense, darlin', but the only person in the entire state of New York I might even consider letting behind the wheel of my car is Melina, and she's not here."

The remark didn't seem to bother Sophy at all, but he would have sworn it somehow made Lynda more distant. Did she still believe he was interested in her friend? Did she care? And why? Did she think Melina deserved better than a carpenter from Georgia?

Or did she want him for herself?

Oh, yeah, sure she did. And his wrist and arm would magically heal, all his sins would be forgiven, and Melina's Bug would beat the GTO head-to-head by a country mile.

"I'll take you in my car," Lynda said in an aloof, standoffish way that set his teeth on edge. He wanted to say no, thanks, don't put yourself out, but truth was, he needed the ride, so he lied instead.

"I would appreciate it." He swung his feet to the ground, then stood up. At the Mercedes, he asked Sophy to lock up the tools in the garage before she left, then eased into the passenger seat with much less grace than Lynda showed. He fastened his seat belt left-handed, then settled back for the ride.

The electronic gate was closing behind them before he broke the silence. "Can we stop by the motel so I can pick up a shirt?"

The look she gave him came from the corner of her eye and barely made contact before drawing back.

"And deprive the female emergency room personnel of admiring you like that?"

He bit back the impulse to tell her that the only female admiration he was interested in was hers. "My grandmother passed on some old-fashioned notions about what was proper. Going out half-dressed didn't qualify."

"Not even if you're injured?"

"Only if you're bleeding from an artery, gut-shot, or having a heart attack. And this cut is just a scratch."

"Where does your grandmother live?"

He fell silent for a moment, the ache in his arm forgotten for one in his chest. "She . . . she passed on a few months ago. She was eighty-seven years old and never slowed down until just before she died. She was quite a woman."

"I'm sorry. I didn't mean to stir up bad memories."

"None of my memories of Emmaline are bad." Except for the knowledge that he'd disappointed her tremendously when he'd broken up with Berry rather than face the responsibility of fatherhood. And that never meeting her great-granddaughter broke her heart.

"Emmaline. That's an unusual name."

He chuckled. "The South is filled with unusual names. It's part of our charm."

"So how is it you wound up named Ben? Did your parents lack imagination?"

"Nah. They just didn't care enough to bother. If Ben E. King's music was good enough for my old man to listen to, then his name was good enough, too." He gazed out the side window, well aware that she was looking at him as much as or more than the road. It was a curious look, a he'd-said-more-than-he'd-intended-and-she-wanted-to-know-even-more look. It made his skin warm and his nerves taut. Finally he irritably said, "Don't do that."

"Do what?"

"Look at me like I'm some sort of bug trapped under your microscope." He turned his head and caught her at it. "My parents and I aren't close. So what? You get along with yours?"

"Of course."

"Of course," he repeated. "Even though your mother spends her time trying to find you a man."

Something about his tone—the insolence, probably—offended her and made her get all stiff and distant again. As far as he was concerned, distant was exactly the best way for her to be. Out of his reach. Too far away to tempt him, to make him think about taking the pins from her hair and letting it fall over his hands, or about removing every single item of her prim and proper clothing and finding out just how *im*proper she could be with the right coaxing.

"You think I can't attract a man on my own?" Now she was keeping her eyes on the road. Her fingers were clenching the steering wheel and her jaw was clamped tight enough to show. "I'm worth a fortune."

He waited for her to name the rest of her attributes. She was gorgeous. Intelligent. Incredibly capable. She put off an air of aloofness that no man who liked a challenge could resist. She had legs a mile long and a voice that could make a strong man weak.

But she didn't go on. She pulled into the motel parking lot, followed his directions to his usual space in front of his room, then shut off the engine. He studied her for a moment before opening the door. Instead of getting out, though, he turned back to her. "You think money is all you have to offer a man?"

The blush that crept into her cheeks was becoming familiar. He wondered how many people in Bethlehem besides him had seen it, wondered how many thought she couldn't possibly be vulnerable enough to blush.

"For a smart woman, you sure have some dumb ideas," he said as he eased out of the car. He emphasized the point with the closing of the door, crossed the sidewalk to his room, and let himself in.

It took about twice as long as usual to maneuver into a clean T-shirt, then run his fingers through his hair. He didn't look so hot in the bathroom mirror—about a dozen shades paler than normal, with deep lines at the corners of his mouth and eyes. Amazing the effect a little thing like a sprained wrist could have on a person. Getting beat up by Peggy Louise's boyfriend had hurt a hell of a lot worse, and so had some of the whippings his parents had given him as a kid. But those times he'd had Emmaline to take care of him, help him manage, comfort him. Now he was alone.

If he left Bethlehem without meeting Alanna, he very well might stay that way.

Grimly he returned to the car, and they made the remainder of the trip in silence. When Lynda pulled up to the emergency room entrance, he glanced at her. "You can go back to work now. I'll get a ride from someone."

"I—I thought . . ." Breaking off, she nodded. "Sure."

"You thought what?"

Her nails tapped a delicate rhythm on the steering wheel before she reluctantly answered. "I thought I'd go in and wait with you. But that's all right. If you'd prefer I didn't—"

"No," he interrupted. "I wouldn't. Go ahead and park while I get checked in." He slid out, then watched her drive away. It was funny how insecure people could be—or was it sad? He'd spent his share of time in emergency rooms, and they weren't places he would voluntarily choose to waste three or four hours, especially when he wasn't the one in pain. Lynda was probably just concerned because the accident had happened on her property.

Or maybe she was just being a decent person.

Footsteps drew his attention away from the parking lot as a young woman in white jeans and a red blouse came out of the hospital, stretched, then looked at him. She gave him a friendly smile before her gaze dropped to his hand. "There are better ways to spend such a beautiful day than getting yourself sent to the emergency room. I'm Dr. Matthews. I'm in charge of this joint this afternoon. What've you got?"

"I thought I would see if I could fly, and took a header off the roof."

She checked his hand, then lifted the edge of his shirt for a look at the cut. "Eww. Lucky for you, I majored in Home Economics so I'd have something to fall back on if the doctor gig fell through. People everywhere will admire the absolutely perfect scar I'm going to give you. Come on in. We've got six rooms, no waiting."

She escorted him to the admissions desk, then excused herself and headed back to the treatment area.

Ben was just getting comfortable in the chair when he heard a distant voice ask, "Can I help you, ma'am?" Turning, he saw Lynda with a blue-haired volunteer just inside the door.

She glanced around, saw him, and gestured in his direction. "Thanks, but I'm with him."

He settled in his chair again. It was just a meaningless phrase. She wasn't really *with* him, not in the important ways a woman could be with a man. But for the moment she was there. For the moment she *was* with him.

And there was nothing in the world meaningless about that.

LYNDA HAD NEVER ACTUALLY MET NOLA Matthews before, though she'd heard about her. She had a reputation as a very good doctor, she was the object of countless middle and high school athletes' fantasies, and she did a thorough, if time consuming, job of patching up sprained wrists and scratches, particularly a "scratch" that, according to the nurse, required sixteen stitches to close.

Wincing inwardly, Lynda got to her feet as Dr. Matthews escorted Ben to the waiting area. He looked pretty ragged, an appearance enhanced by the splint that circled his thumb and extended halfway up his forearm, as well as the bandage that covered the gash below his elbow.

"If you have any problems," the doctor was saying as they joined her, "call the hospital— You know, sometimes I forget this is Bethlehem. I'm in the phone book. Remember, no lifting, no hammering, and no roof-climbing until the stitches are out and you don't have any pain at all in your wrist. And if you get curious again, take my word for it. Superman, Peter Pan, E.T.—it's all special effects." She shifted her attention to Lynda. "Ms. Barone. I'm Nola Matthews."

"Lynda Barone. It's nice to meet you." She was surprised by the strength of Nola's handshake. Physically, the doctor was everything she'd always wanted to be—petite, curvy, blue-eyed, fair-haired, short. And strong, capable, and talented, too. Lynda didn't know whether to admire her or envy her. Feeling decidedly Amazonian—in her heels, she towered a good foot taller than Nola—she opted to go with envy.

"Ben, take better care of yourself. Lynda." With a brisk nod, Nola left them alone.

She and Ben were halfway to the car before she thought of anything to say. "Are you all right?"

"Sure. I've had plenty of sprains and broken bones before. Haven't you?"

"No."

"Not even as a kid? Climbing trees? Riding your bike?" When she shook her head, he mimicked the action. "You've lived a deprived life, Miz Lynda. I bet when you weren't being a perfect student and perfect daughter, you spent your free time playing with Barbie dolls, taking dance lessons, and being prissy."

"I've never played with a Barbie in my life. I did take dance lessons because my mother insisted, but I hated them because I have no sense of rhythm, and how could I be prissy when I looked like the mutated girl from the Planet of the Giants?"

He grinned at her over the roof of the car. "You

have a sense of humor. If I had bet on that, I would've lost."

"Who's joking?" she asked dryly before sliding behind the wheel.

"So topping six feet wasn't on your list of girlish dreams. And since it happened anyway, you wear those heels as a way of making the best of it. You know—when life gives you lemons, make lemonade."

"I wear them because I love heels," she corrected him, then ruefully added, "I used to wear flats, trying to hide the fact that I was tall, but once I reached six foot in my bare feet, little details like inches were no longer important. Kind of like once you get to a certain net worth, it's pointless to keep counting. Is it going to matter to anyone else whether you're worth twenty billion instead of eighteen? Either way, you're rich, period. I was tall, period. So I decided I might as well be tall in great shoes."

"You're not worth twenty billion, too, are you?"

She chuckled. "No, not by a long shot."

He resettled in the seat, put his head back, and closed his eyes. "You know what, Lynda? All those guys you went to high school and college with have grown up now—most of them, at least. Their egos aren't so fragile, and they're not so worried about appearances. A lot of 'em couldn't care less if they fall short in the height contest, as long as they measure up in other ways."

"Not the men I meet."

"Those guys aren't scared off by how tall you are. It's how rich you are. How powerful. How cool. If a man's foolish enough to ignore the Do Not Touch warnings you give off, he's gonna get frostbite. They may not care about height anymore, but they do want to keep their body parts intact."

Lynda pulled into the grocery store lot and parked, then looked at him. "Did Dr. Matthews give you a shot of something that loosened your tongue?"

His laugh was low and rich. "No. If she were alive, Emmaline would tell you that knowing when to keep my mouth shut was never one of my strong suits. But I figure I'm out of a job anyway, so what can you do?"

"Out of a job?"

He raised his hand, started to wiggle his fingers, then winced. "The doctor said the stitches can come out in ten days, but I'll be wearing this splint for a couple weeks. No lifting, no hammering, no climbing . . . that pretty much translates to no working."

"You think I'd fire you because you got injured working on my house?"

"I think you'd hire someone else to finish the job."

His response had neatly avoided the question, but that wasn't what she wanted. "Answer me, please. Do you think I would fire you because of this?" What she really wanted to know was did he think she was that cold, that uncaring. She knew some people thought so—she'd been called heartless on more than one occasion—but that was different. That was business. Ben was . . .

Ben was business, too, as far as he was concerned.

Finally he looked at her. "No. I don't. But it's only reasonable for me to quit so someone else can take over."

An odd sense of relief settled in Lynda's stomach. "Have you forgotten? No one else wanted the job. You were the only taker."

"So I get to keep it by default?" he asked wryly.

"No. You get to keep it because you do good work and you're reliable." And because she'd gotten accustomed to seeing him around. Because she liked knowing where to find him any time of the day. Because she liked all the possibilities he put her in mind of . . . even if most of them were likely *im*possible. She was no more his type than he was hers.

But what did type matter? Her mother thought she'd do just fine with a man named Darnell, or a pretty-boy slacker ten years younger. If she could make *that* relationship work, what did it matter how different she and Ben were?

Of course, there was one not-so-minor flaw in her reasoning. The pretty boy was looking for a rich wife. Ben was merely looking for a good time.

"Why are we sitting in front of the grocery store?" Ben asked.

"I thought I'd pick up some bandages for your arm. Do you need anything?"

He shook his head.

"You want the air conditioner running or the windows down?"

"How about the top and the windows down?"

She did as he suggested, got out, then hesitated. "You . . . Do you want to have dinner?"

"I usually do."

"I meant . . . with me."

When he hesitated, she felt the heat rising under her collar. She would take the invitation back if she possibly could, but since she couldn't, she was seeking some graceful way to say forget it when he finally responded.

"I usually do . . . but I don't know if I'm up to learning to eat with my left hand in public."

"Of course not. Sure." It was a valid excuse, one she should have thought of before asking the question. Granted, she hadn't known she was going to ask until it popped out, but . . .

"How about a picnic? You and me, a blanket in the grass. Common people have them every summer. Try it. You might like it."

"I'm common," she protested. "And I've been on picnics." His unwavering look forced her to go on. "Just not in . . . twenty years or so."

Without moving from her face, his green gaze warmed, and the corners of his mouth curved up in the slightest of smiles. "You're not common. In fact, Miz Lynda, you just might be the most uncommon woman I've ever met."

And that just might be the most pleasing compliment she'd ever been given, Lynda thought . . . at least, until she was inside the market and pushing a cart down the aisle and an earlier remark he'd made drifted into her mind. Do you want to have dinner? she'd asked, and he'd replied, I usually do. With me, she'd clarified, but he'd given the same answer. *I usually do.*

Maybe some of those impossibilities weren't so impossible, after all.

After stocking up on first aid supplies, she headed for the deli section, where she got sandwich makings, chips and dip, and three different kinds of cookies. She added a six-pack of cold beer and another of Diet Coke, then headed for the checkout stand, then the car.

"Okay," she said, once she'd stowed the groceries in the trunk. "Where should we go for this picnic?"

"Surely a town like Bethlehem has a couple of pretty little parks."

They could go to City Park, she thought, and while they were there, she could check out the site for the new swimming pool and . . . Get a grip, Lynda, she silently admonished herself. Ben—the devil in blue jeans—had agreed to have dinner with her, and she was thinking about work? She was pathetic. And she wondered why men weren't beating a path to her door.

"Or we could go to your house. There's a pretty place out at the edge of the front yard. And you're going to have to change clothes anyway."

"All right. My house." She left the top down for the drive home, and he seemed content to let the ride pass in silence. She was content, too, for the first time in . . . she didn't know how long. Half sorry the journey wasn't longer, she parked beside the GTO—the car he would let Melina drive, but not her, she remembered, and a twinge of jealousy pierced her contentment. Of course, she wasn't nuts about cars and engines as Melina was . . . but she feared she was on her way to becoming nuts about the owner of that particular car. It would have been nice, just for her ego's sake, to be included in his vote of confidence.

"Are you sure you feel up to this?" she asked as she retrieved the bags. "We can eat inside or on the porch. It doesn't have to be in the grass."

"Yes, it does. It was my choice, remember?" He eased out of the car, grunting once, whether from general discomfort or the pain in his arm, she couldn't guess. "Do you have a single pair of shorts in that prissy wardrobe of yours?"

"I have several. There's the khaki linen ones that are

cuffed at the knee and have a pretty striped sweater to match. Or the hunter-green velvet ones—I bought them for a Christmas party, but I don't wear them often because they really look best with flats, and we've already discussed my penchant for heels. And let's see . . ."

"Don't you have a pair of cutoffs?"

"Cutoffs?"

His grin said he knew she was teasing—she wasn't very good at it, so she was glad he'd caught on—and was simply playing along. "You know, faded, snug-fitting jeans, cut off high on the thigh and allowed to fray?"

"Jeans?"

There was no playing in the surprise that spread across his face. "You don't own any jeans?" He sounded shocked, as if the mere idea were incomprehensible.

"Actually, I do have a pair. They were a gag gift from Melina. I believe they still have the tags on them." She unlocked the back door, then set the bags on the counter. "Don't worry. I'll find something suitably casual. Make yourself comfortable. I'll be back in five minutes."

Lynda would be the first to admit that she liked clothes. From the day she'd started making enough money to indulge her preference for expensive garments with designer labels, she had, resulting in a wardrobe that filled her own closet, as well as the closets in both guest rooms. She had suits that ranged from severely tailored to unbearably feminine, evening gowns to die for, racks filled with dresses, slacks, skirts, and, yes, a few pairs of dressy shorts . . . and nothing that appealed to her at the moment.

Five minutes had turned into ten by the time she settled on a pair of loose-fitting linen pants the color of caramel, a white ribbed-knit tank top—so called, she was sure, because it clung to her ribs like a second skin, an overshirt of white cotton left unbuttoned with the tails tied at her waist, and a pair of low-heeled jute sandals. The entire outfit was a souvenir of an unexpected layover, sans luggage, in the Bahamas a few dozen business trips ago. It wasn't the sort of casual Ben had been talking about, but it was the best she could do. The next step down would be her loose cotton pajama bottoms, or the skintight Spandex shorts that made up her running wardrobe, and she wasn't quite prepared for either of those.

When she returned downstairs, a quilt folded over her arm, Ben was standing in the foyer, studying the stained-glass sidelights that flanked the door. He turned to watch her with appreciation in his eyes that made her feel . . . special. "That's better."

"Th-thanks." She laid the quilt over the banister, then didn't know what to do with her hands. They fluttered nervously in the direction of the living room. "Have a seat, and I'll—I'll fix the food. It won't take but a minute."

With a silent curse and an uneasy smile, she escaped to the privacy of the kitchen.

Chapter Nine

BEN WATCHED HER WALK DOWN THE hall, admiring the easy way she moved. She'd hated dance classes, she'd said, because she had no sense of rhythm. Malarkey, Emmaline would have said. With an innate grace to every move she made, there was no way she could not be a good dancer. A gesture as simple as tucking a strand of hair behind her ear was elegant and complex—her fingers arching together, gliding smoothly over hair on one side, the curve of her ear on the other, sliding all the way to the lobe with a smooth twist of her wrist, then drifting away. The way she touched things, the way she moved so fluidly, so naturally . . . he could watch her doing something as mundane as making sandwiches and consider it time well spent.

Instead of following her to the kitchen, though, to prove his point, he stepped through the double doorway into the living room. What he'd seen of the house was solid, well built, and meant to last for generations, though the previous owners had apparently lacked the interest or the wherewithal to maintain it. Too many Southern mansions, faced with the same problems as well as relentless sun and unforgiving humidity, fared much worse, crumbling right down to their foundations, but this place had been luckier. He hadn't yet found any damage that wasn't reasonable in a house its age, and Lynda had said cost wasn't a consideration. If he stayed around long enough, and she didn't change her mind, by the time he finished, this old place would look as good as it had brand-new.

He ran his hand over aged wood and cold marble, skirted an antique rug that covered heart-of-pine flooring, looked out intricately designed windows that combined wavy glass that was likely original to the house with stained-glass borders. Except for the electric lighting, the room was so true to its time period that he looked totally out of place. He wondered if Lynda ever felt that way, if she regretted too many fussy flowers on the prints, too many elegantly exaggerated curves on the woods, or the heavy hand with dark, bold colors. She was a simpler, subtler sort of person.

He was standing at the fireplace, studying the ornately framed mirror that hung above it, when she appeared in the hallway, carrying a large wicker basket and the quilt. She looked incredible in the softer, less structured clothes, though, truthfully, she didn't seem totally at ease in them. Of course, she had the body to look incredible in anything . . . or nothing. He doubted she was totally at ease in nothing, either.

"Are you ready?"

For a moment, he studied her in the mirror, trying to imagine her without clothing, but the image refused to form. Just as well. He wasn't sure it was an image he could deal with this evening.

Particularly when he'd decided sometime in the past few hours that he did want to meet Alanna, not as strangers but father to daughter. It was the acknowledgment at the motel that he truly was alone that had made up his mind for him. He'd never needed much in his life as long as he had Emmaline, but without her . . .

A man needed someone to notice he was alive, someone who might wonder what happened if he disappeared from sight, who might give a damn if he died. Even if Alanna hated him for the rest of her life, to which she was surely entitled, at least he would have a connection to another human being.

"Ben?"

At the curious sound of Lynda's voice, he blinked and realized he'd been staring at her reflection, wide-eyed and unresponsive. He managed a grin as he turned to face her. "I was just admiring the view."

"You like looking at yourself?"

"I like looking at you." He complimented women as easily as he breathed. He'd learned at an early age that green eyes and flattery would get him almost anything. With Lynda, it was an added bonus that the flattery was true.

He took the basket, though she protested, and they left through the front door. New wood showed in a dozen places on the porch—where rotted floorboards had been pried up and new ones laid down, railings had been repaired, and spindles and sections of rail caps had been replaced.

Lynda bent to run her fingers over one delicately curved spindle. "It's a perfect match for the others. Where did you find it?"

"Sebastian Knight made it. He's doing about twenty more—mostly for the porch, though three are for the main staircase inside."

"I saw you talking to him Sunday evening."

"The guys at the hardware store said he's good. They weren't sure he'd take the time for a small job, though."

"Gee, where have I heard that before?" Her voice was dry enough to ease the humidity on a steamy Georgia day. "Yet somehow you persuaded him to make time for *your* small job."

"I offered him fair payment for an easy job. Even Sophy could do it—and I prefer to keep her away from power tools."

The yard stretched a hundred feet in front of the house, a broad expanse of emerald green in need of mowing. At the edge, where the hillside dropped away, a system of retaining walls had been built to create a short flight of steps leading to a small grassy promontory. Looking out over the valley and the town, it was private from all but the birds flying overhead.

Once the quilt was spread, he stretched out, resting his head on his left hand. Lynda sat primly, properly, her long spine as straight a line as could be plumbed.

"Can I ask you a personal question?" he asked.

Her gaze shifted to him, away, then back again.

"You can ask anything." Whether she answered was another matter.

"Don't you ever kick back, let down your hair, and relax?"

For a time she concentrated on unpacking the basket. Though they'd come straight from the house, she'd taken the time to wrap each sandwich individually, and she'd included linen napkins, china plates, and an antique silver spoon to serve the dip. It was a start . . . but maybe he'd keep suggesting these picnics until he got her out there with throwaway dishes.

Finally there was nothing left to unpack but the drinks. She offered him a beer and opened a diet soda for herself, then was left with nothing to do but answer his question or change the subject. Surprisingly, she answered. "Until we moved to Bethlehem, working at McKinney Industries was not conducive to kicking back and relaxing. If you wanted to advance in the company, you had to be very good and you had to work very hard. I wanted to advance. I worked eighteen-hour days for years. After a while, I found out that if you live for your job, pretty soon your job becomes your life."

She fell silent, and he didn't prompt her but waited and watched. She stared across the valley, but he would bet she wasn't seeing the trees or the mountains. Her expression was too distant, too pensive. After a time, she faintly smiled, then drew her knees up and wrapped her arms around them. She stared off again for a moment, smiled uneasily, turned her face away from him, then finally faced him. "Who's the bug under the microscope now?"

He grinned. "Does it make you nervous for me to look at you?"

"Of course not," she said, but she lied.

The first time he'd seen her, he wouldn't have believed for an instant that she was even capable of getting nervous. She had been so amazingly aloof, except for the brief bout of intimidation with the baby munchkin, that he would have been more likely to believe she bit the heads off small animals for breakfast . . . and grown men for dinner.

But she got nervous. She blushed. Sometimes she didn't seem to know what to say—at least with him. Which meant what?

"So you lived for your job and your job became your life. Is that what happened with your fiancé?"

"What— How do you— What do you— Melina." Her features shifted into a grimace, then resignation. "What did she tell you? That buying this house was the second biggest mistake in my life, after getting engaged to Doug?"

"Doug," he echoed, deliberately drawing out the vowels a few beats. "She just called him the idiot lawyer."

"That's all she ever called him—that, and pig. Even to his face."

"How did you ever hook up with someone so different from you?"

"We weren't different. In fact, we were very much alike—both ambitious, dedicated to our careers, determined to achieve phenomenal success. . . . You meant Melina, didn't you?"

He nodded. "You're so proper, and she thought nothing of calling her best friend's fiancé 'pig' to his face."

She smiled as she began unwrapping the sandwiches.

"She's an amazing woman. Without her, I probably would have moved into my office years ago and never come out again. She has a real appreciation for life and people that I envy. I can leave her alone for five minutes in a restaurant, and she'll make at least two friends while I'm gone." Her smile took on a regretful cast. "I'm not very people-friendly."

"You're just out of the habit."

"I don't think I ever had the habit."

He sat up to take the plate she offered. The sandwiches were meat and cheese on French rolls, with lettuce, tomatoes, and Italian dressing, and all cut into manageable pieces. He added a handful of chips and a spoonful of onion dip, then asked, "Did you notice that you didn't answer my question about Doug?"

"What was the question?"

"What happened?"

In spite of the drippy dressing, Lynda ate neatly, taking several bites from the sandwich, more to delay answering, Ben figured, than out of hunger. But then she patted her mouth with her napkin—such a prissy gesture, he thought with a grin—and shrugged. "As I said, we were a lot alike. Both ambitious, both working endless hours. Even though we shared an apartment, we really didn't see each other very often."

"You even had to schedule your lovemaking."

As he expected, she blushed heatedly. "I'm going to kill her, I swear. I'm surprised she didn't tell you *everything,* the snot." She took a deep breath, then rushed on, as if that were the only way she could tell something so personal. "Okay, here's the story. We were going to get married as soon as one of us found the time to plan a wedding and both of us could schedule a few days off for the ceremony and a honeymoon of some sort, but we'd been trying for nearly a year without much luck. We had already agreed that marriage wouldn't change our lives. I wouldn't take his name. He didn't want children. We were going to be the quintessential two-career couple."

So what was the point of getting married? Why make a commitment to someone if it didn't mean anything—if you wouldn't share each other's lives?

"We had scheduled a meeting with the goal of setting a wedding date, but he had to cancel—some sort of emergency business involving a client who'd gone to an empty little town out west for his granddaughter's wedding. Doug flew out there and . . . " With a curious smile, she shook her head. "Six hours after getting there, he ran away with the bride. Last I heard, they were still living in that empty little town. He was working for her grandfather, she was teaching kindergarten, and they had twin sons who would be two now."

"And were you heartbroken?" He wouldn't have asked the question if he weren't pretty sure he knew the answer. She and Doug hadn't been planning a marriage—just a merger. She hadn't fallen in love. She'd found a suitable prospective partner who brought his own assets, strengths, and capital to the partnership, someone she could work with and live with but never really be happy with.

"No," she admitted, as if it were a shameful thing. "Truthfully, I was relieved. When I told my mother that he'd run off and married someone else, she drove up from Binghamton and she and Melina gave me a thank-God-the-pig-is-gone party."

A successful lawyer, dedicated, ambitious, hard-working, presumably rich . . . What mother didn't dream of such a catch for her only daughter? For Mama Barone to celebrate losing him, Doug must have been one hell of a loser.

"So . . . that's the whole sordid story—and it's not sordid at all. I can't even get a good tale out of getting dumped for another woman." She finished the last bite of her sandwich, daintily wiped her hands and patted her mouth, then sipped her Diet Coke. "What's your story? Why aren't you married and raising a family?"

"No story. Just no interest. I never thought of myself as the marrying kind."

"Having too much fun being single to give it up? You don't want to tie the knot because you have an aversion to nooses? If God had meant for you to have a wife, he wouldn't have given you a sex drive?"

His gaze narrowing, Ben studied her for a moment before stacking his plate with hers. "Which is it you don't have a very high opinion of? Marriage? Me? Or both?"

Her smile faded, and an uneasy look came into her dark eyes. "I'm sorry. I didn't mean . . . Melina tells me I shouldn't tease until I get more practice at it. This is why *I'm* not married. I'm not very good—"

Without warning, Ben leaned forward, curved his fingers to fit the back of her neck, and kissed her. It wasn't a hot kiss, or passionate or anything else, but the sort of kiss he might have given a girl on their first date back when he was a kid. A sweet kiss that stunned her into silence and made him want so damn much more.

"Are you going to slap me?" he asked, backing away only a few inches.

She shook her head.

"What if I kiss you again—this time with my tongue?"

She swallowed hard as desire and uncertainty flitted through her eyes. He thought for an instant she might find the courage to say, Yes, kiss me . . . or No, don't. He figured instead she would back away, stumble through a few moments' awkward conversation, then announce it was time for him to go home. In the end she did nothing but stare at him, her dark eyes twice their size, reminding him of some skittish creature, wanting to come closer but afraid to give up its distance.

Then she leaned toward him—not a lot, not so much that she even noticed it, but he did, and he decided what the hell. If she wanted to punch him when he was done, she could.

He slid his fingers along her jaw and her lashes fluttered shut. Her skin was too soft for his experience, too soft for the comparisons that came to mind from growing up poor and working in construction. Her hair was soft, too, long strands of black silk that fell loose from their pins and covered his hand as he slowly worked his fingers through the mass.

Somewhere along the way he moved closer, or maybe she did, because he didn't have to lean forward as far, and whenever he shifted at all, his legs bumped hers. His mouth brushed hers side to side, lazily teasing, before he slid his tongue between her lips. She didn't open to him right away—he would have been surprised if she had—but made him wait, so he made her wait, too. He slid his mouth away from hers, leaving kisses along her jaw to the delicate curve of her ear.

"You don't have to sit here all tense and stiff,

darlin'," he murmured, sending shivers through her. "You can come closer. You can touch me. You can have your way with me," he teased . . . or not. Reaching blindly while he continued to kiss her, he found her hand, fisted in her lap, and moved it to his thigh, where he uncurled her fingers and smoothed them out flat. As his mouth claimed hers again, he placed her hand on his shoulder, then slid his fingers back into her warm, silken hair, held her still, and thrust his tongue deep into her mouth.

For the space of one heartbeat, she remained motionless, unresponsive, then the heartbeat ended. She slid both arms around him, her pampered hands with their long, delicate fingers delivering restless caresses that made his muscles tighten and his skin burn. Greedily she sucked at his tongue, as if she'd never been kissed, never gotten hot, never let passion and need overshadow cool aloofness, and his body responded in the same way. His chest grew tight, making air hard to come by, and when he managed a breath, it seared his lungs. His muscles were taut as well, and he was hard and swollen in seconds. Even his injured arm was pulsing with each thud of his heart.

And then it ended. One moment her hands were on his shoulders, his chest, underneath his T-shirt and sliding over his ribs, and he was thinking how much he needed her and wondering how to get them down on the quilt and out of their clothes with only one working hand, and the next she pulled free, backed off, and drew a deep, deep breath. She was staring at him wide-eyed again, and this time he stared back. Her hair was mussed, her lips kissed free of the coral-tinted lipstick she favored, her eyes hazy and confused . . . and heavy with arousal.

For the first time since he'd met her, her movements were lacking grace as she finger-combed her hair, then moistened her lips with the tip of her tongue. The desire to lean forward and say, Let me do that, was strong, but he restrained it.

The ice maiden, the woman at the Starlite had called her last weekend. There was no denying that she was cool on the outside, but he had to admit he was a little surprised by the heat on the inside.

"I—I— What was that?" Her trembling hand gestured in the heavy warm air between them, and her voice wasn't much steadier.

Neither was his. "Damned if I know," he said on a ragged breath. He'd intended it to be a kiss. Just a kiss. Not a prelude to anything. Not a release of passion. Just an intimate kiss of the kind he'd given countless women before walking away from them.

But it had been more, and had held the promise of so much more. And it had convinced him of one fact. No matter how much experience he had at leaving, it was going to be damned hard to walk away from Lynda.

AFTER THE SOCCER GAME ON SATURDAY AFTERnoon, Alanna's team met at Harry's for their usual sundaes-and-milkshakes celebration. They'd won their game, though in Bethlehem, that didn't matter as much as it did other places. Win or lose, everyone got treated pretty much the same . . . but she liked winning, a lot.

She was sitting on a stool at the counter with a chocolate malt in front of her and Susan and their friend Mai on one side. The stool on her other side was empty, and she intended to keep it that way until the Graysons got there.

"Hey, Lannie." Susan leaned over to whisper. "There's that friend of Grandpa Bud's, remember? The one we met at the band concert."

Alanna had just seen Dr. J.D.'s truck park across the street and was trying to tell which of the kids had come with him when Susan nudged her. Annoyed, she turned to look and saw the man from Georgia sitting by himself in the nearest booth, eating a piece of pie and reading the newspaper. "Yeah, that's him," she said, then immediately looked outside again.

"Caleb and Trey are coming with their mom," Susan said smugly. "I saw 'em get in the car with her. And before they come here, they gotta drop off Gracie for Shania Russell's birthday party."

Alanna gave her a dirty look, then glanced back at the guy in the booth. "What's the big deal about him?"

"Susan thinks he's cute," Mai said with a grin, then ignored the poke in her ribs.

Alanna looked at him once more. "He's *old*."

Mai answered again. "She likes older guys. That's why she follows Trey Grayson around like a puppy."

Susan's face got all red, and she gave Mai a shove that pushed her off the stool. "Would you *shut up*? I'm never telling you any secrets again!"

"Oh, like anyone in here doesn't already know you have a crush on Trey. Let's see." Mai climbed onto the stool on her knees and clapped her hands. "Hey, everybody—"

Susan clamped both hands over Mai's mouth and shook her hard while whispering angrily in her ear. Probably threatening to tell everyone about Mai's crush on Kenny Howard. Kenny's father was the pastor of their church, and Alanna had heard Aunt Emilie say he sure proved true that old saying about preachers' kids. He'd given Josie a black eye once, and she was younger and lots littler and a girl besides. And last summer he and his friends had ganged up on Caleb and beat him up. Miss Corinna said Kenny was a bully and a troublemaker, and no one liked him except his troublemaker friends. And Mai.

But even if Susan did tell, it wouldn't matter. There were so many people in the café that no one had even heard Mai clap her hands for attention except the man from Georgia, who'd looked up from his paper and was watching them with a smile.

He was cute, Alanna admitted, for someone his age. But he must be at least thirty, and while liking Trey was okay—he was only a few years older than them—liking someone who was thirty . . . She would have to be at least twenty-eight before she could even think about it, and she was only twelve now. That was forever away.

"What happened to your arm?" she asked while Susan and Mai continued to whisper. Most people probably thought they were telling secrets, but she'd seen Susan pull Mai's hair, and Mai had pinched her back.

He glanced at the splint as if he'd forgotten all about it. "Fell off a roof and sprained my wrist."

"What were you doing on the roof?"

"Working. I'm doing some repairs at Lynda Barone's house."

"I know her. Well, I've met her, but I don't know her. Kinda like you. You talk just like my Aunt Emilie did when she came to live with us in Boston." It had been more than four years ago, but she could still remember how much she'd loved the sound of Emilie's voice, soft and sweet and never angry. Sometimes she'd told them stories until they fell asleep, and Alanna had known that as long as they had Emilie, everything was going to be okay.

"Aunt Emilie from Atlanta?"

"Yeah. How did you— Oh, yeah, Josie. That's my loudmouth sister. She's got a splint just like that. She's around here . . . " Alanna glanced around, then rolled her eyes. "She's gone to Shania's birthday party, too."

Finally knocking it off, Susan and Mai straightened up and Susan jumped into the conversation. "Hey, I saw you at the game last week with a blonde girl. Is that your wife?"

"Or your daughter?" Mai added with a giggle and an elbow poke for Susan.

"She's a friend."

"Are you married?" Mai asked.

"No."

"Hear that, Susan?"

Alanna gave them both the sort of look their teachers got when they were too giggly, then slid to the floor and walked over to his booth. "Aunt Emilie says one girl's fine, two's okay, but three or more, and they get silly. I don't remember your name."

"Ben."

"Did you come here just to work on that lady's house?"

He shook his head, but didn't say why he did come.

She was used to grown-ups not telling her things because she was a kid, but she was more grown up than they thought. She'd practically raised Josie and Brendan until Emilie moved in with them, and she'd just been a little kid herself. Like Caleb. When his father died, he'd taken care of his two brothers and Gracie for weeks until they'd gone to live with Dr. J.D.

"Why did you come here?" Ben asked.

"We were on our way to Georgia, but we had car trouble here, and we stayed." She shrugged. "Is Atlanta nice?"

"If you like big, crowded cities."

She shook her head. "Boston was big and crowded. When we needed help there, the welfare people tried to take us away from Aunt Emilie. When we came to Bethlehem, they were a lot nicer. Everyone wanted to be friends with us and to help." She shook her head once more. "I'm never living in a big city—"

"Lannie!" Susan whispered, wildly waving her back to the counter.

Alanna looked at her, then at the door, where Kelsey Grayson had just walked in. Behind her were Caleb and Trey. "I've gotta go. See ya."

BEN'S BREATHING WAS IRREGULAR, AND HIS stomach was unsettled from the odd sensations rippling through him. Curiously empty, overwhelmed, stunned . . . he felt all that and more. Awed, amazed, and regretful.

And afraid. He knew for a fact he'd made the wrong decision when he'd walked away from Berry all those years ago. He just wished he had some way of knowing that he'd made the right one now. Some little sign, some indication that telling Alanna the truth was right for her, that it wouldn't screw up things worse than he already had.

It wasn't so much to ask, was it?

"WHAT DO YOU MEAN, HE KISSED YOU? AND you're just getting around to telling me?"

Lynda held the phone away from her ear until Melina's shriek faded away. There was a moment of heavy breathing, then her friend's carefully controlled voice. "All right, put the phone back to your ear. I'm not going to get hysterical. It's no big deal. Only the best-looking guy you've ever looked twice at *kissed* you *twice* three *days* ago and you're just now telling me about it! Lyn! Do I keep secrets from you?"

"No, you don't."

"No, I don't! If our situations were reversed, I would have said, 'Hold that thought, darlin',' then run in the house and called you *immediately*. But nooo. Not you. You wait three days, then casually toss it into the conversation. 'Ben reroofed the roof, and he patched the porch and twisted his wrist, and, oh, yes, he stuck his tongue halfway down my throat.' *Ohhh!*"

"It was just . . . " Lynda ate a bite of ice cream, then licked the spoon. Just a kiss? Oh, yeah, right. If that was just a kiss, then she was an innocent schoolgirl who'd never been kissed. It had curled her toes, kinked her hair, made her see stars, and stirred a fever. She had never believed a kiss was just a kiss, and Ben had proven it Wednesday evening.

"Just what, Lynda?" Melina repeated.

She didn't have a clue, and so she gave the same response Ben had. "Damned if I know."

"So . . . how have things been between you since then?"

"I haven't seen him."

"You're kidding. You haven't called him?"

"*He* hasn't called *me.* Remember, I'm the old-fashioned one. I like for the man to make the moves. You, on the other hand, consider it great restraint to find out the guy's name before you molest him."

"But he's injured, Lyn. You should be taking him food, checking on him—hell, you should have moved him into the guest room. After all, he did get hurt on *your* property."

"Apparently, he's getting around just fine. He picked up his car Thursday." She had come home from work to an empty driveway and wondered when he'd come, and how, and if he'd deliberately chosen a time when he'd known she wouldn't be there. Did he regret that he'd kissed her? Did he think she would read more into it than he'd intended? Was he sorry?

"Give me details," Melina demanded. "Is he a great kisser?"

"Oh, honey . . . Granted, my experience is nowhere near as vast as yours, but he's the best I've ever had."

"Did he get . . . you know, turned on?"

Lynda laughed. "Jeez, Lina, what if I said no?"

"I wouldn't believe you. Were you impressed?"

Impressed. Wowed. Stunned. And just a little bit afraid. God, there was a new sensation. When was the last time she'd been afraid? Probably her first day at college, when her parents had kissed her good-bye, then driven away from her dorm, leaving her all alone in a strange place. So long ago, and she could still remember how it felt—a great deep emptiness opening up in her stomach that felt as if it would never go away, as if things would never be right again.

Exactly the way she'd felt since Wednesday.

"I'll take your silence as a hearty yes," Melina said. "Now that you've necked with him, what do you think? Is he worth your Jimmy Choos?"

"Um . . . how about my Jill Sander heels?"

Over her friend's laughter came the sound of a car door closing out back. The emptiness in Lynda's stomach filled with butterflies as she headed toward the kitchen. The only people in town who had the code to the gate were Gloria, Sophy, and the man for whom she'd just volunteered to give up some of her favorite shoes. Since there was no reason for either Gloria or Sophy to show up after five on a Saturday afternoon, that meant . . .

She looked out the kitchen window, and the smile starting to form froze in place. "Oh, my God, Lina, Mom and Dad are here."

"You weren't expecting them?"

"*No.* With Mom on her you're-going-to-be-an-old-maid kick, I would have gone to Malaysia if I'd known they were coming."

"Hey, Janice is nobody's fool. That's why she decided to surprise you. I'll let you go. Give your folks my best."

"I will." Lynda was lowering the phone when she saw the third figure slide out of the car. "Oh, God, Melina? Melina!"

The line was already dead. She disconnected the phone, let it drop to the counter, and murmured disbelievingly, "They've brought someone with them."

A male someone. Handsome and smug. Looked like an underwear model—and was looking at her property as if assessing its value. Please don't let him be Anton, Raphael, or Darnell, she silently prayed as she watched them approach the porch.

Janice rapped sharply at the back door. Lynda took a couple of rapid breaths, then hurried over to open it. "Mom! Dad! How wonderful to see you."

Her mother, looking beautiful and petite and smelling of Chanel, came in, hugged her tightly, then gestured outside. "I see you're finally getting some work done on this place."

"Yes, I am—"

"Say hello to your father, dear."

"Hi, Dad." She bent to accept a hug and a kiss from her father, Phil.

"You've got good help," he said. "The place looks better. You have any beer?"

"In the refrigerator."

"Why do you have beer when you didn't know we were coming?" Janice asked.

"Dad's not the only person who drinks beer."

"Hmph. Is this how you dress for company?"

Lynda glanced down at her tank top and pajama bottoms. "No, this is how I dress when I'm home alone and not expecting anyone. Would you like me to go upstairs and change?"

"You can do it before dinner. Come here, darling, we've brought someone for you to meet." Janice linked her arm through Lynda's and pulled her over to the model-boy. "Lynda, this is Richard Andrews. Richard, our daughter, Lynda. Richard is the youngest partner in the law firm your father uses. You may remember his uncle, George Andrews. He was your father's lawyer and golf partner for years."

And the reason Richard was the youngest partner in the firm, Lynda thought as she held out her hand and smiled politely. "It's nice to meet you, Richard."

"Likewise." His handshake was as impressive as his greeting.

Pulling her hand free the instant it wouldn't be rude, she turned back to her mother. "You guys didn't drive all the way up here just for dinner, did you?"

"It's not *that* far. We thought we'd spend the night, then head back in the morning."

"Oh, Mom, I only have one guest room that's livable."

"Don't worry. Richard was able to get us rooms at the McBride Inn. It helps when you have connections, you know."

Lynda simply stared at Janice. *She* had connections. She knew Holly McBride Flynn and had worked with her husband for years. Probably half of Holly's guests were in town to do business with McKinney Industries, many of them to see Lynda. *She* could have gotten them rooms. "I wish you'd let me know you were coming. I have plans for dinner this evening."

"What? A frozen dinner in front of the computer?" Janice rolled her eyes. "We know how you spend your time, Lynda. Work can wait."

"Actually, I'm meeting someone for dinner." The lie was out before she could stop it, but the surprised look on her mother's face was almost worth the deceit.

"A business dinner, of course."

Lynda shook her head.

"A date? You haven't had a date in . . . heavens, since my hair was this color naturally."

Painfully aware of the lawyer boy—who, she'd decided on sight, wouldn't be worth giving up a headache for—Lynda smiled uneasily. "It hasn't been quite that long, Mom."

"Almost. Well, bring him along." Janice looked around, spotted the phone on the counter, and handed it to her. "Call him. Tell him you'll have three guests with you."

Lynda stared at the phone.

"Well, go on, dear. If he's good enough for you to go out with, then he won't mind a little change in plans. Call him. Tell him to meet us at that steakhouse in . . . oh, an hour. That'll be plenty of time for you to get ready." When Lynda still didn't take the phone, Janice's gaze narrowed. "There *is* a man expecting to have dinner with you tonight, isn't there? You wouldn't lie to your mother about such a thing, would you?"

"Of course not, Mom." There were two men expecting to have dinner with her, and they were both standing right there in the kitchen. But Lynda managed a smile as she took the phone. Who could she call? Ross? Her parents had met him and knew he was married. Tom was out, too, for the same reason. There was a harmless VP in Marketing who had clumsily let her know that he was interested, but he was so short that she could look down on the part in his thinning hair. Her mother would never buy him as a date. Maybe the engineer, Gabe, with whom she'd worked on the Spring Valley project, but he was pretty insistent on spending his off-time with his wife and daughter.

Who was left besides the obvious choice? The unmarried man she knew best in Bethlehem. The only man she had much interest in spending an evening with. The only man she could realistically believe might have some small interest in spending an evening with her.

Either him, or admit to her mother that she'd lied.

Thankful she had a good memory for numbers, she dialed, then walked to the dining table while the phone rang. Janice followed her.

"Angels Lodge, this is Bree. How may I help you?"

Lynda smiled tightly at her mother. "Could I speak to Ben Foster, please?" While Bree put the call through, she politely asked, "Could I have a little privacy here, Mom?"

Janice gave her a whole three feet.

Ben sounded drowsy, as if she'd awakened him. "H'lo."

"Hi, Ben. It's Lynda."

"Thanks for the hint, but I would have figured it out." He was grinning. She could hear it in his voice. "What's up?"

"About dinner tonight . . . I have some unexpected company, and I was hoping you wouldn't mind if I brought them along."

He made a soft *mmm* sound, as if he were stretching. She could all too easily imagine him sliding up on the bed to sit, pillows behind his back, wearing nothing but jeans . . . or, since she was imagining, nothing at all. All that smooth, warm, tanned skin, all those muscles . . . Just the thought was enough to make her hot.

"Dinner tonight. Did I know we were having dinner tonight?"

"Of course."

"Considering how Wednesday's dinner ended, I can't imagine how another meal could possibly have slipped my mind. And here I went and made plans for this evening."

What plans? she wanted to ask. An evening at the Starlite Lounge with someone pretty, flashy, fun? Jealousy knotted in her stomach. "I—I know you've been busy. If you need to cancel"—a few feet away Janice made a sound of protest—"it's all right. I understand."

"Cancel a date I didn't know we had? That wouldn't be polite, would it? Who is this unexpected company?"

"My parents and a—a friend."

"A muscular, oily type friend?"

"Yes. I realize it's short notice—"

"Let me see if I'm awake enough to understand. Your parents showed up without warning, and they brought a man with them, and the man is for you. Huh. I'll bet it never crossed Emmaline's mind to give me a woman."

The amusement in his voice would have been charming if it were at someone else's expense. As it was, she felt foolish. She shouldn't have called him, shouldn't have lied to her mother, shouldn't even have opened the door. Her mom had the code to the gate, but not a key to the house. They would have gone away after a while.

Oh, who was she kidding? Locked doors weren't enough to keep Janice Barone from her goal. "Only because you already had so many of your own," she said, teeth clenched, tone impeccably pleasant, even friendly. "One more would have been superfluous."

"You could just say 'too many.' "

"I knew you'd understand. So . . . if it's not a problem for you, we could meet at six-thirty at McCauley's Steakhouse. . . ."

"And what am I supposed to be?"

She turned her back to her mother and lowered her voice, but heard the floor creak as Janice came closer. "On time would be nice."

"Am I your date? Your boyfriend? The man in your life?"

"You're enjoying this, aren't you?"

"Yes, ma'am. You know, if I'm saving you from an evening with one of your mother's pretty boys, I think the least I deserve is a sweet, husky 'darlin'.' "

"I don't think so."

He yawned again. "You know, I might go back to sleep. . . ."

She drew a deep breath, turned, and found her mother too close and law-boy studying her kitchen with an intensely critical look as if he could already envision it done over in stainless steel and phony space-age surfaces, and she smiled. "Then we'll see you there at six-thirty, darling. Take care."

Carefully she replaced the phone on the table and included her guests in her smile. Before she could think of anything to say, her mother did.

"Tell me about this Ben Foster."

"You're going to meet him in less than an hour. Wouldn't you prefer to judge him for yourself?"

"How old is he?"

"About my age." Actually two years younger, according to the birth date he'd given her, but she wasn't about to quibble.

"What does he do?"

"He works in construction."

"You mean he owns his own company."

"No-oo." It was hard to read her mother. Some days she thought any son-in-law at all was better than none—hence the recommendation in favor of unemployed boy toy Raphael—but most days she was holding out for a man who could *provide.* Lynda had tried to explain that she earned more in a month than most of the doctors and lawyers Janice had tagged as good prospects did in a year, but it didn't sink in. Oh, her mother knew she made very good money. It was just that in her marriage, her friends' and their parents' marriages, the man provided the money and the woman did everything else. It had worked just fine for all of them, and she saw no reason why it shouldn't work for Lynda, too.

"Well, if he doesn't own his own company, then . . . ?"

"For heaven's sake, Jan," Phil said impatiently. "She means he *works.* He's got a job, like a real schmuck. Like her old man."

Lynda smiled broadly at him. She loved her mother, but she related to her father. All he'd ever wanted was for her to be happy. If that meant going to college, and then into business, fine. Working nonstop and traveling so often she couldn't remember what country she was in, great. Making a fortune and having no need for a man in her life, that was okay, too. In fact, the only part of Lynda's dream he hadn't liked was the moving-away-from-home part. He missed her, and she missed him. "You're not a schmuck, Dad," she disagreed.

"Sure I am. But I'm the schmuck she loves." He indicated Janice with his beer, then slid his arm around her waist.

"I'd better get changed if we're going to make it to the restaurant on time. Why don't you go in the living room and have a seat?" Without waiting for a response, she started up the back stairs. She was halfway to the top when her mother's voice floated up after her.

"Oh, stop that, Phil. We've got an audience." Then, "Did she mean this Ben is a *carpenter*? What would she want with a *carpenter*?"

"Maybe she likes him," Phil replied. "Or maybe she's got dry rot."

Dry rot of the brain, Lynda thought as she closed the bedroom door behind her. Why else would she subject herself to dinner with her mother, law-boy, *and* Ben to avoid having dinner with only her mother and law-boy?

Maybe because dinner with Ben would be worth a few hours with Janice and . . . what was his name? Ryan, Rick? No, Richard.

She stopped short, one hand poised to remove a silk tunic in a rich deep coral hue from its hanger. When was the last time she'd forgotten somebody's name? Ever? Never. The realization made her slightly giddy . . . and more than slightly uneasy. She'd never been so distracted that she couldn't remember names. In fact, she never forgot anything. She was single-minded and purposeful to a fault . . . at least, she had been until a handsome green-eyed stranger had come to town.

She'd added ivory pants to the tunic, done her hair up in an intricate roll, added earrings of Mexican fire opals that glowed the same color as her top, and was about to put on her shoes when a tap sounded at the door. "Come on in, Mom."

Janice came to stand in the doorway leading to the dressing room. "You look beautiful, dear, but . . . you're not planning to wear those shoes, are you?"

"No, Mom, I'm putting them on just to admire them, then I plan to take them off and put on my running shoes."

Janice's smile was affectionate. "Don't you smart-mouth me, young lady. You may be a foot taller, but I can still turn you over my knee."

"You've never turned me over your knee."

"You never gave me a reason. You may not have noticed, but Richard's only five-eleven."

"Ben's six-two, and he likes me in heels." Not that he'd ever actually said so, but what was one more lie?

"You know I'm not a snob, dear."

Lynda got the second shoe on, then stood up to check her appearance in the full-length mirror. She looked fine . . . though for one crazy moment, she wondered how the sleeveless coral silk top would look tucked into the snug-fitting jeans in the darkest corner of her closet. Would she look as silly as she thought she would feel? Would Ben appreciate it? Would her mother survive it? Lynda wasn't quite sure, especially coming so soon after the my-daughter-is-dating-a-carpenter shock.

"No, Mom, you're not a snob," she said dutifully, then waited for the *But* . . .

"You and your brother weren't born with a silver spoon in your mouths, and heaven knows, your father and I certainly weren't. But . . . a carpenter? You once dated a senator."

"We went to dinner twice. It hardly qualifies as 'dating.' "

"You were engaged to a lawyer."

"Whom you never liked. You celebrated when he dumped me, remember?"

"You go out with CEOs. Politicians. Actors."

"One actor, Mom, and it was because I was trying to close a deal with him for some property."

"But a carpenter . . . darling . . ."

"Mom, your only problem with this man whom you've never met is his occupation. I think that might be the very definition of a snob." Laying her hands on Janice's shoulders, she turned her toward the door. "Let's hold off on passing judgment until you've at least had a chance to meet Ben. Come along. We don't want to be late."

Chapter Ten

McCauley's Steakhouse was located on a side street in downtown Bethlehem. It was casual and crowded, with booths along the walls, tables in the middle, and customers waiting in the small lobby. When Ben reached the hostess, he automatically returned her smile. "I'm meeting a party that may already be here. Lynda Barone?"

She checked her list, then shook her head. "Maybe she left your name . . . No, no Ben. How many are in the group?"

"Four. Two men, two women. One of the women is . . . " He thought of all the superlatives he could use, then settled for simple. "Tall."

"Oh, like . . . " The hostess raised her arm above her head, waving her fingers in the air up high. "I didn't seat them, but I remember her." Stepping into the dining room, she scanned the room before gesturing toward a distant booth. "Is that your party?"

At the same time Ben saw them, Lynda saw him and left the booth. She moved so gracefully, and she looked so damn beautiful that he simply stood there and watched. Beside him, the hostess was watching, too. "Wow," she murmured admiringly.

Wow, indeed. Then Ben glanced at the girl—short, chubby, with braces, glasses, and enduring a bad-hair moment. Someday the braces would be gone. Weight could be lost, glasses traded for contact lenses, and bad hair fixed. Someday she would be very pretty . . . but not a *wow.* Not like Lynda.

"You could have met me halfway," Lynda said mildly when she joined him.

"And miss watching you walk all the way over here?"

"How's your hand?"

"Sore, but better." He leaned close enough to smell her perfume, to see the dim light glisten on her lipstick. "Do I get to kiss you hello?"

She avoided answering, but she couldn't stop the flush that crept up her neck. "I—I really appreciate your doing this. I had no clue they were going to show up with law-boy in tow."

" 'Law-boy'?"

"Richard Andrews. He's a lawyer. Not that I have anything against lawyers in general . . ."

"Except the one you used to be engaged to."

"But his handshake is limp, and he kept looking at my house as if he were appraising it. I left them downstairs while I changed, and when I went back down, he was *measuring* the doorway into the living room."

"Fifty-eight inches." She gave him a startled look, and he shrugged. "The pocket doors are warped. They need to be replaced, and of course it'll be a custom order." He glanced across the room again. "Are your parents going to hate me?"

"Dad thinks you do good work, and that counts for a lot with him. Mom . . . She'll probably try none too subtly to show that what's-his-name is the better catch." Her smile looked more like a grimace. "We'd better join them before she pushes Dad out of the booth trying to get a better look at you. Feel free to talk. A *lot.*"

As they approached the booth, Ben's gaze shifted to the lawyer. His tan looked as if he spent hours in a tanning bed, and his teeth were too white and even to be natural. Ben would bet money that his perfectly sun-streaked hair was out of a bottle, the intense blue of his eyes was courtesy of contacts, and what muscles he had came from a gym, not from real work like hauling 75-pound bundles of shingles onto roofs. The guy probably took longer than most women to get ready to go out and apparently relied on lots of help to look his phony best. No doubt, most women considered him handsome. Hell, even Ben could admit that *he* thought the guy was handsome.

Even if he was about as real as a three-dollar bill.

Lynda slid onto the bench beside the lawyer, and Ben had barely gotten settled beside her when her mother, sitting opposite, spoke. "So . . . Ben . . . I understand you're a carpenter."

Lynda hastily performed the introductions. Did she know she sounded nervous? Her parents didn't seem to realize it, and Richard Andrews wouldn't figure it out until she started stammering and broke out in a cold sweat. Whatever kind of law he practiced, he didn't appear to be particularly astute.

Janice Barone was an attractive woman—small, blonde, pampered. In his one-minute analysis, she struck him as high maintenance, well intentioned but too certain she was right. After all, hadn't she brought law-boy here, when anyone could tell just looking at him that he wasn't Lynda's type?

Oh, yeah, like you *are?*

Maybe not . . . but he came closer than Richard Andrews ever could.

"Yes, ma'am, I am," he said in response to Janice's statement.

"How . . . helpful. My grandmother always said if you can't marry a man with money, marry one who's handy around the house."

"My grandmother always said there's no shame in honest work. Speaking of honest work . . . Lynda says you're a lawyer, Rick."

"It's Richard," the man said pompously.

"Honest and lawyer. Now there's two words you don't hear together very often, do you, Richard?" Phil Barone teased.

Janice gave her husband a sobering look, then turned on Ben a smile as phony as the lawyer. "You have quite an accent. Where are you from?"

"The great state of Georgia."

"Home of Georgia peaches, rednecks, the Atlanta Braves, and Coca-Cola." Andrews laid his hand over Lynda's and leaned unnecessarily close to scornfully add, "And some people actually think"—he shifted into a really bad Southern accent—"the South's gonna rise again."

Ben could think of one Southerner who just might rise and undo a small fortune in dental work on one obnoxious Yankee . . . but McCauley's wasn't the place for a brawl, and Lynda wasn't the type to take it in stride like most of the women he knew back home. But if the guy didn't let go of her hand . . .

Before the thought was finished, she eased free of Andrews and scooted an inch closer to Ben. Her father didn't notice. Her mother did, and her mouth tightened.

"Tell me, Ben," Janice began, her voice purposeful. "Where did you go to school? Richard graduated from Yale, of course. All the men in the Andrews family attend there. All the men in the Andrews family are lawyers."

"Really. You'd think one lawyer would be more than enough for any family." He smiled as if he felt like it. "I was lucky to finish high school. But then, I chose a field that didn't require seven years of additional schooling."

"And how did you happen to choose that field? Did you grow up wanting to be a carpenter?"

Yeah, sure. And did you grow up wanting to be a bitch? Of course he didn't ask that. Instead, he leaned close to Lynda, bringing his mouth into intimate contact with her ear. "You owe me big-time, darlin'," he whispered, then turned back to her disapproving mother. "No, ma'am, I didn't. But when I graduated from high school, I had to do something. . . ."

WHEN BEN WAS NINE YEARS OLD, HIS MOTHER had gotten herself in enough trouble to bring social services into the picture. They'd placed him in the temporary custody of his grandmother, and subjected Emmaline to interviews, investigations, and home inspections. The social worker, a thin, sour woman, had come to Emmaline's house and criticized damn near everything. She'd been rude, obnoxious, arrogant, and condescending, and Emmaline had taken every insult without comment. *Why?* he'd demanded when the woman was gone, and she'd replied that there was nothing to be gained from sinking to someone else's level. Sometimes the best action was to smile, be polite, and keep your opinions to yourself.

Ben did a lot of smiling and being polite that evening.

Lynda had done her best to redirect the conversation, and so had her father—though Phil, Ben had noticed early on, coped with his wife mostly by backing down. Janice Barone didn't back down at all, and she didn't have a passing acquaintance with subtlety. She liked Richard Andrews and didn't like Ben. She thought Andrews was more suitable, more likely to make her daughter happy and produce lovely grandchildren for her to spoil. Ben thought he was a first-class idiot. But to balance things out, Janice thought Ben wasn't good enough to share her daughter's table . . . although, being a lowly carpenter, he could be allowed to build it.

In the past few minutes, Janice had fallen silent—probably looking for something else about him to insult. She'd taken shots at his background; his education—or lack of; his prospects—or lack of; his income—or . . . Hell, apparently she found everything about him lacking, except possibly his table manners. He figured the splint was all that had saved him there. She didn't want to seem politically incorrect in criticizing the temporarily disabled. She hadn't minded at all, though, making it very clear that she didn't consider him suitable for her daughter—not as a date, not as a lover, and certainly not as a husband.

And the hell of it was, she was right. He *wasn't* suitable. Lynda was filthy rich, while people in his end of the construction business did good to get by. They didn't drive Mercedes or live in big expensive houses or jet halfway around the world on a moment's notice . . . or get involved with women who did.

But that was okay. He wasn't looking to get involved. Dinner Wednesday night had been the boss feeling sorry for the injured employee. Tonight was just the employee doing the boss a favor. And the kisses . . .

They'd been a mistake.

Some part of him wanted to protest. Maybe kissing her hadn't been his brightest idea. Maybe it had been foolish, tempting himself with something he couldn't have. Definitely it had been sweet. Hot. Greedy. Tantalizing. But it hadn't been wrong.

Just . . . not wise.

When the waiter brought the check, Lynda took it before anyone else could. She glanced over it too quickly to read anything, then handed it back, along with a credit card. "This is my treat," she said with an uneasy smile, "since I can't offer you a place to stay tonight."

"Oh, the inn will be fine," Janice said. "Once Ben has completed the work on your house, you can invite us for a visit. When do you think that will be, Ben?"

"I don't know," he replied. With a lazy grin, he parroted Miss Agatha's words. "Work on an old house is never done. As soon as one thing's fixed, another starts showing its age."

"Yes, but sooner or later, all good things must come to an end. You'll be wanting to return to Atlanta before long. Surely you have family and friends there."

"No, ma'am. No family I claim, no friends I miss." He watched her jaw tighten and figured she had noticeably ground down her teeth in dealing with him for an evening. If he were married to Lynda, what fun he could have in a lifetime of tormenting Janice.

If he were married to Lynda. . . .

"Why doesn't that surprise me?" Janice asked dryly as they prepared to leave.

"Because you're an intelligent woman."

Her only response was a snort of the kind Emmaline had given when she'd known he was manipulating her.

Outside the restaurant, they came to an awkward stop, the five of them standing in a loose circle, pretty much not looking at each other. Finally Phil offered his hand. "Nice meeting you, Ben. A lesser man would have left halfway through Janice's assault."

"Phil!" she exclaimed in dismay.

Ignoring his wife, he turned to Lynda. "I'm guessing you want to catch a ride home with your young man. Sorry we surprised you like this."

"I'm glad I got to see you, Dad." Lynda hugged him, then her mother, and politely shook hands with Andrews.

"We'll stop by and say good-bye before we leave in the morning," Janice called as the three of them headed for the Barones' car.

Ben slid his hands in his pockets, then quietly said, "Want to make your mother freak out in the morning? Let me show up before they do. I'll take off my shirt and shoes and come downstairs as if I've just gotten out of bed."

Lynda smiled faintly. As her parents drove past, Phil tapped the horn and she lifted her hand in a halfhearted wave.

Once the car was out of sight, they began walking toward the GTO, parked half a block away.

"I am so sorry," Lynda said.

"For what?"

She gave him a disbelieving look. "The last two hours of smug condescension and insults."

"You insulted me? I must have missed it."

"My mother did, practically nonstop."

"Then let your mother apologize."

She gave the same little snort. Was it a woman thing, or a woman-dealing-with-Ben-Foster thing? "I dragged you into this, and I'm sorry. All I could think about was *not* spending an evening with Mom pushing law-boy at me the whole time. I didn't realize she would be so rude to you."

"You may not have noticed this, but I'm a big boy. I've been saying no for about thirty-one years now. Parental disapproval is nothing new to me. If I had minded facing your mother's, I would have told you no thanks, and stayed home."

She stopped beside the GTO. "Why didn't you?"

He stopped, too, and for a moment just looked at her. He could tell her that he'd had to eat anyway, so he might as well do it with her family, and it would be the truth. Or that he'd wanted an excuse to spend a few hours with her. That was also true. That he'd been thinking about her way too much since Wednesday—

truth. "I figure it can't hurt to have the boss owe me a favor." Also true.

"I think this equals two or three favors."

He glanced at the keys he held, then gestured down the sidewalk. "How about cashing one in? Let's take a walk."

Her smile was surprisingly sweet and pleased. "I'd like that."

They automatically continued the way they'd started, heading toward downtown and the square. "I liked your dad," Ben remarked after half a block.

"Everyone likes my dad. Believe it or not, my mother loves him dearly."

"I believe it." Janice's hostility had all been directed at *him*. Occasionally she'd grown impatient with Phil, but what wife didn't get annoyed with her husband?

"Tell me about your parents."

Ben gave her a wry look. "My family's not like yours. Our lives didn't remotely resemble *The Donna Reed Show.* We're a bit more dysfunctional." After a moment, he took a breath, then launched into a subject he'd never voluntarily discussed with anyone other than Emmaline. He figured he was better off not looking too closely at why he was doing so now.

"My parents got married, had me, and got divorced in less than a year, and they lived apart most of that time. My father had less desire to be a father than he did to be a husband, which was about zero. I've seen him fewer than two dozen times in my life, and then only when he needs something from me—usually money for bail, booze, or to pay off his gambling debts. Jewel Ann, my mother, played at being a mother when it suited her, which wasn't very often. The rest of the time I stayed with her mother, Emmaline. She pretty much raised me and kept me out of serious trouble and out of jail, at least until I was grown. I haven't seen my father in at least five years, and Jewel Ann in . . . maybe three years, and I haven't missed either one."

"Didn't your mother go to your grandmother's funeral?"

He shook his head. "I couldn't locate her. She was always taking off, hooking up with some guy or looking for some dream."

"You must miss Emmaline a lot."

"I do. She had always been there for me, and I'd thought she always would be. I mean, logically, I knew she wasn't going to live forever, but I never really accepted that someday she would be gone."

And he for damn sure hadn't been prepared for the knowledge that she went to her grave knowing that he was less a man than she'd taught him to be.

As they reached the corner, children's voices sounded in the night. The square was just ahead, with parents on the park benches and kids playing in the grass. On the bandstand steps, a young woman with a guitar was giving an impromptu concert to an attentive audience of kids, and on the far side of the square, the lights of the ice-cream parlor shone brightly in the dusk.

"Want an ice-cream cone?"

Lynda smiled. "Do I look like the sort of woman who would pass up ice cream?"

He let his gaze slide over her perfectly proportioned body, from just-right breasts to slender waist to shapely hips, and he slowly smiled. "You look as if not one single sweet has ever crossed your lips. Did I mention you look lovely tonight?"

"No."

"You do."

She murmured thanks as they cut through the square, then crossed the street. They stood in line in the ice-cream parlor, the only adults unaccompanied by kids, then took their cones to a bench in a quiet corner of the square.

The night was cool, the music soothing, the sounds of the children at play oddly relaxing. Occasionally a bird in the trees trilled while lightning bugs flashed in the dark.

They sat in silence for a time. Then Ben leaned forward, elbows resting on his knees, and studied his ice cream as if finishing the cone required his utmost attention. "Why me?" He felt rather than saw her questioning look. "You know other men. Why did you call me this evening?"

Was it because he was so obviously ill-suited that she'd known her mother would spend all her energy getting that fact across and never get a chance to push law-boy on her? Had she been afraid that inviting some other guy who *was* suitable would succeed only in transferring Janice's matchmaking efforts from Andrews to him?

"Which answer do you want?" she asked quietly. "The brush-off? The excuse? The face-saver?"

"How about the truth?" Just as with his answer to her question earlier, he knew there were various truths. He wanted to know with which one she trusted him.

A minute or two passed while she finished her ice cream. She dusted her fingers, blotted her lips, then crumpled the napkin into a tiny ball before facing him.

"I called you because I wanted to see you." A pause, then, "Is that honest enough for you?"

It certainly was, and to prove it, he leaned forward, pulled her close with his good hand, and kissed her. And maybe it was foolish and unwise. Certainly it was sweet, hot, greedy, and tantalizing.

And it was also right.

Amazingly, impossibly right.

MELISSA'S GARDEN WAS ONE OF AGATHA'S FAvorite places in town. The nursery always seemed cool and welcoming, even on the hottest of days, and being surrounded by beautiful growing things soothed her spirit. She'd often thought that if she hadn't taught school, she would have opened her own nursery. But teaching school had been a wonderful career for someone who would never have children of her own. It had been a substitute for the life she'd planned for herself when she was young and unaware of what lay ahead. She'd intended to marry and to devote herself to being a good wife and mother, as her own dear mother had done. She'd thought she would be active in the community, would volunteer at the hospital, the library, the schools, and the church, but most of all she would be a loving wife to Sam and a doting mother to his children.

It was natural to be thinking of Sam that Monday afternoon. After all, if fate hadn't intervened, Melissa Thomas, owner of Melissa's Garden, would have been a cousin by marriage . . . and, after all, she was at the nursery to talk to Melissa about flowers for her wedding to Bud.

The ceremony was less than two weeks away, and at

times the reality of it boggled her mind. After Sam's death on Omaha Beach, she had quickly become Bethlehem's resident old maid. Oh, she'd had her share of suitors, but Sam's dying had changed something inside her. She had loved him so completely and mourned him so deeply. She simply hadn't been able to summon such passion or devotion for any of the men who had come around. She'd thought she would never care so intensely for anyone else ever again.

Until she'd met Bud. Sometimes she felt like a foolish schoolgirl, though there was nothing girlish about her feelings for Bud. He made her feel young and beautiful again, even if those days were fifty-some years past.

After wandering around the nursery for a time, breathing deeply of moist earth, sweet-scented flowers, and fertilizer, Agatha rang the bell on the counter. "Melissa, dear, it's Agatha," she called.

"I'll be right there." The voice filtered from the back room, where no doubt Melissa was up to her ears in her latest shipment. She was devoted to her husband, Alex—Bethlehem's best attorney, in Agatha's unbiased opinion—and her family, friends, and the shop. Unfortunately, that family didn't include any children. The only thing more difficult for Melissa than getting pregnant, it seemed, was carrying a baby to term. It was her greatest sorrow.

But Agatha was living proof that a maternal woman could have a satisfying life without children of her own to love. And sometimes there were rewards. She had the Dalton children and young Michael Bishop, and Bud was the proud grandfather of six. Already the littlest ones called her Grandma—the sweetest name she'd ever known.

Pulling off a pair of muddy gloves, Melissa joined her at the counter, where she gave her a hug and a kiss on the cheek. "I swear, Miss Agatha, you're glowing these days. Isn't love grand?"

Undoubtedly, the blush heating her face added to the glow. "It certainly is. And how is Alex?"

"He's fine. And Bud?"

"Oh, he's fine, too," she replied dreamily, then caught herself and cleared her throat. "Is this a good time to talk flowers?"

"Any time is. Let's get comfortable."

Melissa led the way to a pair of wicker chairs surrounded by lush greenery, and there they debated bouquets, boutonieres, centerpieces, and candelabra until there was nothing left to discuss. Once all the details were finalized and the order form written up, Melissa gave Agatha a copy, then asked, "Have you seen Holly lately?"

"Bud and I saw her when we had dinner at the inn a few days ago. She looked . . . serene."

"Yes, that's a good way to describe her. Can you imagine—our Holly, overseeing the construction of both the new house *and* the motel at the same time, and she hasn't taken anyone's head off yet?"

"It's amazing what the love of a good man can do for a woman's outlook. I understand they're moving into the new house next week."

"Yes, and I heard Emilie and Nathan are—" Her cheeks turning pink, Melissa quickly broke off.

"Emilie and Nathan are what?" Agatha thought of the Bishops as the next best thing to her own children and presumed she knew all the important events in their lives before practically anyone else.

"Oh, nothing. Is there anything else I can do for you today, Miss Agatha?"

Other than giving an honest answer, she couldn't think of anything, and she said so politely.

"Then I'd better get back to those plants in back. I got an entire shipment of hostas crammed into pots so tiny that I could hear them getting root-bound before they were even unloaded. I figure the least I can do is give them a chance at surviving until someone buys them and gives them a good home. You take care, and if there's anything else I can do for you, don't hesitate to call."

Agatha watched her hasty departure, wondering what in the world Emilie and Nathan were up to that *she* wasn't supposed to know. Maybe Emilie was pregnant again and didn't want her friends to spill the beans before she'd had a chance. Or maybe . . .

Agatha simply didn't have a clue.

When she got home, she was surprised to see Bud's car parked on the street out front, along with Nathan's police vehicle. The two men were standing in the driveway next door talking, and they both looked more than a little guilty when she joined them.

"What are you doing here in the middle of the afternoon, Nathan? Is there a problem?"

"No, ma'am. I do live across the street, remember?"

She playfully slapped his arm, then presented her cheek to Bud for a kiss. "This is a pleasant surprise, to see my two favorite men unexpectedly."

"I bet you tell all the men that," Nathan teased. "Better watch out, Bud. I heard she was being coquettish with that new guy in town."

"Coquettish," she repeated with a laugh. "I wasn't flirting with Ben. He was flirting with me. And Bud knows all about it. In fact, he's the one who introduced us."

"Yes, but I was just being friendly," Bud said. "I didn't realize I was going to have to beat him back with my cane."

"I'd better get back to work. Miss Agatha, I'll see you when I pick up the kids. Bud."

"Nathan!" she called before he reached his vehicle. She wasn't a gossip, she assured herself, but she did like knowing what was going on. "Is there anything . . . new with you and Emilie?"

He looked as innocent as young Michael. "Nope. We're both keeping busy with work and the kids, as usual. See you later."

As he drove away, Bud slid his arm around Agatha's waist and started walking her toward the house she shared with Corinna. "What was that about?"

"Oh, nothing. What brings you over this way?"

"You, of course. You don't think I'd come into town without stopping to see my girl, do you?"

She looked up at him and felt a lazy warmth flow through her that had nothing to do with the afternoon sun. "No, I don't think you would. I just wanted to hear you say it."

"Well, I've got a few things I want to hear you say, too. Starting with 'I do' a week from Saturday."

"Oh," she murmured with a satisfied sigh. "I certainly will."

Chapter Eleven

A WEEK AFTER INJURING HIS HAND, BEN RE-turned to work.

Lynda was upstairs, getting ready to leave for work herself, when she heard the familiar rumble of the GTO's engine. By the time she made it downstairs, he was sitting at the kitchen table with a cup of coffee and a plate of sticky buns in front of him. "What are you doing here?" she asked as if she weren't unreasonably pleased to see him. As an afterthought, she added, "Good morning, Gloria."

"Mornin', Ms. Brown."

"Good morning to you, too." Ben grinned, and the emptiness in her stomach was suddenly filled with butterflies. "I've got work to do."

"You've also got a doctor's orders to not do it for another week."

"She said no work until the pain goes away."

"She *said* until the stitches are out and the pain goes away."

Gloria interrupted, giving him a moment's reprieve from responding. "Ms. Lydia, I thought I'd do some heavy-duty spring cleaning today, if that's all right with you."

"Yes, of course."

Humming to herself, the woman picked up a cleaning caddy and left the room. With his foot, Ben pushed out the chair opposite him and gestured for Lynda to sit. She did.

"Look, I'm not used to lying around all day doing nothing. I may be just a carpenter, but I like keeping busy."

"So keep busy with something else."

"I have. I found an apartment and moved in. That took all of an hour and a half. I've watched every one of the fifty-seven channels the local cable service offers—and there's not a fishing or NASCAR channel in the bunch. I'm bored. I need to work."

She thought he was teasing about the fishing part, but wasn't sure. After studying him a moment, she asked, "What is NASCAR?"

Surprise raised his brows. "The National Association for Stock Car Auto Racing."

"Is that a Southern thing?"

His disbelieving look slowly shifted into one of those to-die-for grins. If he'd grinned at her mother like that even once Saturday night, Janice would have forgotten all her complaints and spent the rest of the evening drooling over him. "No, darlin', it's not a Southern thing. The circuit covers the entire country, including your home state of New York. However, down South, we do treat it with the respect it deserves. You people have your churches. We have our speedways."

"Sounds . . . loud."

He shook his head. "You just don't have a proper appreciation for fast cars, do you? Not even after taking a ride in my Goat."

"I take it that's your car."

"Not just my car. All GTOs are Goats. Haven't you ever heard that?" He gave an exaggerated sigh. "You've lived such a deprived life."

She had never felt deprived . . . until he'd come along. Oh, sure, she hadn't had a date in ages, couldn't remember the last time she'd had sex, and had only hazy, dusty memories of being kissed, but she'd had her work. Her house. Melina. And her work.

God, her life had been empty.

"Well, maybe sometime you can take me for a fast ride in your . . . Goat"—she had to force the word out—"and show me what the big deal is. Right now, though, I've got to get to work."

When she stood up, he caught her right hand in his. His grip was fairly strong, considering that he'd worn a splint for the preceding week, but she didn't try to pull away. No sense in testing just how well his sprain had healed . . . or so she told herself.

"How about tonight?" His voice was pitched low, the tone about ten times more serious than usual. "We'll take a drive, get some dinner, and see what I can teach you."

The smart thing would be to pull away, tell him thanks but no thanks, get her briefcase, and go. The smart thing, the prim thing, the prissy, stuffy Lynda thing. She'd been doing it for more years than she wanted to remember, and she was tired of it. She wanted to go with him. Wanted to see how fast they could go. Wanted to see how far they could go.

"All right." Her voice was just as low, just as serious.

He stood up without letting go of her, and though she could easily step back, she didn't. He invaded her personal space, standing closer to her than she normally allowed anyone to get, so close that she could see a few faint flecks of brown in his green eyes and could feel the slight puff from his slow, steady breathing. "Good. I'll pick you up here at six-thirty. Is that okay?"

She nodded, resisting the urge to tell him to make it earlier. In fact, she couldn't think of anything urgent on her calendar for the day. At the moment, though, she couldn't think of anything on her calendar, period.

For one tantalizing moment, he leaned closer, and she thought he was going to kiss her. He didn't, though, leaving her feeling disappointed—and more than a little anticipatory. She was going out on a date with a man whose kisses did funny things to her insides, whose grin gave her butterflies, and whose simplest touch made her tingle.

Melina was going to be *so* jealous.

"I—" Her throat was tight, her voice thick and foreign-sounding. "I'd better go."

For a long moment he simply looked at her. Finally, he released her hand and stepped back. "I'll see you."

She made it as far as the back door before he spoke her name. When she turned, he was wearing an expression of . . . guarded concern was the best way she could describe it. "Don't change your mind."

She smiled faintly before leaving. She was still

smiling faintly when she walked into her office ten minutes later. She went straight to the phone and called Melina in Buffalo. "Ben asked me out," she said in place of a greeting. "Can you believe it?"

There were muffled sounds in the background—the phone hitting the floor—then a grumpy, sleepy voice muttered, "Who is this?"

"Wake up, Melina. This is important."

"Lyn? Do you know what time it is?"

"Past time for you to be up unless . . . Are you alone?"

"Of course I'm alone. That's why I'm cranky. Well, that, plus I ate an entire half gallon of banana pecan ice cream with a whole box of vanilla wafers last night, *and* someone woke me up to gloat at the ungodly hour of"—there were more muffled sounds, probably the alarm clock hitting the floor—"whatever time it is."

"You weren't sleeping. You were comatose from sugar overload. Do you want me to call later when you're feeling better?"

"I'm not planning on feeling better. I wasn't even hungry. I was just watching TV, and I got the munchies, and before I knew it . . . ten thousand calories for dessert. And you've got a date with our Southern hunk. I hate you."

Lynda had roomed with Melina long enough to know that she was sitting up now, pushing her heavy dark curls away from her face, rubbing her eyes to help her wake up. She wasn't a morning person, but could last far longer into the night than Lynda had ever dreamed of.

"Where are you guys going on this date?"

"I don't know. Someplace for dinner."

"You don't know. Okay, who am I *really* talking to? The Lynda Barone I know and love has never let a man take her *anywhere* without knowing all the details first—where, why, who they might see, what they might do, how long they might stay."

It was hard to laugh when the words were so true, but Lynda managed a chuckle. "I wasn't that bad," she lied in her own defense.

"Yes, you were. Now tell me exactly what Ben said when he asked you out."

"He said, 'We'll take a drive, get some dinner, and see what I can teach you.' "

"Oooh. Wear your prettiest, sexiest underwear. You're gonna get lucky. Man, do I hate you."

Sex with Ben. Oh, yeah, she could easily describe that as "getting lucky."

"Get your mind out of the gutter—or the backseat," she chided.

"What do *you* think he meant by see what he could teach you?"

"We were talking about my lack of appreciation for fast cars."

"That may have been what you were discussing, but it's *not* what he was talking about." Melina sighed wistfully. "Why couldn't it have been me? I already appreciate the car, and I'm perfectly ready to appreciate him. Promise you'll call and tell me everything that happens . . . unless, of course, he spends the night. Then you can wait until the morning."

"Darn, Melina, my other line's ringing. I've got to go."

"Remember—sexy undies!" Melina reminded her before she switched lines.

She had plenty of sexy undies, Lynda thought as she worked her way through phone calls, meetings, and reports. She had a taste for silk and satin, for barely-there wisps and see-through softness, often adorned with demure rosebuds and bows. Naughty and nice, wicked and innocent, sexy and sweet. The problem was what to wear over the undies. For their picnic last week, she'd worn the only casual outfit she owned. Ben probably suspected it, but he would know for sure if she showed up wearing it again, and he would be amused.

Unless she went shopping.

No sooner had the idea formed than she'd decided it was a great one. She checked her schedule and found nothing of earthshaking importance, told Tasha she was taking an early lunch, and left her secretary with a dazed and bewildered look on her face. But she was the one who was a little dazed as she walked into one of Bethlehem's few clothing stores less than fifteen minutes later. She felt like a child playing hooky, as if any minute now Ross or Tom would spy her and order her back to the office—or off to the hospital for tests. There were a few hard and fast facts in life—the sun came up in the east, water was wet, grass was green, and Lynda Barone did not play hooky or act on impulse.

But there she was, browsing through racks of summer clothes when she should be negotiating for a new partner in the Malaysia deal, wondering if she would look silly in a mint-green top and denim shorts in a darker shade when she could have been working out the final details in the swimming pool construction.

She was holding a dress at arm's length, a sleeveless

garment with a row of buttons from the V neck all the way to the hem—which wasn't really all that far. It was more fitted than the styles she usually wore, and significantly shorter, but it was still perfectly modest. She could even wear it to the office without getting much more attention than usual, she told herself. Then honesty won out over the need for reassurance. If she walked into the offices at M.I. wearing that dress, heads would turn, tongues would wag, and poor Tasha would probably keel over at her desk. It just wasn't her.

She returned the dress to its rack, then picked up a lightweight summer sweater, soft as a cloud, in pastel ice-creamy colors. She was admiring a pale aqua when a voice spoke behind her.

"There are some white jeans on the other side of this display that would look great with that."

She turned abruptly to find Maggie McKinney, holding Rachel, and Holly Flynn behind her. It was Maggie who had spoken, her tone friendly, giving no hint of her true feelings toward Lynda. The boss's wife couldn't possibly think too highly of her, and with good reason, Lynda was ashamed to admit. Back when Maggie and Ross's marriage had been on a rapid downhill slide, Lynda had taken her cues on how to treat Maggie from Ross. To say she had been inexcusably rude would be an understatement, and the fact that Ross had been even ruder didn't change things.

But if Maggie harbored any resentment, it didn't show. It baffled Lynda and made her uncomfortable as she fumbled the sweater back onto the display. "Hello, Maggie, Holly, Rachel."

"I don't believe I've ever seen you outside the office during the day for anything but a business meeting, and here you are shopping," Maggie said. "I didn't know you even shopped here in town. Special occasion?"

"N-no. I—I was just looking for something . . . casual." She saw Maggie's gaze shift from the dress to the sweaters, and her cheeks warmed. Okay, so her definition of casual was a tad different from Maggie's. She wore shorts, a T-shirt, and thick-soled sandals, looked comfortable, cool, and relaxed, and Lynda couldn't pull off the look in public to save her life.

"The sweater's great, but with your coloring, you should try the lavender instead. Here, Holly, hold Rachel for a minute."

"Yeah, right." Holly gave her a chastening look. "I don't hold infants."

"Oh, come on. It's not as if she spits up on command or anything," Maggie said.

"But it'd be a neat trick if she could," added a new voice. "I'll hold her. C'mere, munchkin."

Lynda's faint blush turned deep crimson as Ben took Rachel from her mother. Just what she needed—an audience of people she hardly knew to watch her buy a simple outfit for a date, and now the date was there, too, on the verge of charming everyone within fifty feet. "Ben," she said awkwardly. "What are you doing here?"

"We had to pick up some supplies, and Sophy wanted to come in here for some T-shirts." He gestured, and across the room, Sophy grinned, waved, then went back to her browsing.

"You must be the handsome Southerner I've heard so much about," Holly said. "It's hard to believe you've been in town more than a few hours and this is the first time I've laid eyes on you. How did that happen?"

He looked pointedly at the ring on her left hand. "Maybe you've been paying more attention to your husband than to the other men in town."

"My husband," Holly repeated. "Words no one *ever* thought would cross my lips. It's an amazing thing."

"Tom's an amazing man," Lynda said.

Holly's perfectly-shaped mouth curved into a smug, secretive smile. "He most certainly is. So . . . Ben, is it? How long will you be staying in Bethlehem?"

"As long as I have a reason."

Maggie nudged Lynda toward the end of the rack and away from Ben and Holly. "The lavender sweater's down here. It's all right to leave him alone with Holly. Her devotion to Tom has rendered her harmless to the opposite sex. He's awfully handsome," she went on, her voice pitched low so it wouldn't carry. "And look at him with Rachel. Who can resist a man who's so comfortable with a baby?"

They did make a sweet picture, Lynda thought, sneaking a few glances their way. His hair was tousled, his grin wide, his stance at ease, as if cradling chubby drooling little girls was an everyday thing. As for Rachel, she looked as if she couldn't imagine anyplace more comfortable than snuggled against his chest, listening to the lazy, honeyed sound of his voice. Smart child.

Maggie picked up a lavender sweater, shook it out, and held it up to Lynda, then turned her toward a mirror in the corner. "So how long have you been seeing him?"

Lynda almost dropped the sweater. "I— We aren't— Ben works for me."

Maggie deliberately misunderstood. "A man *should*

expend a little effort to win the woman he wants. It's only fair."

"No, I mean—"

"I know what you mean, Lynda," Maggie said with a laugh, then waved toward the mirror. "This is a really good color for you. Add a pair of jeans or trousers, maybe a short little denim skirt. . . . He won't be able to take his eyes off you, which he's hardly done anyway."

Lynda resisted taking a peek at him in the mirror for all of thirty seconds, then angled to one side where she could see that Maggie was right. He did keep glancing in their direction. And that could mean anything. Or nothing.

She was so preoccupied with watching him that when Maggie turned her around, it caught her off guard, and when Maggie spoke, her voice raised to carry, Lynda was totally unprepared. "Ben, what do you think of this color on Lynda?" she asked, swinging the sweater side to side before settling it over Lynda's chest.

Lynda felt her face turn crimson. The last time she'd asked a man's opinion on clothing, she'd been dressed up for her one and only formal high school dance, and the man had been her father. He'd told her she was beautiful, even though the flats she wore had ruined the whole effect and she'd faced an entire evening of awkward dancing with a boy whose nose came right smack in the middle of her cleavage.

But Ben wasn't sixteen years old, he reached considerably higher than her chest, and sometimes when he grinned at her, she felt as beautiful as her father had insisted she was.

He came a few feet closer, and his gaze moved over the sweater . . . slowly. "At my grandmother's house in Atlanta, there was a big old oak tree outside my bedroom window wrapped in a wisteria vine as thick as my arm. Every spring it was loaded with so many blossoms that it turned the entire oak that same shade of purple. That wisteria was the first thing I saw when I woke up and the last thing I saw when I went to sleep. That's been one of my favorite colors ever since."

There was a moment's silence, then, at the same time, all three women gave a soft sigh. It wasn't his words so much as his voice—soft, rounded vowels flowing into lazy consonants, so very Southern and smooth and sexy as hell. And he probably knew it, too, Lynda thought. She looked at him, expecting to see that grin, but it wasn't there. In its place he wore the faintest of smiles, the most serious of expressions. When he caught her looking, the smile broadened slightly, privately, somehow meant for her alone.

Then he shifted his attention to Rachel. "Your mama says you can't spit up on command, munchkin. How about if I teach you to burp on cue? You know, when you can't walk or talk, you've gotta do something besides look cute to earn your keep."

"You're very good with her," Maggie remarked. "Do you have children of your own?"

It took him a moment or two to look up, and finally he was grinning. "I haven't been in town long enough to accept responsibility for anyone but myself."

Which begged the question, Lynda thought. If the answer was no, why not simply say so? And if he did have a child, why not simply say so?

Her first thought was that another call to Melina

was in order when she returned to the office. Her second thought was something new and different, at least for her. Instead of paying a private investigator to snoop around once more in his personal life, especially when she had no professional reason for wanting the information, why not ask him? She knew an incredible amount of information about her coworkers, neighbors, and strangers, and virtually all of it came secondhand. Why not, for once, go straight to the source? It would be so normal, so expected—so *un*expected from her. It would be an entirely new experience.

And who knew? He might even give her an answer.

SOPHY SWUNG HER SHOPPING BAG AS SHE AND Ben walked down the sidewalk toward the GTO. She was chattering about clothes and summer colors versus fall ones, but he was paying little attention. At least five minutes had passed since he'd given the baby back to her mother, but he swore he could still feel her weight pressing against him, could still smell the sweet baby-powder scent of her and feel the warmth seeping from her chubby little body.

Was that how Alanna had felt and smelled when she was tiny? Had she dazzled Berry with those goofy, sleepy smiles? Had she made Berry feel connected? Incredibly fortunate? Would she have made him feel that way twelve years ago?

He wasn't proud to admit that the answer was probably not. He'd been twenty years old and living for the moment. He'd had no goals beyond enjoying himself, no needs other than a place to live, beer to party, and money for his car. He hadn't been able to comprehend the enormous responsibility of parenthood, though Emmaline had done her best to make him understand. All he'd known was that he didn't want to be a father, tie himself down with Berry, curtail his social life, or grow up in the ways that having a baby would require. It was easier to kiss Berry goodbye. He would have stopped seeing her before long anyway. Her getting pregnant had just moved up the inevitable by a few weeks.

But in the past twelve years he'd finally done the growing up he'd wanted to avoid. He knew he'd been selfish and irresponsible—knew it was most likely too late to have a real relationship with Alanna. But he could let her know he was sorry. He could make sure she understood the problems were his and Berry's, and so was the blame. He could assure her she'd deserved better parents.

If he ever figured out how or when to approach her.

"Hey. Yoo-hoo. Earth to Ben."

Five long slender fingers waved in front of his face, then snapped, making him blink. Sophy stood in the street in front of him, and he'd stopped short on the curb, staring blindly across the street . . . where a half-dozen young girls spilled out of a store, talking and laughing.

Alanna was in their midst.

Sophy looked from him to the girls, then called, "Hey, Angels! When's your next game?"

"Saturday at one," several of them replied together.

"Good luck." Sophy nudged Ben, and he slowly stepped off the curb. "I love soccer. Where I come from, we didn't have it."

He forced his gaze away from Alanna, wearing

shorts that came halfway to her knees, a Seraphim T-shirt, and her blonde hair in a ponytail. "And where do you come from?"

"Ohio."

"They don't have soccer in Ohio?"

Either she didn't hear his dry question or chose to ignore it. "Where are you taking Ms. Barone for dinner tonight?"

"How do you know I'm taking her to dinner?"

"People talk," she said with a shrug.

He didn't talk, and he'd bet Lynda didn't, either. Since no one else knew— "You mean, Gloria talks."

She shrugged again. "So where are you going?"

"I don't know."

"You don't *know*?" She circled to the passenger side of the car, then frowned at him over the roof. "Maybe that's how you do it down home, but Ms. Barone's different. You can't just go cruising around until you pass some hamburger joint that smells appetizing and pull in on the spur of the moment."

"Why not?" he challenged. "Lynda has her entire life planned out in her daily organizer. She can tell you today what time she intends to go to bed a year and five months from now. It might do her a little good to just go cruising around with no destination in mind. An occasional surprise is good for the soul."

She blinked, opened her mouth, then closed it again. It was the first time he'd seen her at a loss for words, and it made him grouchy. "What?" he asked finally, not liking the blank way she was staring at him.

"You're right."

"Of course I am." Then, "About what?"

"An occasional surprise *is* good for the soul. I wasn't aware you knew very much about souls."

He scowled at her, then slid behind the wheel. As soon as she was settled in beside him, he headed for Lynda's house.

"So your plan for this evening is no plan at all."

"Pretty much." Except when the evening was over. He most definitely planned to get another kiss or three from her. Kisses he could have without compromising his no-involvement rule. After all, there was a world of difference between kissing someone and having an affair with her. Lynda too-rich-too-beautiful-too-everything-for-the-likes-of-him Barone was about as likely to have an affair with him as Alanna was to throw her arms around his neck and cry, "Welcome home, Daddy, I've missed you so much!"

Both plain, hard facts left an achy feeling deep in his gut.

He and Sophy worked until six o'clock. She left with Gloria, and he followed them down the hill, then drove the few blocks to the apartment he'd rented. Each unit had a living/dining room, a kitchen, a bedroom, and a bathroom, and came with furniture that, as far as he could tell, had never had a prime to be past. Number 7 was only slightly larger than Lynda's living room, but it was suitable for his needs. It wasn't as if he'd be bringing women home with him, or have his kid there for the weekend.

After showering, he dressed in jeans and a white shirt. With the tails tucked in and the sleeves rolled up, it was about as dressy as he ever got, except for the black suit he'd bought for Emmaline's funeral. It had been his first time wearing a suit, and he wouldn't mind at all if it was also his last.

Unless someday, by some miracle, he got invited to Alanna's wedding. Unless, by some bigger miracle, he had a wedding of his own.

At precisely six-thirty, he parked beside Lynda's Mercedes and shut off the engine. He wondered if she'd be wearing the wisteria-colored shirt the baby's mom had picked out for her, wondered where she expected him to take her and if maybe he should have taken Sophy's advice and planned ahead.

He couldn't afford the sort of places she was accustomed to going on dates, not on a regular basis, which was okay, since the closest one was probably a hundred miles away. Besides, he couldn't pretend to be something he wasn't. If she couldn't unbend enough to enjoy a simple evening with him, she would tell him no the next time he asked, or he wouldn't be foolish enough to ask again.

Too bad.

He rang the back doorbell, and after a moment she opened the door. She *was* wearing the lavender sweater. It looked as soft as spun cotton and clung to her breasts before ending just below the waistband of— "You're wearing jeans."

"I—I thought— Do I look like an idiot?"

"Oh, darlin', far from it." She looked . . . incredible. "Are you ready to go?"

She locked up, and then he had the pleasure of watching her walk down the steps and across the path to the car. Every other woman he knew should look so good in white denim. It was enough to make his own jeans suddenly feel snugger.

"Is there anyplace in particular you'd like to go?" he asked as he backed around the Mercedes.

She shook her head. "Surprise me."

He grinned. "I think I can do that."

It was a good night for a drive. The windows were down, and it was warm, but not stifling. There was little traffic on the road, B. B. King was on the stereo, and she'd fixed her hair in some sort of braid that looked as if it could withstand a hurricane, so there was no complaining about the wind. He would give an awful lot, before the evening was over, to remove the elastic band, let her hair fall over his hands like threads of silk, and comb it smooth with his fingers . . . right before he mussed it again.

Maybe. If he was lucky.

He drove through downtown Bethlehem, then took the highway out of town. It curved up the mountainside and out of the valley, and led to a town about twice the size of Bethlehem, named Howland. When he'd finally arrived in this part of the state a few weeks ago, he'd stopped there to get gas, have a cup of coffee, and entertain tempting thoughts about turning around and heading home before it was too late. Emmaline was dead, and delivering the pendant could be better done by mail, he'd reasoned. Alanna had gotten along just fine without him for her entire life. There was no reason to think she couldn't do just as well without him for the rest of it.

Funny. She *would* do just fine without him. He wasn't so sure how well he'd get along without her.

"When I saw you that night at the concert . . . "

He glanced over in time to see Lynda smile sheepishly. "What?" he prompted when she didn't go on.

She shrugged, then gestured toward the stereo. "I thought then that you probably liked the blues."

"You want to change it?"

"No, it's fine."

"What do you like? Wagner, Schubert?"

"God, no. I like George Strait. Garth Brooks. Trisha Yearwood."

Ben grinned. "So you're a country girl at heart."

"It's good music," she protested.

"I'm not arguing with you. I'm just pleasantly surprised."

"I like most kinds of music. But not classical. Or rap. Opera drives me nuts. Some of the stuff young people listen to strikes me as mostly noise."

"Young people," he repeated. "Like you're so old. You must be all of . . . what? Thirty? Thirty-two?"

"You're a brave man, guessing a woman's age. Let's say I'm older than you and leave it at that."

"Let's not. How much older than me?"

She took a moment as if she needed to do the calculations, but he suspected she already knew, to the day. "Two and a half years or so." She brushed her hair back, though it didn't need it. Ben figured it was just something to occupy the moment it took her to quietly ask, "Does it matter?"

"Not to me." Only one age had ever been of much importance to him, and that was the age of consent. They'd both passed that years ago. Besides, they were just going out. No dinner reservations, no plans, nothing more than a few good-night kisses at the door when it was over—hardly even a real date. This was no different from taking Sophy or Melina to dinner . . . except that he had zero desire to kiss Sophy or Melina.

"You've never been out with a man who's younger than you, have you?"

Lynda shook her head.

"Has anyone ever suggested that you need to loosen up a bit, Ms. Barone?"

"Melina does all the time. But I couldn't be like her."

"I'm not sure many people could. What do your parents think of her?" If Phil and Janice Barone didn't like her and Lynda was best friends with her anyway, then . . . What? It might not be important that her mother hated the thought of her daughter with him? Since Lynda would never be *with him,* it didn't matter.

"My dad loves her. He says she's the daughter he never had." She gave him a quick look with an uneasy smile. "It's his idea of a joke, because Melina's so feminine and so clearly adores men and I . . . I have my career."

Not much of a joke, Ben thought. "And your mother?"

"Mom likes her, though she doesn't exactly approve of her. She thinks Melina's too wild, too aggressive, too brash . . . but she also thinks Melina's going to make her mother a grandmother long before she'll be one."

"The woman who's planning a website called marrymydaughterplease.com thinks someone else is too aggressive?"

Crimson stained not just her cheeks but her entire face and down her throat, and her voice came out choked and dismayed. "She *told* you about that?"

"Actually, she was discussing it with law-boy when you left the table Saturday night. For all practical purposes I became invisible when you walked away." He grinned. "Hey, you were the one who had to go to the bathroom. You should have known better. So . . . tell me again about Anton, of the green eyes and oily muscles. Exactly what product is he selling? It wouldn't happen to be himself, would it?"

She covered her eyes with one hand, but underneath it, he could see the corners of her mouth twitching with a barely restrained smile. "Yes, as a matter of fact, he is. The magazine is called *Prospects,* and it's a—a—"

"Mail-order groom catalog?"

Her hand slid away. "Basically, yes. I guess some of the guys are decent guys, but they look like underwear models. They can't hold jobs because they're spending too much time in the gym working on their bodies, and they're looking for the perfect Ms. Right who will take care of them well into the future."

And Janice thought those guys were preferable over him. She'd rather see Lynda with someone who wanted her for her money than with some undereducated carpenter who wanted her for herself. For himself. Not that he wanted her . . .

Oh, hell.

LYNDA GOT THE FAST RIDE FIRST, TIRES SQUEALing on pavement, the car hugging the road as if Ben knew it intimately. The one time she dared look at the speedometer, she'd practically shrieked. Since she didn't think startling him when they were traveling in excess of a hundred miles an hour was wise, she didn't look again.

As they approached Howland, he slowed down to

the speed limit, sending a great shudder of relief through her, then grinned at her. "What do you think?"

She thought she probably didn't have to raise her brows much to appear wide-eyed. "I'm impressed."

He patted the dash. "All the girls say that. My Goat's a good car."

"Actually, I meant your driving. After all, we're alive." Thank God.

"Hey, I'm fast, not reckless. I wouldn't go looking for an accident. You know how much time and money I have in this baby? I'm awfully fond of her."

Her laugh sounded nervous. "Gee, I'm concerned about the damage to my body, and all you can worry about is the *car*?"

His gaze moved over her like a caress. "I'll concern myself with your body, too, if you have no objection."

Her smile froze on her face, and her heart stopped beating for a moment, two, more. Then he grinned and looked away, and her unsteady heartbeat resumed.

As they drove into the main part of town, Ben gestured. "Is there any place in particular you'd like to have dinner?"

She shook her head, all the while considering that he'd asked her out without even choosing a restaurant. Shameful, her mother would say. Poor planning, lawboy would add. Spontaneous, Melina would disagree, and spontaneous was good. The men Lynda had dated when she lived in Buffalo had been even less spontaneous than she was. Her last dinner date had been to a restaurant so exclusive it required connections to even get a reservation, major connections to get in with less than a month's notice. Her date, powerful as he was, hadn't managed. She'd had to mention Ross's name to get them in.

Ben was taking her to a fast-food drive-in, and it was neither shameful nor a result of poor planning. In fact—she took a deep breath that smelled of fried onions—the way her mouth was already starting to water, it seemed a very good idea.

All the spaces close to the street were taken up by teenagers celebrating the warm weather and the start of summer. He parked near the back, away from their laughter and music, and shut off the engine. They sat for a moment in a cozy sort of quiet before he looked at her. "Is this okay?"

"It smells great."

They ordered cheeseburgers and fries. He asked for a vanilla malt. She debated, then settled on a Diet Coke. She would have to run a lot of miles to burn off the meal without adding ice cream to it.

While they waited for the food, he settled comfortably in the seat. The neon lights that hung beneath the tin roof hummed, and one on the wall blinked regularly, switching from *onion* to *on on* every few seconds. A car filled with teenagers crept past with music blaring, then pulled into an empty space on the other side, and everyone spilled out to join their friends.

"Do you remember ever being that young?" Ben asked.

"It doesn't seem so long ago, until you realize that we're practically old enough to be their parents." Looking away, she grimaced. "I mean, not *us,* but you and me. I mean—"

"I know what you mean." His voice was low, warm, and something else. Affectionate? Tolerant? Indulgent?

Whatever it was, she decided the chance was as good as she was going to get to bring up a discussion left unfinished that afternoon. Careful to not look at him, to sound casual and careless as if she were making idle conversation, she said, "In the store today . . . you avoided answering Maggie's question about whether you have any kids of your own. Why?"

"Maggie . . . that's the munchkin's mom, right?"

"Uh-huh."

"And your boss's wife."

"Uh-huh. And you're avoiding my question now."

"Uh-huh."

She studied him for a moment in the dim light before speaking. "You do, don't you? You have a child, or children, someplace. Otherwise, you would simply say no."

Before he could answer—or not—a pretty teenage girl brought out their food. He cranked up the window a few inches to hold the tray, paid the girl, then handed Lynda one cheeseburger, one paper bag of fries, and her diet drink. For a few moments they busied themselves with packets of salt and ketchup, with spreading out napkins and balancing food on knees and the dash. Finally, when she figured he'd successfully avoided answering again, he asked the same question she'd asked earlier. "Does it matter?"

So it was true. Ben was a father. Though she'd dated divorced men and men whose sex lives were far more active than her own, she'd never been involved, even on the most casual basis, with a man who had children. It was a curiously difficult concept to grasp. Somewhere out there was a little boy or girl, maybe blond-haired, maybe green-eyed, with Ben's blood flowing through his or her veins. Maybe with his grin, his lazy Southern speech, his mannerisms. And maybe more than one little boy or girl.

Did it matter? Employer to employee, of course not. Friend to friend, maybe not. Woman to man . . . she honestly didn't know.

Since she couldn't offer an answer she didn't have, she remained silent, and when she remained silent, he became that way, too. They ate without speaking, and when they were finished, he gathered the trash onto the tray and set it all on the shelf underneath the menu. Instead of starting the car, though, he turned slightly to face her. "I was nineteen. I met this woman in a bar, took her home, and . . . she stayed. We were together three or four months. I was about to end it when she found out she was pregnant. I was a dumb kid. All I could think was no way was I sticking it out with her. My parents had gone through that and made each other's lives and everyone else's hell. I told her so long, it was fun, I'm outta here. And I never saw her again."

Not wanting him to see the emotions in her eyes—not sure what emotions *were* in her eyes—Lynda avoided looking at him. "What about the baby?"

"It was a girl. She's twelve now. She lives with her family, and she's happy, cared for, and well loved. She probably doesn't know I exist, and she probably doesn't care."

He'd turned his back on his own child. The idea was appalling. Indefensible. Astoundingly selfish.

But he'd been a kid himself. Nineteen, raised by a grandmother who clearly loved him, and ignored by parents who hadn't wanted him. He'd merely followed the example they'd set for him.

But he'd known firsthand how hurtful a parent's abandonment could be, and he'd done it to his own child anyway.

"I know I screwed up," he said quietly. "I was selfish. But for whatever it's worth, she was better off without me. I would have been a lousy father. I was a kid, and all I cared about was having fun. There's no way I could have dealt with her, her mother, and marriage."

But you could have tried, Lynda wanted to say. Her mother was a kid, too, but she hadn't had the option of walking away. She'd grown up quickly, had the baby, loved her, raised her, and helped her become that happy, cared-for twelve-year-old.

When she still didn't say anything, he muttered something under his breath, started the engine, and backed out of the space. Once they were out of town, he settled in at about ten miles above the speed limit, turned the stereo loud to combat the wind—and to make conversation impossible—and seemed to forget that she was there. She wanted to break the silence but couldn't, wanted to pretend she'd never asked the question and he'd never answered but couldn't do that, either. Perversely, she wanted to ask other questions—*Have you ever seen her? What's her name? Where does she live? Don't you feel even the slightest longing to know her the way a father should?*

And one other. *Is she the only one?*

The trip home seemed to fly past, and yet, when he parked beside her car and she climbed out into the warm, quiet night, her entire body ached, as if she'd been wound taut as a spring for hours. She expected to say good night right there, but he got out of the car and silently walked to the back door with her.

She unlocked the door, then faced him with an uneasy smile in the dim glow of the porch light. "I'm afraid I'll never share your appreciation for fast driving. I guess I'm just a tad fainthearted. But I enjoyed the evening."

"Yeah, I could tell by all that nonstop chatter."

She wasn't sure whether the bitterness in his voice was directed at her or perhaps himself. Did he regret telling her the truth? Did he wish he'd told her it was none of her business or just flat-out lied?

He walked as far as the top of the steps, then turned back. "Emmaline used to say don't ask a question if you aren't prepared for the answer. You weren't prepared for that one, were you?"

For hearing that the man she was attracted to had abandoned his own baby girl? How could she ever be prepared for that? "No, I wasn't."

"You know what, Lynda? People make mistakes. We screw up, and when that happens, we can't undo it. We can only try to make it right."

"What have you done to make it right?" She'd tried to hold the question in, but it popped out anyway. "Have you tried to be a father to your daughter? Have you accepted any responsibility for her support and upbringing? Have you apologized to her for ignoring her existence for twelve years?"

The look he gave her was harsh. "No." And that was all he said. Not, I'm planning to. Not even, The thought crossed my mind. Just, *No.*

"People *do* make mistakes. I understand that. But when it involves a child, it's just . . . You know how it felt to be abandoned by your father, and yet you did exactly the same thing to your daughter."

"And she was better off for it, just like I was better off without my old man." Anger sharpened his voice and gave a rough edge to his accent.

"Why do you get to make that decision for her?"

"Parents do that. It's what being a parent is about."

"No. Being a parent is about loving your child and being there for her, protecting her, teaching her, and setting a good example for her."

"And where does your mother fit in that definition? She treats you like a commodity that has to be given away before you get too old to be of any childbearing use to her. She doesn't care what you want. She doesn't give a damn about your career. She looks at you and sees her only daughter, nearly thirty-five, still single, and not likely to find a good husband on her own, which makes you a failure in the grandchild-producing department, too. She's convinced she can pick a better man for you than you can—and she's probably right, since her only requirements seem to be an impressive bank account and the willingness to breed you like a prize mare. If that's loving, protecting, and setting a good example, I'm damned lucky to have escaped my parents, and my daughter's damned lucky to have escaped hers."

For one stiff, chilly moment, they stared at each other, then she smiled her best drop-dead smile. "Go to hell, Ben," she said politely before going inside the house and closing the door. For good measure she turned off the porch light, leaving him standing alone in the dark.

Chapter Twelve

BEN AWAKENED THURSDAY MORNING WITH a headache and a killer case of heartburn. He would have liked to blame them both on the greasy burger with fried onions, but it was too early in the morning to try to fool himself. Last night's dinner had nothing to do with the way he felt. The after-dinner conversation did.

He would have guessed that it wasn't yet dawn, but a glance at the alarm clock showed that it was a few minutes after seven and a look out the window explained the darkness. Clouds hung low over the valley, bringing rain in sheets that fell from the roof like a flood-swollen river. It was the first rain since he and Sophy had finished their work on Lynda's roof, and he wondered—

Remembering that icy smile she'd turned on him, he groaned and turned over facedown in the bed. He wasn't sure which had hurt worse—that smile, the *Go to hell,* or her turning off the light while he still stood there. There had been something so disdainful, so dismissive, in leaving him there in the dark. He'd felt . . . hell, he didn't know exactly what he'd felt. Like he didn't matter. Like he didn't deserve the simple courtesy of a light to show him the way out.

A rumble of thunder brought his head up out of the pillow. There was plenty of inside work to keep him and Sophy busy at the site. Otherwise, this would have been a goof-off-without-pay day, thanks to the weather. It could still end up that way. Lynda very well might have changed the security code on the gate and instructed Gloria to have him bodily removed by the sheriff if he showed his face up on the hill.

And he couldn't blame her. What had possessed him to say those things about her mother? And what in hell had made him tell her the truth about Alanna?

That was what had hurt most—her reaction. He'd never told anyone about Alanna, not even Emmaline. Berry had taken care of that. He hadn't wanted to acknowledge what a bastard he'd been, hadn't wanted to face the guilt he'd managed all on his own, heaped on top of Emmaline's censure and disappointment. It was his greatest regret, his greatest shame, and he'd never trusted anyone with it. But he'd trusted Lynda.

He should have lied, should have grinned and said, *You volunteering, darlin'?* If he had, he might have gotten those kisses he'd been planning on.

But he hadn't lied, and in choosing not to, the only thing he'd accomplished was changing her opinion of him. Before, she'd thought he was maybe worth some kind of fling, if nothing else. Now she knew him for what he really was.

He watched the storm, brooded, and kept track of the time until eight o'clock had come and gone and eight-thirty was quickly approaching. Sure that she had long since arrived at her office, he finally got up, dressed, and dashed through the rain to the GTO. The interior of the car was warm, steamy, and smelled faintly of burgers, onions, and something more expensive, more exotic. Perfume? Or Lynda herself?

After a detour to the doughnut shop, where the clerk now knew his name and had his order ready when he walked in the door, he headed for the Hope house. His only hope that morning, with his mood as dark as the weather, was that he still had a job to go to.

He was halfway up the hill when he slowed to a stop. Sophy, in shorts and a slicker, with the hood down and her blonde curls dripping, greeted him with a brilliant smile. "Isn't it a beautiful morning?"

"Oh, yeah, sure. When I went to bed last night, I told God, Let's have a beautiful morning—you know, clouds, rain, thunder." A bright flash made him scowl and add, "Lightning."

"You did not," she said with a good-naturedly accusing look. "You didn't talk to God at all last night."

That was easy enough to guess. People could look at him and rightly assume he was not a praying man. Other than his grandmother, he'd never had anyone in his life he cared about enough, or wanted anything badly enough, to resort to prayer. "Hop in. I'll give you a ride."

After a moment's hesitation, she obeyed him. "I actually like walking in the rain," she said as he moved his foot off the brake. "Everything smells so fresh and clean, and I run into some special people."

"The only people you're likely to meet out here in the rain are trespassers."

"You're not a trespasser."

Oh, but he was. He didn't belong there. Truth was, with Emmaline gone, he didn't really belong anywhere.

"How did your date go?"

His jaw tightened until his teeth hurt, but the memory of Janice Barone grinding her teeth trying to get through a meal with him made him ease the pressure. "Ladies and gentlemen, we have a winner in this week's Date from Hell."

"Let's see if I can guess what went wrong. Everything was fine right up until you finished breaking every traffic law in the state of New York, then you . . . " Thoughtfully she tapped her finger against her lips, then her eyes brightened. "Then you dropped a major surprise in her lap that she didn't know how to react to and you ended up arguing."

Ben gave her a long look. "How did you—?" *Gloria.* Lynda must have told her what happened or—more likely—the housekeeper had overheard her talking on the phone to Melina. "She didn't have any problems reacting. And there wasn't an argument. We just exchanged a few words."

"Hurtful words."

"She'll get over it," he said with an indifference he didn't feel.

"But will you?"

Before he could respond to Sophy's quiet question, they crested the hill and he swore under his breath. The clunker Gloria drove was in its usual spot, and right beside it was the Mercedes. Great. Lynda had delayed going to work so she could fire him face-to-face. And he hadn't expected anything more personal than a message passed through Gloria.

The muscles in his neck were knotted when he followed Sophy into the kitchen, but there was no sign of Lynda. Good. Maybe he could manage to be working elsewhere when she came down to leave.

"Morning, Gloria," Sophy said cheerfully.

"And isn't it a beautiful one? Good morning, Ken. Have a seat and I'll have your coffee ready in a flash."

He shrugged out of his jacket and left it hanging in the laundry room, then looked warily up the back stairs, and down the hall toward the office.

"Miss Lydia's still upstairs," Gloria said as she brought him a mug of coffee. "The power went off when the storm started and she overslept. At least, that's what she said. Truth to tell, though, she looked like she hadn't slept a wink all night. She was sitting right there where you are when I came in this morning, just staring out the window and eating ice cream. Something was troubling her."

Sophy looked at him, one brow raised. He pointedly ignored her. "Tell me something, Gloria. How is it you can't remember names, but you have no problem remembering exactly how I like my coffee?"

The housekeeper's hands fluttered in the air in a brush-off. "Give me a decade or two, and I'll have your name down pat. But who can wait that long for good coffee?"

Carrying a plate and saucers, Sophy slid into the chair across from Ben. "What do you think was troubling Lynda, Gloria?"

"Oh, hon, I don't know."

"Me, either. Oh, gee, Ben, you saw her last night, didn't you? What do you think is the problem?"

Scowling at her, he dumped sticky buns and glazed doughnuts onto a plate, then crumpled the bakery sack. "I don't know. Maybe there are too many nosy people in her life."

"No, I don't think so. I think it's something more personal, like . . . oh, I don't know. Going out on a date and having an argument instead."

"You know, Sophy," he began sourly, "I hired you. I can fire you, too."

She wasn't the least bit intimidated. "For all you know, maybe *you've* been fired," she said cheerfully. "Anyway, you wouldn't fire me. We work so well together."

"No one's getting fired," Gloria said. "Let's get back to the subject. Did you and Miss Lindy have an argument last night?"

"What happened between Miss Lindy—Lydia—" Shaking his head, he muttered a curse. "What happened between us last night—"

"Is no one else's business."

As one, they all looked toward the stairs, where Lynda stood stiff and mannequinlike on the bottom step. If she'd had trouble sleeping last night, Ben couldn't see any evidence of it. She wore a plain suit that was flattering only because she could make a plastic trash bag look like high fashion, and her hair was pulled back and up, pinned and clipped so tightly that he was surprised she was able to blink. She looked hard, stern, and uncompromising. And beautiful.

"Is there any particular reason you people are sitting around gossiping over coffee instead of doing the jobs you were hired to do?"

Gloria beat a quick path to the counter and poured a cup of coffee for Lynda. "Mornin' again, Miss Lily. Here you go. This will help soothe you."

"I'm not in need of soothing, and my name is *Lynda.*"

"Well, of course it is, hon." Gloria made the coffee disappear in the sink as Lynda stopped beside the worktable.

"What will you be working on today?"

Rankled by the *you people* comment, Ben shrugged, and replied, "I thought we'd start on the plumbing."

"Why don't you finish replacing those second-floor windows before starting something else?"

He glanced at the rain, then back at her, and made the muscles in her jaw twitch. "Replacing the windows means removing them. Down where I come from, we try not to remove windows in the middle of a heavy rain, 'cause if you do, things tend to get a little wet inside. We also try to avoid climbing out on the roof with metal tools in a thunderstorm—you know, water, lightning, a disaster waiting to happen? Of course, we're all dumb rednecks. What do we know about anything?"

Her dark gaze narrowed and sharpened. "I wonder about that myself sometimes. Please get to work. This is my time you're wasting, and I don't appreciate it." Spinning on her heel, she started down the hall, toward the front of the house.

"Even a slave got a break for meals," Ben called after her.

She stopped, stiffened, then continued past the office and the front stairs to the living room. Suddenly, Gloria dropped the dish towel she'd been fiddling with and started toward the door. "Oh, Miss Lynette, you might want to—"

The rest of the suggestion was lost in a crash. Wood hit wood, glass broke, and hard objects thudded against other hard objects. Ben pushed past Gloria and raced to the living room with Sophy right behind him and the housekeeper bringing up the rear. He skidded to a stop in the doorway, narrowly avoiding a collision with a massive table that hadn't stood there the last time he'd looked . . . or, apparently, the last time Lynda looked, either. Running into the table had thrown her off balance, and she'd taken a chair, a smaller table, and everything it held to the floor with her. She was still there, half lying, half sitting, staring at the room.

Ben looked around, too. "Wow, Gloria. When you said you were going to do some heavy-duty cleaning, you weren't kidding, were you? Tell me you cleaned all that ugly, uncomfortable furniture and found this great stuff underneath."

"Of course not. I found all this in the guest house out back. It's so much better suited to the house, don't you think?"

He agreed. The sofas and chairs were soft, upholstered in pastels, and looked perfect for relaxing or napping. The tables were good wood and proportioned to the overstuffed sofas, and the lamps were sleek, tall, and very definitely modern. Even the wallpaper looked cleaner, newer, less obnoxious, with the changes.

"You did all this yourself?" Except for the smallest tables, all the pieces were substantial, and if asked, he wouldn't guess Gloria could lift even one end of one sofa.

"Oh, no. I had some help. You were gone to town with Sophy. It didn't take long." Abruptly, the pleasure drained from her face. "Oh, Miss Lynda! I am so sorry! Are you all right?"

"My antiques," Lynda murmured, sounding as dazed as she looked.

"Are in the guest house. Everything's fine—no nicks, no scratches, nothing broken. Well, except what you knocked over here. I'll get a dustpan and broom. Sophy, can you help me?"

Ben crouched down, elbows braced on his thighs, fingers laced together. "Are you all right?"

She eased herself into a sitting position, avoiding slivers of glass from what looked like two vases that had shattered. "My antiques . . . "

"Were almost as uncomfortable as having no furniture at all. If you're honest, you'll admit you didn't like them. You just thought they were appropriate." And being appropriate was, for her, more important than being comfortable or likable. "Did you hit anything when you fell?"

"Only the floor."

She moved as if to get up, and he easily stood, then offered her a hand. For a moment he thought she might refuse to take it, but then she wrapped her fingers around his. He pulled her to her feet and considered holding on tightly, but instead he watched as she withdrew her hand, brushed her clothes, then tried to surreptitiously rub her left knee. "Do you need to see a doctor?"

"No. I'm fine. You can get back to work." Then she feigned surprise. "Oh, I forgot. You haven't *started* working yet. Please do. And when you turn in your hours this week, don't forget you got a late start today."

The sweet sarcasm in her voice got under his skin damn near as much as her inference that he might collect wages for more hours than he'd actually worked. In his head he could hear Emmaline warning him to smile, be polite, and keep his opinions to himself. He managed the smile and turned away without saying anything at all, since that was the only way to ensure politeness, then abruptly swung back around. "You're out of line, Ms. Barone. I've never cheated my employers. I've never padded invoices or falsified a time card or taken so much as a damned nail home from a job site, and you have no right to even hint that I might. If you don't like the choices I made when I was a kid, that's your problem. It's got nothing to do with the work I'm doing for you."

Like him, she started to turn away. Like him, emotion got the better of her. "It's got everything to do with the kind of man you are. You make it sound so simple, so harmless—the 'choices' you made. Put it in plain English, Ben. You *abandoned* your own baby. You helped create a new life, then said, 'Oh, hey, I was just looking for sex. This father gig is more than I bargained for. I'm outta here.' And you walked away and never looked back. You left her mother feeling used. You let your own daughter grow up *knowing* you didn't give a damn about her. And you broke your grandmother's heart."

He stared at her, his face hot, his chest so tight that taking a normal breath was impossible. At his side, the fingers of his right hand curved into an impotent fist, sending a dull throb through his hand and wrist that did nothing to lessen the ache in his gut.

He stared at her so long, so hard, that her anger faded and her damnably cool civility took over. "I'm sorry. I shouldn't have said that. I think it would be best if we both went to work and forgot—"

"No."

She looked startled. "Excuse me?"

"I said no. Sorry I can't give notice, but yesterday was my last day. Since you apparently have doubts about my honesty, my integrity, and my character, keep the money you owe me. That ought to cover anything you think I cheated on."

This time when he turned, he walked past Sophy and Gloria, both staring openmouthed, down the hall, across the kitchen, and out the door, and he never looked back.

AFTER THE SOCCER GAME SATURDAY AFTERnoon, Alanna was nursing a sore rib where she'd collided with one of the other team's players, and she was hot and sweaty, but she couldn't have felt better. The Seraphim were undefeated, she'd been asked to help out at Miss Agatha's wedding shower that night, and—best of all—Caleb would be there, too. They would be watching the little kids with Susan, Trey, and some of the others, and when it was over, Dr. J.D. was treating them all to dinner. Of course, it wasn't a date—Uncle Nathan told her she couldn't date until she was twenty-one, and Aunt Emilie said he was just teasing, but Alanna wasn't so sure, because he got that stern-policeman look in his eyes. But it was going to be a lot of fun anyway.

When she got to the bleachers where everyone was gathered, Aunt Emilie bent to kiss her forehead. "You did a great job, Lannie."

"Thanks." Soccer wasn't the most important thing in her life, but she was glad she was good at it. When they'd lived with their mom, they'd never stayed anywhere long enough or had the money for her to take part in sports or anything. She'd been jealous of kids who played soccer, took gymnastics, or were in Scouts, because she was lucky to steal enough money from her mom to buy food before Berry had spent it all on drugs. All she'd wanted back then was to have a normal life—a home, enough food, someone who loved them, and friends.

And she had it all now.

With Aunt Emilie and the kids, Alanna started toward the parking lot. People they passed patted her on the back and said they were lucky to have her, and she smiled politely. She wouldn't admit it to anyone, but the after-the-game part was almost as much fun as the game itself.

They were practically at the car when she saw Ben Foster walking toward his car. "Hey," she said in greeting. "Where's your friend?"

"She couldn't make it. You did good. Congratulations."

"Thanks." She waved as Aunt Emilie turned from unlocking the doors.

"Who was that, Alanna?"

"A friend of Miss Agatha's and Grandpa Bud's. His name is Ben, and he's from Georgia."

"Does he know someone on the team?"

Alanna shrugged.

"Do you run into him very often?"

"Nah. Just at the band concert. And he was at our game one day. And Susan and Mai and I talked to him at Harry's last weekend. Oh, and we saw him when we went to the fabric store last week. And today. That's all. Oh, yeah, and he came by Miss Corinna's one day, asking for directions. Can I wear my new dress tonight, or do I have to save it for church?"

"We'll see."

Josie was already buckled in the front seat, so Alanna got in back with Brendan and Michael. She made sure Brendan's seat belt was fastened tight, then checked the straps on Michael's car seat before fastening her own seat belt. Finally, Aunt Emilie got in and started the car.

"If you see this man again, Alanna, let me know," she said as she backed out of the parking space.

"Is he a bad man?" Josie asked. "If he is, Uncle Nathan can shoot him with his gun."

"How can I know if he's a bad man if I don't know him?" Aunt Emilie asked. "I'd just like to meet him and welcome him to Bethlehem the way everyone welcomed us. Do you remember?"

"You're gonna make him cinnamon rolls and hot cocoa? That's what Miss C'rinna and Miss Agatha did for us." Josie made a face. "No offense, Aunt Emilie, but I don't think you can make cinnamon rolls as good as they can. You prob'ly better buy 'em instead, or ask Miss C'rinna to bake 'em."

Aunt Emilie laughed, and said, "I'll keep that in mind." But she took a long time to pull out of the parking lot, because she was watching the man's car drive away, and when she looked at Alanna in the rearview mirror, she had a funny look in her eyes. Kind of a worried look.

Alanna wondered why.

MELINA HAD HAD ONE HELL OF A WEEK, SO when it was over, she did what came naturally—she packed a bag, gassed up the Bug, and headed for Bethlehem. She loved her brief trips—the long drive with the top down and music blaring, the lazy nothing-to-do-unless-she-wanted-to attitude once she got there, the catching-up with Lynda. The only downer was having to leave again. She had actually, a time or two, given thought to staying. Not that the town could support her business, but it could be handled long-distance.

But she wasn't moving. She hadn't kidded when she'd told Lyn on her last visit that she wanted love, marriage, commitment—all those things that had come automatically for her mother's generation, that her generation wasn't supposed to care so much about. Well, *she* cared, and there were a lot more marriageable men in a city like Buffalo than in a hamlet the size of Bethlehem.

But all it took, her mother was fond of saying, was one.

She'd just turned off Main Street when she saw a familiar car approaching from the opposite direction. She slowed to a stop, then raised both arms over her head in exuberant greeting. "Ben!"

Rumbling like the powerful machine it was, the GTO stopped beside her, and the driver gave her what would be a smile from anyone else. But she'd seen Ben Foster smile, and that was a poor substitute for the real thing.

"You look like hell. What's wrong?"

"Nothing. I got my stitches out. It's a beautiful day. What could be wrong?"

"How's Lynda?"

"You'll have to ask her when you see her."

"You had a date with her Wednesday." And Melina hadn't heard from her since. She'd meant to call her, but that hellacious week had gotten in the way—one employee quitting, having to fire another, bailing two more out of jail as well as dealing with demanding clients. It had been a fun couple of days. "What did Lyn do wrong?"

"She didn't do anything. The evening was fine. She was fine. Everything's fine. Listen, I've got to go."

"Wait. How about dinner . . . " She let the words trail off as he drove away with a wave.

Her face felt as if it had settled into a permanent scowl by the time she reached Lynda's house. She let herself in, then bellowed Lynda's name.

"Melina? What are you doing here?"

The voice came from the office. By the time Lynda got to her feet, Melina was already striding through the doorway. She assumed she looked as fierce as she'd been aiming for, because after one look at her, Lynda sank back down into her chair and put on a scowl of her own. "What a pleasant surprise."

"Don't try to get on my good side. What happened on your date Wednesday night?"

Lynda's eyes hardened. "The usual stuff. I let him take me in that car of his. We drove a hundred-ten miles an hour over mountain roads, and had hamburgers and fries at a drive-in plagued by neon, teenagers, and fifties' music."

Something had definitely gone wrong, because Lynda wasn't a snob, not about things like cars and restaurants. One of her favorite places in Buffalo had been a hole-in-the-wall burger joint where the aroma of fried onions made your eyes water a block away, and the only problem she had with riding in the Bug was when the top was up and her head bumped the roof. "Did you let him kiss you good night?"

Lynda suddenly found it imperative that she give the computer a command at that very instant. Then, finally she grudgingly admitted, "By the time the evening was over, he wasn't interested in a kiss or anything else."

It took a few minutes to coax an explanation from her, and even then, it wasn't complete. All she would say was that they'd argued over something he'd done years earlier. What that was, she wouldn't admit.

"I didn't want him to quit," she said moodily.

"I don't know. You accuse an honest man of ripping you off just because your nose is out of joint, you gotta expect a similar reaction. I mean, what kind of respect could you have for the guy if he stuck around after you said something so insulting?"

"He made insults, too," Lynda said defensively.

"What did he say?"

"That my mother doesn't give a damn about my career. That she sees me as a failure because I haven't found a husband and given her grandchildren. That she wants to breed me like a prize mare."

Melina sat down and propped her feet on the edge of the desk. "You know I adore your mother, but all she ever wanted you to be was a housewife and mother, just like her. She wanted you to finish college so you would have something to fall back on if your husband left you for a younger woman, but she never wanted you to have a career. Besides . . . you subjected him to two hours of Janice's insults. At least he had the decency to not say his peace to her face, like she did with him."

Lynda saved her file, then leaned back in the chair. "There's a reason I don't get involved with anyone—"

"Yeah, you're socially stunted and a coward."

"I'm not socially stunted. I just choose to not be burdened by personal relationships. And I'm not a coward. I don't really want a relationship. I don't want to get married. I have enough going on career-wise that I want my personal life to be quiet and uneventful."

"Yeah, sure. And every night when you go to bed, you pray to grow four inches taller, to gain fifty pounds, and to have your mother live with you for the rest of your unnatural life." Melina made an irritated gesture. "Save the lies for someone who'll believe them."

"*I* believe them."

"Yeah, well, you think you don't want a hot, steamy fling with Ben Foster. You're obviously delusional." She gazed out the window for a moment, then said, "You know, Lyn, it's possible to disapprove of someone's actions and like or love him anyway. I don't like everything you do, but I still love you."

Lynda gave her a sour look that didn't encourage that line of conversation, so Melina got to her feet. "Come on. Treat me to dinner at the Starlite, then we can drown our sorrows in a couple of beers . . . or a couple of good-looking pickups."

She was surprised when Lynda readily agreed. No argument, no trying to beg off, just a sighed "All right."

It was a few minutes after six when they arrived at the tavern, but the parking lot was half-full. Melina parked the Bug near the door and hopped out, buzzing with energy, while Lynda dragged out. She swore, if she met Mr. Right tonight and had to turn him down because of Ms. Sad Sack over there, she was giving up forever her attempts to help Lyn enjoy life. All future visits would be restricted to activities suited to a stuffy, prissy thirty-four-year-old old maid.

There was a nice crowd in the tavern. The dance floor was mostly empty, though a sign on the stage announced live music in an hour. Melina stood just inside the door, sizing up the men, and decided there were decent pickin's tonight. She might not get lucky, but she would have some fun.

"See that big guy in the last booth?" It was tricky business, pitching her voice loud enough for Lynda to hear but not so loud that she could get caught shouting at the end of a song. "If I weren't here visiting you, I'd take him home with me tonight."

"That's Sebastian Knight. He was at Harry's last time you were here."

Oh, yeah. Carpenter, lived outside town, wife had run off and left him and their little girl. Somehow, the fact that he was so amazingly masculine had escaped her that night—probably because Lynda and Ben had both been in pissy moods and she'd been trying to keep them from each other's throats.

The man looked as if he stood close to six and a half

feet tall. His shoulders were broad, his hair dark brown and stylishly casual, and his features were rugged. She wouldn't say he was particularly handsome, but macho? Yeah. Impressively male? Absolutely. He looked quiet, steady, and strong—and those were the ones a girl had to watch out for.

She followed Lynda to a booth and took a seat facing Sebastian. They ordered burgers, and beer for Melina, Diet Coke for Lynda, and they talked about nothing in particular. More people wandered in, the noise level increased, and a few minutes before seven, the band took the stage.

"I'm going to ask Sebastian to dance," Melina said, sliding from the booth. "Want me to get his companion for you?"

"No, thanks."

She wound her way between tables and past the pool table, where some guy got fresh. Looking back, she smiled warningly. "Do that again, sweetheart, and I'll . . . buy you a beer."

The guy moved as if he would do it again, but she was quicker. To the sound of his friends' laughter, she approached the back booth . . . where she received a pleasant surprise, along with a not-so-pleasant one. Sebastian's companion was none other than Ben Foster, and *his* companion was Kelli. "I didn't know you were here, darlin'."

Ben responded with his heaviest drawl. "It's a Saturday night in the squeaky-clean town of Bethlehem. Where else would an unattached man go?"

"Last Saturday night you went to dinner with Lyn and her parents."

"Lucky for me, that'll never happen again." He took

a drink from his beer, his green gaze never wavering from her face. "Did she send you over here?"

"She doesn't know you're here. If she did, she would have walked out a long time ago."

"Then what do you want?"

"Nothing from you." Deliberately shifting away from him, she gave Sebastian her best smile, the kind that made friends of men and small children and caused women to hate her irrationally. Judging by the way Kelli wrapped herself possessively around Ben, it was working. "Hi. I'm Melina Dimitris, and I surely would like to dance with you."

Sebastian's gaze moved over her, from the top of her wild curly hair over her short, snug red dress, all the way down to her heels and red-painted toes. Appreciation darkened his hazel eyes as, without a word, he slid from the bench and took her hand.

Before walking away, she managed to unobtrusively bring one heel down hard on Ben's foot. "Y'all have fun," she said sweetly. "I certainly intend to."

Chapter Thirteen

FRESH AIR. QUIET. HER PAJAMAS. A COOL breeze. Ice cream.

Lynda sat in the booth, not giving even half an ear to the man who'd invited himself to join her, and made a mental list of the things that would bring her pleasure at that very moment. It was a short list, and incomplete, but it made her long to walk out of the Starlite and set about fulfilling it. If only Melina would come back, and Mickey, Ricky, or whatever the hell his name was, would take the hint that she wasn't interested and go away. But he'd been there long enough for her to finish her drink and showed no signs of leaving.

She was debating ordering another drink, maybe even beer, when Ben stopped beside the booth. "Melina just waltzed out the door with Sebastian, and I don't think she's coming back. Do you have a ride home?"

Lynda stared at him, disconcerted by the facts that he'd been in the same room all this time and she hadn't known it, that Melina had left her on her own, and that Kelli was plastered to his side. "I . . . No, we came in her car."

"Hey, no problem, doll," the guy across from her said. "I'll take you home."

Ben's gaze shifted from her to him and narrowed. "I don't think so."

The man took her hand as if staking his claim. "Look, pal, this is between the lady and me."

Ben easily removed her hand from his grip. "No, *pal,* it's between you and me. The last guy I argued with in a bar couldn't eat solid food for six weeks. Don't mess with me. Come on, Lynda."

"Why don't we let her decide?" the guy challenged, and Kelli chimed in, "Ben, I thought we were going to my place. Let him take her. Mickey's harmless, aren't you, hon? At least, most of the time," she clarified with a giggle.

"I can find my own—" The look Ben shot her was so forbidding that Lynda's words ended abruptly.

"Kelli, I told you I would take you home. I also told you I wasn't staying," Ben said impatiently. "Mickey, stay the hell away from her. Lynda, come on."

It didn't strike her as a particularly good time to argue, especially when he was offering what she'd just been longing for. She grabbed her handbag and slid to her feet, and, with his hand at the small of her back, was unceremoniously hustled from the bar.

Kelli accompanied them only to the parking lot. "You're serious? You weren't planning to spend the night?"

"That's what 'no thanks' means where I come from," Ben said irritably. "Do you want a ride or not?"

She planted one hand on her hip. "I have my own car here. Jeez, did you think I walked? You know, Ben, for an unattached man, you certainly seem attached to the ice queen there. Well, you're welcome to her, sweetheart. You've blown your last chance with me. As far as I'm concerned, you can go to hell."

Lynda watched over her shoulder as Kelli spun around and flounced back inside. Though she resented the ice queen remark, she admired the very feminine show of temper. She couldn't toss her head, spin around, or flounce like that any more than she could sidle up to a stranger and say, Hey, baby, wanna take me home?

But maybe she didn't need that questionable skill. After all, Kelli was very good at it, but she'd tried it twice with Ben and failed both times.

He opened the GTO's door for her—because he didn't trust her to get in on her own, she suspected—then slid in beside her. He remained silent all the way to her house, a fierce scowl marring his features as if he were mad at the world . . . or her.

When he stopped next to her car, she sat motionless a moment. She owed him several apologies, but couldn't find the words. She got out, then bent to speak through the window. "Thank you for the ride. Though it wasn't necessary. I could have made it home on my own. And I could have dealt with Mickey on my own, too. Still, thank you." Figuring she'd said more than enough, she started toward the house.

She was at the steps when the car door slammed, then Ben's angry voice called out. "How? How would you have dealt with Mickey? Would you have let him bring you home, then given him a prissy little 'Thank you for the ride,' and expect him to be a good boy and leave again?"

She unlocked the door as he took the steps two at a time.

"Would you have tried to intimidate him into leaving without something for his trouble? Would you have gone into your frigid, aloof, so damn superior routine to keep him at arm's length? 'Cause I'll tell you something, darlin'. It wouldn't have worked." As he spoke, he advanced on her, his voice growing softer as the distance between them narrowed. "A guy like Mickey is too stupid to be intimidated, macho enough to take your untouchable act as a challenge, and egotistical enough to believe you'll enjoy it so much once he gets started that you'll forget the force that was necessary to change your mind."

She retreated until the door was against her back. He stopped only when mere millimeters separated them, so close she could feel his breath on her skin. She could smell Kelli's cologne on him and feel the heat radiating through him, could feel when his anger shifted into tension of a different sort. Though he wasn't touching her, her body responded as if he were. Her breasts grew heavy, her nipples swelling, and heat pooled deep in her belly. Her nerves tingled, and her skin rippled in anticipation of the warm, calloused feel of his hands on her.

He breathed shallowly, unsteadily. She found it difficult to breathe at all. She wanted to open the door at her back, run inside, and lock it between them. More than that, she wanted to grab hold of his shirt, yank him those few millimeters closer, and kiss him like she'd never kissed a man—greedily, hungrily, demanding, claiming. She didn't do either, because Melina was right. She was a coward.

"You don't have an answer, do you?" Ben murmured, his breath caressing her cheek. "The incredibly competent, efficient, all-knowing machine doesn't have a clue, does she?"

She managed to find her voice, though it was husky. "Your girlfriend says he's harmless."

"Kelli's never said no to a man in her life. She doesn't know what can happen. Neither do you. You're so used to dealing with puppets you can control that you don't know what it's like to be with a real man."

Then show me. She'd thought she'd spoken aloud, but the words had gotten lost somewhere between her brain and her mouth, which he was now touching, brushing his lips lightly over hers. With a trembling breath, she tried again. "Show me."

His mouth stilled, and for a moment he stared at her. She could feel his gaze, though she couldn't meet it. She had no idea how he might respond to her request, whether he would be willing or if she left him as cold as Kelli apparently did. When he remained still and quiet moment after long moment, she felt a sick, embarrassed queasiness building in her stomach. He was just playing with her, teaching her a lesson for her own good, for his own amusement.

She was trying to find a way to pretend she'd been joking when she felt a tug around her middle. Looking down, she saw that he'd unfastened the bottom button on her blouse, and finally the touch she'd been waiting for came. It was slight, just the tip of one finger, sliding underneath her shirt and gliding back and forth along the waistband of her slacks. Gentle pressure, gentle warmth, and it made her eyes flutter shut and her breath catch in her chest.

"I don't think it would be a very good idea," he murmured even as he moved a step closer, even as his hands slid around to her hips to press her against his arousal. "Your mother was right about me. I'm not what you need."

She raised her hands to his shoulders, then slid her arms around his neck. "You're wrong, Ben. You're exactly what I need . . . exactly what I wan—"

He kissed her then—none of that tantalizing rubbing and teasing, but a serious, greedy, blood-stirring kiss that made her knees weak and sent a rush of heat sizzling through her body. He thrust his tongue into her mouth, probing, tasting, stroking, and ground his hips against hers. In some small still-functioning part of her brain, she remembered Melina pointing out that the two of them would be a perfect match in their bare feet, and she was right. Lynda wasn't too tall. He wasn't too short.

He smelled of wanton woman and tasted of beer, and his body was warm, hard, his muscles finely honed from years of physical labor. She slid her hands over his back, tugged his shirt free of his jeans, and spread her palms flat on heated silken skin. She wanted to touch him everywhere, wanted to see him, taste him, feel him inside her, but she couldn't bring herself to end the kiss, to give up the sweet, greedy claiming, not even when her lungs threatened to burst for just one breath of searing air.

A moment later he broke off the kiss, but he didn't pull away. He rested his forehead against hers, drew a few heavy breaths, then rubbed his mouth side to side over hers. "This is your second chance, sugar, and I don't give third chances. If you're gonna change your mind, now's the time to do it. Tell me to go. If you don't, I'm gonna take you upstairs to your bedroom"—he kissed her cheek —"and get rid of these clothes"—then her jaw—"and make love to you"—then left a trail of wet, hot kisses down her throat to the vee of her blouse—"at least eight or ten times." Thrusting his hips against hers, he made her moan. Finding and teasing her nipple through her blouse, he made her whimper, then he brought his mouth close to her ear, making her shudder. "And then I'm gonna do it all over again. It's your decision. What do you want?"

"You," she murmured, her mouth seeking his for another kiss. He indulged her for a moment, one brief press of his mouth against hers, one intimate thrust of his tongue, before pulling back.

"Open your eyes and say that again," he commanded. "Look at me and say it."

He wanted to be sure she was choosing him—not merely giving in to need and desire, but to need and desire for *him*. She understood that insecurity, opened her eyes, and cupped her hands to his cheeks. "I want you, Ben E-doesn't-stand-for-anything-or-maybe-it-stands-for-everything Foster. I want you to kiss me again and again. I want you to go upstairs to my bedroom with me—or, hell, right here on the porch is fine—and get rid of these clothes. I want you inside me."

He stroked her breast, ending with a little pinch on her nipple, then did it over and over, making her eyes close, her breath catch, and she lost track of what she was saying for one tantalizing moment. When her brain was able to send commands again, when she could put a coherent thought together, she opened her eyes and grinned at him in that wicked way of his that she loved so much. "I want to get nekkid with you, Ben."

He kissed her once more, a hard, demanding kiss that bordered on punishing, then reached past her and opened the door. Only the light above the sink was burning to show their way, but neither of them was watching where they were going. They stumbled up the back stairs, bumped the wall on their way down the hall, then finally reached the cool, quiet darkness of her bedroom.

He turned on the bedside lamp, then held her, hands on her waist, at arm's length. "Last chance, darlin'."

"You only give second chances, remember? And I told you what I want." She studied his face, so handsome and serious. Arousal made his eyes a few shades darker and tightened the skin across his cheekbones and the line of his jaw, as if he was relying on great reserves of self-control. She found the idea one hell of a turn-on, but she didn't move closer, didn't touch him any more than she already was. "This is *your* second chance, Ben. If you don't want this . . . "

He reached for her hand and pressed it to his chest, where his heart thudded rapidly, then slid it slowly over his ribs, from soft cotton shirt to softer faded denim, not stopping until her fingers were insinuated between his legs, curving and stretching to mold his erection. "Does that feel like I don't want you?" he asked hoarsely.

You, he said. Not *this,* as she had. It was a small difference, but it touched her deep inside. *This* could mean any woman touching him so intimately. *You* narrowed it down, made it special, made *her* special. When was the last time a man had made her feel special? She couldn't recall.

Gently flexing her fingers, she made his breath catch, then rush out on a harsh groan. A feeling of power swept over her that, for the first time in memory, had nothing to do with her career, her authority, or her fortune, and everything with being a woman. For the first time, she felt beautiful, utterly feminine, even delicate. She *didn't* feel six feet tall, coldhearted, or an ice maiden.

Curling her fingers around the hem of his T-shirt, she peeled it up and over his head, tousling his blond hair, then brought both hands to his chest. Somewhere there was a hunk-of-the-month calendar waiting for a photograph of him just like this. His skin was golden brown, hot, and stretched taut over well-defined muscles, and it quivered when she caressed it. His small, flat nipples hardened under her touch, and his muscles constricted tighter when she dragged her tongue across them.

She unbuttoned his jeans without faltering, slid the zipper down, then started pushing both jeans and briefs over his hips, until she got lost somewhere along the way. As she cradled him in both hands, he sucked in an edgy breath and muttered, "Damn, sugar." His voice was thick, ragged, his accent so pronounced it added additional syllables to the words. She stroked him, caressed, tenderly explored until, with a groan, he pulled her hands away, dragged her close, and took her mouth. His tongue plunged inside before she had a chance to protest, then with a new bout of fever spreading through her, she forgot what she wanted to protest.

He finished removing his clothes one-handed while, with his other hand, he held her for his kiss. She freed her mouth, moved out of reach of his. "Now," she demanded. Pleaded.

"In a minute." He began lazily unbuttoning her blouse. When she tried to help, he pushed her hands away. When she started to unfasten her trousers, he claimed both hands and settled them on his shoulders. "I've been wanting to undress you since about two minutes after I first saw you. Let me do this."

"I can't wait."

He chuckled softly, gently, wickedly. "Trust me, darlin', it'll be worth it." He slid her blouse off her shoulders so slowly that her skin felt raw, as if every nerve ending were exposed. Just as slowly he removed her bra, wrapping the wisp of lace and ribbons around his big dark hand before dropping it to the floor. By the time her slacks joined the other clothes on the floor, her skin was on fire, burning, tingling, and need throbbed inside her with an urgency that made her damn near incoherent.

He cupped her through her panties, no more substantial than her bra, then rubbed hard and made her sink against him for support. "Please," she whispered.

"Please what?" He slid his hand underneath the lace and stroked one finger inside her.

"Now."

"What do you want now?"

"You. Inside me. Please, Ben."

Still tormenting her, he lowered her onto the bed, then stripped off her panties. She tried to help, but couldn't manage more than raising her hips. Her legs were too weak, her muscles too unsteady. Her entire body was hypersensitive, quivering wherever he touched her. When he bent to suckle her nipple, she cried out, tried to push him away, then pulled him closer. When he settled between her legs, she moved restlessly, achingly, until he'd filled her, stretched her, made her feel incredibly whole.

Bracing himself on his elbows, he leaned over until they were practically nose to nose. "Okay, darlin', I'm inside you." He shuddered as she tightened her muscles around him, and his voice sounded significantly less controlled. "What do you want now?"

She raised her hands to his face, touching his cheeks, his jaw, his mouth. He automatically opened, taking the tip of her finger inside, nipping it, sucking it, making her body convulse around his again. "Teach me," she murmured.

"Teach you what?"

"Everything you know."

Slowly he grinned, and it was sexy, charming, and endearing as hell. "It might take a while, but it'll damn sure be fun."

"I could use some fun, and I've got a while." A night, a day, a weekend . . . the rest of her life.

"Hold on tight, sugar," he murmured against her mouth. "I'm gonna take you for the ride of your life."

BEN LAY ON HIS BACK, UTTERLY EXHAUSTED, and stared at the faint patterns created on the opposite wall by moonlight through the windows. His breathing was finally as close to normal as it was ever going to be again, and the sweat had dried from his body, but he felt weak, spent, even achy in some places he hadn't thought possible. He hadn't yet decided if he'd just made the biggest mistake of his life . . . or just done the *right*est thing in his life. Probably both. Only time would tell just *how* right and wrong.

Lynda lay beside him, curled on her side, her dark gaze on him. He knew he should be next to her, holding her, but after the last time, they'd both been so hot, slick with sweat, and barely able to breathe. He'd sprawled on his back on one side of the mattress. She'd chosen to lie on the other.

He could hear her breathing—quiet little puffs, a drastic change from the desperate gasps that had racked her earlier. It had been quite an experience—the oh-so-aloof-and-cool Ms. Barone looking, sounding, and behaving thoroughly wild.

The mattress shifted as she did, then her voice, quiet but not quite controlled, drifted across the bed to him. "It's all right if you regret it."

Surprised, he turned to look at her. The lamplight fell over her shoulder, lighting part of her face, casting the rest in shadow. She looked beautiful, serene . . . except for the insecurity in her eyes. He rolled onto his side, stuffed a pillow under his head, then reached for her. His first impulse was to cup her perfect small breast, to see if he could make her nipple swell again with nothing more than his fingers. Instead, he rested his palm against her cheek. "You're the only part of my life I don't have any regrets about, sugar." Except he wished he were *more.* More acceptable. More her type. He wished there was something he could give her besides long nights of good sex, wished he could have some value in her life.

After a moment, he gave in to his own insecurities. "Are you having regrets?"

"Oh, no. You're the best time I've ever had." The smile that curved her lips was one he'd never seen before—playful, seductive, innocent, and sinful. "By my count, that was only three times. You promised at least eight or ten. Can we do it again?"

He drew her close and tucked her body against his. "So you're pretty and sexy and greedy, too, hmm?"

"I can't help being greedy. I've lived a deprived life, remember? It didn't have you in it."

A few days ago she hadn't wanted him in her life. A few hours from now, she might feel the same. Or she might decide it was all right to keep him around as long as their relationship remained private.

"Lyn . . . " He hesitated, wishing if he could have mastered one of Emmaline's lessons, it would have been knowing when to speak and when to shut the hell up. He shouldn't say what he was about to, but he couldn't not say it. "I'm the same man you told to go to hell Wednesday night. The same one whose integrity and character you questioned Thursday morning. Nothing's changed. You know that, don't you?"

She hid her face against his shoulder. With his fingers on her chin, he gently forced her to meet his gaze. "I'm not looking for an apology." But he did want to hear her say that she trusted him, that she *knew* he wouldn't cheat her in any way, that she thought better of him than that. "I just want you to understand that the things you don't like or respect about me are still there. Whatever it is you don't trust about me is there, too."

She laid her palm along his jaw, stroking his skin, making him want to rub against her. "Do you think you'd be here right now if I didn't trust you with my life?" she asked regretfully. "The things I said Thursday morning . . . I was upset. Embarrassed. Disappointed."

"I'm pretty good at that. I kept Emmaline in a constant state of disappointment, right up to the day she died."

"I don't believe that. She loved you."

"And she was disappointed in me."

"Melina says just because you disapprove of a person's actions, that doesn't mean you disapprove of the person, too."

"So you can think I'm lacking in character, but still want to have sex with me." He tried to sound as if he were teasing, but it didn't sound very convincing to him. Apparently to her, either, because she pulled away from him, found a corner of the covers rumpled beneath them, and pulled it over her when she sat up.

"I don't think you're lacking in character, and I'm truly sorry I ever suggested it. It's just . . . I don't understand how the man I know could turn his back on the woman pregnant with his child. I don't understand how you could weigh a baby's needs against your own and decide yours are more important. It's so selfish, so immature."

"You're right. It is. And if you remember, I told you that Wednesday night. I screwed up. I was selfish. But you're right about one other thing, darlin'. The man you know didn't—wouldn't—do those things. I was nineteen years old, still a kid in most people's eyes. Do you remember what it was like to be nineteen? Did you ever do anything then that you wouldn't dream of doing today?"

"Of course. But . . . a baby who needed you . . . "

Feeling as if he were arguing a losing battle, Ben sat up, too, but didn't bother with the cover. There was nothing left to be modest about. "This may surprise you, darlin', but I'm not the only teenage father who didn't stick around to change diapers and give bottles. Kids can grow up perfectly fine with one parent or one relative to love them. You're judging me based on your own experience of a perfect childhood, the perfect family, a father who worked and supported the family, and a mother who stayed home and had cookies and milk waiting for you after school. I bet you never saw your parents fight, or come home stinking drunk with some stranger, or lie, cheat, and steal on a regular basis. I bet your mother never got tired of you and disappeared for days at a time, and I'm damn sure she never knocked you around just because she needed a target and you were handy."

She stared at him, her brown eyes huge and glittery as they filled with tears. "Oh, Ben," she whispered.

"Aw, don't do that. It was a long time ago, and it's not worth crying over." He wiped a tear from her cheek, and felt it, hot and damp, on his fingertips. "My point is that while what I did was unforgivable in your experience, it was pretty normal in mine. It's not the choice I would make today, but I'm not a kid anymore. I've learned what's important."

She furtively wiped her eyes, then drew her hand through her hair. He'd had the incredible pleasure the second time they'd made love of removing the pins that held it and tangling his hands in it. It was as silky as he'd imagined, and had wrapped around his fingers before sliding free. When she'd kissed him, it had brushed his face and tickled, and when she'd curled up in his arms, it had tantalized him with its softness and its exotic fragrance.

"So . . . what's important?"

Alanna was. Making connections. Having ties. Not being alone. Mattering to someone.

And Lynda. He'd never meant for her to become important. She was way out of his league. She needed someone who could fit into her world, someone she could take to those parties and dinners with congressmen and every last hotshot on the East Coast. Someone with a hell of a lot more status than a mere carpenter—smarter, better educated, better everything than he could ever be.

"People are important," he said slowly. "Leaving someone to notice when you're gone. And being able to live with the choices you've made. Knowing you've done your best."

"Then why haven't you contacted your daughter?" she asked in little more than a whisper. "Why haven't you tried to make up to her for not being there the first twelve years of her life?"

He studied her a long time, debating how much he could afford to trust her. His chest felt tight, and there was a sick feeling in his gut, reminding him that the last time he'd confided in her, all he'd accomplished was lowering her opinion of him. Could he afford another disappointment?

Could he afford to not take the risk?

He reached for her hand, lacing his fingers through hers. "Did I mention that you're the only person I've ever told about my daughter?"

She shook her head.

"You are. You're the only one I've ever trusted enough. . . . " He swallowed hard, cleared his throat, then went on. "That's why I'm in Bethlehem—to see her. To meet her. To tell her I'm sorry."

"You mean . . . ?"

He nodded. "She lives here."

LYNDA COULDN'T REMEMBER EVER IN HER LIFE staying in bed past nine o'clock, but it was after twelve before hunger dragged her out Sunday afternoon. She felt thoroughly lazy and decadent as she dried off from her shower and dressed in a short, sleeveless summer dress, then pulled her hair back in a ponytail, before heading down the back stairs barefooted.

Ben stood at the stove, wearing nothing but jeans, stirring the contents of a cast-iron pan and looking about a thousand miles away. She wondered if he was thinking about his daughter, who lived there in town, or her mother, his former lover, who presumably also lived here in town. He hadn't offered any names, and she hadn't pressed for them. It was his secret, and only he could decide when and what to tell her. That he'd told her so much already touched her deeply.

After he'd fallen asleep last night, though, she'd tried to make a mental list of every girl about the right age. It hadn't taken long to realize that she was only vaguely familiar with the pre-teen-age set in town. And, truthfully, she'd been as interested in the mother as the daughter. He'd wanted her once, lived with her, created a child with her. Had he seen her yet? What if he discovered he still had feelings for her? What if the sense of responsibility and commitment he'd gained with age extended to making a real family for their daughter—with her mother?

She hesitated on the last step, suddenly unsure how to act. What she really wanted to do was sneak up behind him and see if she could interest him in yet another round of lovemaking. Or just wrap her arms around him and count on him to do the same, simply holding her for a minute. In her experience, though, men weren't fond of just holding. They wanted either sex or separation.

In the end, she didn't do anything she wouldn't have done a week ago. She walked into the room as if it were any other morning, smiled politely, and said, "Whatever you're making, it smells good."

She was walking past him to reach the coffeemaker when he snaked his arm around her waist, snuggled her close, and kissed her. It was a sweet, warm, lazy kiss, not the kind that led straight to hot, passionate sex, but it could get there . . . eventually.

"Good morning," he said when he lifted his head.

"Oh, yeah," she murmured, clinging to him.

His chuckle was knowing and amused. "Breakfast will be ready in a couple minutes. Emmaline Bodine's best butter-dredged biscuits and sausage gravy."

She turned to look at the gravy, bubbling in the iron skillet. "You haven't had time to go to the store."

"No."

"Then how could you make biscuits and sausage gravy when I didn't have biscuits, sausage, or gravy?"

"You had flour, baking powder, and cream, and I brought the sausage the day I sprained my wrist because Gloria wanted to learn to make gravy. She put it in the freezer to wait until I came back." He grinned at her. "Just for the record, we would have had the cooking lesson on our own time, not yours. And who knows? We might even have shared with you."

She leaned her forehead against his shoulder. "I'm sorry, I'm sorry, I'm sorry. I know you've put in more hours than you've billed me for, and I'm sorry I ever opened my mouth. I normally never say stupid things like that."

"But you normally don't let emotion get in your way."

That was true. But from the first time she'd seen Ben, it was as if somewhere a switch had been flipped, pushing her pragmatic side to the back and bringing the long-neglected emotional side to the forefront.

And for the most part she'd enjoyed it. Tremendously.

"Will you come back to work? I promise I won't be stupid again."

His smile was sweet. "Sorry, darlin'. I've already accepted a job with Sebastian. Sophy and I start tomorrow."

She nodded once. She had no one to blame but herself, but she would deal with it. She would eventually find someone else to work for her. And who knew? She might still see Ben from time to time. Every night would sound fine to start.

He ushered her to a seat at the dining table, already set for two, then joined her a moment later with a bowl of gravy and a tin of biscuits. The biscuits were golden and crusty on top and bottom and tender inside, and the gravy was too good to even think about the calories until she'd taken the last bite.

Leaning back in her chair, she sighed. "You're handy around the house—"

"And handier in bed."

"You're handsome as sin, and you cook, too. Why aren't you married? Don't those Southern belles know a good thing when they see it?"

"I've had my chances. I've just been waiting for the right one."

And what constituted *right* for him? Was there any chance it might include a born-and-bred Yankee career woman who couldn't think of any better way to pass her nights—or her days—than with him?

"Actually, I never planned on getting married. It doesn't seem to mix too well with folks in my family."

"You marry the wrong person, and of course it's not going to last—or if it does, it's going to be miserable. But if you choose the right person . . . " She gave a sigh that sounded equal parts satisfaction and wistfulness.

"But how many people have thought they were marrying the right person, only to find out down the line that they were all wrong?"

"How many have married the right person, only to realize when the first problem came along that it was easier to give up, divorce, and try again with someone else than to compromise and sacrifice to make the marriage work?"

"Spoken like the product of a long, happy marriage."

"And you sound like the cynic who's survived his parents' unhappy marriage."

He carried their dishes to the sink and began filling it with hot soapy water. "I'm not a cynic, darlin'," he said when she joined him. "If I were, I would have accepted that my kid more than likely wants nothing to do with me, I would have stayed in Georgia, and I never would have presumed that I could show you anything. In fact, all things considered, I'd say I'm a damned-fool optimist."

Something about his tone, or maybe it was the look in his eyes that bordered on bleakness, made Lynda ache to wrap her arms around him. Instead, she set aside her coffee, picked up a dish towel, and helped him with the dishes. When the phone rang as they were finishing up, she answered, expecting Melina. It was Janice. "Hi, Mom."

Ben grimaced as he wrung out a cloth to wipe the stove and countertop.

"I called earlier and got your machine. Screening your mother's calls?"

"I must have missed it, Mom. I slept late."

"Are you sick?"

"Oh, no, I feel fine. How are you and Daddy?"

"We're fine, too. Listen, dear, I was wondering if you could come down here next weekend. I met the most interesting woman yesterday while playing tennis at the club. Turns out, her husband plays golf with your father, and they have a son who is to die for. He's a pediatric cardiovascular surgeon, he has black hair, blue eyes, and the cutest dimple, and his name is Travis Colton. Could you have come up with a better name if you'd named him yourself?"

Making a face, Lynda turned to Ben and gestured for him to say something. He dropped the washcloth in the sink, dried his hands, then wrapped his arms around her from behind and leaned close to the receiver. "Hey, Mrs. Barone," he said as he pulled Lynda suggestively against him.

There was a moment's silence at the other end, then Janice's less friendly voice. "Is that—that carpenter person there?"

"Of course he is, Mom."

"What do you mean, of course? He's not *living* with you, is he?"

"Technically, no. He's got his own place."

Janice took a moment to process that, then called, "Phil! Your daughter is practically *living* with that carpenter!"

Her father's voice came back, distant and distracted. "That's nice, Jan. Maybe he'll cut her a good deal on the rest of the repairs on that old place."

"Did you hear that?" Janice demanded. "Your father's not happy about this, not happy at all."

"He didn't sound unhappy to me."

"That's because you don't know him the way I do. Trust me, he's not thrilled to hear that his little girl is living with a carpenter."

"Mom, this may come as a surprise to you, but—"

Sometime in the last minute Ben had eased down the zipper on her dress. Now he tilted the phone up to push her dress off one shoulder, then let it fall from the other shoulder. Pressing his erection against her bottom, he slid his hands underneath the fabric and covered her breasts, kneading, caressing, while his mouth on her ear sent shivers ricocheting through her.

"But what, dear?" Janice asked impatiently. "What's your surprise?"

"I—I—" Lynda gasped when he gently pinched her nipples, and she arched her back, forcing her breasts hard against his palms. "I don't—"

His mouth directly above her ear, Ben whispered, "Tell her you have to go so I can make love to you. Tell her if I have to wait another second to get inside you, I'm going to explode."

"Can I—" Her voice was high, unsteady, strangled. "Mom, can I c-call you back?"

"But what about next weekend and Travis? Lynda? Lynda!"

She disconnected and let the phone fall to the counter. Behind her, Ben lifted the hem of her dress, swept her panties down far enough that when he let go, they fell to the floor, then opened his jeans and thrust inside her with one long, easy stroke.

The marble countertop was cold in front of her, and Ben was hot behind her. With one hand he played with her breasts, while the other slid between her legs to torment her there. He took her hard and made her come fast, and the instant the shudders that made her entire body clench eased, he came, too, filling her with a groan of pure pleasure.

When he withdrew from her body, he turned her around and gave her a fierce, claiming kiss that sent all new tingles through her. Finally he lifted his head to take a breath, and she smiled lazily at him. "You are a wicked man."

He didn't grin or joke, but stared at her intently. "Tell your mother I don't share."

She became just as serious. "I don't, either."

"Good."

"Good."

Feeling incredibly wanton—with both neck and hem of her dress bunched around her waist, her underwear gone, and swollen, damp, and still quivering—she was reaching for him again when he caught her hands.

"I'd love to, sugar, but Melina just pulled in out back. She's gonna be in here in about sixty seconds."

Lynda glanced out the window as Melina got out of the Bug. While Ben took care of himself, she tugged her dress up, shimmied the skirt down, then jammed the long zipper running up her back. "Aw, hell," she muttered as the key rattled in the back door. She made a dash for the stairs, then belatedly remembered the underwear gone missing. Since the door was swinging open, it was too late to do anything besides hope that Melina was less than her usual observant self that afternoon.

Ben listened to Lynda's bare feet on the wooden stairs, not even noticeable if a person didn't know what he was hearing, while he wished for a shirt and at least a little time to prepare for Melina. His body was taking its sweet time recovering from the already familiar steamy heat of Lynda's body, and a woman as experienced as Melina probably wouldn't miss any of the signs. Not that he cared for himself, but it wasn't his place to tell anyone, even her best friend, that he'd made love with her.

Melina stopped short when she saw him, and a sexy, teasing smile touched her full mouth. "Well, well, handsome. Don't you look right at home? Your hair hasn't been combed. You haven't shaved. No shirt." Her gaze traveled down. "No shoes and . . . hmm. Do my eyes deceive me, or is that a pair of Lyn's favorite satin panties there on the floor beside you? Indulging in a little kitchen delight, hmm?"

Ben felt the heat of embarrassment flood his face as he glanced down. The bit of deep crimson fabric had landed right in the middle of a black tile on the checkerboard floor, impossible for even a blind person to miss. "I, uh . . . don't . . . "

Melina's whoop pierced his ears. "Lyn, make yourself decent, 'cause if you don't come down in the next minute, I'm coming up after you."

To Ben, it seemed forever under Melina's smug looks before Lynda returned downstairs, but he imagined it hadn't been more than a minute or so. Her dress wasn't wrinkled at all, she'd put on shoes, and she looked cool and controlled, as if he hadn't just brought her to a toe-curling orgasm right there beside the sink. The transformation unnerved him.

Then she smiled at him as she came to lean against the counter beside him, and the tightness in his gut eased. "It's about time you wandered back, Lina. Is Sebastian still alive?"

"Alive and well, and looking about as satisfied as young Ben here. You naughty, naughty girl. I was going to apologize for leaving you without a ride last night, but apparently you got one—or several, by the looks of things."

"Hah. You didn't give me a single thought last night. You forgot I existed."

"I plead guilty. But that's about how much thought you gave me when you were tangled in the sheets with Ben, isn't it?" Melina gave him a long, lingering look, then slyly added, "In fact, I'd be surprised if you were even capable of thought, with Big Ben here to play with."

This time the flush didn't stop with Ben's face. It spread down his throat and crept across his chest.

"You are hopelessly crude," Lynda announced arrogantly. "Go make yourself comfortable in the living room. We'll be in in a minute."

"Unfinished business, huh?" Melina called over her shoulder as she strolled from the kitchen. "Do try to be quiet about it, will you?"

After a moment's silence, Lynda glanced at him. "I'd say our best bets for privacy are outside or in my room."

He gestured toward the door, and she led the way onto the porch. She turned right, going to the corner, then leaned against the railing he and Sophy had repaired earlier. He leaned there, too, a few feet away, looking out over the valley while she faced the house.

"I, uh . . . I'm not very good with people." She smiled faintly. "Big surprise, huh? You probably figured that out by the second time we met."

It was the first time, actually, when he'd watched her freeze at being left alone with the munchkin, but he didn't say so.

"My point is . . . I guess what I'm trying to say . . . Is this a one-night thing? I mean, when you leave, are you coming back, or is this it?"

She was probably the smartest, most competent and capable woman Ben had ever met, and yet she couldn't tell that he wanted every possible moment he could have with her. She couldn't see that he was crazy about her, and a whole lot more.

"I don't do one-night stands, darlin', unless that's all you're willing to give me. I don't do secrets too well, either, but you're the one with a reputation to protect, so if you're willing, that's up to you."

"What do you mean, secrets?"

"I mean, keep what's between us *between us*—and Melina, since she already figured it out. If you don't want anyone else to know . . . " He couldn't say it was all right with him, because it wasn't. "That's your decision."

She stared at him, eyes slowly widening as understanding sank in, then slapped his upper arm just hard enough to let him know he'd been smacked. "You mean if I'm *ashamed* to be seen with you? If I only want to acknowledge you in private, when no one else is around?" She slapped his arm again. "You—you—!"

He moved to stand intimately close in front of her and lifted her to sit on the rail. Her arms automatically wrapped around his neck, her legs around his hips, and his body automatically responded. "You think you're tough, huh? But you're not. I can make you curl up and purr like a pretty, pouty, sleek little satisfied kitten."

"Big deal. I can make you tremble like a leaf in the wind."

"You certainly can, darlin'," he murmured, nuzzling her throat.

"And I can make you impossibly hard with only four words."

"That's not saying much, since you can make me hard without any words at all. Just one look, sugar . . . " He lifted her, turned so the rail was behind him, then settled her where her slightest move rubbed his growing erection. He intended to make it grow more, to find some quick pleasure for both of them, and had just slid his tongue inside her mouth when Melina spoke from the back door.

"Some people have no sense of decorum. Don't you agree?"

Lynda tensed and would have retreated in a struggle for dignity if Ben hadn't been holding her so tightly. Deliberately he finished the kiss, then let her slide slowly to the floor. "And some people have no sense about minding their own business."

"First the bedroom, then the kitchen, now on the porch. Where will it be next time?"

"Anyplace you aren't, darlin'. Hey, Sebastian." Ben glanced at Lynda, blushing furiously. He claimed her hand tightly in his and drew her toward the other couple. "You two haven't met, have you? Lynda Barone, Sebastian Knight."

"Nice to meet you," Sebastian said, barely restraining his amusement.

Lynda managed little more than a strangled sound.

"Did I forget to mention that Sebastian was coming over?" Melina asked innocently. "I must have, or you would have at least taken this show around the corner. You'll have to excuse them, Sebastian. They're like kids who've discovered new toys to play with. Let's go inside and get comfortable—while remaining decent if we can."

She and Sebastian went inside, but Lynda turned with a groan to press her face against the wall. Ben slid his hand around her neck, massaging the muscles there. "Hey, she's just having some fun with you. Trust me, they hit the sheets long before we did—if they even made it to a bed the first time."

She tilted her head to one side and smiled ruefully. "She's teased me since the day we met. She says I'm stuffy."

"I don't think she'll say it anymore. Come on, before she comes back to see what's taking us so long." Hands on her shoulders, he pulled her away from the wall and steered her to the door. There he hesitated before opening it. "What four words?"

She looked utterly innocent.

"You said you can make me impossibly hard with only four words. What words?"

Though they were alone, she leaned close and whispered, "I'm not wearing panties," then turned to follow the others.

And damned if she didn't leave him standing there, greedily, desperately, impossibly hard.

Chapter Fourteen

It was hot Wednesday afternoon at soccer practice, so the coaches divided the team in two groups, one resting and drinking Gatorade while the other worked out. When it was Alanna's turn to rest, she sank down underneath a shade tree with a towel and a bottle. She was soaked with sweat, and her hair was falling out of its ponytail, but it was so wet that it didn't get in her way.

Susan dropped down beside her, her face red. "Tell me again why we decided to go out for soccer instead of swimming."

"Because Bethlehem doesn't have a swimming pool."

"Oh, yeah. I heard we're gettin' one, though. Mr. McKinney's company's gonna build one over in City Park. My mom heard it at work."

Susan's mom was a nurse. Alanna wasn't sure why the hospital heard all the news in town first, but they usually did. "When will it be open?"

"I dunno. Soon, I hope. At least when it gets really hot next month, we'll be at Camp Woe-Is-Me. They've got a lake *and* a pool, and there's a boys' camp across the lake, and I'm gonna steal a canoe and sneak over there some night."

If anyone would do it, it was Susan. But since Caleb wasn't going to be at the camp across the lake, Alanna didn't care.

"How's your ribs?"

"Okay."

"You guys about ready to move?"

"Yeah. We start Sunday after church." It was supposed to be a secret that they were moving. Aunt Emilie and Uncle Nathan had been talking about it for a long time, 'cause the house was awfully crowded, and they wanted to have another baby, and nobody believed Berry was ever going to get well enough to take care of her own kids. Even if she did, Alanna wasn't going with her. Emilie was the only real mother she had, or wanted.

Anyway, they'd talked about moving to a bigger house, then one day Grandpa Bud bought the big house across the street—the one they'd borrowed when they first came to Bethlehem—and he wanted to sorta trade with them, so he and Miss Agatha would live in their house after they married and they would live in his house.

"Maybe I'll come and help," Susan said. "Does Miss Agatha know yet?"

"No. It's a surprise. She won't know until they come back from their honeymoon."

Susan scrunched up her face. "Don't you think they're awfully old to have a honeymoon and go to Niagara Falls? I mean, they're, like, geezers."

"They are not! If they don't think they're too old for a honeymoon, then they're not."

"Jeez, don't get crabby. Are you excited about being in the wedding Saturday?"

Leaning back against the tree trunk, Alanna smiled. She was going to be a bridesmaid. She had a long, pretty dress, and there was a brand-new pair of heels in her closet—well, little ones—and she was going to wear pantyhose and makeup and everything. Aunt Emilie said she was going to be beautiful and Caleb, who was one of Grandpa Bud's groomsmen, was going to be dazzled. She knew Caleb liked her without heels, pantyhose, and makeup, but she thought it would be fun to see him dazzled, just once.

"Yeah," she replied. "It's going to be fun."

"You don't sound like it. What's wrong?"

Alanna dug a place in the dirt with her heel before finally answering. "We got a letter from our mom. She said she can't come see us this month because she's got to find a new place to live, but she'll *definitely* come next month." Usually, *finding a new place to live* for Berry meant being evicted, arrested, or threatened, and it might be across the street or to another state. She might write to them next month, if she remembered, but she wasn't gonna come see them.

"I'm sorry." That was what Susan always said when they talked about Berry. She couldn't imagine what it was like having a mom like that. She'd always lived with both her mom and dad, and she had two sets of grandparents in Bethlehem, and uncles and aunts and lots of cousins. At their last family party, they'd had nearly a hundred relatives.

Alanna didn't have any grandparents—at least, none who wanted to be. Emilie was her only aunt, Michael her only cousin. Unless her father had brothers or sisters or parents, her entire family came to less than ten people. Even if her father did have a family, it didn't matter, 'cause they weren't *her* family.

"I don't care what Berry does," she said. "I never believed she would come, but Josie did and she cried. She thinks Berry *wants* to be a good mom but can't, so she can't even get mad at her 'cause it's not her fault. So instead she gets real sad, and it makes *me* real mad."

"I'm sorry," Susan repeated. After a moment, she pointed toward the street. "There's Ben. Boy, he must really like soccer to come watch practice."

Alanna turned to look at the blue car parked across the street. It was him, all right, and he *was* watching. Other people came and watched, too, but they were mostly relatives, and they sat on the bleachers instead of in their cars. Ben wasn't related to anyone on the team that she knew of.

She tried to pretend he wasn't there, or like he was just a friend of Grandpa Bud's, but she kept remembering the worried look in Aunt Emilie's eyes last week. She'd told Josie she wanted to welcome him to town, but Alanna knew that wasn't true. Aunt Emilie hadn't liked him hanging around. But Aunt Emilie wasn't there.

When she looked up for the third time and he was still watching her, she told Susan to wait there, and she headed for the bleachers. Shelley Walker, Susan's aunt, was sitting on the first row, with her little girl, Becky, on her lap. She came to practices when Susan's mom couldn't get off, and her husband was the chief of police.

Alanna straddled the bench beside them. "Miss Shelley, can I talk to you?"

"Sure, Alanna. What's up?"

"See that car across the street? Aunt Emilie told me the next time I saw that man to let her know, but she's not here—Josie's got karate tonight—and Uncle Nathan's working late."

Shelley looked at Ben, then back at her. "You've seen him before?"

"Lots of times. He's always around, but Aunt Emilie's never met him, and she wanted to know."

"Okay, hon. You go on back and don't worry about it, okay? I'll call your uncle and see what he says."

"Okay." Alanna felt better as she returned to the shade tree, but she felt kind of bad, too. Ben had always been nice, and she figured Uncle Nathan would probably arrest him or something. But she couldn't have just ignored him, because Aunt Emilie had *said* . . . With a big sigh, she dropped to the ground where facing Susan meant having her back to Ben.

If he wasn't doing anything wrong, then telling wouldn't matter, she told herself.

And if he was . . . well, then she'd done the right thing.

BEN WAS TAPPING HIS FINGERS ON THE STEERing wheel, wishing Sophy would hurry, when a once familiar sight appeared in his rearview mirror—the flashing lights atop a police car. Back home the lights were blue instead of the red, blue, and amber used in Bethlehem, but everything else was the same, including the dread tightening his gut.

One officer approached on the left side of the car, one on the right. They were both bigger than him, armed, and serious. The one on his side bent to speak through the open window. "Can I see your license and registration, please?"

Ben handed them over without comment. The officer glanced at them, then handed them to the other cop, who returned to the car with them.

"Can I ask what you're doing here?"

"I'm waiting for a friend." Sophy had asked him to drop her off at home, wait while she changed clothes, then give her a lift to the inn. Since he was headed that way anyway to meet Lynda, Melina, and Sebastian for dinner, he'd agreed.

"What is this friend's name?"

"Sophy Jones."

"And she supposedly lives around here?"

"I assume so, since she told me to let her out right here."

"So you dropped her off." When Ben nodded, the officer's gaze narrowed. "But you don't know which of these houses is hers."

Ben shook his head. He hadn't looked to see which house she'd gone into because the soccer team across the street had caught his attention.

The cop looked at his partner, then stepped back. "We'd like to ask you to come down to the police station with us, Mr. Foster."

"For what? Sitting in my car on a public street?"

"We're not placing you under arrest. Our sergeant would simply like to speak to you."

Ben wanted to refuse. Going to the station would make him even later for dinner than he already was, and surely Sophy would return any minute now. But there was no sign of her, and he'd learned a few painful lessons when he was a kid about what happened when you didn't do what a cop wanted. "Can I follow you in my car?"

"We'd prefer you come with us. Your car will be fine here."

After rolling up the windows and locking the doors, Ben got out. He could feel the curious gazes from across the street—from Alanna and her friends—and the heat of embarrassment crept up his neck.

"Do you have any weapons on you?" the second cop asked.

"No."

"For your safety and ours, do you mind if I search you?"

Again, he wanted to refuse—desperately—but he knew how they thought. If he had nothing to hide, why would he object? It was a line of reasoning that could be embraced only by someone who'd never found himself bent over the hood of a police car, subjected to the indignity of being patted down. If he were guilty of some crime, that was one thing, but all he'd done was sit in his car on a damned public street!

And watch Alanna.

"Sure," he said flatly. "Go ahead."

The pat-down was quick, thorough, and then he was put in the backseat of the patrol unit. Lights still flashing but no siren—thank God for small favors—the driver made a U-turn and headed downtown.

As the car drove past, Sophy stepped out from behind the massive oak trunk that had hidden her from Ben's view. Once he and the officers were out of sight, everyone at the park slowly returned to their activities . . . except Alanna. For a long time, she stood motionless, staring down the street. Then Susan tapped her on the shoulder, grabbed her arm, and dragged her onto the field. She laughed, but her heart didn't seem to be in it—kicked the ball, but without much care.

Leaning back against the tree, Sophy gave a heartfelt sigh.

Sitting at a table for four on the terrace outside the McBride Inn dining room, Lynda glanced at her watch for the tenth time in twenty minutes. Dinner tonight had been Melina's suggestion—a way for the two of them to spend some time together. Even though she had extended her visit from Buffalo indefinitely, she'd been with Sebastian every minute he wasn't working, which was all right, because every minute Lynda and Ben weren't working, they were together, too. It had been incredible. The best time of Lynda's life.

At least until he and Sebastian had stood them up.

Five minutes ago she'd called his apartment. There was no answer. Next Melina called Sebastian's workshop. No answer there, either. They'd made small talk for a few minutes before falling silent.

The terrace was the loveliest place in all of Bethlehem in summer. Old faded brick laid in a herringbone pattern created the patio and supported pale green wicker tables and chairs. Snowy linen cloths covered the tables, with white-and-green cushions on the chairs. Chinese maples provided dappled shade, and flowers growing in beds scattered among the tables offered sweet fragrance. With tall candles in clear hurricane globes providing illumination, it was welcoming and romantic—the perfect place for a date.

Not so perfect for two women whose dates, apparently, had forgotten them.

"Well?" Lynda asked dryly. "How long do we wait before we accept that we've been stood up?"

"They'll come. Something must have happened." Melina sounded confident and lighthearted, but worry made her eyes darker than usual. "Did I mention that I'm going to marry Sebastian?"

Lynda's eyes widened. "He asked you to *marry* him? After only four days?"

"Not yet. But he will. And when he does, I'm going to say yes."

"Oh, man, he must be something." Lynda hadn't seen enough of the man to know. He wasn't particularly handsome, in her opinion, or particularly charming. He was quiet, not outgoing, not flashy—in general, not Melina's type. But surely there was more to him than she was seeing. Melina had obviously fallen hard for the guy, and Ben seemed to like and respect him. That was enough for Lynda.

"You gonna marry Ben?"

"Call me silly, but I think I'll wait until I'm asked before I make a decision." Truth was, if Ben asked, she would jump at the chance. It would be a dream come true. But she honestly didn't think he had any intention of asking. Gut instinct said he might want her, care for her, even come to love her, but he wouldn't marry her. And if thirteen years in business had taught her anything, it was to trust her instincts.

Melina reached for her cell phone. "Call Ben's apartment again. I'll try Sebastian."

No answers.

"You don't think something happened?"

Lynda smiled faintly. "To both of them? Ben was already home when he called me after work. He was taking Sophy home, and then he said he would be here."

"Can you trust this Sophy?"

There was no denying that Sophy was pretty, but there was also no denying that she trusted Ben. He said he wasn't interested in Sophy, and she believed him. "I trust her. What about Sebastian? What were his plans?"

"He was supposed to take Chrissy to her grandmother's house, then meet us here."

"Can you trust this Chrissy?" Lynda asked with a smile.

Melina answered in all seriousness. "I don't know. She's a pretty little girl, sweet, smart. I don't think she dislikes me, but I don't think she likes me, either."

"You know, making a successful marriage with a man who's already a father can be difficult, to say the least." It was advice Lynda had gotten from her mother, that she'd never paid much attention to . . . until now. Would Ben's daughter make a difference in their lives? Would seeing her mother again after all these years affect them?

Six-thirty came and went. The waitress who'd been serving them wine and keeping Lynda's water glass filled was way past sympathetic looks and knee-deep in pity for them when she slid into what should have been Ben's chair. "Maybe there was some sort of mix-up."

Lynda smiled tautly as Melina drained her wine. "I'm sure there was."

"Would you like to go ahead and order? We have some wonderful specials this evening, and the desserts here are to die for."

Somewhere in the last half hour, Lynda's appetite had disappeared. She looked at Melina, who nodded, and at the same time they said, "Ice cream." Lynda added, "The richer, the better."

The waitress left, then returned in minutes with two ice cream, chocolate, and fresh fruit concoctions. *To die for* was right. If the dish had one calorie less than a thousand, Lynda would be surprised.

They both dove right in.

By seven o'clock, they'd paid their check and were halfway home when Melina suddenly spoke. "Take me by Sebastian's house."

Lynda wanted to protest that he lived five miles out in the country, that finding out he was home but not answering his phone wouldn't help anything, but instead she turned at the next corner and followed Main Street out of town.

The Knight farm had been in the family for generations, though none of them worked the land now. Sebastian had turned the barn into a workshop for his carpentry business, which apparently was more successful than ever, since he'd taken on two new employees in Ben and Sophy.

When Lynda pulled into the driveway, Sebastian and Chrissy were playing catch in the front yard, with a big red setter running happily back and forth between them. Sebastian dropped the ball the instant he saw Melina, and a terrible look of guilt came across his face.

"Chrissy, go in the house," he said, his voice carrying in the still evening, and she obediently trotted off.

"Bastard," Melina murmured as she got out of the car. "You never intended to come to dinner tonight, did you?"

The guilt intensified. "No."

"Why didn't you say so?"

For a long time he simply stared at her, then he lowered his gaze to his left hand, stroking the gold band on his ring finger. His wedding ring. It hadn't been there the other times Lynda had seen him, and she was fairly certain it hadn't been there with Melina, either. "Not showing up seemed the easiest way to get the message across," he replied, uneasily, ashamed, and Lynda whispered her own vehement, "Bastard."

Melina stalked across the yard toward the house. When he caught her arm, she jerked free. "You touch me again, and I'll shoot you, you son of a bitch."

Lynda wondered if he knew Melina carried a .380 in the beaded purse worn bandolier-style across her chest, or if she'd told him she was a better shot than most men ever dreamed of being. Maybe, because he did back off.

Melina stormed inside the house, slamming the screen door behind her, then reappeared almost immediately with her overnight bag. She walked past Sebastian without so much as a glance, got in the

Mercedes, and said tight-lipped, "Get me the hell out of here."

"Melina . . . " The rest of Sebastian's words were lost in a spray of gravel as Lynda accelerated out of the drive and onto the road back home.

NEARLY AN HOUR HAD PASSED SINCE BEN HAD been escorted into a conference room at the police station, then left there alone with an officer stationed at the door. Once, one of the cops who'd brought him had offered him coffee and an apology for the delay, but when Ben had asked to use the phone, he'd been told, "Sorry, not yet."

Finally, the door opened and two men walked in. One sat down across from him, and the other tossed a manila folder on the tabletop with enough force that the computer printouts inside spilled half out. Arrest records, Ben recognized.

The seated man introduced himself as Mitch Walker, chief of police. Under other circumstances, Ben would have asked if he was any relation to Susan. Under *these* circumstances, he wisely kept his mouth shut.

The second man, the one who'd tossed down the file, was Nathan Bishop.

"I'm sorry it's taken us so long to get back to you," Walker said. "Things got a little hectic. Is there anything you need?"

"You know, for a man who's not under arrest, I certainly feel like I am," Ben remarked. After a moment, he replied to the question. "A phone, and a telephone book. I was on my way to meet someone. If she hasn't given up by now, I'd like to let her know I can't make it."

Walker left, then returned with a telephone and a directory. Ben called McBride Inn and asked for Lynda. The clerk put him on hold, giving him a moment to notice the assessing looks Walker and Bishop were giving him, then came back. "Ms. Barone's not here, sir. The waitress said she and her friend left about twenty minutes ago."

"Thanks." He hung up and pushed the phone to the center of the table.

"You want to call Ms. Barone at home?" Walker asked.

"No." He preferred to do his groveling without an audience. "Do I need a lawyer?"

"You're not a suspect in anything. We'd just like to ask a few questions."

"Yes, but if I talk to you now, and later you decide to hang something on me, you'll have gotten a free interrogation to twist any way you choose."

"Sounds like you've had some experience with the way the system works."

He looked pointedly at the folder. "You know I have."

Until then, Nathan Bishop had remained in the background, leaning against the wall behind the chief. Now he came forward, resting his palms on the table, bending menacingly close. "What's your interest in Alanna Dalton?"

This wasn't the way Ben had wanted the truth to come out. He'd thought he might meet privately with Emilie Bishop, or write her a letter to help pave the way. He'd briefly considered asking Miss Agatha to talk to her for him, or Lynda. He'd even thought he might let things drag along until somehow, miraculously, the information came out on its own. But thanks to his own carelessness, the choice had been taken from him, unless he wanted to be branded some sort of pervert. He tried once, though, to avoid the truth just a little longer. "It's personal."

The answer infuriated Bishop. His eyes grew darker and colder, his tone more ominous. "Like hell it is. Alanna is my niece. She's like a daughter to me. No one has an interest in her that my wife and I don't know about."

The silence in the room was heavy, threatening. Ben wished he could run back time a bit and tell Sophy she'd have to find another ride, or maybe even go back to his first day in town, but all he could do was sit there with two armed men, one very angry, and tell the truth.

"She may be like a daughter to you, Sergeant Bishop," he said quietly. "But she *is* a daughter to me. I'm Alanna's father."

Both men stared at him. Bishop started to speak, but couldn't. Walker cleared his throat. "Do you have any proof?"

"Other than a baby picture in my car, no." That, and the gut feeling he'd had since the first time he'd seen her. "But you can ask her mother. Berry's word ought to count for something."

"Are you listed on her birth certificate?" the chief asked.

"I don't know. Berry and I broke up—" Ben took a deep breath, then started over. "I broke up with her as soon as I found out she was pregnant. I haven't seen her since, but she sent a birth announcement to my grandmother, with a picture of Alanna."

Bishop reached for the phone, dialed a number, and, without a greeting, curtly asked, "Who's listed as the father on Alanna's birth certificate?"

There was a long silence, presumably while his wife went to check. Wouldn't it be a hoot if she came back with a different name? If he saw the pictures as nearly identical because he wanted them to be? If Berry had lied to him all those years ago?

Then Bishop's mouth tightened. "Why don't you drop the kids off with the Winchesters and come down to the station?" he suggested. She must have asked why, because he coldly added, "Ben Foster is sitting across from me right now."

After he hung up, the three of them sat in silence. Ben wondered whether Lynda was more angry or hurt, whether she would be embarrassed to hear he'd been rousted by the cops. Obsessing over her was easier than wondering what Alanna was going to think when she found out that the man she'd watched taken off by the cops—the man all her friends had seen hauled off—was her father. If Lynda was embarrassed, Alanna would be mortified. As if being a kid wasn't tough enough, she'd have to deal with public humiliation, too.

He'd screwed up big-time. But what was new?

There was a knock at the door, then Emilie Dalton Bishop let herself in. She greeted her husband and Mitch before turning her attention to him. Though they were both blue-eyed blondes, she was about as different from Berry as two women could be. She was younger by a couple years, but had always been more mature. Where Berry was weak and fragile, Emilie damn near glowed with good health. While Berry had turned her back on her own children, Emilie had loved them like her own. The bad mother and the good mother.

And he and Nathan could be the bad father and the good father.

Emilie studied him for a moment, then offered her hand. "Berry used to have a few pictures of the two of you. You were both so young then."

He shook her hand, then, under Bishop's watchful eye, drew back.

"So . . . Alanna got that stubborn jaw from you."

"Or you."

"And those high cheekbones . . . Berry and I would have loved to have bones like that." After another silence, she bluntly said, "You can't take her away from us."

Of course that would be one of her concerns. She had sacrificed everything for those kids, and to risk losing one now to the father who hadn't given a damn . . . "That's not why I'm here." Not that he didn't like the idea of someday having a home and a family—Alanna and Lynda and any kids they might have. But that was just a dream. He might be Alanna's father, but the Daltons and the Bishops were her family.

"Then why?"

"I was pretty much raised by my grandmother, Emmaline Bodine. Emmaline always wanted to meet her only great-grandchild. When her health started failing, I hired a private detective, but she died before he found Alanna. Her last wish was for Alanna to have her locket. It dates back to the Civil War, and it's the only thing the Bodine family ever had worth keeping."

"So you came here to deliver the locket and . . . ?"

He glanced at the two men, then fixed his gaze on Emilie again. "You understand the importance of family better than Berry or I ever did. It took the death of the only person who ever gave a damn about me to make me realize what I'd done all those years ago, to make me understand that . . . being alone is not an easy thing. I came here intending to give the locket to you, then go back to Georgia, but the first night I was in town, I met Alanna and . . . she was real. In all those years, she'd never been real to me. She was this faceless, shapeless problem that all I had to do to get rid of was break up with Berry. But then I met her and . . . " He broke off and shrugged.

"What is it you want?"

"To apologize to her. To get to know her."

"You understand she may not have any interest in knowing you."

Though her quiet remark caused a stab of pain, he didn't let it show. "I know, and I wouldn't blame her at all. But I'd still like to try if . . . if you think it's all right."

Emilie looked at Nathan. It was clear from his expression what he thought. Given a choice, Bishop would escort him to the state line, with orders to never return under threat of imprisonment. Ben couldn't blame him, either. How hard would it be for a cop who loved a stranger's child as his own to let that stranger waltz back in, especially with a string of arrests and character flaws dogging his every step?

"I'll be honest with you, Ben," Emilie said. "This is a difficult time for Alanna. She's developed a fair amount of anger and hostility toward her mother, and

I'm not sure it's the best time to introduce her to her father. But, if you have no objection, I'll talk to a friend of ours who's a psychiatrist. His specialty is children, and he knows ours quite well." She smiled at the implication and clarified, "Though not as patients. If J.D. sees no problem with it, then we'll decide where to go from there. Fair enough?"

Ben nodded. J.D. must be Dr. J.D., Bud Grayson's son, young Caleb's father.

"If J.D. wants to talk to you first, would you be willing?"

"Sure." He'd never been on a shrink's couch before, but there was a first time for everything. Like wanting to be a father. Volunteering to accept responsibility for himself. Falling in love.

Emilie nodded once, then stood. Ben and Mitch Walker did the same.

"Am I free to go now?" Ben asked.

"Yes," Walker replied. "I can give you a ride back to your car."

"No, thanks. I'd rather walk." He acknowledged them all with a curt nod, then left. One step outside the courthouse doors, and the night felt warmer, the air smelled sweeter, and life was better. He'd spent way too much time in police stations, jail cells, and courtrooms, but no more. He was too old for it. Too tired of it. Too sure he wanted more.

Chapter Fifteen

MELINA WAS RIGHT ABOUT THE STARS, Lynda thought. Bethlehem did have far more than its share. They brightened every inch of the night sky, from horizon to horizon, shining brightly here, barely twinkling there. They offered comforting constancy—there tonight, tomorrow night, and ten thousand nights from tomorrow.

Too bad people weren't as reliable.

She was lying in one of two Adirondack chairs dragged into the center of the backyard, legs stretched out, head tilted back to the sky. Beside her Melina occupied the second chair, snoring softly under the cover of a navy-blue sheet.

The sound of the GTO's engine carried in the still night before it was even halfway up the hill. She automatically glanced at her watch, though it was too dark to see the time. It was about nine, she estimated, maybe later.

What was Ben's excuse for missing dinner? Was it going to be as hurtful as Sebastian's?

His headlights swept across her and Melina as he parked between their cars. The instant the engine shut off, heavy silence fell over the hillside again, broken a moment later by the closing of the car door.

He came across the yard to stand at the foot of her chair, so close that if she stretched her toes out, they would brush his khaki trousers. His white dress shirt glowed with moonlight, but his face was in shadow as he studied her.

She crossed one leg over the other, leaving room for him to sit, then calmly said, "I must say, Ben Foster, my dates with you are certainly . . . different."

After a moment's hesitation, he sat down. He rested one hand outside her legs, where her knee brushed the inside of his wrist. "I'm sorry."

"I figured you were."

With a nod, he indicated Melina. "Is she all right?"

"She's sleeping off the effects of three glasses of wine at the restaurant, four beers when we got back here, and . . . oh, yes, half a bottle of scotch that a grateful associate gave me last spring."

"Hasn't she ever heard that you shouldn't mix your alcohols?"

"She'll have a pretty strong reminder in the morning." She glanced at Melina, curled in a position sure to give her a backache and a stiff neck to go with the hangover. "Did you know Sebastian was going to dump her?"

"You're kidding. I thought he really liked her."

"He liked having sex with her. Once he'd gotten enough, he wrote her off. He didn't show up for dinner this evening because he figured that would be the

easiest way to get the message across—easiest for *him*."
After a moment, she leaned forward, touched his hand. "Why didn't you show up?"

He turned his hand to lace his fingers with her. "Not because I wanted a way to write you off." His tone was hard, fierce, challenging her to not believe him. Then, with a heavy sigh, he went on. "I've spent the evening in the company of several of Bethlehem's finest."

"You were *arrested*?"

"No. Just questioned."

"About *what*?"

He was silent for a long time, as if debating what to tell her, or maybe how. With another of those weighted sighs, he began. "I told you my daughter lives here. I happened to meet her my first night in town, at the band concert, and I—I've gone out of my way to see her from time to time. I was just curious and . . . a little overwhelmed. But eventually someone realized there was a strange man conveniently running into a twelve-year-old girl, and they called the police."

A perfectly understandable response, Lynda thought. "So you were watching her this evening?"

"No. Yes. Not deliberately. Sophy asked me to take her home and wait while she changed. Her house is across the street from the soccer field, and the team was practicing. I had no idea, I swear. I was just waiting for Sophy, and I glanced across the street and . . . " He ended with a shrug.

"You told the police the truth?" Of course he did, or he wouldn't be sitting there. He would be locked up in one of the cells underneath the courthouse and the key would have already been thrown away. "And they . . . what? Called her parents?"

"I think it was her uncle who had me picked up. He's a cop—Nathan Bishop."

Lynda stared at him in the dim light. "*Alanna?* Alanna Dalton is your daughter?"

He nodded once.

Alanna Dalton. It was perfectly logical—she was the right age, she had Ben's coloring, her mother and her aunt were from Atlanta, and it was common knowledge that all three Dalton children's fathers had abandoned them either before or shortly after their births.

Still, it was hard to grasp that she *knew* his daughter. That *he* was one of the parents everyone condemned for the children's abysmal experiences. That he hadn't turned his back on a young woman who'd been forced to grow up quickly, accept responsibility for his child, and love her, raise her, and sacrifice for her. He'd walked away from Berry Dalton, an alcoholic, drug-addicted, self-absorbed, despicable excuse for a person. Because *he* hadn't wanted to be bothered, he'd left his baby in the care of a woman incapable of caring for anyone but herself, and not even that half the time.

"Well . . . " Her voice sounded shaky even to her. "You're just full of surprises, aren't you?"

"That's my last one."

"Good. I'm not sure how many more I could take."

He seemed to sense that she wasn't merely teasing, and his mood grew somber. After the silence drew out, one minute into another, he abruptly said, "Come around front with me."

"But Melina—"

"She'll be all right." He stood up and offered his hand. When she didn't take it right away, he relented. "I'll carry her inside to the sofa, okay?"

"Thank you." Lynda let him help her up, then watched as he picked up her friend's limp body. Melina's head rolled back, and her arm flopped nervelessly before settling around his neck. Leave it to Melina, even unconscious, to know when a handsome man was nearby and to grab hold.

"She looks like she might weigh seventy-five pounds soaking wet," Ben said with a grunt as he got a better grip on her. "But this ain't no seventy-five pounds."

Lynda hurried up the steps and opened, then closed, the door for him. Once he dropped his load on the couch, he looked at her. "You're a good woman, Lynda."

It was a simple compliment, but she couldn't recall ever hearing it before. It made her smile unsteady but warm. "Thank you."

"Now come out front with me." He started to straighten, but Melina grabbed his wrist.

"It's okay, S'bastian," she murmured, rubbing her cheek against his hand. "I still love you, even if you are a bastard."

Ben gently freed his hand, then combed her hair back from her face. "Go to sleep, darlin'. If you're lucky, you'll be so sick in the morning, you'll hate everyone, including Sebastian. At least that'll get you through the first few hours." After tucking the sheet around her, he followed Lynda out the front door and down the steps. He gestured toward the promontory where they'd shared their picnic—and their first kiss—and they strolled in that direction.

Thinking about how gentle he'd been with Melina, she asked, "Have you ever had your heart broken before?"

"Only when Emmaline died." At the bottom of the

steps cut into the hillside, Lynda sat down on the retaining wall on one side. He sat on the other side, facing her. "But I have this funny feeling that you're about to teach me all about it."

Because she didn't believe such a thing was remotely possible, she brushed off the comment and changed the subject—or maybe it was just a different aspect of the same subject. "What was Berry Dalton like when you lived with her?"

He took a moment to consider his answer. "She was funny. Sexy. A hell of a lot more experienced than I was. She was wild, reckless, and always ready to take a chance. And she was needy. She was raised in foster homes and had virtually no contact with Emilie until they were both grown. Where Emilie came out of it strong and independent, Berry had learned that the way to make people happy was to do anything and everything they wanted. She'd been sleeping with foster fathers and foster brothers and any other guy who wanted since she was fourteen. She was the easiest, neediest, most difficult person I've ever known."

"She drank."

"She liked to party. Most girls her age did."

"And she used drugs."

Gazing out over the valley, he nodded. "She had a lot to deal with, and for her the easiest way to do it was to escape. When she was wasted, she didn't have to be poor Berry Dalton, abandoned by her mother in death and her father in indifference, and used, then discarded, by practically every other person in her life."

"And did you use drugs with her?"

He smiled, but there was nothing pleasant or amused about it. "Beer had been good enough for generations of Bodines and Fosters before me, and by God, it was good enough for me, too. Besides, I had enough run-ins with the police without adding illegal substances into the mix." After studying her a moment, he asked, "Why don't you go ahead and say it, Lyn?"

"Say what?"

"What you're trying so hard *not* to say. 'She was a sick, sad, sorry woman. She wasn't capable of caring for herself, much less a helpless baby. How could you leave her to take care of your child alone? My God, what kind of man are you?' " The silence was still, expectant, as if he'd caught his breath and was holding it. The tightness in her chest felt the same way. Then he loudly exhaled. "Does that about cover it?"

Tears filled her eyes. "I guess it does."

He knelt on the grass in front of her. "Berry had some problems I recognized, some I didn't, and some I just didn't care much about. Our relationship, on my part, at least, was your typical nineteen-year-old-getting-laid-regularly thing. I didn't love her. Sometimes I didn't even like her. Mostly I just used her, and mostly she was just using me. If that makes me less of a man today in your eyes, I'm sorry, but it's in the past. I can't change it. But I can tell you that I'm not that kid anymore. I've been telling you that . . . but you just don't seem to agree."

For a moment, Lynda thought the lump in her throat would prevent her from speaking, but she managed. "It's not that I don't agree, Ben. I just need time. . . ."

"Time for what? To accept that I made a mistake thirteen years ago? To acknowledge that I'm trying to make it right? Or to determine whether *you* made a mistake in getting involved with me?"

She didn't have an answer.

And that was answer enough for him. He sat back on his heels and stared at her for a long time, then breathed out heavily. "Maybe the mistake wasn't yours. Maybe it was mine for thinking a woman like you could have an honest relationship with someone like me. Well, don't worry about it, darlin'. I've been dumped enough times to know how it works. But it was fun while it lasted, wasn't it? Now you can find somebody more suitable, and I can find someone less perfect and more human, and we'll both be happier for it."

He stood up, slid his fingers around her neck, then bent to kiss her. Not a simple, chaste good-bye kiss, but a hungry, demanding I-want-you sort of kiss, and she kissed him back in the same way. And then he walked away.

As she sat there, eyes closed, tears silently streaming down her cheeks, she knew he was wrong. Her mistake hadn't been getting involved with him. It was letting him go. And she had no doubt in her heart she would live to regret it.

MELINA AWOKE TO THE SOUND OF A LOW, tortured moan, and slowly reached the realization that it was coming from her. Opening one eye, she winced at the spotlight aimed at her face. Sunlight, coming through the god-awful lead glass Lyn insisted on keeping in her windows. Antique, schmantique, it distorted everything and increased the brilliance of a sunbeam to blinding, aneurysm-inducing intensity.

Why did she feel like something fallen off the back of a garbage truck, and why was she fully dressed and sacked out on the sofa? Had she been stricken by some bug that left her too sick to climb the stairs last night? Had that incredible dessert given her food poisoning? That would explain her headache, queasy stomach, and the stiffness in her joints.

Then she burped—oh, so ladylike—and knew it was no virus or ice-cream attack. She was hungover. But she wasn't a heavy drinker, and she hadn't had a hangover since finding out about Rico the rat, and that—

A whimper escaped her as she remembered. Dinner, a double date, a double stand-up, and Sebastian . . . He was worse than Rico the rat had ever been. He was a rat bastard, and she hated him.

"Are you awake?"

With one eye still tightly closed, she turned to see Lyn sitting a half-dozen feet away. "I don't know. Do you have a pile of fuzzy purple strings in your lap?"

"Yes, I do."

"Then I'm awake." Holding her head with both hands, Melina slowly sat up. When she tried to scoot back on the couch, her legs slid out from under her and she landed on her butt on the floor, the sofa at her back. It was good enough for the moment.

"You look awful."

She worked her other eye open to scowl at Lynda. "You're no prize this morning, either. Still in your jammies, and the sun's high, high, in the sky. Did that rat bastard Ben dump you, too?"

"Oh, no. *She* dumped *him*." That came from Gloria, dusting a corner cabinet filled with Lladró. Melina winced, wishing she would do it more quietly.

"My head's awfully stuffy. It sounded like she said you dumped Ben."

"I did," Gloria replied, "and so did she."

"Why?" Melina winced again at her own shriek. "What did he do?"

"Got a girl pregnant, then turned his back on her." Gloria stabbed the air with her feather duster. "Didn't marry her, didn't stick around until his baby was born and take her away from her mama, and didn't give up everything to go off and ruin his life along with her mama."

"Gloria."

"Sorry, Ms. Lydia."

Melina looked from one to the other. "Ben got someone pregnant? He hasn't even been in town very long."

"Not here. In Atlanta."

"You mean . . . before he came here?" Okay, so hungover wasn't Melina's finest state. She tended to catch on more quickly when she hadn't downed enough booze to fill a bathtub. But it wasn't fair for Lynda to be deliberately obscure. "So . . . before Ben knew you existed, he got someone pregnant, and you're mad about it?"

"As she should be," Gloria put in. "It goes to his character. You can't love a man of poor character, and Mr. Forester is a man of poor character. He was selfish and uncaring, and the fact that he was a mere nineteen years old at the time doesn't change things one whit. No, sir, Ms. Lynette, it doesn't."

From somewhere Melina found the strength to push herself back onto the sofa. With cushions at her back, she felt the slightest bit steadier, which was good, because mentally she was on shaky ground. "So . . . when Ben was a kid back in Georgia, his girlfriend got pregnant and he skipped out. And that's why you broke up with him now. And what the hell is that purple string?"

Lynda picked up a handful of fuzz and looked at it as if she wasn't quite sure where it had come from. "It used to be a sweater the color of wisteria."

"And what happened to it?"

In her other hand, she held up a pair of eyebrow scissors.

"Did you finish off the scotch last night?" Melina asked suspiciously, but Lynda shook her head. "I was afraid of that. I make more sense stinking drunk than you do stone-cold sober. Put the scissors down and *rationally* explain this whole Ben thing."

For a moment Lynda acted as if she hadn't heard her, concentrating instead on cutting small pieces of yarn into smaller pieces. Then, with a deep breath, she launched into an explanation that made little sense. The best Melina could figure was that, for Lynda, there was forgivable teenage-boy behavior and then there was the unforgivable. Abandoning a pregnant girlfriend who was smart and capable was regrettable but forgivable. Abandoning a pregnant girlfriend who was needy, insecure, and got wasted too often wasn't.

"Now do you understand?"

Melina gave a bewildered shrug, then immediately stopped because the movement made her stomach heave. "But he was *nineteen*. For God's sake, Lyn, don't you remember being nineteen?"

"I *never* would have done what he did."

Of course she wouldn't have, but then, things had been different for her. Her family had been close-knit. Even when her parents hadn't approved of her decisions, they'd supported her fully. But Ben hadn't been so lucky. Lynda knew more about his background than Melina did, but she knew his parents lived in

Atlanta and yet he'd been raised by his grandmother. Enough said.

"I'm sorry, Lyn, but I don't see the unforgivable sin here. When he was a kid, he did something selfish—something that countless kids do every day. Now he's a man, and he regrets it, and he wants to fix it. I think that's admirable. You know, he could have chosen to give up the search after his grandmother died. Granny's dead—she'd never know he hadn't fulfilled her dying wish."

Lynda glared at her. "Whose side are you on?"

"Yours, of course. I just think you're being unreasonable."

"Unreasonable?" Lynda jumped to her feet so quickly that purple yarn flew everywhere. Still dusting the same shelf of Lladró, Gloria clucked her tongue, and Melina cringed. "Those Dalton kids have lived awful lives! They've lived in shelters and gone to bed hungry! They never had a safe, secure home or someone to love them in their entire lives until Emilie took responsibility for them, and Ben helped make all that happen! And you think I'm being *unreasonable*?"

Melina had to admit it was harder to defend him when she put it that way, but she tried anyway. "He didn't know what his daughter's life was going to be like back when he left her mother. You can't blame him for that."

"He knew Berry Dalton wasn't capable of taking care of an infant. He knew the odds of her becoming a good mother were—were—"

"As poor as the odds his own mother had faced," Gloria put in.

"That's right," Lynda said triumphantly.

The housekeeper went on with both her dusting and

her speech. "And look at him. Even with a bad mother and a worse father, he turned out all right, and he had no reason to think that his daughter wouldn't be fine, too."

"That's—" The triumph disappeared. "That's not right. He had no reason to think she *would* be fine. Berry Dalton is a drug addict and an alcoholic. She abandoned her children so many times she lost them for good. She's an unfit mother and a poor excuse for a human being."

"That's the Sherry Dalton of today," Gloria disagreed. "Ben doesn't even know that Sherry. The one he knew was a pretty blonde with the bluest eyes. She loved to laugh and dance and flirt with the boys. She was the life of every party. When she was happy, she was vivacious and outgoing and oh, so much fun. And when the happiness passed, she was insecure, depressed, demanding, and shrewish. She couldn't keep a relationship for more than a few months. Young Len stayed for nearly four months—long after he should have left—and that was a record for her. He knew she had problems. He just wasn't grown up enough to know how serious they were, or how much worse they would get. If he'd understood, I believe he would have handled things differently, I truly do. He might have been a wild young man, but he had a good heart. And he still does. It's a bit sore this morning, but it's good."

Melina looked from her to Lynda, who was staring, then back to Gloria. "How do you know all that?"

"Oh, if you listen enough, you learn all sorts of things. Besides, I've got friends in Atlanta." She rolled her eyes heavenward. "*Lots* of friends. Can I get you something for that headache, Miss Melanie? It'll settle your stomach, too."

"Yes, please."

With a smile, Gloria left the room. Lynda stood motionless a long time, then bent to pick up all the yarn. She looked around for a place to put it, then stuffed it in a vase on the side table before starting for the stairs.

"Where are you going?" Melina asked.

"Home." Lynda didn't slow her steps. "I'm going home."

J. D. GRAYSON'S OFFICE WAS ON THE FIRST floor of Bethlehem Memorial, a small room filled with hospital-issue furniture and enclosed by walls in need of paint. The only source of bright color in the room was the family photographs that hung on all four walls, overshadowing the degree from Harvard Medical School in its elegant frame.

Emilie Bishop had wasted no time in contacting her psychiatrist friend. Ben had been on his way out the door this morning when Grayson called, suggesting an eleven A.M. meeting. It was two minutes after, now.

Though the man seated across the desk wasn't much older than him, Ben felt the way he had when he was back in school and had gotten sent—again—to the principal's office. Wary. Inadequate. He didn't like other people having control over his life—didn't like that this stranger got to decide whether he should even have a place in his daughter's life right now. Oh, he knew he had options if Grayson told Emilie to deny him access to Alanna. He could always sue for visitation rights. But how would the good people of Bethlehem feel about him after that? More important, how would Alanna feel about him after having her personal life dragged into court for everyone to gossip about?

Grayson started. "I think you should know up front that Emilie and Nathan Bishop and I are good friends. So are our kids."

"She told me that."

"They're not trying to be difficult. They only want what's best for the kids."

"I know."

"Would you like anything before we start? A cup of coffee, a soft drink?"

Ben shook his head. His palms were clammy, and his nerves were less than steady. He hadn't slept well last night, and he'd been on edge all morning, waiting for this meeting to roll around. He hoped he had all the right answers, but some little voice kept reminding him that he'd always done poorly on tests—and this looked to be the most important test he would ever take.

"How long have you been in Bethlehem?" Grayson asked.

"About a month."

"And you're from Atlanta. What do you do there?"

"I work in construction."

"You have anyone special waiting for you back home?"

Ben shook his head.

"What about your parents?"

"We've never been close."

"Never? Not even when you were young?"

"Taking care of a kid didn't rank high on their lists of priorities. I lived with my grandmother most of the time."

"What about her?"

What about her? He'd loved her, she'd loved him, and she was dead. He said as much to the doctor, though not quite so bluntly.

"Do you have a job here?"

"I started working for Sebastian Knight this week. Before that, I did some work for Lynda Barone."

"Why did you change jobs?"

Ben wanted very much to tell him it was none of his business, but the moment he'd agreed to talk to the shrink, everything in his life had become the doctor's business. "We had a . . . personal relationship, which wasn't exactly compatible with my working for her."

"I imagine not," Grayson said with a grin. "When I met my wife, she was the social worker assigned to my foster kids. It didn't make things any easier. How's the relationship now that you've found another job?"

It was over before it had even gotten a chance. His natural impulse was to take the blame for it himself, but some small stubborn part of him refused. She was being unfair. She couldn't make decisions about their relationship at this time based on his behavior thirteen years ago. It was just plain wrong.

Which didn't change the fact that it hurt like hell. He felt about as bruised and defeated as he'd ever been.

"She . . . ended it last night."

"I'm sorry. Do you mind if I ask why?"

The answer he gave was short, blunt, and honest. Of course, every answer gave rise to another question. Before the interview started drawing to a close, they'd covered every aspect of his failed relationships and practically every aspect, it seemed, of his life in general.

Though their scheduled time had ended ten minutes

earlier, Grayson wasn't quite finished. "If Lynda called you and said, I'm sorry, I overreacted, I want to try again, but I don't want your daughter around . . . what would you say? Would you give up the chance of a relationship with Alanna to continue your relationship with Lynda?"

There would be only one reason for Lynda to not want Alanna around—because that made it impossible for her to forget that he wasn't the man she'd thought he was. He didn't want her if she had to pretend he was something he wasn't. He'd never claimed to be perfect, but at least he deserved credit for what he was. A man who made mistakes. Who took a while longer to figure out what was important in life but eventually did figure it out. A man who was doing the best he could, even if she didn't think so.

"I know it's a tough question."

"No," Ben said quietly. "It's not so tough. If our relationship isn't strong enough to survive the fact that I have a daughter, and that I'd like to meet her, then it's not strong enough to survive, period. But she was right about one thing. I knew what it was like to grow up with a father who wanted nothing to do with me. I learned a lesson from it—that fathers aren't important. That as long as a kid has somebody, they can grow up just fine. Unfortunately, it was the wrong lesson. The right one, the one Emmaline tried to teach me, the one Lyn wanted me to understand, was that family should be more important than that. It didn't matter that my parents weren't worth a damn, because I had Emmaline. There was nothing in the world she wouldn't have done for me. I know it's a long shot, but I'd like to think that someday maybe Alanna could feel that way about me."

Grayson sat silently a long time before glancing at his watch. "One more question, and then I'll let you go. Are you planning to stay in Bethlehem, or will that be determined by the state of things with Alanna?"

"I plan to stay," Ben replied, deciding at that moment. "I like the town and the people, and with Emmaline gone, there's no reason to go back to Georgia."

"But you'll be running into Lynda on a regular basis."

"Don't count on it," Ben said with a wry grin. "How often do *you* run into her?"

"Very rarely, now that I think of it." Grayson stood up, then opened the door. "Come on. I'll walk out with you."

When they reached the lobby, the entire Grayson family was waiting, and not one of the six kids was the least bit shy about greeting their father affectionately. He introduced each of them to Ben, including Caleb, then his wife Kelsey, who was holding the baby—at least until the kid dove headfirst into Ben's arms. He caught her as her mother released her legs, and settled her close. In spite of his mood, he couldn't resist her toothless grin. "You're not the least bit shy, are you, darlin'? Keep that up, and when you're about twenty, you're going to be awfully popular with the men."

"I taught her to do that," Kelsey responded. "Only with handsome men, of course. So, Ben . . . I've heard about you."

"Really?" What he wanted to say was, Heard what? And, From whom?

"I thought Maggie and Holly were exaggerating, but obviously not. The available women in town are going to love you."

Not the one he was interested in.

"You'd better run while you can, Ben." Bud Grayson slapped him on the shoulder. "I don't know what it is about a happily married woman, but she just can't stand having single folk around."

"We just want everyone to share in our happiness, Bud," Kelsey said with a broad smile. "*You* certainly didn't run."

"Yep, and look what's happening. I'm getting married day after tomorrow, Ben, to the prettiest lady in the whole state. We'd be honored to see you there."

Bud gave the time and the address of the church, and Ben said he would try to make it, though he had no interest in anyone's wedding at the moment. After giving the baby back to her mother, he said good-bye, and left, but he hadn't gone ten feet when a sweet, girlishly soft voice called his name. It was Gracie Brown-Grayson, six years old and about as far from the ringlets-ribbons-and-lace image her voice conjured. She wore short overalls with one strap dangling, her sneakers were scuffed and both knees scraped, and her pigtails stuck out under a backward baseball cap. He crouched down to her level.

"My daddy said to tell you that Lannie's gonna be in Grandpa Bud's wedding—so am I, I'm gonna be the flower girl—an' . . . an' you should come."

"Thank you, Gracie."

"Uh-huh." She raced for the door, then spun around and raced back. "I mean, you're welcome."

He watched her run back once more, then headed across the parking lot to his car. Looked like he was going to a wedding Saturday. And maybe he'd just go and shoot himself Sunday. It couldn't hurt any worse.

He was halfway to the car when he realized that the reason for his telling Dr. Grayson every secret he'd ever had was still unresolved. Would he get the opportunity to meet Alanna? Or had his life gone all to hell just for the fun of it?

When he was a dozen feet from the car, he noticed Sophy leaning against it. In her short overalls and scuffed shoes, she looked like a slightly grown-up version of Gracie. Shoving her hands deep in her pockets, she straightened. "Hi."

"Hey, Soph." He unlocked the driver's door, then glanced at her. "What are you doing here?"

"I had some things to take care of this morning. Sebastian said I could probably catch a ride with you."

He slid inside, then leaned across to unlock the other door. By the time she got in, he'd started the engine and was cranking his window down. "Where'd you disappear to last night?"

"I was going to ask you the same thing. Your car was there but you were gone."

"I got picked up by the police. They thought my hanging around the girls' soccer field waiting on someone they'd never heard of seemed a bit suspicious." He backed out of the parking space, then glanced at her. "Why hasn't anyone ever heard of you?"

Her shrug was airy and unconcerned. "I imagine I'm a bit on the forgettable side."

Forgettable? He doubted anyone who'd ever spoken to her more than once would ever forget her.

Then she looked at him with a knowing smile. "Trust me, Ben. I'm easily forgotten. The day will come when I'm not even a faint whisper in your memory. How did Ms. Barone take getting stood up?"

His mouth tightened, and so did his fingers on the steering wheel. "She didn't mind that. She wasn't happy with the reason why."

"Ouch. She dumped you, didn't she?"

"Yes, she did. How do I feel about it? Pretty damned lousy. What am I gonna do about it? Not a damn thing. How does she feel about it? Hell, who knows if she even *has* feelings? Am I gonna answer any more questions? Not only no, but hell no."

"You shouldn't swear so much," she said mildly. "Dr. Grayson's only trying to help."

They traveled the distance to Sebastian's house in silence. When he shut off the engine, Ben reached across to catch Sophy's hand. "I'm sorry. It's just . . . I had this stupid idea that maybe I could belong here with Lynda and have a home and a family and live a normal life. . . . Instead I get rousted by the cops, Lynda decides she has no respect for me, the police think I'm some sort of pervert, half the people in town, including my kid, see me frisked and put in the back of a police car, and I have to spend the morning being interviewed by a shrink to determine whether I'm fit to be in the same state as my daughter." He grinned bleakly. "It hasn't been the best twenty-four hours."

"Things will work out, Ben. Just give it time."

Time. That was what Lynda wanted. Time to figure out if she could forgive him for the choices he'd made thirteen years ago—choices that were her business only because he wanted both her and Alanna in his life.

But he knew a lot about wanting things he couldn't have. Lynda was one more thing he could add to the list.

He prayed Alanna wasn't another.

Chapter Sixteen

At the age of eighteen, Lynda had gone away to college and, effectively, left home for good. In all those years, little had changed. The dark gold carpeting was now beige, and the walnut cabinets in the kitchen had been painted, but her old bedroom was still done in pink with white furniture, including a canopy bed that had been too short for her by her fourteenth birthday. The room had been decorated by her mother, and Lynda had gone through stages with it, loving it, hating it, not even noticing it. Late on a warm Saturday afternoon, as she gazed at herself in the mirror atop the pink-skirted makeup table, she decided it was comforting. She had changed, but the safe haven this room represented hadn't.

Janice knocked at the door, then came in. "He's here— Oh, honey, you're more beautiful than the bride ever dreamed of being."

Lynda smiled faintly. In a moment of insanity, she'd asked her mother to set up that date for her with Travis Colton, the pediatric cardiovascular surgeon to die for. She wasn't sure exactly why—whether she was being a good daughter, trying to prove that Ben wasn't so important, or merely looking for someone to take her mind off him.

Unfortunately, though Dr. Gorgeous didn't mind the last-minute setup, there was just one small thing he had to take care of first—attending the wedding of one of his fellow physicians. And since Lynda had gone to school with both bride and groom, Janice and Travis had decided she should go to the wedding with him, and then they could go straight to dinner.

Great. Trying to forget the man she'd dreamed of marrying by going to someone else's wedding with a handsome stranger. It made tons of sense.

Lynda adjusted the deep vee of her new crimson-colored dress for the last time, then held up two pairs of shoes. "How tall is Dr. Gorgeous?"

"About five eleven. Maybe six feet if he stretched."

She laid the three-and-a-half-inch heels aside and started to put on the one-and-a-half-inch ones instead, but Janice pulled them from her. "You like the others better. Wear them. Let the good doctor get a crick in his neck."

That wasn't a good sign. Lynda couldn't recall Janice ever saying it was all right for her to tower over a date, especially one she'd handpicked. She didn't argue, though. She didn't have the energy.

"I'll wait up for you, dear. We'll have ice cream and talk."

"What if I get an overnight invitation too tempting to resist?"

"You'll turn it down." Janice sounded sure of herself, but didn't say why. Lynda didn't have the energy to ask that, either.

They went downstairs together, where Phil was supposed to be entertaining the doctor. With his newspaper folded in his lap and his baseball game going unwatched on the television, he looked befuddled and unsure why this stranger was in his house.

Travis Colton was everything Janice had promised—black-haired, blue-eyed, dimpled, and breathtakingly handsome. He looked like an actor who played a doctor on TV . . . and he left Lynda cold. His accent—the one she'd grown up with, the same as hers and her parents'—sounded harsh and blunt, and his smile struck her as so much more practiced and less charming than a simple grin. And although he was impeccably polite, once the door closed behind them and they were settled in his BMW, she couldn't think of anything to say to him.

The uncomfortable stiffness between them made her grateful for the wedding. At least there, once the ceremony started, they wouldn't be expected to actually speak to each other. Unfortunately, there were those few minutes before the ceremony started.

"Your mother was rather vague," Travis remarked after they'd been seated at the end of a pew. "You do something in business?"

"I work for McKinney Industries. Ross McKinney, Tom Flynn, and I run the company."

"Huh. So you're like . . . their secretary."

Handsome, a medical whiz, but otherwise dumber than dirt. "No, no more than you're like . . . a nurse's aide."

"No, hon, I'm a pediatric cardiovascular surgeon. I heal sick babies." He carefully enunciated his response, as if speaking slowly might enable her feeble brain to understand. When she didn't respond, he fell silent, though not for long enough. "You're a tall one."

Lynda was suddenly glad her mother had pushed the high heels. "I'd say that depends on your perspective. From where I sit, you're rather short."

The dimple disappeared and the blue eyes narrowed. "Most tall women would never wear heels that high."

"Really?" She crossed one leg over the other and extended her foot to display the shoe. "I had these made in Italy—stopped off to get measured on a business trip to Athens, then picked them up the next time the company jet was free for a few days. I'm really very fond of them, and so are most of the men I go out with." It wasn't exactly a lie. If she'd gone out with many men, she was sure they would have loved the heels . . . as long as they were taller than five-eleven or as self-confident as Ben. "Of course, most of them aren't . . . short."

His eyes narrowed even more. "I'm six foot one."

She looked him over, from head to toe. "In your dreams."

After another silence, he tried again to impress her. "Your mother may have mentioned that I just bought a place at the beach."

"No, I don't believe she did." Or maybe she had. Lynda hadn't had the easiest time concentrating the last few days.

"I'm having my house remodeled and needed someplace to stay for the first few weeks, while the heavy-duty work is being done. Since I hadn't had a vacation in nearly a year, I decided to stay at the beach, and after looking at a few rentals, it obviously made more sense to just buy my own. So I cashed in some investments, and took the plunge." He shrugged. "It was a little pricey, but it was worth it to not have one of those tacky houses you always find near the beach. And, of course, it *is* oceanfront property."

"Good hurricane target, huh?"

This time not only did his eyes narrow, but tiny lines formed at the corners of his mouth and a nerve in his jaw started to twitch.

Lynda turned her attention to the church. It was relatively new and, according to Janice, attended mostly by hypocrites. Barones might not show up in church often, but when they did, it was because they needed prayer, a little saving grace, or just a quiet time of worship—and they *didn't* come to this church. Here the message seemed to be See and be seen. In one look around the large, incredibly ugly modern room, she'd recognized a number of faces, and all of them fitted Janice's description perfectly.

If she was going to spend an hour or two in a church this evening, she'd much rather be in the First Church of Bethlehem, where Agatha Winchester and Bud Grayson were being married tonight. There were none of these odd angles and massive expanses of brightly colored walls, no bright patterns or trendy color schemes in the two-hundred-year-old church. It looked exactly the way . . .

. . . A CHURCH SHOULD LOOK, BEN THOUGHT AS he claimed a space at the back in the standing-room-only crowd. Solid. Enduring. The stained-glass windows depicted Bible verses familiar to him in spite of the long years that had passed since he'd regularly attended Sunday school, and the hymnals most likely were filled with familiar songs.

"When's it gonna start?" the restless kid beside him asked.

"Soon," the boy's mother replied.

"Why can't we sit down?"

"Because all the seats are taken."

"What's it the First Church of?"

"Bethlehem."

"But what's it *of*? Is it the First Baptist Church?"

"No, babe."

"First Christian?"

"No."

"First—"

"It's just the First Church. Years ago, when Bethlehem became a town, this was the very first church the people built, and that's how it got its name." The mother gave Ben a harried smile. "Aren't kids fun?"

Not feeling exactly qualified to give an opinion, he shrugged instead.

The boy looked up. "Miss Agatha's my Sunday school teacher. Was she your Sunday school teacher, too?"

"No. I just moved here."

"From where?"

"Atlanta."

"Where's that?"

"Georgia."

"Is that why you talk funny?"

"Kyle!" his mother admonished.

Ben crouched beside him. "Down in Georgia, everyone talks like me. We'd think *you* talk funny."

"My name's Kyle."

"Mine's Ben." He accepted the hand the boy stuck out and shook it. Feeling a steady gaze on his back, he glanced over his shoulder and saw Nathan Bishop watching him. Feeling guilty, he released the boy's hand and stood up.

By the time the heat that had risen on his neck had gone away, the ceremony had started. Ben couldn't remember the last wedding he'd gone to. Most of his friends back home were single, and the few who married were more likely to do it in front of a judge than in a church with all the formalities. Like them, he'd figured why fuss?

But as the Grayson men filed in at the front, Ben thought all the fuss wasn't so bad. Getting married was a big step, and it deserved better than a hurried trip to the courthouse. Like any other special occasion, it deserved to *be* special. If a man couldn't put a little effort into marrying the woman he loved, how much effort could he be counted on to put into the marriage?

With a grand swell, the organ music seemed to fill the cavernous room . . .

. . . BUT IT LACKED THE GREAT FLOURISH IT should have had. That, Lynda noticed, was because it wasn't a real organ, but rather an electronic one that anybody—or nobody at all, in fact—could play. All the money the congregation had spent on soaring ceilings and odd architectural details, a person would think they would have invested in a real organ and a real person to play it.

Not that it was any of her concern as, with everyone around her leading the way, she stood up for the bridal party's grand entrance. Craning his neck to give her a look that was rather disdainful, Travis leaned close. "Did I mention I've got a new Porsche on order?" he murmured. "The first bridesmaid there—her father owns the local dealership."

Lynda debated answering. If she pretended interest, she was in for a *boring* evening. If she said what she wanted, at least it would be a short evening. The second bridesmaid, the third, then three more did a slow step down the aisle before she finally decided. Leaning close, she murmured her response in his ear, then watched him blanch with some satisfaction.

The ceremony was touching, even if she didn't belong there. It made her wish for a white gown of her own, for a handsome groom in a tux— She glanced sideways at Travis in his custom-tailored suit and corrected that thought. For Ben, in a tux, a suit, or jeans and a T-shirt. What he wore wouldn't matter. How sincere he was would.

She'd never known him to be insincere about anything.

When the ceremony ended and the wedding party started passing by, Lynda caught a glimpse as Travis slid his hand in his jacket pocket. An instant later, his pager started beeping. With a look of incredible relief tempered only slightly by feigned regret, he pulled it out, then pretended to look at the number that wasn't there.

She waited until he opened his mouth, then said, "Emergency call?"

"Yes, as a matter of fact it is."

"Don't worry about me. I'll catch a cab home."

"Would you? I'd appreciate it."

As soon as the exit was clear, Lynda left the church. The western sky was shades of pink, blue, and purple, the eastern sky deep velvety blue. It was a warm evening, and she wasn't far from her parents' house. Instead of calling for a cab, she set off for a leisurely stroll.

For the first few blocks, all she could feel was relief at leaving Travis behind. She forgot him soon enough, though, in favor of thoughts about what a lovely evening it was, and how much more she would have enjoyed Agatha Winchester's wedding than this one. Of course, Ben would have been there, and that would have been difficult . . . or maybe not. Maybe, even with the entire town there, she would have found the courage to approach him and tell him how much she missed him, how much she loved him, and how sorry she was for judging him. It all would have been true.

But it had been true Wednesday night, too. It just hadn't changed anything.

She was home before she realized it. No, not home. It still felt dear and familiar, but her home was in Bethlehem, in her needy old house on the hill. She was halfway up the sidewalk when her mother spoke from the front porch.

"Lyn? Darling, is that you?"

"In the flesh." After climbing the stairs, she sat down on the swing next to Janice. "What are you doing?"

"I sit out here every evening. It's a nice way to wind up the day. Where is that rat Travis?"

Lynda gave her a brief rundown of the disastrous date, ending with the faked page and the false emergency. Janice shook her head in disgust. "As if *my* daughter wouldn't know that old trick? Does he think you're beautiful but dumb?"

"No telling. *I* thought *he* was." Lynda raised her hands to her face for a moment, as if she could rub away the weariness, then leaned back.

"You want to talk about him?"

"Travis? There's nothing else to say."

Her mother's look was reproving. "Ben. You've been here two days, and you haven't mentioned his name. What happened?"

She was going to be cool about it. They had some irreconcilable differences. It happened all the time. She smiled breezily in the dusky light and said, "It's no big deal. You tried to warn me that he wasn't my type, and you were right," but her voice was less than steady.

Janice made a dismissive gesture. "Who's foolish enough to believe in types? If a man makes you happy, that's all that matters." She hesitated, then delicately said, "He did make you happy, didn't he?"

"I'm thirty-four years old. I have a great job, a great house, the best friend in the world, and the best family. I don't need a man to be happy."

The sound her mother made was rude and expressed a world of doubt. "All those 'great' things are pretty cold comfort when you're all alone. You know, you can be so independent, intelligent, and capable it's scary, and still need a loving, giving, sharing relationship with a man. It's human nature. Look at Adam and Eve, Romeo and Juliet, Rhett and Scarlett. People need people. It's a fact of life."

"No, people *used* to need people. Now all we're supposed to want is success—the jobs, the promotions, the big bucks. We're not supposed to settle for a person until we've achieved everything there is to achieve."

"First problem." Janice stabbed one finger in her direction. "You haven't let anyone tell you what you want or need since you were about three years old—and seeing as I was usually the one trying to do the telling, believe me, I know. Second—who says success applies only to careers? Do you know how hard it is to find the right man? And even once you've found him, it doesn't get easier. You have to compromise and learn and fight and give in, and that's fine, as long as you don't give up. And if you have children—God forgive me, I mean *when* you have children—you have a lifetime of worrying about them. A successful career is a snap compared to a successful marriage and family." After a moment's silence, she went on. "What's the real problem with Ben?"

Lynda knew she couldn't outwait Janice. Her mother was the most incredibly patient person in the world. So, after staring off into the distance for a time, she fortified herself with a deep breath, then told her all about Alanna, Ben, and Berry. She used the simplest, bluntest terms—didn't sugarcoat it, didn't try to make it better or worse. There was no need. Janice was a reasonable woman. She would listen to the details and be as appalled as Lynda had been. She certainly wouldn't want Ben for the father of her grandchildren.

She finished the story and waited for a response. When it came, she nearly fell off the swing.

"For heaven's sake, Lyn, he was a *boy*. Yes, what he did was wrong, but Lord help us if people start judging us now by things we did when we were teenagers.

We're all in big trouble—well, except you. What's the real problem here?"

"That *is* the problem."

"Are you afraid of being hurt? Did you get in deeper than you'd intended and risk more than you'd decided was safe?"

"Mom, he walked away from his own baby! He left her with a woman who couldn't be a decent mother to save her life!"

"Yes, and it was wrong, and you say he regrets it and feels guilty for it. But has he done it again lately? Does he make a habit of walking away from his children? Has he turned his back on someone who was counting on him in recent years?"

"No." He'd promised there were no more secrets, and she believed him.

"So he made a mistake, he regrets it, and he's atoning for it. Now . . . What's your problem? Why are you being so unreasonable about this? Are you jealous?"

"Of his affair with Berry? Of course not. That ended years ago."

"Are you jealous of his daughter? Are you afraid you can't love another woman's child?"

"No!" Lynda kicked off her shoes and drew her feet onto the swing, but getting more comfortable didn't ease her scowl. "This isn't about me, Mom. I don't have a problem. I'm not jealous. I'm not afraid."

"Have you told him you love him?"

The sudden knot in Lynda's stomach made a lie of her last words. It certainly felt like fear. Tasted like it. Hurt like it. "N-no."

"Has he told you he loves you?"

"No." The answer slipped out, even though she hadn't wanted to give it, and that one small word was overflowing with a wealth of emotion that she couldn't stem.

"Why do you think that is?"

The irrational urge to cry swept over Lynda and propelled her to her feet to pace the length of the porch. She found a safe place in the shadows, folded her arms across her chest, and tried for a careless response. "I assume it's because he doesn't love me."

"So he can safely assume that you don't love him, either. After all, you haven't told him so." Janice sighed. "I do hate to use old clichés, but you know what they say about assuming things."

"That it makes an ass of you and me," Lynda said sarcastically.

"Leave me out of it. I'm not the one being unreasonable. I have to say, though, I'm tickled pink to see that you are, Lyn. You're the smartest, most capable and perceptive woman I've ever met. But toss in a little emotion like love, and you become as fallible and insecure as the rest of us. I'm glad."

"I'm miserable, and you're *glad*?"

"Yes. Because it proves you're human. Sometimes I wonder about that." Janice spoke naturally, calmly, in a way that was difficult to take offense with. Ben's tone had been similar, though regretful, when he'd made a like comment. *Now you can find somebody more suitable, and I can find someone less perfect and more human.*

"I'm human." If she weren't, she wouldn't have gone out with Dr. Gorgeous. She wouldn't have run away from home. She wouldn't be hurting so.

Janice patted the swing beside her. "Come sit down, Lynnie."

Though she hated the old childhood nickname, she obeyed.

"We've already established that you're smart. Prove it now. Look into your heart and tell me you honestly think less of Ben because the girlfriend he walked out on was this Berry person and not someone bright and capable like you."

Lynda's automatic response was yes, but when she opened her mouth to say so, Janice raised one hand. "You can't look into your heart that quickly."

Clamping her mouth shut again, Lynda gazed off into the distance. She thought abandoning your pregnant girlfriend, no matter how well suited she was for being a single mother, was terribly selfish, juvenile, and immature . . . but wasn't that pretty much the definition of a young man? And wasn't a person entitled to make a mistake or two? Didn't everyone deserve a second chance? If not, why would anyone ever change? Why make any effort at redemption if you couldn't be forgiven past sins?

By his own account, by Gloria's account, he hadn't abandoned the sad, pathetic woman Berry Dalton was today. She'd had problems, everyone agreed, but didn't a lot of young women? And didn't a lot of them, when faced with impending motherhood, often grow up, find help, and straighten out themselves as well as their priorities?

Did she ever ask him for help? Did she ever contact Ben and say, I need money, a place to stay, someone to watch our daughter for a while? She was the one who'd moved, not him. It took his private detective weeks to find her, but she always knew where to find him. She knew where to go for help, and if she had he would have given it. He wouldn't have turned away from her a second time.

The voice was a murmur inside Lynda's head, solid, real, yet lacking substance. It sounded like the gentlest breeze rustling through the leaves. Like the delicate tinkle of glass chimes far away or the distant echo of some long-forgotten memory.

Actually, she amended, it sounded an awful lot like Gloria.

She gave a shake of her head to clear it, listened, and heard nothing out of the ordinary—traffic a few blocks away, crickets in the darkness, the muted sound of her father's TV.

And her mother's subdued prodding. "Well?"

"I can't say what he did was all right."

"No one's asking you to."

"But . . . it's not fair to blame him for everything that went wrong in Alanna's and Berry's lives. She was the primary caregiver for those kids, and she screwed up. And he does regret it."

"And he deserves a second chance, just like everyone else who's ever made a mistake. Just like you."

Lynda's eyes grew misty. "He's already given me a second chance, and I blew it. He doesn't give third chances. He said so."

"If he loves you, he'll give you three hundred chances if that's what it takes to get it right . . . though I'm hoping you're more competent than that."

If he loves you . . . That was part of the problem. He'd never said he loved her, never talked about their future, had never seemed to be in it for more than a little fun and a little sex—which was all he'd ever wanted from Berry Dalton, too.

A little fun? the whispering, tinkling Gloria-voice mocked. *You're hardly the logical choice for any man looking for a little fun.*

Lynda scowled. Gloria's voice. Melina's sentiments.

"I feel like such an idiot, Mom."

"You should. But you swallow your pride and you explain it to Ben the best you can. And then you tell him the truth—that you have a history of irrational behavior when it comes to men."

"That's not true," Lynda said, her defensiveness only partly feigned.

"It most certainly is. Remember Doug? Did you tell Ben about him?"

"Yes, I did." And a short time later, he'd kissed her for the first time—the sweetest kiss she'd ever been given. And then he'd kissed her again and curled her toes.

"I've heard you tell it several times, and you always say it the same way. You and Doug had scheduled a meeting with the goal of setting a wedding date, but he had to cancel due to an emergency involving one of his clients."

"Yes? And your point?"

"Doug didn't *have* to cancel. You urged him to. You *sent* him to that empty little town out west, where you knew he would run into that granddaughter whom he'd met before, whom he'd admitted an attraction to before. You *sent* him, Lynda. At worst, you'd get a temporary reprieve from planning a wedding. At best, you'd get out of having to have a wedding at all."

Lynda wanted to say, No, you're wrong, that's not the way it happened. But that was exactly the way it had happened. "So you're saying I sent Ben away because I didn't want to be involved with him?"

"No. I'm saying you got scared, just like you got scared with Doug, except there wasn't another woman handy into whose arms you could push him and hope for nature to take its course, and so you developed this fixation on his past behavior."

"If it were true, that would be ridiculous."

Janice smiled affectionately. "That's my point, darling. You're not exactly rational in your dealings with men."

"And you are? You hated Ben on sight. You were shoving law-boy into my arms, and if that didn't work, you were perfectly willing to marry me off to Anton or Darnell or Raphael, who doesn't even have a job . . . but not Ben, because he's a carpenter, because he didn't go to Harvard."

"I never expected you to marry any of the men in that magazine. I would have been appalled if you'd shown even the slightest interest. I just wanted to get your hormones stirred up a bit—remind you of the differences between men and women and why they're so good. And who knows? Maybe it worked. Your hormones certainly got stirred up."

"I believe that was thanks to Ben, not the men in the magazine."

"Maybe. Maybe not." Janice got to her feet. "Time to head inside and dish up your father's nightly ice cream. Want some?"

"No, thanks, Mom."

From the other side of the screen door, Janice looked back. "What did you say to the rat Travis to shut him up?"

Lynda had to think for a moment, to shift gears from the disaster of her relationship with Ben to the disaster of her date with Travis. "Nothing much. I just leaned close and whispered, 'Depending on my stock options and the current quarter's earnings, I'm going to make between two-point-one and three-point-eight million dollars this year.' "

Janice laughed, then sobered. "I love you, Lyn, and if you love Ben, then I will, too. By the way, do you suppose he could fix that window over the kitchen sink? It's always sticking, you know, and your father—Well, don't get me started on your father."

"What about her father?" Phil called from the living room.

"Nothing, dear. I was just telling her you'd be happy to give her away at the wedding. Two-point-one to three-point-eight million dollars. . . . Is that true?"

Lynda merely shrugged. Actually, it should be a bit more.

And she would give up every penny of it for another chance with Ben.

BY THE TIME MISS AGATHA AND BUD HAD exchanged vows, the air in the old church had grown warm. Ben remembered hot summer evenings in church as a kid, when Emmaline had kept them both cool with paper fans, printed on one side with a Bible picture, on the other with a verse. He hadn't minded church then, when he'd been too young to feel guilty setting foot through the doors.

He'd paid little attention to the service this evening, and had hardly noticed the music. Instead, he'd watched

Alanna, studying her intently as if he might commit every detail to memory. She stood on the bride's left, wearing a formal-length gown of deep green and her long blonde hair done up on her head. Caleb's jaw had practically hit the floor when she'd come down the aisle, and Ben's reaction hadn't been much more subtle. She was amazingly, incredibly beautiful. It was hard to believe he and Berry had turned out a child so perfect.

As the recessional started, he tracked Alanna's progress, feeling a twinge when she met Caleb in the center aisle and accepted the arm he offered. She looked older than her age, and so incredible. She was practically grown, and he'd missed it all.

"Isn't she beautiful?" a voice murmured in his ear.

Glancing over his shoulder, he found Holly Flynn. "They all are," he agreed. He let his gaze settle on Miss Agatha, wearing a pale green dress with a floppy-brimmed hat of the sort Emmaline had always favored, then Emilie, Alanna, Josie, and Gracie.

"Miss Agatha asked me to tell you to be sure to come to the reception. It's at the inn. Do you need directions?"

He shook his head. Lynda had told him how to find it for their failed dinner date. He didn't have much interest in going when she wasn't there, but no point telling Holly that. It wasn't as if anyone would miss him in this crowd.

"Good," Holly said with a smile. "Then we'll see you there."

Once the wedding party was out of the sanctuary, most people stood around chatting. Feeling more like an outsider than ever, Ben left and headed down the block to his car.

"Hey, Ben."

He turned to see Sophy hurrying to catch up. In her pale dress and with her blonde curls, she looked as young and lovely as Alanna. "I didn't know you were coming to the wedding," he remarked, pausing for her.

"I wouldn't have missed it for anything. Didn't Miss Agatha look radiant? And Bud . . . They both looked so happy and so much in love."

"Bully for them," Ben muttered.

She gave him a measuring look. "I take it Lynda's not back yet from visiting her parents."

"I didn't know she had gone. Want a ride somewhere?"

"Yes, to the inn, please. That was a quick change of subject there. Is Lynda a sore topic with you?"

She'd definitely made his heart sore. "Yes, so don't mention her again."

"Okay. Can we talk about Alanna?"

He glanced at her before opening the car door for her. What did she know about Alanna? He'd mentioned his daughter to her as they were leaving the hospital, but she hadn't picked up on it, or so he'd thought. Was she guessing, or had she heard some gossip?

"Truthfully, Soph, I'm not much in the mood for talking at all. I'm just going to drop you off, then go on home."

"Oh, you can't do that. In fact, you might say my job is to make sure you show up."

And who'd given her this job? he wanted to know as he slid behind the wheel. Had Agatha thought her request wouldn't be enough? Had Holly decided his agreement had been less enthusiastic than she'd wanted, so she'd sent Sophy along as insurance?

"Turn left at the first intersection," she directed, and he obeyed. She sat quietly, her arm half out the open window, a serene look on her face. When was the last time he'd known such utter contentment? Probably never . . . until last Saturday, when he'd fallen asleep holding Lynda in his arms. That had been pretty damned peaceful.

He should have known it wouldn't last.

To change the subject, he dredged up an old memory. "Emmaline had an angel she put on top of the Christmas tree every year that had a smile just like that. She wore a dress that color, and had curly blonde hair and—heck, put a pair of feathery wings on you, and you'd look just like her."

"Angels don't need wings."

"Sure they do. How would they get around if they didn't have wings?"

"Well, feet work just fine most of the time." She wiggled her feet on the floorboard, then smiled as if speaking to a child or a dim-witted adult. "They're heavenly beings, Ben. They have heavenly powers."

"All the angels I've seen have wings."

"All the representations you've seen," she corrected him. "None of the real angels you've run into have had them."

"Real angels," he scoffed. As if such things existed.

"They do." When he gave her a sharp look, she smiled and shrugged. "They do exist. Trust me. I know. Turn left at the next intersection."

He did so, following the street to its end, then drove through a gate and along a narrow wooded lane. The inn sat at the end of the lane—a simple old farmhouse that had been expanded to several times its original size, but without losing its simplicity.

When Ben would have pulled up to the porte cochere at the main entrance, Sophy gestured. "There's a parking space over there."

"I'm dropping you off, remember?"

"Oh, come on in and have a glass of champagne. At least give your best wishes to the happy couple. Miss Agatha would be hurt if you didn't."

Miss Agatha would be surrounded by so many well-wishers that she couldn't possibly notice he wasn't among them. Still, since being alone in a crowd sounded less painful than being alone alone, he pulled into a space at the end of the gravel lot, and he and Sophy strolled toward the door.

"Isn't it romantic?" she asked, practically swooning over the lights, the flowers, the quiet music barely audible in the night. "Your dinner here with Lynda would have been so perfect if you hadn't gotten arrested instead."

"Not arrested. Picked up for questioning. Trust me, there's a difference." The dinner *would* have been perfect, he was forced to admit. The terrace, where dozens of candles burned and the wedding cake presided from its own table, was just the place for an intimate dinner. From there they would have gone to her house for an intimate feast of another sort.

"Hi, Ben." Bree Aiken, from the motel, greeted him as they entered the lobby. "Wasn't the wedding wonderful?"

"Yeah," he agreed. "Wonderful." He turned to introduce Sophy and saw that she'd made a beeline for the far side of the sweeping staircase, where she was studying portraits on the wall by the time he caught up with her. "Don't take off like that."

"Like what?" she asked innocently, but before he could respond, the first wave of guests came through the doors.

He spent the next hour wishing he were elsewhere, wondering what had persuaded Lynda to go home, curious whether Janice had taken advantage of the opportunity to set up as many dates as she could with suitable men. Binghamton was full of candidates, since he was pretty sure Janice's new definition of suitable was *men who weren't Ben Foster.* Standing on the terrace, apart from the other guests, he wondered when Lynda would come home, and how much trouble she would go to to avoid him, and—

"Hello, Ben."

Turning, he found himself face-to-face with Emilie Bishop. She offered her hand, and he accepted it with a wary glance around for her husband.

"I was hoping to catch you before you left, but I was afraid I'd already missed you. Will you come inside so we can talk in private?"

His mouth went dry. He wanted to say, sorry, but this wasn't a good time. Too many people, too much noise, better wait until next week, next month, next year. But all he really said was, "All right." He set his punch cup on the nearest table and followed her inside the inn and into the library. It opened off the lobby, and looked like every rich person's library he'd ever seen, with the exception that the books in this one looked as if they'd actually been read. He didn't care about the books, though, or the amazingly detailed woodwork, or the furniture. He just wanted to hear what Emilie had to say.

She sat in a wingback chair, and he took a seat on

the sofa. He couldn't get comfortable, though. But why should he be comfortable when she was about to either give him some bit of hope, or take away what little had survived Lynda?

"I realize this isn't the ideal time or place to discuss this, but I also understand that you must be anxious to hear J.D.'s recommendation." She smiled faintly. "I've lived with Berry's kids for more than four years and have had custody of them most of that time. Sometimes I worry about Berry getting better, convincing a judge to return the children to her, and taking them off to another city, another state. Sometimes I don't think I could bear it if that happened. I couldn't love them more if I'd given birth to them, and I don't think I could live without them.

"But I never considered the possibility that *you* might show up. I just assumed that because you had no interest in being a father thirteen years ago, you never would. I didn't consider that in those years, you would grow up and realize what's important in life."

His fingers were knotted so tightly that the muscles began to cramp. He wanted to jump to his feet and pace, wanted to demand a blunt answer—yes, he could see Alanna, or no, he couldn't. No explanations or rationalization. Just yes or no.

"J.D. and I have spent much of the past few days talking. So have Nathan and I. It seems like an easy decision. A parent has a right to see his child. But when he abandons that child, he gives up his rights. We all make mistakes and deserve second chances, but do we deserve those second chances at our children's expense?" She smiled faintly. "There are good arguments on both sides, and believe me, we've covered every one of them. Nathan's not too happy with the idea of giving you access to Alanna. He's not . . . um, impressed with your background. J.D. is a big believer in second chances. Family and forgiveness are important to him."

"And what about you?" Ben's voice was husky, a good match for the tightness in his chest and the queasiness in his stomach. "What's important to you?"

"Family. Forgiveness. Protecting the kids from anyone who might harm them."

And did she think Alanna needed protection from *him*? The possibility hurt somewhere deep down inside, and the fact that he'd given her reason to think it hurt even worse. "I would never do anything to harm Alanna. I know you have no reason to believe me, but I swear . . ."

"Actually, Ben, I do believe you. Berry said you were the best of the many that got away. She remembers you—which is something in itself—with affection."

That made him feel guilty, especially when, for thirteen years, he'd tried not to remember her at all.

"You understand this is going to be a big shock for Alanna, don't you? She seems to like you well enough as the nice guy who comes to her soccer games, but finding out you're her father will change everything. She hasn't had an easy life, and part of that can be traced to the fact that you weren't a part of it. I imagine she's got some anger and resentment built up toward you. She might be able to deal with you and it at the same time, or she might want nothing to do with you—and if that's her choice, I won't force her to see you anyway."

"I wouldn't expect you to." He would have hated it if Emmaline had forced him to spend time with his father when he was twelve. He'd had zero need and even less desire for any sort of relationship with his old man. Like Alanna.

"All right." Emilie's voice took on a cheerier let's-get-this-wrapped-up tone. "I think it would be easier if we tell Alanna the news together, the sooner, the better. The longer she thinks of you as just a friend, the more the deception is going to hurt, I think. Also, the quicker she hears who you really are, the sooner she can start dealing with it—and we'll all do our best to help her with that. I'd like to suggest a meeting tomorrow afternoon—you, Alanna, Nathan, and me. We'll break the news to her, and see where we go from there. How does that sound?"

Scary as hell, Ben thought. He wanted to say, Nope, I've changed my mind, forget about it, almost as much as he wanted to agree. He wasn't on a winning streak at the moment. He'd lost Emmaline, then Lynda. Alanna was the only person left in his life who mattered. If she hated him, as she was surely entitled to, he would be truly alone.

"All right." He cleared his throat to give his voice some substance. "What time and where?"

"Two o'clock? Our house?"

He nodded.

When she stood up, so did he. With a gentle smile, she laid her hand on his shoulder. "It will be all right, Ben. It may take some time, but everything will work out for the best. I'm sure of it."

"I wish I was."

She laughed. "Don't look so grim. You're in Bethlehem, where angels and miracles abound."

It would take something spectacular, like angels with their pockets full of miracles, to make things work out best for him, he thought as he followed her from the library. Angels might abound—Sophy thought so—but surely they were too busy helping people who deserved their help to bother with him. After all, every bit of the blame for his problems rested squarely on him.

In the lobby, Emilie waved good-bye and turned into the dining room. He made his way past people way too happy for his mood. He wondered if he should tell Sophy he was leaving, then figured she could find her own way home. Surely fifteen or twenty generous souls there were going her way, but at the moment, he couldn't play chauffeur or even friend. At the moment all he could think of was escape.

SECONDS TICKED PAST AUDIBLY FROM THE OLD clock on the fireplace mantel. After a minute's worth or more, the high-backed chair that faced the windows slowly swiveled halfway around before coming to a sharp stop. Alanna stared across the empty room, feeling numb and sick and tearful and mad, and about a million other things all at once.

Ben Foster was her *father.* The man who'd wanted nothing to do with her all her life. The man Berry had told her about when she was drunk—handsome as sin and with the devil's eyes. Then she'd always said, Or was that Josie's daddy? And then she'd laughed and said it didn't matter. *All* their daddies were handsome and had the devil's eyes. All liars, all no good, all selfish, and she'd bet Ben was the biggest liar of them all. Every time she'd seen him, everything he'd said . . . all lies.

Maybe this was a lie, too. Maybe he wasn't really her father and was just saying so. Maybe he used to know her father, and he'd fooled Aunt Emilie and Uncle Nathan and everyone else into believing he was him. Maybe he'd *never* known her father—had never even known her mother—and he was just playing some stupid game of let's-pretend, or maybe he was crazy, or . . . or . . .

Or maybe it was true. Maybe he was the father who'd never wanted her. Never cared what happened to her. Never loved her or even cared that she existed.

The first tear plopped on her arm, leaving a hot, wet trail as it slid off. Drawing her feet onto the seat, she rested her arms on her knees, buried her face, and cried.

THE TENSION INSIDE BEN MADE HIM FEEL AS IF he were going to pop, and he was envisioning a hundred-mile-an-hour drive to ease it when he saw the car parked behind the GTO, blocking him in. It was an old Caddie, a convertible with the top down. He didn't have a clue who owned it and was considering how much he *didn't* want to track down the owner in a crowd of hundreds when a voice spoke from the shadows.

"Somebody blocked your car. That was rude."

Lynda. He searched the darkness until he spotted a shadow too dark and curvy to be anything else. He came to a stop beside the Caddie, slid his hands into his pockets, and simply looked.

She strolled out of the shadows, stopping a half-dozen feet in front of him. It was too dark to make out the color of her dress, but he had no problem seeing that it fitted like a second skin, that the neck dipped low and the skirt was slit up high. She was wearing higher-than-usual heels, since she was taller than him than usual.

"You look like you're dressed for a party," he remarked.

"For a date, actually."

His gut knotted with jealousy. "Did he tell you you look beautiful?"

"No. He said I shouldn't wear such high heels."

He looked down again. "I like your heels."

"Thank you." She hesitated, and a measure of her aloofness slipped. "Would you go someplace with me?"

"Where?"

"It's just a place I'd like to show you."

He shrugged and started around the Caddie. "Whose car?"

"It's a rental. Isn't it great?"

Nobody in Bethlehem rented cars like that, which meant she'd made the owner an offer he couldn't refuse for the use of his car. Why, Ben had no idea.

She slid behind the wheel, then started the engine and backed up. "Can't you just see me tooling down some Georgia back road in this?"

With the sun shining hot and the air heavy with the fragrance of magnolia, with the countryside lush and green and the kudzu creating living sculptures out of any object in its path. Oh, yeah, he could see it. "You'd have to take your hair down."

She drove through the gate onto the street, then reached up and removed the clip that held her hair off her neck. With a grin she tossed it out the window, then shook her hair free. The sight made his fingers itch to grab handfuls of it, made his groin tighten and his throat go dry.

For a time she drove in silence—through the mostly deserted town, turning onto a street that ran through an older neighborhood, then into a brand-new one, still under construction. They passed the last building sites and continued to follow the road as it climbed out of the valley. The road narrowed and became typical of mountain roads everywhere, curving this way and that, seeking the easiest route.

Finally, they reached the top, where the road ended in a clearing. She shut off the engine, combed her fingers through her hair, then gestured out over the valley. "Isn't it a great view?"

"Great," he agreed without taking his gaze from her. "What are we doing here?"

She looked down at the valley, at him, then up at the sky, before turning to face him. He leaned back against the door and did the same, and there was still enough seat to put two people between them. It was a shame. Any man lucky enough to go for a ride on a night like this in a car like this with a woman like Lynda should have one hand on the wheel and the other arm around his girl.

"I went to see my parents," Lynda announced.

"How are they?"

"Fine."

"When did you get back?" He wouldn't mention the date. He didn't want to know what kind of Mr. Right Janice had found for her this time, didn't want to know where they'd gone or what they'd done or anything except that she wasn't seeing him again.

"About ten minutes before I showed up at the inn. I flew back."

"Lynda the fainthearted who never breaks the speed limit?"

A breeze swept a strand of hair across her face, and she brushed it aside, but not in time to stop him from wanting to do it himself. "No, I mean I *flew.* I chartered a helicopter. I felt the need to get back as quickly as possible."

He didn't waste time wondering how expensive a proposition that was. She could afford it, and it got her away from Janice's latest prospect. That made it fine with him. "Why the rush?"

After staring over the valley for another moment, she launched into her response. The longer she talked, the faster she went, as if she had to spit it all out before her courage failed her. "There's something I need to tell you. I'm really great with words most of the time, but I'm not very good with emotions because—well, you know why. But I really am sorry for the things I said and the way I acted, but you scare me to death—or, at least, the way I feel about you does, and not knowing how you feel about me. Mom says I'm irrational when it comes to men, and maybe she's right, because I really didn't want to marry Doug, so I pushed him away, and I really did want to marry you, except you never asked, but I pushed you away, too. The truth is, I know you were just a kid, and you have a good heart, and maybe I really was just scared that you didn't want any more from me than you wanted from Berry, and I—"

Finally she breathed, and the starved sensation in Ben's own lungs eased. She looked at him, so damned beautiful in the moonlight, her features so delicate and perfect. "I keep telling myself and everyone else what a great life I have," she said quietly. "The truth is, it's lonely and sad without you. I don't have any experience at being in love, and I've got this pride issue about not doing things that I'm not good at, and I'm really not good at this, but—"

He stretched his arm along the back of the seat, and his fingertips grazed her bare shoulder, silencing her. "Will it help if I tell you first?"

She gave him a sidelong look that lingered, then shifted to head-on. She was tempted, but she shook her head. "No. I mean, yes, it would help, but . . . I really need to say this first. I'm sorry. I'm sorry I judged you. I'm sorry I was unfair to you. I'm sorry I was unreasonable. I'm sorry I'm difficult." Her expression grew even more serious. "I love you, Ben."

Before the words had faded between them, she was going on. "You don't have to say it back. You don't have to say anything at all. I just thought it was time I told you, because otherwise—"

Catching hold of her arm, he pulled her across the seat, wrapped his arms tightly around her, and cut off her words with his mouth. He slid his tongue inside her mouth and tasted sweet heat and hunger and love. He took it needily and gave it back readily.

When he finally ended the kiss, he continued to hold her close. He combed his fingers through her hair, tangled them in the silky strands, then stroked the fine skin stretched across her jaw. "Can I speak now?"

She nodded.

"I accept your apology, and I want to marry you, too, and I don't want much from you—just your body, your love, and a place in your life for the next sixty or seventy years." Then he grew somber. "But your mom was right about one thing. I *am* just a carpenter. I can't afford a house like yours, or a car like yours, or more than a few of these dresses and shoes you do such justice to."

"Ben, most of the men I've dated have wanted me only for my money. Please don't break my heart just because of the money."

"I'm not going to break your heart. I have a healthy ego. I don't care about the money. But other people will say—"

" 'Look how happy they are. We should be so lucky.' "

He cupped her face in his palms, looked intently into her eyes, and said, "I do love you, Lynda."

Her smile was enough to make an arrogant man humble. He felt so much more than lucky. Blessed. It had been one of Emmaline's favorite words, and it described his feelings perfectly.

She kissed him sweetly, then gave a deep satisfied sigh as she rested her head on his chest. After holding her for a time, he tilted her head back. "Why did you want me to see this place?"

Though he didn't want to let her go, she gave him no choice when she sat up. "We're at the top of the world," she said, opening her arms wide to take in the valley.

"And that has what significance?"

She kicked off her shoes, maneuvered to stand in the seat, then stepped carefully into the backseat. There she reached behind her to undo the zipper of her dress. "It's a balmy summer night, the top is down, at least one of us is stripped down naked"—she stepped out of the dress and tossed it over the seat, then eased off a pair of tiny, naughty panties—"and we're about to make hot, lazy, crazy love under the stars. That is"—she looked suddenly shy and innocent in spite of the fact that she stood naked in the backseat of a rented Caddie—"if you're willing."

With a laugh, Ben ignored the buttons and pulled his dress shirt over his head, then joined her in the back, where four hands made not-so-quick work of—but created lots of incredible pleasure in—removing the rest of his clothes. As they sank down into the seat, he sank down inside her, filling her, and he knew that he truly was blessed. After thirty-two years of searching, he'd found the place he belonged.

And her name was Lynda.

Epilogue

The long corridor that led to the Sunday school classrooms in the First Church of Bethlehem was wide, paneled on one side and with lots of windows on the other, and was carpeted with the same dark red carpet that filled the rooms. Four doors opened on the paneled side—one leading to the ladies' room and three to classrooms. The other classrooms and the men's room were off an identical hall on the other side of the church.

As the last of the kids went into their classes, Alanna looked at Caleb. He looked kinda sick, like all he wanted was to go on to Sunday school like he was supposed to. His fingers were holding his backpack strap so tight that they'd turned white, and there was a scared look in his eyes.

She was scared, too, but she wasn't changing her mind. He could stay if he wanted, but her best chance at getting to Providence was leaving town in less than thirty minutes, and she was going to grab it.

Her hands were sweaty when she wrapped them around the bar that would open the metal door. Quickly she looked left, then right, then at Caleb once more before shoving the door open and stepping outside. He waited a bit—so long that she thought he wasn't coming—then slipped through just as the door started to swing shut again. Together they hurried down the steps and started toward Fourth Street.

"This is a bad idea," Caleb announced.

"You said that before." Last night, when she'd suggested it. This morning, before church started. "If you're afraid to go with me—"

"I'm not afraid. I just think it's a bad idea. Providence is a long way from here. We're gonna get caught. And I don't understand why you can't just tell your Aunt Emilie that you have to talk to your mother. She'll take you there."

"And what if she doesn't?"

"But she will."

"But what if she doesn't? What if she doesn't understand . . . ?"

"*I* don't understand," he muttered. "I don't think even you understand."

There was nothing to understand. She wanted to see her mother, period. She needed answers that only Berry could give her, and she needed to look into her eyes when she gave them, so she would know Berry was telling the truth. And the only way she could do that was to go to Providence, where Berry lived.

Alanna stopped at the first intersection, looked both ways, then looked at him. "If you want to go back,

Caleb, go on. But if you tell anyone where I am or what I'm going to do, we'll never be friends again. I'll hate you forever." She started walking again, faster than before, so she wouldn't have to see that hurt look in his eyes. She would apologize later, when all this was over, but right then she didn't have time to worry about his feelings. She didn't need him to go with her. She could do this all by herself if she had to.

But she was relieved when he caught up with her again.

"I'm not going back," he said in a hard voice. "I know you think you can do it all by yourself, but you can't. You don't know what it's like to be all alone in a strange place. It's dangerous and scary."

She guessed he knew from when he'd run away last year, and she *was* scared. But she wasn't gonna let him know it. "Then it's a good thing you're coming, isn't it?"

Her house came into sight up ahead, and her stomach started hurting. What if something happened and she never saw it again? If she never saw her family again? What if Emilie and Nathan got so mad at her that they wouldn't let her come back?

No, that would never happen. They might just be her aunt and uncle, but they loved her the way parents were supposed to. They would understand that this was something she had to do, and they would forgive her.

Parked in the driveway across the street from her house was a pickup truck with a big travel-trailer hooked on behind. It belonged to Miss Corinna's cousins from Utica that had come for the wedding, and they were going back home around eleven. From there, she figured, they could catch a bus or a train, and be well on their way to Providence before anyone even remembered the travel-trailer had been there.

"Wait here," she whispered when they reached the trailer, even though no one was around to hear. She ran across the street, retrieved her backpack from the bushes where she'd hidden it before church, and laid her Bible and Sunday school lesson book on the porch. There was a letter inside to Emilie that had taken Alanna a long time to write, especially since she'd kept starting over.

She unfolded the paper and read it quickly:

Dear Aunt Emilie, I know about the man claiming to be my father, and I've gone to see my mother. Don't worry about me. I'll be safe. I love you and Uncle Nathan very much.

And one last line:

I'm so sorry.

Wishing she could say something more but not sure of what it would be, she folded the letter again and stuck it back in the Bible where the top part showed, then left the Bible where it couldn't be missed.

Sliding one backpack strap over her arm, she ran across the yard and the street and joined Caleb at the trailer door. His hand was on the handle, but he didn't turn it right away. "I still think this is a really bad idea," he said glumly.

A lump formed in Alanna's throat as she looked back at her house. Then she laid her hand over his and opened the door. "Come on, Caleb," she said quietly. "It's time to go."

About the Author

Known for her intensely emotional stories, Marilyn Pappano is the author of nearly fifty books with more than six million copies in print. She has made regular appearances on bestseller lists and has received recognition for her work with numerous awards. Though her husband's Navy career took them across the United States, they now live in Oklahoma, high on a hill that overlooks her home town. They have one son.

Be sure to watch for

HEAVEN ON EARTH

the next unforgettable story in

Marilyn Pappano's series of romantic novels

set in the heartwarming town of

Bethlehem, N.Y.

On sale in

January 2002.

Read on for a preview...

THE DOUGHNUTS SHE'D BOUGHT THE NIGHT before were stale, the coffee in the thermos was lukewarm and bitter, and every bone in Melina Dimitris's body ached from spending ten hours in the cramped seat of an 80s vintage Mustang. She was definitely too old for these all-nighters, she thought as she rubbed her gritty eyes. She wasn't a two-bit P.I. trying to make ends meet. She owned the biggest and best investigations firm in all of Buffalo, so what was she doing hunkered down outside a sleazy motel watching the room where her client's sleazy husband was holed up with his girlfriend of the week? Why wasn't one of her employees doing this while she spent a lovely, comfortable night in her lovely, comfortable condo?

One of her employees had been doing it, honesty forced her to acknowledge, until she'd shown up in the wee hours of morning, unable to sleep and in need of a distraction, and had sent him home. She couldn't keep doing it, though. She wasn't as young as she used to be, and her body didn't bounce back the way it used to. Just because Sebastian Knight had broken her heart, the rat bastard, didn't mean she had to let him break her body and spirit. Instead of moping around like some lovesick schoolgirl, she would deal with him properly, starting today. She would finish up here, shower, then go to her folks' house for the weekly Dimitris family get-together, and there she was going to ask her brother Nikos to set her up with one of his friends. Greek, Italian, or hell, maybe even plain old white-bread American—she didn't care, as long as he wasn't six foot five, incredibly broad-shouldered, ruggedly handsome, and didn't have intense hazel eyes and amazingly strong, gentle hands.

As long as he wasn't someone she could fall for. That falling was tough business, especially when you landed. She'd done it twice now, and she wasn't inclined at the moment to ever do it again. If she wanted that kind of pain, she could just shoot herself and recover a whole lot faster.

Movement at the motel drew her attention across the street. The door to room 16 opened, and the sleaze stepped out. She raised the camera with its telephoto lens and snapped off several pictures as Miss June appeared in the doorway, showing an incredible amount of tanned skin, and examined the rat's tonsils with her tongue.

Now all Melina had to do was follow him home, where he would tell his wife all about his weekend business trip to Chicago—the difficult client and the lousy hotel that left him badly in need of an afternoon's sleep. Then she would be free to tend to her own business. Meeting family obligations. Finding a new guy. Getting Sebastian the pig out of her system.

The sleaze pulled onto the street, and after a moment, she followed. She was thinking about her client, who'd trusted this man enough to make him the father of her children, and about what an amazing risk love and marriage were for any woman, when too late she realized she'd been spotted. Instead of trying to lose her, though, the bastard slammed to a stop, his car angled across the quiet residential street, and he jumped out, grabbed a baseball bat from the backseat, and ran toward her.

"What the hell are you doing following me?" he shouted, his face mottled. "Did my wife hire you? Do you really think I'm stupid enough to let you give her evidence against me so that bitch can divorce me and take everything I have?" He smashed the bat against the Mustang's driver's door, rocking the entire car, then leaned in the open window, forcing her back in the seat and making a grab for the camera.

His fingers were knotted around the camera strap when Melina brought her weapon up and pressed the barrel against his temple. The Sig Sauer was warm and hard, and it made his eyes practically pop out of their sockets. "Go ahead," she said softly. "Give me a reason. Threaten me with a bat. Steal my camera. Breathe too loudly."

He froze, and beads of sweat broke out along his forehead. She could smell his fear, along with Miss June's perfume, a hint of Cool Water cologne, and the stink of sex. "I—I—"

"Let go of my camera."

He did.

"Drop the bat."

He did that, too, and it landed with a clatter before rolling to a stop.

"Now back away. Slowly." Keeping the gun aimed at him, she grabbed her cell phone, then got out of the car. The door panel was crumpled from top to bottom, side to side, and was so flat at the point of impact that odds were, the window was shattered, too.

As she dialed 911, she gestured with the pistol. "Get on the ground. Face down." Under different circumstances, she might let the bastard go, or at least get his wife's opinion before she had him hauled off to jail, but if he was angry enough to take a bat to a stranger's car, who knew what he might do to his wife given the chance? Besides, she was nursing a healthy dislike for anyone with testosterone this morning. He'd be lucky if she didn't shoot him before the cops arrived.

The officer arrived within minutes, a female cop whom Melina knew and had tried on several occasions to hire away from the department. Faced with two women with guns, the sleaze stayed sullen and silent. Once he was handcuffed in the backseat of the patrol car and a wrecker arrived to hook up his car, the officer approached Melina. "Still stirring up men wherever you go, huh?"

"All men are bastards."

"Ain't that the truth. But like the saying says, we can't live with 'em and we can't live without 'em."

"I thought the saying was we can't live with 'em and we can't just shoot 'em." They both laughed, then

Melina went on. "Speak for yourself. I intend to live a long, happy life without 'em. Except," she added wickedly, "on occasion."

"Tell me, Melina, you ever wonder what you're doing in a job where people come after you with a baseball bat?"

"The thought has crossed my mind a time or two." Or twenty. She spent more time with sad people and lowlifes than anyone ever should. She'd been shot at, threatened, punched a few times, and run off the road. She'd feared for her life and had fought against becoming overly cynical. And she loved her job. How was that for weird?

"You know the routine," the cop said. "I'll need a written complaint from you to attach to my report, then it'll go to the D.A. tomorrow."

"Who will look at it and say, 'Felony assault on a woman with a baseball bat? Throw the book at him. Oh, wait, it was Dimitris. She probably provoked him. Give him a better weapon and her home address, and let him go.' "

Again they laughed. Though she got along well with most Buffalo cops, her relationship with District Attorney Milligan was less than congenial. She blamed several factors—his distrust of private investigators in general, his dislike of capable, independent women, and, most important, the fact that she had gathered evidence for his ex-wife to use in their much-publicized divorce a few years earlier. He'd gotten caught with his pants down, and he'd hated Melina for it ever since.

"If you ever decide you want better hours, a better salary, and much cooler weapons, give me a call,"

Melina said as she gingerly opened the banged-up door, then slid behind the wheel.

"I'll keep that in mind."

Once the wrecker had driven away, Melina returned to the high-rise that housed Dimitris Investigations, typed a quick report, left instructions to get an estimate on the Mustang, then headed home. Within two hours of the crack of the baseball bat against her door, she was walking into her mother's house, greeting relatives and exchanging hugs for kisses as she went. Anyone coming from a normal background could be forgiven for thinking it must be a special occasion to bring fifty or sixty relatives together for dinner, but the Dimitrises weren't a normal family. They were Greek, which pretty much explained everything.

The closer she got to the kitchen, the more amazing the aromas became. Nobody could cook like a good Greek mother, and at the moment, there were about ten of them in her mother's kitchen, putting together a feast. It was a good thing the dress she wore fitted too snugly to accommodate one single excess pound. It was the only way she knew to keep from growing as round as the other women in the family.

As if reading her mind, one aunt shook her finger as she passed. "I wouldn't allow my Mona to wear such a dress in public."

"Aw, Aunt Saba, you'd wear it yourself if Uncle Gene would let you out of the house."

"Tell me one thing," Aunt Olympia requested. "Where do you hide your gun with a dress like that?"

"You'd be surprised." Melina gave her a wink and a smile. "Yaya Rosa!" Bending, she kissed her grandmother's cheeks. There had been a time when Rosa had cooked for a crowd this size single-handedly, but these days, she supervised from a comfortable chair at the kitchen table. She was about eighty years old, frail in body but not in mind, and was most definitely the matriarch of the Dimitris family.

Rosa peered up at her through thick lenses. "How many criminals have you locked up since last we saw you?"

"Only one. But we caught four cheating husbands"—five, counting this morning's loser—"and two deadbeat dads."

"Good for you, *koretsi mou*." Rosa applauded. "With a busy week like that, have you had time to meet any men?"

Every time Melina saw her grandmother—or her mother, any of her aunts, or most of her female cousins—she got the same question, but it usually didn't stir a twinge of pain in her gut. This time, as an image of Sebastian formed in her mind, it did. She'd had such hopes for him—such silly, romantic fantasies—and he'd destroyed them. "Nope," she lied. "You have to remember, the people I run into at work aren't exactly the sort I'd consider settling down with."

"Not the crooks, cheating husbands, or deadbeat dads," her cousin Antonia agreed. "But surely there's a petty thief or two. A white-collar criminal. Maybe an industrial spy?"

Melina gave her a phony smile as she circled the island to reach her mother. Antonia was a year older than she, had gotten married right out of high school, and had three kids by the time Melina had graduated from college. She'd added three more in the years since and was the accomplishment Olympia lorded over Melina's mother most often. As if producing a daughter who could breed like a rabbit was something to be proud of, Livia Dimitris groused. Deep in her heart, though, Livia was longing for grandbabies of her own, and none of her three children showed any sign of providing them just yet.

Truth was, Melina was longing for them, too. At thirty-four, she still had plenty of time, but she'd always hoped to have a few years to settle into a committed, permanent, happily-ever-after marriage before she started a family. With that in mind, time was about to get short.

She kissed her mother's cheek, then bent to inhale deeply of the fabulous aromas coming from the pan Livia was stirring on the stove top.

"You look hungry," Livia said. "Eat."

Obediently Melina scooped up a triangle of baklava from a nearby tray. The flaky phyllo dough was golden brown and buttery, the layers filled with nuts and redolent with honey. Like everything else that came out of this kitchen, it was incredible.

"How was your week?" Livia asked.

"Busy." It wasn't entirely a lie. She'd spent a good part of Sunday, Monday, Tuesday, and Wednesday making wild, passionate love with Sebastian. Then he'd dumped her. No excuses, no explanations, just a heartlessly cold kiss-off.

No, that wasn't exactly true, either. There'd been an explanation—the wedding band he'd been wearing for the kiss-off. She'd thought he was divorced. It was common knowledge in Bethlehem that he'd been alone since his wife left him four years ago. At the moment, she neither knew nor cared about the status of his marriage. She hated him, and that was all that mattered.

"I called your office Tuesday, and they said you were out of town. On business?"

"Everything in my life is business, Mama."

"More's the pity. How are you sleeping? You look tired. Are you getting enough rest?"

"I'm fine. Is there anything I can do?"

Just as Livia opened her mouth, the cell phone in Melina's handbag trilled. "You can get the phone," Livia suggested. "I think we have enough cooks in the kitchen today."

"I'll be right back." Melina hugged her mother, then fished out the phone as she headed for the back door and a bit of quiet. Only a bit, though, since all the cousins under twelve were playing in the backyard. Taking a seat on the top step, she pressed the phone to her ear. "This is Melina."

"Hi. Are you busy?" It was Lynda Barone, her best friend since their first day of college, and she sounded about as down as Melina felt. She was having man problems, too, except hers were vastly different. Ben Foster was handsome, charming, and sexy as hell, and he clearly loved her, but she'd chosen to punish him for being immature, selfish, and human thirteen years ago. Melina had to admit, she found it a lot easier to see Ben's side of things than Lynda's. So he'd gotten a girlfriend pregnant. So he'd broken up with her rather than accept the responsibilities of fatherhood. It was a long time ago, and he'd grown up and was trying to make things right.

Of course, having been recently dumped herself, it was easier to relate to another dump-ee rather than the dump-er.

"I'm at my folks' house. We're about to sit down to enough souvlaki, tyropitta, and kadaifi to feed a small country. What's up?"

"You remember I told you that Ben has a daughter."

"Uh-huh."

"She ran away this morning. Two other children are also missing. One is a good friend of Alanna's, and the other apparently chose to tag along. The authorities have been notified, but we want you to look for them, Melina, please."

She gazed across the backyard, where a dozen or so kids played. What would it be like to have a child of your own, then lose him? Like losing the better part of yourself, she imagined. "All right. Do you think your boss would have one of his pilots pick me up?" It was a five-hour drive from Buffalo to Bethlehem, and she'd rather not waste all that time.

"Not a problem."

"I'll get a suitcase at home, then head for the airport. Set up a meeting with the parents. Ask them to bring recent photographs of their kids. If they have any idea where the kids went or why, I want to know. I'll also need lists of their friends and relatives, both in town and out, and the best guess they can make at what the kids took with them—clothing, a toy, any photographs or money that's missing, everything. If they left notes, I want to see them. Any clue where they're headed?"

"Providence. Alanna's mother lives there."

"Providence . . . I'll see if I know anyone who works there." She paused and softened her voice. "Is Ben okay?"

"He's worried, and he's blaming himself. Apparently, Alanna found out by accident that he's her father, and she was upset. If anything happens to her—"

"Nothing will," Melina promised, though she was far from sure. "What about you? Are you okay?"

"Sure. Just worried about the kids and Ben." Lynda made an obvious effort to lighten up. "Hey, he asked me to marry him, or maybe I asked him. I don't remember. Anyway, we're getting married. He loves me, Melina. Can you believe that?"

The wonder and awe in her voice brought a sheen to Melina's eyes. That was how she'd felt with Sebastian. She'd thought she was the luckiest woman around. Turned out she was merely the biggest sucker around.

She swallowed the lump in her throat and forced an excited whoop. "Of course he loves you, darlin'. The only one who doubted it was you. Congratulations! After we find the kids, we'll celebrate properly. Now I've got to go and pack before I turn pea green with envy. I'll see you in a few hours."

After disconnecting, she sat motionless on the stoop. *She* was the one who'd announced not long ago that she wanted to settle down, get married, and have kids, and Lynda had been cynical. They were modern women. They had careers, money, travel, and excitement to keep them happy. They didn't need men or marriage. Now the cynic was getting married and would probably be pregnant before she could say "impending motherhood," and the wanna-be bride was farther from commitment than she'd ever been.

Life just wasn't fair.

But if it was, she would be out of a job that paid very well and supported her in the way she wanted to be supported. After all, it was the schemers and deceivers who kept her in business.

As she reentered the kitchen, Livia looked up, subjecting her to a moment of study before her full mouth flattened. "Something's come up, and you don't even have time for a bite of food with your family. What is it this time? Another straying husband? A bad-check artist? Someone stealing from wealthy old women?"

"Three missing kids." She knew that would silence any complaints from Livia. Though her mother adored Lynda, Melina also knew not to tell her about the engagement. *She found a man in that burg where she lives?* Livia would complain. *And you can't find one in the entire city of Buffalo? That's all it takes, you know. Just one.* "I'm going to head out the back. Make my apologies to Papa and everyone, will you?"

"You be careful. And keep in touch with your mother, you hear?"

"I will, Mama. Love you." Slipping out the back door, Melina made her way around the house and down the street, where her Bug fit right in with the second-hand cars that surrounded it. It was a classic car, older than Melina, a convertible, and in better shape than most people its age. Though she could afford virtually any car on the market, the Bug had been a sixteenth-birthday present, and she loved it dearly.

Above her, the sun went behind a cloud, cooling the air briefly. That was why she felt a shiver down her spine, Melina told herself. Not because this new case involved children, and kids-in-danger cases were always tough. Not because it involved Ben's kid, and she adored Ben and would have married him herself if Lynda hadn't accepted his proposal. And certainly not because she was going back to Bethlehem, where she could conceivably run into Sebastian long before she was emotionally ready to face him again.

But she *wasn't* going to run into Sebastian. He was pretty much a loner, and his only daughter was too young to be a friend of Alanna Dalton's, and surely, after his behavior last week, he would be no more eager to see her than she was to see him. The rest of her life might be filled with surprises and unexpected events, but she was pretty sure it was never going to be filled with Sebastian again. He didn't want her.

He'd made that painfully clear.